S0-BXG-014

DARK SEDUCTION

"Nicole," Freya said, "didn't you tell me that one of the happiest periods of your childhood was when you were having your wolf-dreams? In your dreams, you accepted your wolf-nature. You loved being a wolf! Yet you retained enough of your human consciousness to remain in control, if need be."

Freya's voice had softened, and Nicole found herself listening intently. "That's the key, Nicole. As long as you fight your wolf-nature, you will be a divided, suffering person. But when you fully accept the wolf in yourself, when you embrace her, when you learn to revel in being what you really are, then you will find yourself fully in control.

"But you must accept every aspect of yourself . . . the hungers, the cravings . . . the instinct to defend yourself and your territory . . . the urge, if need be, to kill. . . ."

To kill? Never. What was Freya saying? Nicole could never do that.

And yet . . .

Freya's voice sank lower. "Of course, it will probably never come to that. But when they threaten you . . . don't fight the urge to attack . . . let it grow . . . enjoy it, savor it . . . and then . . ." The words were little more than a whisper. ". . . and then, let them see your teeth."

John R. Holt

Wolf Moon

BANTAM BOOKS
NEW YORK TORONTO
LONDON SYDNEY AUCKLAND

WOLF MOON

A Bantam Book / August 1997

All rights reserved.
Copyright © 1997 by John R. Holt.
Cover art copyright © 1997 by John Dismukes.

No part of this book may be reproduced or transmitted in any
form or by any means, electronic or mechanical, including
photocopying, recording, or by any information storage and
retrieval system, without permission in writing from the publisher.
For information address: Bantam Books.

If you purchased this book without a cover you should be aware that
this book is stolen property. It was reported as "unsold and
destroyed" to the publisher and neither the author nor the publisher
has received any payment for this "stripped book."

ISBN 0-553-29198-X

Published simultaneously in the United States and Canada

Bantam Books are published by Bantam Books, a division of Bantam Doubleday
Dell Publishing Group, Inc. Its trademark, consisting of the words "Bantam
Books" and the portrayal of a rooster, is Registered in U.S. Patent and
Trademark Office and in other countries. Marca Registrada. Bantam Books, 1540
Broadway, New York, New York 10036.

PRINTED IN THE UNITED STATES OF AMERICA

OPM   10 9 8 7 6 5 4 3 2 1

Once again to
Peg
with love
and with thanks for her long patience
and her sharp pencil

(and thanks to our daughter Helen
for applying her "acid test")

". . . not all demons are fallen angels . . .
I think the worst demons, the very worst of all,
are people, just like you and me."

—ELSPETH CROWN TREMAINE

Wolf Moon

Prologue

THE PACT

Even now, the doctor thought, the girl was beautiful.

Her raven-black hair, neatly brushed and glossy, lay spread out over the white pillow. Her face was as pale as if drained of all blood, but that did not detract from the fineness of her high cheekbones, her straight delicate nose, her perfect, faintly parted lips.

A clear plastic tube encircling her head brought oxygen to her nostrils. Other tubes, extending from plastic bags hanging from a metal tree, conveyed glucose, antibiotics, and nutrients to a needle taped into her left arm. Wires attached to her body sent the message of the still-beating heart to a monitor at the nurses' station in the hall. Others attached to her head searched in vain for signs of conscious life.

The girl was dead.

What a waste, what a waste, Dr. Frank Stranger thought. A seventeen-year-old girl with everything going for her and so much to give, a girl so beautiful and bright and beloved, snatched away from her father and friends in a matter of days, of hours.

Frank was only dimly aware that the others, doctors and nurses, were quietly departing. In their white clinical jackets and uniforms, they melted away like snow. He found himself alone with the girl, and there was nothing, nothing more in the world, he could do for her.

Reluctantly, because her father had yet to be faced, the doctor left the room. He found the man leaning heavily against a file-cluttered desk, looking like an ancient Goliath struck by the fatal stone and on the verge of collapse. For an instant the doctor hardly recognized him. On Tuesday evening, he had been a tall, brawny, ruggedly handsome man, apparently in his mid-forties, with silver-streaked hair and dark, bristling eyebrows, and an electric gaze that could cut steel and shatter diamonds. He had been vigorous and alert and determined to save his daughter, by sheer willpower if necessary. In the next forty-eight hours he had aged twenty years and become groping, hesitant, vulnerable. Now, on the morning of the fifth day, he might easily be in his eighties—dazed, diminished, humbled. Even his physical stature seemed reduced, and he gazed at the doctor with despairing eyes.

What was Frank to say? Your daughter is dead? He was certain that Timothy Balthazar had known that intuitively from the very moment his daughter had gone beyond reach or return. Those empty, banal words, I'm sorry? Timothy must surely know that no words could express the sympathy his old friend felt.

The words he did say were just as empty and banal: "Timothy, we did all we could."

But Timothy didn't seem to hear, and he looked toward the doctor, blind-eyed. "Why did he do this to me, Frank? Why did he let her be taken from me?"

Frank shook his head. Only the god they both acknowledged could answer that. Why? Why . . . ?

Ordinarily, a diabetic coma developed slowly, over a period of days or weeks. But dear God, a coma could strike the young so swiftly—a child could go from insulin deficiency to coma in a day or less. But even so, the girl shouldn't have died! She had been given immediate and proper emergency treatment—Frank couldn't understand what had gone wrong.

It was almost as if an angry god had reached out to snatch her away from her father.

The thought that that might literally be true terrified Frank.

He recalled Timothy's telephone call, calm but urgent: "She's terribly flushed and she's vomiting violently. She has a constant thirst, if that's important. She's had a long day of travel, up from New York, and she's been in an emotional state all evening, laughing but on the verge of tears. She has difficulty breathing, and, Frank, her breath is . . . odd."

In making a diagnosis, Frank always tried to avoid leading questions. "Odd in what way?" he asked carefully.

"It has a chemical smell, like . . . acetone, perhaps. Frank, I don't want to play doctor, but doesn't that suggest . . . ?"

Yes, it did. They were the classic symptoms of Type I diabetes mellitus, and thank God that Timothy had recognized their significance. Not that that had saved the child. "Get her to Emergency at St. Claire Memorial as fast as you can, Timothy. I'll phone them that you're coming and tell them what to expect. I'll meet you there."

When Frank arrived at the hospital, he found the girl, as he had feared, barely conscious and in DKA—diabetic keto-acidosis. They had already put her on saline solution for the dehydration, and Frank ordered forty units of insulin. They were taking throat tests and urine cultures, of course—at this point they had to be on guard against everything from strep throat to meningitis.

"Don't worry," he had told Timothy. "Everything is un-der control, and she'll come out of it in a few hours."

But she had not come out of it. She had only sunk ever deeper into irreversible coma. The lines penned by the elec-troencephalograph had come to resemble a crumbled desert landscape, desolate and abandoned.

The hours had become a day, a day and a half, two days. Blood sugar levels were constantly monitored and the insulin-glucose balance was carefully adjusted. And yet the girl re-mained unconscious.

What the hell was wrong?

Frank briefly considered the possibility of a brain tumor

and ordered a CAT scan, but there was absolutely no sign of any such thing.

Three days passed.

Four.

The girl's heart faltered.

Code Blue.

They had kept her heart beating, had kept her breathing. But now it was over.

"May I see her, Frank?" An old man's voice, high, thin, and tremulous.

"Of course."

As the man straightened and tottered toward his daughter's room, Frank had an impulse to take his elbow and steady him. But that wouldn't do. Even now, Timothy Balthazar would not endure the indignity of accepting help. But the doctor remained in the doorway until Timothy was seated at his daughter's bedside and gazing at her waxen face.

He was about to turn away and give the man his privacy, when Timothy motioned for him to come in. He went to the bedside and stood by his friend's shoulder.

"Why did he let this happen, Frank?"

Frank, unable to answer, shook his head. He knew that Timothy was referring to their god, the god of this world, but who could know the ways of a god?

As if he had read Frank's thoughts, and perhaps he had, Timothy protested, "But she's still breathing, Frank. Why?"

What could he say now? *I don't know. She's gone, even so.*

"Her heart is still beating."

Yes, Timothy, Frank thought, *but she's a vegetable. A mindless organism, artificially sustained. Do you want her to remain in this state forever?*

"I want her back, Frank. I want her back!"

Frank put his hand on the man's shoulder.

Timothy slowly turned his head and looked up at him. The strange colorless eyes seemed to regain their determination, and some of the age fell away from the face.

"They do sometimes come back, don't they, Frank? I've read of cases where after months, even years . . ."

Frank shook his head. He couldn't lie to his friend or offer him false hope. "Timothy, that is so rare . . ."

Timothy brushed the words away. "Keep her breathing, Frank. Keep her heart beating. Do whatever you have to do to keep her body alive. Because I'm going to have her back. I don't care how long it takes or what it costs—a fortune in medical research or a deal with the devil—*I'm going to have her back!*"

Frank patted Timothy's shoulder, comfortingly, he hoped. He expected Timothy to break down at any moment, but though his mouth twisted with pain and his lips trembled, Timothy did not. He slowly stood up.

"Take care of her, Frank."

He gazed down at his daughter and, after a moment, bent down and kissed her forehead.

"I'll have you back, darling," he whispered.

Without another look at his daughter or the doctor, he left the room.

Why, O Lord, why?

Why have you taken her from me? Or allowed her to be taken?

Why? . . .

The silence of Timothy Balthazar's god was like angry thunder.

The limousine glided through the streets of St. Claire, New York, like a submarine through sunlit waters, while Timothy stared unseeing through its ports. He seemed enclosed in silence. He heard no sound of traffic, not even the roar of a truck or the howl of a siren. Like exotic marine specimens, other cars passed, a cyclist or two sped by, pedestrians crossed before the limousine at a stoplight, but he saw none of them. He was alone.

Why, O Lord, why?

And still he received only the angry reproof of silence.

But that was wrong. The sheer injustice of Alida's fate aroused Timothy's own anger, and he found himself abandoning all caution.

For years I have served you faithfully! For you, I have built the mightiest convocation in the country. I have brought together respected senators and governors, leading scientists and academics, even bishops of the church—all with psychic abilities pledged to you. For over forty years I have dedicated my every act to you, always putting you first before all others, always, always . . .

Timothy felt a sudden sense of deflation, a sharp uneasiness.

Always? . . .

Had he always put his god first?

Of course he had. Knowing what he did of the ways of his god, he would have been a fool not to.

And yet the feeling of uneasiness would not leave him. Indeed, it grew stronger.

What have I done? he asked in anguish. *How have I failed you?*

His god or his conscience, which may or may not have been the same thing, answered.

You are a fool, Timothy Balthazar, an arrogant fool. You say you have served me faithfully, putting me before all others, but in truth you have always thought you could use me for your own ends.

Perhaps that was true, but wasn't it only natural and right? Self-interest was a law of nature, and—

Self-interest be damned, you have thought yourself my equal. More than my equal! In your arrogance you have thought that you could trick the devil himself into doing your will—

That's not true!

It is true. And I have been patient, I have bided my time, I have never ceased to shower my blessings on you as I waited for you to shed your arrogance and pay me proper respect. But the time of waiting has come to an end. I will humble you at last and exact full payment for all I have given you. All! All! All!

The center would not hold. Timothy felt his world crumbling, falling apart, coming to an end.

"But not my daughter," he cried out aloud. "Not my daughter!"

His plea went unheeded. Once again his god was silent.

The beauty of the spring day mocked him. The temperature was in the seventies, and Lake St. Claire, long and narrow and cradled in ancient mountains, reflected a cloudless delft-blue sky. Though the water was still cold, the public beaches at each end were crowded, and small sailboats wandered about lazily, except for two or three catamarans that darted in short bursts of speed like colorful water bugs.

Lake St. Claire. St. Claire State Park. The town of St. Claire in St. Claire County. This was Timothy Balthazar's kingdom. He had long ago driven out, almost fortuitously, the last of the St. Claires, and yet their name remained everywhere, as if to taunt him.

Leaving town, Heinrich, Timothy's butler-chauffeur, took the south branch of the road that circled the lake. They passed a number of country estates, including the old St. Claire place, on the left, and, farther along on the right, lakeside vacation cabins. Near the far end of the lake, set back in solitary grandeur on the highest mountaintop, stood his own great four-story fortress of a home. From its aerie, he could look out over his kingdom.

He had completely rebuilt the house in the fifties, and it had been further enlarged and refurbished since. The last major rebuilding had taken place sixteen years ago, shortly after Alida's mother, pursued by the same angry god who now punished Timothy, lapsed into madness and catatonia. As far as Timothy was concerned, the woman was dead, and he had taught Alida to think of her in the same way. "Alida, your mother is dead. What remains is an empty shell." But, dear God, must he now think of Alida in the same way? No! He refused!

A long curving drive of crushed stone led from the front gate up the mountainside to the house. Heinrich let him out under the portico at the side entrance. The ever-attentive Heinrich had probably known Alida's fate even before seeing Timothy's face at the hospital, and now old Minna, his housekeeper-cook, knew it the moment he stepped into the foyer. But she wisely said nothing. She merely clutched at her heart, closed her eyes, and sighed, and then embraced him for a moment.

Gently detaching himself from her, Timothy looked about. Five evenings ago these rooms had been filled with the laughter of Alida and her two friends. Yes, even Alida, though she had been flushed and exhausted and her voice tremulous.

He had thought that that had been only the result of excitement and the fatigue of the trip back from New York City. To celebrate her seventeenth birthday, he had given Alida and her friends a long weekend of fine restaurants, theater, and shopping. But the very night of their return, the vomiting had begun . . . and now five days later Alida lay in the hospital . . . dead. . . .

No! He would not accept that. She was not dead, not to him, and he would have her back. He would have her back, whatever the cost!

He shook his head. "I must be alone for a time, Minna. You understand."

Of course she did. She was a wise and perceptive woman whom he had made very wealthy indeed. She was paid to understand. And she was of the faith. . . .

Leaving Minna, he went to the back of the house and down a flight of stairs. *Orpheus descending,* he thought with grim humor. At the foot of the stairs he opened a door and flipped a switch that turned on a few concealed and softly glowing lights.

The lights revealed a room, perhaps twelve by twenty-four feet, with walls and ceiling of black—Timothy's private chapel. Oak pews occupied most of what might be called the nave. They faced a dais on which stood a long black-lacquered altar, separated from the nave by a communion rail. No cross, crucifix, or other common religious symbol appeared over the altar, but its backdrop was a brilliantly colored tapestry of a griffin—or at least a griffinlike creature—of the most extraordinary beauty. The torso was human, but the arms and legs were furred and armed with claws, and the eagle head seemed to mask something both temptingly human and repellently monstrous. It was a great bronze-winged beast-angel.

Timothy gazed at it for a moment, and then went to a closet. He took out a long black cloak, threw it over his shoulders, and fastened it on with a griffin-embossed clasp. He drew its hood up over his head. He then lit black candles that were in sconces along the walls, and two on the ends of the altar. He turned off the electric lights and sat down in the front pew.

At last, huddled within his cloak and its hood, he could be alone again with his god.

The candlelight glittered on the more-than-human blue eyes of the griffin, giving Timothy a focal point for his meditation. *My God, my God, if I have offended you, I am heartily sorry and beg forgiveness. Tell me what I must do. That's all I ask. Tell me what I must do to be reconciled!*

Reconciled.

Timothy knew at once that that was the key word. He knew that his god was speaking to him.

Any of the god's people who betrayed him must be reconciled—or punished. Any who broke the vows of obedience or silence or sacrifice.

But I have never broken any vows, except, perhaps, in putting my daughter before you—and since I have promised her to you, I haven't even really done that!

A pathetic defense, he knew. Yes, he had promised Alida to the god, but he had done little to prepare her for membership in the convocation. Something had held him back, some strange reluctance to see her lose her innocence, and he had told himself that there was plenty of time. . . .

All right, I shall prepare her to become your bride at once. Give her back to me so that I can do so. Just tell me what to do!

At length, out of the long silence that followed, came a single soft word in a woman's voice, his own name, sweetly, almost mockingly drawn out: *"Timothy!"*

Opening his eyes, Timothy slowly raised his head.

She stood before him, leaning back at ease against the communion rail, a tall blond woman, agelessly beautiful, dressed in white: Freya Kellgren, once his lover and always his rival, second only to him in the convocation. In the candlelight, Freya's face was indistinct, but she seemed to be smiling. Come to gloat, Timothy thought.

But he only said, "What do you want, Freya?"

"I've heard, of course. I've come to help you."

Timothy laughed weakly. "You? Help me?"

Freya was indeed smiling. "I've helped you before, and you know it. You could never have become what you are without my help—"

"All right, all right," Timothy said impatiently, "what do you have to say?"

"You want her back—"

"*Of course I want her back!*" Timothy's rage was explosive, his voice a harsh roar, and he half rose in his pew as if to fling himself at Freya. "*Of course I want her back, and I'm going to have her back!*"

Freya was as calm and unruffled as if a tornado had not just passed over her. She nodded. "Yes. Yes, you're going to have her back. And I am here to help you. We have had our differences, but we have come a long way together, Timothy, and believe me, I only want to help you."

Timothy doubted that. Freya would always have her own objectives, her own agenda. But it wouldn't hurt to hear her out. He sank back into his pew.

"What do you suggest?"

Freya did not answer at once. Leaving the communion rail, she entered Timothy's pew, and sat down nearby, facing him. Now he could clearly see her smiling face in all its fine-boned Nordic beauty.

"Timothy," she said, "the time has come for you to rectify a very serious mistake."

"And what would that be?"

"The Holland coven."

Surprised, Timothy was silent. He knew what Freya was talking about, but the matter seemed utterly insignificant compared to the loss of Alida.

Nevertheless, he finally asked, "What about the Holland coven?"

"Timothy, I have been doing a great deal of fasting and praying these last few days, and I have been given the answer to your problem. If the convocation is purged of the Holland coven, Alida may well be returned to you."

Timothy shook his head in exasperation. "Freya, the Holland coven is a pimple on Satan's butt."

"No, Timothy, not a pimple, but a boil, and a very painful one. . . ."

The Holland coven . . . a half-dozen teenagers who, seven years ago, had dabbled in Luciferianism for a few months, before going their separate ways. Timothy had kept track of them to some extent, but they were unimportant.

Except, perhaps, for Bradford Holland, the leader of the coven. Bradford, so Timothy had heard, had not simply lost interest in the faith and abandoned it—Bradford had spat upon his vows and become an enemy. Yes, the god of this world might well wish to see him punished and destroyed. Very well, Timothy could see to that. But the rest of the coven?

". . . call them back. We can start calling them back tonight if you wish."

Call them back? What was Freya talking about? Timothy had been lost in his own thoughts.

Freya smiled at his bafflement. "The vow they took at my insistence, don't you remember? To impress upon them the importance of what they were doing. Their promise that if they ever turned away from our lord and master they would return to St. Claire within seven years to be reconciled—or punished. Do you remember, Timothy?"

Timothy shrugged. "If any come back and are reconciled, fine. I very much doubt that Bradford will, and he's by far the most important. Leave him to me."

Freya's voice hardened. "You aren't listening, Timothy. They must return to St. Claire for their judgment and punishment. If necessary, they must be *made* to return. The terms of the vow must be fulfilled."

The woman was tedious. "My dear Freya, you don't know what you're talking about. In any case, it's most unwise to foul one's own nest. They cannot be punished here—"

"Timothy, do you want your daughter back or not?"

Timothy stared. The woman had spoken the words like an ultimatum. And it was true that he was the one out of favor with their god, not she. He had the terrible feeling that at this moment she spoke for their god.

"It may not be possible to draw them all back."

Freya smiled thinly. "It will be easy. Lily Bains is already here, and Derek and Joanne come back every summer. I'm making arrangements for the Johnson boy to come back, and that leaves only Bradford and the Lindquist girl in question. I'm sure we can manage them."

Timothy was no longer listening to Freya. He was gazing at her in mute dismay.

"I'm making arrangements for the Johnson boy to come back. . . ."

The Johnson boy . . . who, he had been told, was now living in New York City with Nicole St. Claire. If for any reason Duffy Johnson were to return to St. Claire, it was not unlikely that Nicole would return with him. And that, Timothy did not want. He still felt a spark of fear as he recalled Nicole's grandmother, Julia St. Claire, warning him more than forty years ago: *"I want you to know, Timothy, that if you ever try to hurt one of my family, or anyone close to us, I will use the power of anathema against you. I promise you."*

It had been no idle threat. The Balthazars had felt that power before.

Julia St. Claire was dead now. Did the power of the St. Claire anathema extend beyond the grave?

Had Nicole St. Claire inherited her grandmother's power? The notorious "Wolf Girl of St. Claire."

Now he understood. Freya saw this as the occasion of his possible destruction, a chance to even old scores. He who so often foresaw the future, why had he not foreseen this?

But suddenly words uttered by his grandfather on his deathbed came back to him, words repeated by his father and burned into Timothy's brain: *"Remember: The anathema is their strength, but the wolf will become their weakness. Through the wolf you will be ended . . . or triumph!"*

And the wolf had indeed "become their weakness."

Perhaps . . .

The first intimations of a plan, vague, as yet shapeless, began to form in Timothy's brain. Yes, perhaps . . .

Timothy felt as if Satan himself were looking at him, grinning and nodding encouragingly.

He turned back to Freya. "You're right," he said mildly. "The coven must be brought back here and its members reconciled or punished. And of course we must rid ourselves of the last of the St. Claires once and for all. Isn't that what you had in mind?"

Surprised at his suddenly taking this tack, Freya smiled uncertainly and then attempted a sneer. "It did occur to me that it might be amusing to observe the faltering old warlock versus the vital young witch."

Timothy merely smiled. With a horny fingernail, he traced a faint wrinkle at the corner of Freya's eye. "You're right, my dear. Obviously neither of us is getting any younger."

Hissing like a cat, Freya slapped his hand away.

For the first time in days, Timothy laughed. "Don't worry, my dear. If we succeed—and we will—you will get your fondest wish."

And I will get mine, he added silently, speaking to his master. *I'll destroy Nicole St. Claire, I'll destroy her as certainly as I did her father and her grandfather. But I will destroy her in such a way that St. Claire itself will forever curse her name. And in return* you *will give me back my daughter. Nicole St. Claire for my daughter. Are we agreed?*

Still smiling, Satan nodded.

The Tale

A Daughter
of Wolves

Part One

Timothy
The
Rapture

CHAPTER 1

She was a happy little girl.

Her mother had departed for heaven when Nicole was four, but she had a grandmother to take care of her, and a father who came from the city to visit, and a number of playmates, both real and imaginary.

And a pet white mouse named Snowflake.

Nicole was a pretty little thing, with shining brown hair, bobbed short, and sparkling brown eyes, and she was never the cause of trouble at her kindergarten. The most frequent inconvenience she caused at home was taking all the pots and pans out of the lower kitchen cabinets and then not putting them back. The pots and pans were soon forgotten, when she went off to play with Snowflake.

She frequently forgot to put Snowflake back too. Snowflake lived in an aquarium that had once housed goldfish, but as often as not he was to be found roaming the house—exploring closets and cupboards, nibbling at Nicole's toenails, or having midnight conversations with Grandma. For Snowflake was every bit as friendly and trusting as Nicole.

Snowflake lived for well over a year.

Not bad, for a mouse.

Nicole would never forget the day that Snowflake joined Mommy in heaven. On returning from kindergarten, she had had her lunch and then gone upstairs to her bedroom to play with Snowflake. The spring day was as sunny as Nicole's disposition, and when she knelt to look into the aquarium, the wooden floor and the old rag throw rug were pleasantly warm. Snowflake immediately scampered out of his piles of shredded newspaper and stood up against the glass wall, wiggling his nose and pleading to be taken out. Nicole took the screen lid off of the aquarium and reached in for him, and he hopped into the palm of her hand.

Snowflake was a little bundle of pleasure, plump and silken. He turned this way and that, sniffing at her palm. He nibbled at her thumbnail. He sat up on her palm and licked his little paws and groomed his whiskers. Mice are clean little creatures, Nicole had learned, and Snowflake was as neat as they came. Snowflake sniffed and sniffed, and ran up her arm, enjoying his freedom, and ran back down. He sat up again, and looked at her, cocking his head as if he were talking to her. He was her friend and she was his. She fed him mouse food from the pet store and gave him fresh water and let him run free. He liked her grandma and her daddy, but he had been Nicole's since he was a baby, and he preferred and trusted her beyond all others.

She put him down on the faded brown and red throw rug. He slowly crept a few mouse-paces, sniffing as if he had never explored the rug before.

Nicole sniffed too.

She smelled Snowflake. She had smelled him before, of course, but never as acutely as now. He had a peculiarly pungent odor, a smell that excited her, a warm, wet brown and yellow and red smell that seemed to fill her head.

She picked Snowflake up yet again, and the smell grew even stronger. It was a yummy smell, *such* a yummy smell, and suddenly her tongue was so wet that she had to swallow.

She felt a trickle of moisture on her fingers and realized that Snowflake was peeing. That meant he was frightened, and for a moment Nicole was puzzled. Snowflake had never been afraid of her before; why should he be afraid now? She wanted to laugh at the poor thing and, at the same time, to reassure him. *Snowflake, don't be frightened! I love you!* She was growing increasingly excited—she didn't think she had ever before been excited quite like this.

She brought the little mouse to her face, holding it with both hands. She snuggled her nose into his warm body. Mmm, so good. She could feel his rapidly pulsing life. She could smell it, so rich and raw, so yummy, she had never smelled anything so excitingly, dizzyingly yummy ever before. She didn't want to hurt Snowflake, she just wanted to . . .

She opened her mouth.

The little mouse screamed as she bit down. Screamed just once. . . .

She seemed to be in a delirium, in a feverish state in which she hardly knew what had happened or what she was doing. She was simply a creature feeding, mindlessly feeding, with infinite pleasure. But gradually full consciousness returned. She realized that she was sitting on the old rag throw rug in her bedroom and that her grandmother was standing just within the doorway—her grandmother, with her eyes so wide and sunken and dark as night, her thin face white as milk, hardly breathing, staring at her in horror. Her grandmother, staring at Nicole's hands.

Nicole looked at her hands, at first uncomprehendingly. She saw the ragged remains of the small carcass, and the blood. She felt the blood on her face and tasted it in her mouth.

Then her own horror welled up. She understood. She had done this terrible thing, she had destroyed the pet she loved. Snowflake was dead, he had died horribly and she was soaked in his blood, and she could hear only the rise of her own shrill screams.

Her grandmother called their family doctor, who actually came, because, short of an ambulance, there was no way she could get this hysterical child to his office. The doctor gave Nicole a sedative, and her grandmother tucked her into bed. Her grandmother promised to call her father in New York that very evening.

As Nicole lay in bed, she wept for Snowflake. How could she have hurt a pet that loved and trusted her? She hid her face in her pillow and promised her daddy and her grandmother and her mommy in heaven that she would never, never be bad again. And yet . . .

And yet, as she drifted into sleep, the faint taste of blood lingered in her mouth like that of the wonderful red wine her father sometimes let her sip.

ST. CLAIRE, 1981

Daniel St. Claire first met Freya Kellgren in, of all places, the St. Claire public library. He was there, on a hot July afternoon, in the forlorn hope that he might learn more about his daughter's illness from the latest medical publications.

It seemed to Daniel that he had known about—but very little about—Freya Kellgren for as long as he could remember. No one seemed to know much about Freya. She was the last, apparently, of one of the wealthiest families in St. Claire County. (But where had the wealth come from? Timber? Railroads? No one could say for sure.) For years she had lived reclusively in that great Victorian mansion out west of town and north of Lake St. Claire. (Or was it her mother one remembered living there? Or her aunt?) In more recent years she was said to travel extensively and to live somewhere on Long Island or in New York City, but she reappeared in St. Claire for at least a few weeks each summer.

Or was it the daughter who came back, or a granddaughter, or a niece? Identities are hard to lose in the Information Age, they construct themselves ceaselessly if often incorrectly, and yet nobody seemed *quite* to know who Freya Kellgren was. All anyone really knew was that the Kellgren women, married or single, kept the family name and there always seemed to be a Freya Kellgren.

Daniel remembered seeing Freya on the streets of St. Claire when he was a boy—a tall, handsome, blond woman, usually dressed in white, who always seemed to know where she was going but who never lingered anywhere; a woman who cast friendly smiles about but who said little and never raised her voice. She had seemed remote, like a movie star of a previous generation, an object of desire, but a prize beyond reach and not to be dreamed of . . . always cool and slightly aloof. She was the eternal stranger.

But no longer. Not to Daniel. Now, on this sunny afternoon in early summer, a shadow fell across the library table where he sat reading, he heard his name spoken softly, and before he even looked up, he had a sense that some momentous and totally unexpected change was about to take place in his life.

She stood before him, a vision in white, smiling at him across the table. Her short-sleeved dress of some soft cotton fabric molded a slim, lithe, perfect figure. Under a classic broad-brimmed sun hat, her high cheeks glowed a natural rose, and her eyes sparkled, violet as amethysts. "Hello, Daniel," she said in a low, faintly husky voice. "How nice to see you back in St. Claire."

As he stood up, he had a moment of disorientation. He remembered Freya Kellgren from his boyhood as a mature woman, an adult. But this woman surely could be little older than he, somewhere in her thirties. Had the Freya of his boyhood had a daughter? She must have, but how could he have forgotten . . . ?

"Freya Kellgren," she said, as if prompting his memory, and she extended her hand.

"Yes," he said.

For a moment, he could only stare—stare at the slender fingers, the lightly tanned arms, the amused, half-suppressed smile that played on Freya Kellgren's face—and suddenly, for all its brightness, the day seemed charged with thunder. He felt an involuntary sensual heightening, and when he took Freya's hand, cool and dry in his, it was as if he had seized sweet lightning. The charge went right through him. He literally felt it race up his arm. It sped directly to his manhood and to his brain, dazzling him. When his head cleared, he found himself stunned and breathless, and from that moment, Daniel St. Claire wanted Freya Kellgren as he had wanted no other woman in years.

But as he let her hand slip away from his, he only said, "Of course. How are you, Miss Kellgren?"

"Freya," she said, taking off her hat and sitting down across from him. "I'm fine. It's good to be back home again, isn't it? Tell me about yourself, Daniel. How have you been?"

He told her.

Who wouldn't have told this warm and radiantly beautiful woman? And why had he ever thought that he didn't "know" Freya Kellgren? Now he thought he understood why Freya had seemed so much older than he. Since she had been sent away to school, he had never seen her in a school corridor or on a playground, and to a child even a few years can seem an enormous gap. But what were three or four years now? Freya actually seemed younger than he.

He told her about his work. He was the art director of a small but very successful Manhattan advertising agency. Unfortunately, his job kept him so busy, and St. Claire was far enough from the city, that he got back all too seldom.

She was so easy to talk to. He told her about his daughter and her malady, a subject he was ordinarily loath to discuss. Nicole's mother had died of "a heart condition" when the child was four, and Daniel had put her in her grandmother's care. She had seemed to adjust quite well, but after some months she had inexplicably killed a beloved pet mouse. Had literally bit it to death. There had been no other such incidents—she was carefully watched—but soon after that, Nicole had developed a compulsive desire for raw meat. Preferably blood-red.

"Daniel, you don't mean she suffers from . . ." Freya, her eyes grave with concern, hesitated to say the dread word.

Daniel nodded grimly. "Lycanthropy." He tried to speak calmly and dispassionately, as if quoting from a textbook. " 'A severe psychotic condition in which the patient displays animalistic, wolflike behavior . . . and may actually think himself transformed.' "

"That poor child!"

"In Nicole's case, the doctors don't know what triggers the episodes, but I'm inclined to think it has to do with feelings of insecurity and depression. Evidently it runs in the family, going way back. It's never touched me, but I remember how my dad suffered from it."

"The Werewolves of St. Claire," Freya said softly.

"Oh, Christ, those old stories." Daniel shook his head in weary disgust. "You can be sure that Nicole has heard them from her schoolmates by now—how Great-great-grandpa Stephen St. Claire howled at the moon and Great-uncle Fred got shot with a silver bullet. And of course they tease her because of her St. Claire looks. Call her Fox Face and Dog Ears and— *Spock,* of course—and I don't know what all."

"She is a very beautiful child."

"She is that. She just looks . . . a little different."

"She looks like her father."

Daniel realized, with a little glow of pleasure, that Freya knew his daughter on sight. He said, "I take that as a terrific compliment."

"And the doctors have no idea . . . ?"

"Oh, they have all kinds of ideas. I've taken her to every qualified doctor I could find, to specialists in Boston and New York, and they all have ideas—but a cure is something else. Freya, we have tried everything from antidepressants and hypnoanalysis to prayer and holy water—literally."

"But you're not giving up."

"No. I'll never give up. That's why I keep dropping in to bookstores and libraries—hoping I'll find a new book or one I've overlooked that will tell me something helpful."

Freya was silent for a long moment, while she stared at her hands on the table before her.

"Daniel," she said without looking up, "perhaps this is out of line, but may I suggest something that may not have occurred to you? Something . . . rather radical?"

"Of course."

She raised her eyes to his. "You've tried all the approved, conventional treatments, medical, psychological, even religious—and they've failed. But there are other, less conventional sources of healing power, available to a fortunate few. Would you be willing to try one? For Nicole's sake?" Freya smiled tentatively. "Put the 'rules' aside and make a 'deal with the devil'?"

.   .   .

For a moment, Daniel's heart sank. He had been speaking to Freya Kellgren of things he ordinarily discussed only with his daughter's doctors and his mother, and he certainly didn't need another crank cure, not another hoodoo guru selling snake oil. But at that very moment Freya reached out and covered his hand with hers, and he felt such compassion flowing from her that he could not simply dismiss her. All he could do was gaze into those beautiful violet eyes that seemed, almost, to hold him in thrall.

Still, he was skeptical about any "deal with the devil."

"What exactly do you have in mind?" he asked.

Freya looked away, as if unsure of how to tell him. "There is in the West," she said slowly, "a tradition known as 'the laying on of hands.' I'm sure you've heard of it. It's usually associated with religion, but I'm told that it's increasingly employed by doctors and nurses, even nonbelievers."

Daniel nodded. "I've heard of it. Of course."

Freya looked encouraged. "Then you probably know that it's the power to ease suffering and encourage healing and in some cases to bring about cures. It's a very real power, and whether you call it psychic or psychological or something else really doesn't matter, as long as you can make it work for you."

Freya paused, as if gauging his reaction to her words.

"And?"

"And it occurs to me that by mastering that power you might be able to cure your daughter yourself." Freya hesitated. "You're thinking, Crackpot stuff."

Actually, he very nearly was. But he said, "No, I'm thinking, This sounds like 'miracle cures' and nothing new, but what do I have to lose?"

"Shall I go on, then?"

"Please do."

Freya nodded. "You're a psychic, aren't you, Daniel."

"No."

Freya shook her head. "I pride myself that I can often detect them. From time to time, not always, you can read minds, Daniel, you know what the other person is thinking—"

"I'm a fair judge of character, that's all. I can read a situation, pick up vibes. Say I'm pretty intuitive."

"That will do nicely. I would guess that from time to time you have shared dreams with someone else . . . with your wife, most likely, when you were apart."

Daniel stared for a moment. He felt invaded. What she said was true, but the dreams he had shared with his wife were a very private matter, often intimately erotic, their own sweet secret. How could Freya possibly know about them?

The flush of her cheeks deepened, as if she were reading his thoughts. "I'm sorry," she said. "If I've offended . . ."

"No," he said, "but what you're talking about wasn't psychic, it was psychological. We were attuned. It was a good marriage."

"I'm sure. But however you explain it, Daniel, you are the kind of person who is an excellent channel for the power."

"You mean . . . for the laying on of hands?"

"Among other things. The power I'm speaking of takes many forms, from the ability to read minds to the power to amass wealth. I see that possibility in you. If you'll let me, I think I can help you develop it."

Daniel sat back in his chair. He continued to stare at Freya.

"I can see you're skeptical." Freya started to rise. "But think over what I've told you, Daniel."

Daniel extended a staying hand. "No. Please. Let's get to the bottom line: Sure, I'm skeptical, but I would do anything to help my daughter. And I wish you'd make clear to me just what this power, this proverbial devil of yours, is."

Freya leaned forward over the table and touched his hand again. She smiled. She looked as if she had just won a small but important victory and now she was ready to share some great secret with him.

But at that moment, Mrs. Bains, the head librarian, approached their table and touched Freya's shoulder. "Miss Kellgren, isn't it? There's a telephone call for you. You can take it in my office."

The woman walked away, as if assuming Freya would follow. Freya looked wide-eyed at Daniel and shrugged to signal her surprise and incomprehension. "Please wait, Daniel. I'll be right back." She stood up and followed after the librarian.

Daniel thought that Freya might have a good idea of who was calling her. She seemed to leave a trail of anger in her wake.

She was gone for several minutes, and Daniel had the feeling that she had not spent them all on the telephone. She had spent the last of them composing herself before her return.

As she came back to the table, her stride was quick and purposeful; her smile was brief and her eyes were hard. A woman determined to hold her own, Daniel thought.

"That was an old friend of your family," she said. "He would like to get reacquainted with you. His name is Timothy Balthazar, and he fancies himself an intimate friend of the devil."

Timothy Balthazar. Lawyer. Businessman. Councilman and off-and-on mayor of St. Claire. Multimillionaire, said to be the richest man in St. Claire County.

He was another person of whom Daniel seemed to have been aware all of his life. Balthazar had helped manage his father's estate.

He must have been around sixty, but he looked at least twenty years younger, and he radiated vitality. He was tall and solidly built, with a broad carved-in-granite face. His eyes were narrow, cold, and colorless under dark, bristling brows, and his hair was streaked with silver. To young Daniel St. Claire, Timothy Balthazar had always looked more like a Cossack cavalry officer than an American businessman. He still did.

Timothy greeted Daniel cordially, as the son of old friends, and he smiled at Freya; but Daniel sensed that the smile masked annoyance, even anger.

"I gather from what Freya told me on the telephone that she hopes to give you certain . . . much needed help."

Balthazar was seated behind a massive walnut desk in his study. Daniel, seated in a deep, comfortable chair, faced him from across the room. Freya sat between them, but off to one side.

"Help . . . ?" Daniel felt a momentary irritation with Freya for having said anything to Balthazar about a matter so private. "With all respect, sir, if I discussed any such thing with Freya, that's between her and me."

Freya looked apologetically at Daniel, and he nodded his understanding.

"Of course." Balthazar also nodded. "I don't mean to be intrusive, but I would be curious to know what she told you about us."

The cryptic *us* had an almost institutional ring. Again, Daniel felt slightly irritated. "I don't know who *us* is supposed to refer to, sir, but she told me that *you* consider yourself 'an intimate friend of the devil.' "

To Daniel's surprise, Balthazar gave a sharp barking laugh and for an instant actually looked jolly.

"Yes, and perhaps I am. And no doubt you're wondering why suddenly and out of the blue I asked you both here."

"I'm wondering how you could be here and yet know that Freya, or Freya and I, were at the library."

"I'm psychic," Balthazar said dryly, "but it wasn't that. I just happened to look out across the town square from my office window and saw you go into the library. Later, as I was leaving my office, I saw Freya enter the library. I didn't even know if you were still there, Daniel, but the thought that you *might* still be there . . . the growing certainty that you were *both* still there . . . kept eating at me. . . ."

"I'm sorry, but I don't understand. Why should that be of any concern to you?"

Balthazar looked at Freya. "Would you care to explain, my dear?"

Freya had her eyes closed and was wearily pinching the bridge of her nose. She shook her head, as if to declare herself out of the discussion. But then she opened her eyes and spoke defiantly. "Timothy, all I did was talk to Daniel about his daughter's difficulties and suggest that perhaps together we could find a way to alleviate or cure them. I was thinking of using psychic techniques. If he had agreed, I would have entered him in my current class after we both got back to New York, or perhaps given him private instruction. That is absolutely all."

"That is not all," Balthazar said. "If he had seemed at all receptive, you would have tried to proselytize him. You would have let him begin his novitiate without ever consulting me. At the time of his final vows, you would have presented me with a fait accompli—your own pet supporter in your own little coven."

While Freya protested to Balthazar that she had had no such intention and Balthazar insisted that indeed she did, Daniel looked from one to the other. Novitiate? Final vows? *Coven*, for God's sake? What the *hell* were they talking about?

Balthazar noticed Daniel's puzzled frown, his look of irritation. "I'm sorry, Daniel," he said, "we're being very rude. You're right, you're entitled to some answers. Freya?"

"Daniel," Freya said defiantly, "I never had anything in mind other than to help your daughter."

Balthazar sighed. "Very well, *I* shall explain. Daniel, there is no need to go into details, but Freya and I happen to belong to a small group of people . . ."

"Not so small," Freya said.

". . . bound together by certain . . . qualities"—Balthazar gestured vaguely—"generally by high intelligence . . . exceptional talents . . . and what you might call intuitive abilities—"

"Psychic abilities," Freya said flatly. "If you're going to tell him, tell him."

Balthazar ignored her. "We are by no means the only such group, though most are regional, while ours draws its membership from all over the country. It's a rather distinguished membership, if I may say so."

"A kind of psychic Mensa?" Daniel asked.

"You might call it that, yes, but more. While it has no officially formulated philosophy, its members do accept certain commonsense beliefs. We believe in the doctrine of enlightened self-interest, for instance. We believe that the ruling principle of the universe, from the Big Bang to the daily search for sustenance, is power. In fact, we believe this so firmly that it has an almost religious aspect, which is ritualized and which involves taking certain vows. You see, Daniel, we do not believe that this world is ruled by some Unknown God or his Prince of Peace. That is clearly untrue. No, this world is quite obviously ruled by the Prince of Power, and unto him we vow our—"

"Oh, my God!" A bubble of delight filled Daniel's chest as he realized where Balthazar was going. "My God," he chortled, "don't tell me you're Luciferians!"

For a moment, in the face of laughter, Balthazar looked disconcerted. But then he smiled.

"Yes, as a matter of fact, we are, of a sort. But we never refer to ourselves as Luciferians to outsiders except in jest. Unfortunately, Luciferianism is too often confused with a vulgar satanism. But we do not conduct black masses, Daniel, or defecate on altars or otherwise desecrate churches. Such practices are utterly repugnant to us."

Daniel nodded. "I understand that. To you, Lucifer is the Light-Bearer, the Promethean who brings the gifts of understanding and power to mankind. He is not the devil of the Bible or the Church Fathers or Luther and Calvin. It's an entirely different set of symbols, often with positive, life-affirming values. Am I right?"

"I'm delighted that you're so well informed. It makes matters easier."

Daniel shrugged. "I've read a book or two."

"Then you must realize that Luciferianism is not for everybody. And, knowing your family background, I very much doubt that it's for you."

Daniel had been sitting upright, enjoying the conversation. Now he relaxed back in his chair and regarded Balthazar and Freya. Balthazar, his elbows on his desk, was church-steepling his fingers and regarding Daniel gravely. Freya looked at Daniel as if imploring him for understanding, then looked away and closed her eyes. Daniel recalled the magical moment when they first touched hands. He recalled Freya's profound sympathy when he told her about his daughter's plight. He recalled the glimmer of hope, however absurd, that she had given him when she spoke of his psychic powers and the laying on of hands.

"Mr. Balthazar, it's true that Luciferianism, as I understand it, doesn't exactly ring my bells. Life has given me a somewhat darker view. But my concern is for my daughter. If

I decide that Luciferianism offers me hope for her, then I sure as hell am going to take up Luciferianism."

Balthazar sighed audibly, and his church steeple collapsed. "In that case, I'm going to ask one thing of you. Before you go ahead with this, if that's your intention, consult your mother. I confess that I ask this knowing perfectly well that Julia will oppose your having anything whatsoever to do with us. But despite our differences, your mother is a very wise woman whom I admire profoundly, and she will marshal the arguments against your joining us far better than I ever could. Listen to her, Daniel. And, *please,* make it perfectly clear to her that I had absolutely nothing to do with proselytizing you and in fact oppose it. I repeat, *Luciferianism is not for everyone,* and I foresee . . ."

Balthazar's voice faded as if he knew his words were futile, and he turned away from Daniel. He appeared to sigh. He looked at Freya.

"You should have consulted me," he said after another moment.

"Timothy—"

He looked again at Daniel. "You realize that everything we have said in this room is confidential. Except that having to do with your mother."

"Of course, sir. I'll respect that."

To Freya: "You'll be responsible for him."

"Of course."

"His training, his vows, everything."

"Naturally. I have several other novices in Manhattan. He can start training with them as soon as we get back." She looked at Daniel. "I'm sure he's very talented. He should be ready in two or three months. Probably less."

"We'll see."

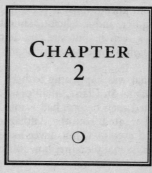

CHAPTER 2

Freya had driven them out to Timothy's citadel in her car, and she was in no hurry to deliver Daniel back to his, parked near the library. She was in no hurry at all, and she didn't touch the accelerator, but allowed her Mercedes convertible to drift down the rugged old mountainside, touching the brake now and then to slow their descent. The sunlight still beat down through crystal-clear air, and when she looked up at the cloudless sky, it seemed to her that they might be floating down out of it, floating down toward the lake and the dense green forests and the little toylike houses below. This sky, these forests, the lake, and the houses were a world in themselves, perfect, the terrarium of some godlike child, separate from the chaos of the rest of the universe. She felt as if in some mysterious way Daniel had transformed it, made it over into something magical and special. Just for her.

She looked straight ahead at the long, slightly winding gravel drive that led to the road circling the lake. Daniel sat turned slightly, facing her. She needed no peripheral vision to tell her that he was looking at her. Her hands were on the wheel at ten and two o'clock, and she felt his gaze on her right hand. She felt it on the large onyx cameo ring on her middle finger. She felt his gaze move to her right ear, with its matching onyx earring. She felt it trace her profile, felt it drifting slowly down her body . . . and then felt it moving along her half-bare thigh from knee to hip, as if his fingertips were ever so lightly touching her, and a delicious shudder went through her—he must have seen it, but she couldn't stop it—as she brought her legs tightly together against the abrupt surge of hot desire.

Dear God, what was happening to her?

How could Daniel St. Claire, of all people, do this to her?

She had wanted men before, had wanted them badly. At one time she had wanted Timothy Balthazar more than any other man she had ever met. But never like this. In the past, physical attraction, sexual pleasure, however intense, had been a mere by-product, a dividend. Now it seemed to be both an end in itself and a means to penetrate some other mystery, something that she now seemed to sense and yet could not quite conceive of. . . .

Body chemistry, she thought, almost despairingly. Hormones, nothing more. The god of this world used hormones to bring certain people together . . . or to keep them apart. It was as simple as that.

But still . . .

Until this afternoon, it had all seemed so simple. Not necessarily easy, but simple. Daniel had first caught her attention one Saturday morning in spring, almost twenty years ago. She had been in Pearson's drugstore, browsing at the perfume counter. Then as now, she had felt a gaze upon her—the wistful gaze of a young adolescent who, when she turned and smiled at him, blushed and quickly looked away. He had frowned and pretended to be deeply absorbed in the magazine rack. Amused and pleasantly flattered, she had been about to turn her attention back to the perfume, when, almost simultaneously, a handful of impressions struck her with breathtaking force. She was in the presence of an exceptional intelligence. This boy, this *child*, might "guess" her thoughts if she didn't mask them. He might put into her mind thoughts that she might or might not welcome. He himself was aware of this ability only dimly, if at all. Moreover, he had a very creative mind, visually creative, one that could construct the most complex three-dimensional image in his imagination like a hologram, turning it and viewing it from all angles . . . and transmit that image to another mind.

And then all those impressions, and others, were gone, as if the boy had self-protectively, if unwittingly, masked his mind. Only one impression remained . . . more than an impression, a fact.

This boy was a St. Claire.

There were other children with paranormal abilities in the community. In Freya's experience, there were a few such people, children and adults, in most communities of any size, and St. Claire had more than its share. But she had detected no others who had Daniel's potential. To Freya, that meant he was a resource, someone who might one day be useful. All the more so because he was a St. Claire and as such would be scorned by Timothy Balthazar. She would keep an eye on this boy.

Thereafter they saw each other occasionally on the streets of the town. She learned his name: Daniel. He became aware that she was that somewhat enigmatic young woman, Freya Kellgren, who lived in the big old house out north of the lake. She was older than he, but not all *that* old, and she tried to plant the suggestion in his mind that she was younger still. It wasn't difficult—like so many young men, where women were concerned, Daniel often saw what he wanted to see.

And so they sometimes ever so slightly smiled at each other and ever so slightly nodded, acknowledging that each knew who the other was. But they had never actually met until this afternoon.

She had not foreseen what was going to happen this afternoon. She did sometimes foresee the future, though not as accurately as Timothy did. His pre-visions of possible and probable futures were sometimes amazing. But she didn't think that even Timothy could have predicted what had happened this afternoon.

She had seen Daniel at a distance a couple of times since he had returned home this summer, but he had not seen her. That little girl of his had seen her, however, and that made her uneasy. Children didn't often take to her, and they didn't seem to understand that *they* frightened *her*. They looked at her with such *seeing* eyes. No, she did not wish to approach Daniel while little Nicole St. Claire was with him.

But he had been alone on this particular afternoon.

She had gone to the St. Claire library to return some books. As she laid them on the counter and turned away, there alone at one of the library tables sat Daniel . . . that long, lean, handsome wolf of a man. . . .

She had known that the time had come. Oh, how exquisite was her sense of the timing! The man was in near-despair, unguarded. Something to do with his daughter . . . the family curse . . .

She knew immediately how she would approach him. She would comfort him. She would offer him compassion, warmth . . . and hope.

She could do that. She would make him hers. She would make him her servant and ally, part of her own little coven within the larger convocation. And, oh, what a coup! A St. Claire within the convocation, and he would be *hers* and not Timothy's!

But that was yet to come. Now she moved silently through the stillness of the library toward Daniel's table, already *making* herself feel the concern, the compassion, the warmth she wished to project, *making* herself feel it even as her other self, her true self, looked on quite dispassionately . . . *Daniel, you are mine!*

Her shadow fell across the table, slid toward Daniel. "Daniel," she said softly.

But then, when he stood and took her hand, something quite extraordinary happened, something she could never have anticipated, something she never in this world would have wanted to happen.

She felt her feigned warmth, her feigned love, go out to him. She saw it seize him like an electric current. She saw it grip his heart, his mind, his manhood. All that, she would have expected.

But not what happened next.

She felt all that concern, compassion, warmth coming back to her—he was sharing it with her.

And it was real!

As if some last guttering candle in her cold soul had suddenly flared back to life, she *cared* about this man. She *cared* about his child. Why in the world should she *not* care about them? When had it ever been forbidden? And by whom?—by Timothy, that envious old fool? What had Timothy to compare to the St. Claire magic? She had heard of it for years, this mysterious allegiance they commanded from so many people. But never had she experienced it, never perhaps been given the chance. But now she knew what it was like, the St. Claire magic. She had offered Daniel fool's gold and he had made it real and offered it back. She had offered him cold darkness disguised as love, and he had given her warm radiance. Nothing was at all as she had expected.

"Tell me about yourself, Daniel," she said as they sat down facing each other. "How have you been?" And she truly wanted to know.

But another, colder voice deep within was saying, *Yes, he's mine now, Timothy. Mine, all mine. And just you watch out!*

She could still feel his eyes on her as they drove along the lake road, and she gave him a quick sideways look and a small purse-lipped smile. She knew what he was thinking: *I'd like to take you to bed.*

It was a temptation. Just to drive around the lake to her house, to take him up to her bedroom and spend the rest of the day, the evening, the night making love. She would have liked that—to seal their love with physical union within their first few hours together. She didn't think it would do any harm. . . .

But no. It was best not to take any chances of destroying the magic, and she knew that haste all too often did that for a man—much as he might deny it. She did not believe that that would happen with Daniel, did not want to believe it, but even so . . .

Earlier this afternoon, her instincts had told her it was time to make her move on Daniel. The same instincts would tell her when it was time to consummate their passion.

Dear Lord, had anything remotely like this happened to her before? She thought not, not even as an adolescent. Since then, she had had many adventures in many places, so many that there were years and adventures that faded in and out of memory, but no . . . nothing like this had happened to her before.

"You've never met my mother, have you?" Daniel asked. "Or my daughter? Why don't we stop by the house? You could stay for supper . . ."

Alarms went off, shrill and brazen, almost drowning out Daniel's words. *No,* she dared not "stop by the house," not now, not yet! Not until she was prepared. She would have been hard put to say why she didn't dare, except that it was almost as if her love for Daniel had rendered her vulnerable, and if she had to face that old woman, *she did not know what would happen.* That old woman and the little child would see through her. *She might even see through herself!* She wasn't sure what that meant, some strange and terrible revelation about herself, but at this time, she didn't think she could bear it.

She forced a smile as she pressed down on the accelerator. "Another time. I have an appointment, things I have to do. Perhaps in a day or two . . ."

She would leave St. Claire in the morning. She would send Daniel a note. An excuse, an apology, an emergency had come up. She would include her Manhattan address and telephone number. . . .

The car roared past the St. Claire house as if she were fleeing for her life.

Nicole was out on the big front veranda when the car went by.

Duffy Johnson was with her. Her grandmother had telephoned Duffy and asked him to come over and look after Nicole while she ran in to town. Of course, Nicole didn't think she really needed a baby-sitter—she was going on nine and would be in the fourth grade in the fall—but Duffy was fun.

Like when he taught her judo tricks and karate and something called *jeet kune do,* which he had learned from his father about as soon as he could walk. She didn't do *real* judo, of course—she didn't want to hurt anybody, even accidentally, and Duffy said it was just for sport. But Duffy taught her how to break a fall, which was useful, and some trip-ups, and a simple hip-roll throw. The hip throw, especially, was fun. She would grab his arm and throw an arm over his chest, then shift her hip behind his and lean forward, and suddenly Duffy was flying through the air, to land—"Aaugh!"—in the grass.

Of course, she knew perfectly well that he was *helping* her to do it, that she could never have done it on her own. But even so, he made her practice it over and over, about a hundred times, it seemed like, with her right hip and two hundred times with her left, until it was almost like she *was* doing it all by herself. Then he taught her what to do when *he* threw *her*—how to use his throw to flip herself up in the air in a kind of backward somersault and land on her feet in front of him. It was more like acrobatic dancing than combat, and Duffy told her she had the makings of an *outstanding* gymnast!

Duffy was very athletic. He was twelve and big for his age and what her grandmother called "as towheaded and open-faced as you can get," and he never minded coming over and staying with her for a while. He would have done it even if her grandmother—Aunt Julia, to Duffy—hadn't slipped him a dollar or two now and then. Her grandmother said he was Nicole's cousin, a third-cousin-once-removed. Whatever that meant. She said he was family, and he might not have the St. Claire name, but he was a St. Claire by several lines of descent, and more a St. Claire than a lot of people who *called* themselves St. Claire. And there was nothing wrong with being a Johnson, either!

When Nicole had told Duffy that, he had just shrugged and said, "Aw, so what?" but she could tell that he was pleased, and somehow that had made *her* feel good.

She didn't like Duffy's friends nearly as much as she did Duffy. His friends were mainly Brad Holland and Derek Anderson. Brad was the smallest of the three, and the darkest, with shiny black hair and dark eyes, and he was very . . . *intense.* Once, when she and Duffy were sitting around the kitchen while her grandmother made sandwiches and deviled eggs for lunch, her grandmother had made a slip. Without thinking, she had referred to Brad as "the Evil Elf." Duffy had laughed so hard that he fell off of his chair and rolled across the floor. Her grandmother had said, "Now, that was just a joke! Don't you go repeating that!" But Duffy had started calling Brad the Evil Elf anyway, and the name had stuck. Actually, Brad seemed to like it. For a while he had gone around acting spooky and saying, "Beware, beware! For I am the Evil Elf!"

Duffy's other friend, Derek, was the tallest and skinniest and prettiest of the three. The girls all made eyes at him, big girls and little girls alike, and when they weren't doing that, they were being rude and mean to him, just to get his attention. Derek would blush and stutter and mumble about "what a dumb jerk I am," and generally act so impossibly modest that it was downright painful. Though she never said so to anybody, Nicole knew that all along Derek was very busily, positively, absolutely *madly* adoring himself.

So why did Duffy hang out with these creeps?

Nicole knew why.

Because they really weren't all that bad. They were just *kids,* for God's sake, as her father sometimes remarked. And they had what her grandmother called *rapport* with one another. Sometimes the same funny thought would occur to all three of them at the same moment, and they would break out laughing together without having said a word. Duffy once told Nicole that when he was taking a geography quiz and couldn't remember an answer, sometimes all he had to do was look at Brad or Derek, and somehow the answer would come to him. Not always, but sometimes.

Not that Duffy hung out with the other two *all* the time. Duffy was the kind of boy who needed to be alone a lot, to think and brood and figure things out. And Nicole gave him an excuse to do that. Not long ago he had told her, "Being with you is the next best thing to being alone." To *being alone?* That was an insult! But they both knew he hadn't meant it that way, and in the next instant they were both laughing.

That was the same day, as a matter of fact, that Duffy had one of his fights with Derek and the Evil Elf.

Derek and Brad had planned to bicycle to the beach at the far end of the lake, explore the woods for a while and go for a swim, and then ride back. Not finding Duffy at home, they had come looking for him here. But Duffy hadn't been in the mood for any such expedition.

"I've got to look after Nicole," he said. It hadn't been true, but it had been as good an excuse as any.

"Whaddya mean?" the Elf said. "Her grandma's here, I saw her."

"She's busy. And she may have to go somewhere. I've got to look after Nicole."

"Ah, Chrissake," Derek mumbled, "goddamn fuckin' baby-sitter."

"Watch your language," Duffy said.

"Yeah, fuckin' baby-sitter," the Elf said defiantly. "What're you, a *girl*, you gotta baby-sit? It's a fuckin' goddamn *girl's* job!"

Suddenly Duffy was leaning forward with his arms out from his side and his eyes were wide and unblinking, and he seemed to *loom*.

His voice was soft and he sounded breathless, but he spoke very distinctly. "I said, watch your language, you little prick, or I'll wrap that goddamn bike around your neck."

For a long moment, Duffy and the Elf stared into each other's eyes unblinking. Then, with feigned casualness, the Elf looked away and swung his leg over his bike. "Ah, what the hell," he said, "Duffy's in a *mood* again. Got his *period*, maybe. Let's get the hell out of here."

Duffy never moved as the other two rode off, but Nicole seemed to hear his heart beating. He stared after them until they were out of sight. Then he took a deep breath and said, "Sometimes I get so sick of those fuckin' dorks, I could throw up!"

At her giggle, he quickly turned around. "You never heard that. I never said it and you never heard it!"

"Baby-sitter," she jeered. "Baby-sitter, girl, girl, nyah, nyah, nyah!"

"I'll *jeet kune do* your little ass!" Duffy said, striking a Bruce Lee pose, and in the next moment she was off her feet and in his arms, and he was whirling her around and around.

Perhaps that was the first time she realized, the first time that she had really known, that Duffy loved her.

And that she loved Duffy.

And he was with her now, when she needed him.

• • •

It was like a dream in which everything is bright and clear and beautiful, the sunlight falling through the trees and over the green lawn, over the blacktop road and the little beach below, and the green and gray and purple mountains beyond the lake, the air so clear and everything late-afternoon bright, and yet suddenly suffused with awfulness.

It was like looking at a painfully beautiful landscape on a movie screen and knowing that in the next few moments something bad was going to happen, and your heart begins to pound.

Through the trees she saw the dark convertible, its top down, coming along the road. It was coming from the west, and at that moment it was the only car in sight. Nicole had no reason to notice it, cars passed by all the time, but for some reason this car held her transfixed.

She had excellent eyesight. But it seemed to her that she recognized her daddy, sitting in the passenger seat, before she could even make out his face—her daddy, coming closer and closer in that car.

But that made no sense. Her daddy had gone into town. He should be coming from the other direction, and in his own car.

This car, she saw with dismay, was being driven by the Lady in White.

Twice this summer, when they were in town, she had seen the Lady in White looking at her father from a distance. Miss Kellgren. Her father hadn't noticed, but Nicole had. It had happened last summer too. Each time, Nicole had had a bad feeling.

And now, as in a bad dream, her father was riding in the dark spectral car with the Lady in White, and the feeling was worse than ever.

As the car went by, her father smiled and waved at her. Miss Kellgren did not. She kept her head tucked down and looked straight ahead all the time. It seemed to Nicole that the car speeded up as it went by.

Then it was winding down the road and out of sight.

It was a moment before Nicole realized that Duffy was teasing her. "Daddy's got a girlfriend. Daddy's got a girlfriend. Nyah, nyah, nyah, nyah, Daddy's got a girlfriend!"

Duffy, her grandmother said, hadn't a mean bone in his body. He undoubtedly expected Nicole to retaliate with pounding fists and gibes of her own and a tussle that would end in laughter. Instead, she abruptly broke down in a paroxysm of sobs and scalding, blinding tears.

At once, Duffy's arms were around her. "Hey, Nickie, I was just teasing, I didn't mean anything, don't feel bad, Nickie. . . ."

By then, her grandmother had returned from town, and Duffy called to her: "Aunt Julia, could you come out here, please?" But by the time her grandmother arrived on the veranda, Nicole was feeling much better. Thanks to Duffy. She couldn't even have explained exactly why she had cried, and she didn't want to talk about it. But Duffy told about her daddy and Miss Kellgren, and her grandmother seemed to think she understood exactly. "Well, I suppose it's only natural," she said.

But Nicole wondered if she really knew about the Lady in White.

Daniel St. Claire asked himself what in hell, actually, he was getting into.

He hadn't got such an erotic charge from a woman since he had fallen in love with Mary, his own dear sweet Mary, more than a dozen years ago. But that situation had been entirely different. He had known Mary, if from a distance, all of his life. He hardly knew Freya Kellgren.

True, Freya had shown him enormous sympathy and understanding, and the erotic attraction seemed to be mutual. But Daniel was not so stupid or naive as to mistake the pyrotechnics of sex for eternal love.

But it was a damned good beginning, and he planned to see a lot more of Freya Kellgren.

If only he knew more about her. It occurred to him that she had seemed to know quite a bit about the St. Claires, and certainly he had prattled on and on about his daughter, but she had told him almost nothing about herself. And he hadn't asked. God, what an egocentric fool he must have seemed. . . .

"Mom, what do you know about the Kellgrens?"

They were in the living room. His mother was at her escritoire, penning a note to an old friend before starting supper, and he had been thumbing through *Newsweek* without really seeing it.

His mother put down his dad's old Montblanc and looked at him sharply. "The Kellgrens? Why do you ask?"

"I ran into Freya Kellgren at the library this afternoon. We've had a nodding acquaintance for years, but never really met. We talked for a while, and she seemed quite nice. But afterward it occurred to me that I really know very little about her. I'm curious."

His mother was silent for a moment, as if considering the matter. "I really can't tell you much. I know the family's been around these parts a long time. I recall meeting a Freya Kellgren, or maybe it was a Greta Kellgren, at a party old Benjamin Balthazar gave for Timothy years ago. I suppose your current Freya could be her daughter, or a niece, possibly. People seem to know *of* the Kellgrens without knowing a great deal *about* them . . . perhaps because they've never really been a part of the community."

"How so?"

His mother smiled ruefully. "I'm sorry, that sounds snobbish. As if my own little circle of friends and acquaintances were the only ones who counted. But the fact remains that the Kellgren women have always avoided involvement in town affairs. The couple of times I tried to get acquainted with a Greta or a Freya through social causes, I got hefty contributions, but my invitations were refused. Almost as if they were paying to be left alone. My impression is that a great deal of the time, they're not even here. Freya, Greta, whoever, they come and stay a few weeks or months and then vanish, almost like the summer people. It's as if their house here were just a place to stop off at for a while between travels."

"What about the Kellgren men?"

"Seldom seen. Presumably off somewhere, attending their affairs. For all I know, there may not even *be* any Kellgren men. My mother once told me that the Kellgren women hyphenated. Magda Kellgren-Smith. Lulu Kellgren-Jones. And at death or divorce or just plain whim, they dropped the Smith or Jones. At the time, back in the forties, that seemed both

scandalous and pretentious. One more thing to keep the Kellgrens at a remove from the rest of us. By the way . . ." His
mother hesitated. "Duffy told me he and Nicole saw you and
Freya drive by this afternoon."

Daniel hated the idea of lying to his mother. But if he told
her that he and Freya had gone to talk to Timothy Balthazar,
she would naturally be curious as to why; and despite Timothy's admonitions, he had absolutely no intention of telling
her. He was certain that she would disapprove, and he was not
going to put that burden of worry on her.

"Freya has a new car, a Mercedes convertible. We took it
for a spin around the lake."

He didn't like the steady, unsmiling way his mother was
looking at him, as if she were reading his mind. But she merely
said, "Too bad you didn't stop by. I'd like to have made Miss
Kellgren's acquaintance after all this time. And meeting her
might have allayed Nicole's anxieties."

Daniel felt himself tensing. "What do you mean?"

"Nothing to be alarmed about, I'm sure. It was just that
thing between motherless little girls and their daddies. Apparently the sight of you and Miss Kellgren brought on a momentary shower of tears."

"Oh, my God," Daniel said, truly dismayed. He stood up
and began to pace.

"Now, it's nothing to worry about. Duffy had her calmed
down before I even got out on the veranda."

"God bless that kid. He has the touch."

"Indeed. If he doesn't grow up to be a doctor, I shall be
very disappointed."

"But he can't cure Nicole," Daniel said despairingly,
"nothing can cure Nicole."

His mother frowned at that, but held her peace. She knew
there was no comfort in vague talk of medical progress and
future cures. The lycanthropic gene, if there was such a thing,
seemed to be dying out of the family, but that was no help to
Nicole. Daniel could only hope and pray that she wouldn't
suffer as his father had suffered.

His father, dead at forty-eight of booze and tranquilizers,
the only thing that gave him relief. Again and again, drinking
and doping himself into a sodden mess to escape some long-

ing, some pain, that Daniel could not even imagine. But he remembered well his own small-boy terror at his father's howls of anguish on moonlit nights. He remembered his father's self-loathing at being a drunk and his painful efforts at resisting his affliction without the use of alcohol and drugs. He remembered his father's tearing off his clothes as if *they* were driving him to madness, and he remembered the nights when his father fled from the house to roam the woods and his mother and grandparents could only pray for his safe return. He remembered the dawn when he awakened early and found his father sleeping naked on the back porch with blood on his face and body.

He remembered the worst night of all.

He had been about Nicole's age, eight. Usually, when his father had his attacks, Daniel was confined to his bedroom, and he willingly stayed there, hands to his ears and his eyes tightly closed, praying for silence and sleep. But on that particular night there came a point when he could stand his father's sobs and moans no longer. He wanted only to throw himself into his father's arms and hold him and try to comfort him. So, tears running down his face, he slipped out of bed and into the dimly lit hallway and went silently toward his parents' bedroom, where light escaped from the half-open door. He looked into the room, and the scene was burned into his memory forever.

His father was sitting on the edge of the bed, his pajamas torn open. His mother, in her nightgown, was kneeling behind him and appeared to be hugging him with all her strength. His father released a long animal sob.

Daniel had never before seen his father like this. His head was thrown back as if he were baying, and even as Daniel watched, he seemed to be turning into something monstrous. His unshaven face was distorted, twisting out of shape, almost as if it were growing a snout, a muzzle. His mouth opened wide, as he cried out, and Daniel saw fangs, long and sharp.

The sight lasted only a few seconds. While Daniel stood there, staring in shock at the unbelievable, his mother saw him. She instantly leaped from the bed and came running out into the hall, pulling the door closed behind her.

Daniel could not stop the words or disguise his horror: "He's turning into a *wolf!*"

"No!" His mother dropped to her knees so that she could better look him in the eyes. She reached for his shoulders. "Now, listen to me—"

"But he's turning—"

"No, no, no, no!" She gave him a shake. "Daniel, that's just your imagination. You've heard stories, and sometimes when we're frightened, we *think* we see things—"

"But, Mom—"

She shook him again. "Listen to me! Daniel, you must never tell anyone what you—what you *thought* you saw. There are ignorant people who would try to hurt your father if they knew! And others who would try to have him locked up. You saw nothing, and you must never, never tell. It was all your imagination!"

For years he had told himself that his mother was right, that the transformation he had witnessed had never really happened. He had never seen it again, had *never allowed* himself to see it again. He had wanted to put it out of mind, had wanted to forget it entirely. But at the first sign of Nicole's affliction, it had all come back to him vividly, in every detail.

He still did not want to believe it had happened.

But a little voice in the back of his mind, a voice that could not be silenced, insisted without the slightest doubt: *It happened.*

Your father was a wolf.

The old stories about the St. Claire werewolves are true.

And what happened to your father is going to happen to your daughter!

But no, no, no, he would not believe that. That would be too awful to be true. He simply could not bear the thought of it.

His father's affliction had grown progressively worse with the years. It had struck most often, though not always, at the full moon, and hiding from the moon had had little effect. The tides of madness rose even in the dark.

He would not, could not, let that happen to Nicole. He would lay down his life before he let that happen to Nicole.

"Daniel?" his mother said softly.

Daniel realized his eyes were wet, and he wiped them before turning to his mother. "I was just thinking," he said, trying to sound cheerful though his throat was clogged, "you've heard of the laying on of hands?"

"Of course. You've experienced it yourself, at your confirmation. It's also part of ordination and ministering to the sick—Holy Unction. What about it?"

"Somehow it came up in conversation with Freya Kellgren, and I was wondering . . ."

His mother ever so slightly frowned. "You discussed Nicole with Freya?"

Daniel shrugged. "Briefly." He knew the lie was transparent.

"Daniel, I don't know exactly what you have in mind, but you must know that Nicole has received unction a number of times. I believe she has benefited from it. After all, her attacks have become rare."

"But she isn't cured."

"No, she isn't cured. But she is in God's hands."

"Oh, sure." Daniel was suddenly angry. "A god that lets little children die of bullets and brain tumors and maybe even lunatic lycanthropy. Maybe we should elect a new god—one that exercises some *power* in this world!"

His mother stared at him for a moment, and he regretted his words. "I'm sorry. I didn't mean to insult your faith."

"I was just thinking . . . how much you sound like . . . Timothy Balthazar."

Daniel was startled. Sometimes he still felt as if his mother could read his mind. He felt as guilty as a small boy who has lied by omission.

"How so?" he asked.

"Oh, Timothy has always liked to joke about being a Luciferian, 'like my old horse-thief grandfather,' he'll say. 'I may worship as a Christian, Julia,' he'll say, 'but it was the Luciferian in me that got a new roof put on the church.' Then he'll chortle as if he's said something oh-so-witty. But I suspect that like his 'old horse-thief grandfather,' he really is a Luciferian, and he jokes to cover the fact."

"Does he know you see through him?" Daniel asked,

thinking of Timothy's insistence that he consult with his mother.

"He probably suspects as much. And incidentally, there was at least one exception to the Kellgrens' rule of not making themselves a part of the community."

"And that was?"

"The Freya or Greta that I remember from long ago was apparently quite close to Timothy. They were, as they say, an item."

"So?" Again, Daniel felt guilty.

"Oh, nothing much." His mother rose from her chair and came to him. "Except that you were speaking of the laying on of hands. Remember that it can be dangerous. Choose the wrong source of power, and you can do great damage. What's more, it can turn on you."

Daniel smiled, remembering things his mother had taught him. "Like the power of anathema," he said.

She nodded gravely. "Like the power of anathema. Daniel, I am not joking."

"I know. And Mother knows best."

"Of course she does. After all . . ." His mother leaned forward and kissed him lightly. "Mother is a witch!"

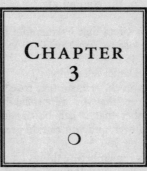

CHAPTER
3

Timothy took the elevator to the fourth-floor tower room—his aerie, as he thought of it. By the time he got there, Freya and Daniel had reached the main road, and he could see the car moving east toward the town. *Damned insolent bitch!* he thought. Did she really think she could do it? Convert a St. Claire to Luciferianism, to the enemy camp, as it were? And behind his back! He had a bad feeling—this could mean trouble. He would have to keep careful watch.

He wondered if Daniel would do as he had asked and consult his mother. Probably not, but he hoped so. Julia would have her suspicions about his Luciferianism confirmed, of course, but so what? These days, the One True Faith could, if necessary, put on the face of harmless eccentricity, something no more serious than Yokel Atheism. The important thing was that he must not earn Julia's enmity. They had been friends of sorts for many years now, for most of their lives, in fact, and he wanted to keep it that way. She had been suspicious of him from time to time, and if she were ever to confirm that he had been her enemy . . .

"I will use the power of anathema against you," she had said, all those years ago. *"I promise you."*

Timothy had not the slightest doubt that Julia had the power and that under certain circumstances she would indeed use it.

Christ, the woman was truly a witch!

She had the most extraordinary ability to get her own way. He thought of an incident that had occurred a few years earlier. Timothy owned a Honda agency, the largest and most successful in that part of the state. Successful, that is, until the manager, a man named Caldwell who had been with him from the beginning, began to slack off. His wife had been fighting a losing battle against cancer, and no doubt it drained the man, but that wasn't Timothy's fault. Meanwhile, the sales force fell apart, Caldwell lost his best mechanics, the plant wasn't being properly maintained, and Timothy saw his business going down the drain. He warned Caldwell several times, with no results, and then decided he would just have to get rid of the man.

He had no sooner reached that decision than he got a telephone call from Julia, who had become aware of the situation. The result? He had somehow wound up giving Caldwell a small raise and time off to be with his wife until her death.

What else could he have done? Put Julia off and fired Caldwell, obviously. Then why hadn't he done that? Why instead had he done exactly what Julia had told him he should do? Was it because he *feared* Julia? Was it because somewhere deep in his soul after all these years he still wanted to *please* Julia? He didn't know. All he had known, with gut-certainty, was that he had damned well better do as Julia said or he could be in deep trouble. And Timothy had to admit that thereafter Caldwell had put the agency back on top and had turned out to be one of the best managers he had ever employed. But even so . . .

There had been other incidents, so many of them.

Julia had promoted the new wing on the public library—paid for largely out of Timothy's pocket.

And he had also paid, thanks to Julia, for much of the new imaging equipment at the hospital.

Incident after incident. Not that Julia constantly interfered—she did not. But when she got interested in some person or project, she usually got things done and done her way.

And Timothy, exasperated, then wanted to know, Who the hell runs St. Claire, anyway? Timothy Balthazar or Julia St. Claire?

"Boy," his father had said, "listen to what I have to say, and always remember it. The St. Claires *owed* your Grandfather Isaac. They would never have been what they became, if not for him. They owed him till the day he died, and as far as I'm concerned, they owe him still and they always will."

He could still hear his father's voice, as they had sat together from time to time, out on the second-floor veranda, where they could look down across the forested land toward the St. Claire house to the east. Except for a strip of lakeside cabins owned by his father, most of the land between the two houses was state parkland, so they had a clear view. The Balthazar house, being on the crest of Balthazar's Mountain, was higher than the St. Claire house. Somehow that was important.

Benjamin Balthazar had been handsomer than his son, or his father. With his longer, narrower face and finer, more lupine features he actually looked more like a St. Claire than a Balthazar, though Timothy would never have dreamed of calling this to his father's attention.

His father had spoken of the St. Claires with an odd mixture of envy, admiration, and anger.

"Give them credit. They came to America before the Revolution and started the St. Claire Northwest Company to supply furs to their New York City business . . . discovered this valley, which was still relatively isolated, and turned it into a thriving little community. The Indians in these parts tended to regard white men as poachers, but the St. Claires got along with them just fine. The Indians said the St. Claires, some of 'em, were shape-changers, wolves mostly, and as a wolf, a St. Claire could travel farther and faster than any man, to seek out deer and other game and lead the Indians to it. Sounds like an Indian tall tale, but I have reason to believe there was truth in it."

Timothy would always remember that autumn afternoon

when he was thirteen and he and his father sat out on the upstairs veranda, looking down at the burnished gold and bronze and copper leaves of autumn, and his father told him the story of Isaac Balthazar and the St. Claire betrayal. His father's face had darkened and hardened and seemed to grow wider as his jaw clenched, and for the first time he looked to Timothy more like a Balthazar than a St. Clair.

"So the St. Claires did well, all things considered, but it was your grandfather Isaac who built their fortune.

"It may be hard for you to believe, but your grandfather was born in the eighteenth century, in 1797, and he was still a young man when he went to work for the St. Claires. He went to work for old Roussell St. Claire as an ordinary bookkeeper, and within a few years he was the chief financial officer for the entire organization. It was he, Isaac, who persuaded them to open their New York City leather goods factories with modern machinery, he who began opening up foreign markets for St. Claire goods, he who landed the big military contracts. Under his stewardship, the St. Claire fortunes grew as never before.

"Then he made the biggest mistake of his life.

"Your grandfather had the gift of prescience. Prescience, Timothy, is the ability to see, on little or no evidence, but very clearly, possible and probable futures. You and I and every successful horseplayer have it, and it can be cultivated. But it's tricky. You must learn never to let yourself be fooled by wishful thinking.

"Perhaps that's what your grandfather did. I don't know. All I really know is that in 1855, at the age of fifty-eight, your grandfather married for the first time. And he married a St. Claire, Miss Melinda St. Claire. He married her both to provide himself with an heir and to further assure that heir's position. His son was, by God, going to be tied to the St. Claires by blood. *I* was going to be Benjamin *St. Claire* Balthazar.

"I don't want to say much about my mother, Timothy. She was a plain-faced old maid of thirty-one when she married my father, and he must have seemed like her last and best chance. She seemed like a sweet lady, a little simpleminded, maybe, but harmless.

"In 1856, she gave birth to me. By that time, old Roussell

St. Claire was dead, and his grandson, Stephen Morgan St. Claire, was the head of the family and the business. Melinda and Stephen were cousins and almost as close as brother and sister, which may have been one of the reasons my father married her.

"Then came the war. Stephen Morgan St. Claire was off to save the Union and free the slaves, leaving your grandfather Isaac in unquestioned charge of everything.

"The war finally ended, and in the spring of 1865 Stephen Morgan came home. That was the beginning of the end for my father.

"It's hard to believe he didn't see it coming. He knew Stephen was looking over the books, something he had seldom done with any thoroughness before the war—the financial details were my father's province. And a month or so later, he must have known that Stephen had ordered a thorough auditing of the books, not just for the time he had been away, but for many years back. No, I am certain that my father honestly believed that he had served the St. Claires well and that he could justify anything that Stephen Morgan chose to question.

"You see, Timothy, your grandfather was a very sharp businessman. One of the things he taught me (remember this!) is that money makes money. But you never use your own money when you can use someone else's.

"Now, from the very beginning your grandfather had determined that he, by God, was not going to wind up being no more than somebody's glorified bookkeeper. If he was going to make the St. Claires richer than ever, *they*, by God, were going to make *him* rich!

"So he borrowed from them from time to time. At a nominal rate of interest.

"There was nothing wrong with this, Timothy. It was simply business. If he was going to look out for the St. Claires' interests, he was entitled to whatever he could get in exchange for doing so. Business!

"What did he put his money into? All kinds of things, as Stephen Morgan found out, but mortgages mostly. Your grandfather turned foreclosure into a fine art. But it was business, Timothy, simply business!

"Of course, when it came to business, he had an edge. He

had early on discovered the One True Faith and sworn himself to the god of this world. And as you know, the god rewards those who act in his name. My father had even drawn together a half-dozen or so like-minded people from around here into his own coven. If he hadn't grown careless . . .

"Timothy, I try to see my mother's point of view. Maybe she tried to stay in her place and mind her own affairs, as a good wife should. But she was not quite the simpleminded soul she seemed, and no doubt over a period of time my father grew careless. I myself remember him using phrases like 'praise Lucifer' as if he were joking, and I remember his referring to a circle of his friends as 'the satanic brotherhood.' Always with a laugh. But at some point my mother began to suspect . . .

"Good Christian that she was, she must have secretly been in agony. Her husband was a 'servant of Satan.' Who could she turn to? She decided she should wait and pray for the return of the one person she could trust to help her, her cousin, Stephen Morgan St. Claire.

"My mother told me none of this, you understand, Timothy. To my recollection, she never said a word to me against my father. But I was a smart, observant kid, and I pretty much figured out on my own what had happened.

"When Stephen Morgan came back, she told him everything she knew or suspected. She identified the members of the 'satanic brotherhood.' I later learned that at least two of them, a St. Claire accountant and a leading lawyer, had testified to my father's Luciferianism. Apparently they were a hell of a lot more frightened of Stephen Morgan, when confronted, than they were of the god of this world.

"My mother's accusations put everything else about my father in question, and that was why Stephen Morgan had the books audited.

"I never asked your grandfather—it was too painful—but, yes, I'm sure he foresaw *some* of what was coming. He simply didn't foresee all of it or when it would come.

"It came on a Wednesday evening at an evening prayer service at the Episcopal Church. St. Jude's, the same church we still attend.

"Your grandparents and I were seated in our usual pew,

up front and to the right, on the epistle side. Stephen Morgan and his family were across the aisle on the gospel side. It was evident all through the service that something was wrong—the minister was pale-faced and faltering, as if he might collapse at any moment. Then, after the final blessing, while the organ was playing and the congregation was rising to leave, the minister raised his hands and said, 'Wait, please! There is an announcement! An important announcement! I think that under the circumstances the chief warden of the vestry should make it. Colonel St. Claire, if you please!'

"I remember a kind of surprised murmur as the music stopped and the congregation sat down again. Stephen Morgan marched right up to the pulpit and gazed down at us. He was a prematurely gray man by that time, with a long, pointed mustache that bristled and steely eyes. He glared at my father for a moment, and I was surprised to see my mother lower her face and cover it with her hands. Then Stephen Morgan spoke the words that I shall never forget.

" 'Brothers and sisters in Christ,' he said, 'I regret that I am the bearer of bad news. Satan has come to St. Claire. *By invitation!*'

"I remember the stir that went through the congregation.

" 'We have among us,' Stephen Morgan went on, 'one who is a thief, a conniving hypocrite, and a blasphemer. But far more terrible, brothers and sisters, we have among us one who has pledged his very soul to the unholy trinity of Lucifer, Satan, and Beelzebub—and yet has dared to take the bread and wine, the Body and Blood of our Lord Jesus Christ, into his filthy mouth—'

"By the time Stephen Morgan had gotten that far, my father had grabbed me by the wrist and was dragging me down the aisle and out of the church, leaving my mother behind.

"The next thing I knew, my father had knocked aside the boy who was looking after our horse and carriage, and we had climbed into the carriage and were riding hell for leather through the moonlight toward the house that my father had built on this mountain. I still remember the crack of the whip and the sparks from the horse's shoes as we thundered along that road. Again and again, my father cursed from between

clenched teeth, 'That bitch! That damned treacherous . . .'
Later it seemed to me that I had heard Stephen Morgan's
words following us, even as we fled them: 'I put my curse on
you, son of Satan!' I could even see the minister's shocked
face: he hadn't expected this. 'Unless you renounce your evil
god and repay all you have cheated and stolen from others,
may you lose all you have, everything! This is the anathema
that I lay upon you and all the members of your coven from
this moment forth. . . .'

"Of course, my father had known at once that my mother
had betrayed him. In that sudden moment of clarity, he must
have thought of a hundred instances when he had treated her
as if she were deaf or blind or feebleminded, and thus in a
sense had betrayed himself.

"He was finished in St. Claire and he knew it, and he left
for New York City that very night. I stood by, frightened and
confused, while he threw clothes into a couple of old carpet-
bags and got out his old Colt revolving pistol. I begged him:
'Please, Daddy, can't I go with you?'

" 'No,' he said, 'a boy your age belongs with his mother.
And no matter what she's done to me, she's a damned good
mother to you, and don't you forget it. But don't you forget,
either, that *you're my son.*' He gave me a reassuring smile.
'Don't you worry,' he said, 'I'm going to go right on taking
care of you. And when you're old enough, I'm going to teach
you about power! Power, the only thing worth having. But
that's between you and me, Benjamin, our secret. Let 'em
think you've fallen for that Sweet Jesus stuff they teach you in
Sunday school. But don't you ever forget *whose son you really
are!*'

"I carried a lamp and one of the small bags out to the
stable for him, and he loaded up the carriage. He had just
finished harnessing a fresh horse when my mother arrived.
She was driven by an elderly member of the parish whom I
recognized as a Mr. Addison. We heard her calling to us before
we even saw her, 'Benjamin! Mr. Balthazar!' and then the
buggy pulled out of the pine shadows into the moonlit stable
yard.

"At the sight of my mother, all my father's anger returned. I don't think he heard a thing she said as she jumped

out of that buggy and ran to him. 'Mr. Balthazar, they're coming for you, you've got to get away! You've got to go, they'll be here at any minute! Mr. Balthazar—'

"I think that was the only time I ever saw my father completely out of control. He said, 'Woman, I'm going to give you what you deserve,' then threw her down so hard that she rolled in the dirt of the stable yard. As she tried to get up, he reached into the carriage for his whip.

"That broke my paralysis. I was my father's son, yes, but I could not let him whip my mother. I hurled myself at him, grabbing his whip arm and screaming, 'No, no, no!' while Mr. Addison seized his other arm and said, 'My God, Mr. Balthazar, you can't do that!'

"My father, by that time, was in his sixties, but he flung us both off as easily as if he had been half his age. He raised the whip high, it snaked across the moon, and I saw his shoulders bunching up as he gathered his strength for that first blow.

"It never fell.

"At that moment there came the longest, loudest, most bloodcurdling wolf howl I had ever heard. It seemed to come from our very midst, a sound so close and loud that it drowned out every thought and left only terror. The fresh horse my father had harnessed started as if it were about to bolt, and the others in the stable stomped and whinnied with fear.

"As the howl faded, a dozen more sounded, near and far, in different pitches, a chorus of howling wolves saluting their leader.

"My father threw the whip back in the carriage, but not because he was afraid. When he drew his pistol, he was grinning and his eyes glittered. 'Show yourself, Stephen Morgan,' he shouted, 'show yourself if you dare! I've got five silver bullets waiting for you—I've been carrying them for years!'

" 'No,' my mother cried, 'no, no, no! Mr. Balthazar, Cousin Stephen doesn't want to hurt you. But there's a lynch mob coming, and they do! You've got to leave, Mr. Balthazar, leave right now. They'll be here any minute!'

"But my father didn't want to run. He tried one more

time. 'Stephen Morgan, show yourself! Come and get me, you yellow-bellied son of a St. Claire bitch!'

"Not a sound.

"Except for my father's harsh laugh of triumph.

"And then, from some distance, shouts.

" 'Mr. Balthazar,' my mother said, 'go! Take the back road! We'll try to detain them here if we can.'

" 'She's right, Mr. Balthazar,' Mr. Addison said, 'you'd best leave right now, while you've still got some head start.'

"So my father finally heaved a big sigh and holstered his pistol. But he was damned if he was going to be *run* off. Taking his own good time, he gave me a big hug and assured me again that he would see me soon. Then he climbed into the carriage and waved to me, and drove off in a leisurely fashion, as if he had all the time in the world."

Timothy had heard the story before, but he never tired of it.

"The mob arrived a few minutes later, riffraff and rabble, drunk and bored, who'd heard that Benjamin Balthazar was 'in league with the devil.' A fine excuse to make trouble for their betters. We were back in the house by then, in the dark, and I could see them from a window. They had come in buggies and carriages and some on foot. A few carried torches, and the flickering light made them look like grinning, blood-thirsty goblins in a holiday mood. I couldn't tell how many there were—a few dozen, I suppose, but my small boy's imagination multiplied that to hundreds.

"Someone fired a pistol into the air and yelled, 'Death to the witch!' And someone else, brandishing a torch, yelled, 'If they won't come out, burn 'em out!'

"At that moment I saw with utter clarity that unless this mob were stopped, they would indeed set our house on fire and burn it down. This was not something I *felt* or *feared*, this was something I *saw* and *heard* . . . my mother screaming, as those hate-crazed brutes tore her clothes off and dragged her away.

"So I wasn't being brave when I ran out across the veranda and down onto the lawn. I was in mortal terror, and I was trying to save my mother and our house. I heard myself yelling at them to go away, to go away and leave my mother alone!

"Then one I recognized stepped into the torchlight, a man called Billy Taggart. He was a dark, hollow-eyed, thin-faced man with a scraggly mustache and a ragged hat, a tenant farmer who had had dealings with my father. In debt to my father, probably, and bitter with defeat. He shook his rifle in the air and pointed a finger at me and said, 'It's the witch's kid! Grab him! He's the spawn of the devil! Don't let him get away!'

"I was ready to run at Billy Taggart, to kick and pummel him, but my mother grabbed me from behind. 'Don't you dare touch this boy,' she yelled back, frightened and angry, 'don't you dare!'

"Something about her voice, her presence, quieted the mob a bit, and someone spoke up, 'We ain't here to hurt you or the boy, ma'am. We just want Mr. Benjamin Balthazar, and you know why. He ain't fit to live among decent folks.'

"The noise started up again. 'Run him off!' 'Tar and feather him!' 'String him up!' *'Thou shalt not suffer a witch to live!'*

"The mob started circling our flanks so we couldn't get away, and my mother could hardly make herself heard. 'Listen! Listen to me! Mr. Balthazar isn't here! Mr. Balthazar has gone away! Come in the house, some of you, and see for yourselves! *Mr. Balthazar isn't here!*'

"Her words finally penet0rated, and the mob seemed to hesitate. But then Mr. Billy Taggart, who was apparently the leader, said loudly, 'Well, boys, if we ain't got the witch, we still got the witch's bitch and the witch's whelp, and I reckon they ain't no better than he is. So let's show 'em what we do with witches in these parts!'

"I tell you, Timothy, no pack of savages—and they were savages at that point—ever howled their approval louder. I could barely hear my own cries of fear, as I turned to my mother and clung to her, my eyes closed and my face hidden in her bosom, expecting the first shot, the first blow. Someone yelled, 'Get 'em! Get 'em!'—and those were the last words we heard before there came the most threatening sound you could possibly imagine.

"It instantly struck that crowd silent again. I raised my face from my mother's breasts and saw that they were all looking about apprehensively for the source of that sound.

"It wasn't a howl this time. It was a great harsh growl, a growl so loud that it seemed to come out of the shadows and surround us; seemed to *contain* us, it was so huge; and it kept changing its timbre, as if nostrils were flaring and jaws were opening and hot breath were flowing over a wet tongue. I listened, as frightened as anyone there.

"After a moment, Billy Taggart said uncertainly, 'It ain't nothin'. Just a dog. They got a guard dog somewhere 'round here.'

"'Goddamn *big* dog,' someone else said. 'Sounds like a goddamn *freight* train!'

"'It's a dog,' Billy Taggart said louder, 'just a goddamn dog! What's a dog against us! We got us a nest o' witches to deal with!'

"And it started again: 'Whip 'em!' 'String 'em up!' 'Thou shalt not suffer a witch to live!'

"Billy Taggart looked straight into my mother's eyes and said, 'You're gonna die, witch! And you ain't gonna die easy. You're gonna die slow and hard, you're gonna die—'

"That was as far as he got. From somewhere out of the shadows, that 'dog,' that immense wolf or whatever it was, those hundreds of pounds of bone and muscle and shining fangs, came hurtling through the air so fast it seemed to appear out of nowhere. With one immense leap, it came flying at shoulder height straight at Billy Taggart.

"Now, bear in mind, Timothy, that what happened next took only a few seconds. That beast hit Billy Taggart a rib-crushing blow that knocked him at least twenty feet down the slope of the lawn. It landed on top of him, its fangs raking Billy's face and throat. Billy screamed and tried to beat the animal away, but it was no use. Those big jaws closed on Billy Taggart's belly, the teeth tearing through fabric and flesh like they were cutthroat razors, ripping him open from sternum to groin. And while Billy screamed, that beast literally *threw* his torn guts into the air.

"By then, Billy was a dead man, of course—he just didn't know it. By some supreme effort, he actually managed to roll over onto his torn belly, and it seemed to me he was trying to crawl away. But the wolf's jaw closed on his back, breaking his ribs and crushing his spine, and Billy gave his last long terrible scream. Then, mercifully, the wolf put him out of his misery. The jaws clamped down just once more, on the back of Billy's neck. That wolf lifted Billy from the ground, shook him as easily as another wolf might shake a rabbit; shook him, blood spraying, and flung him away.

"And then the wolf turned on the others.

"They were running, screaming. Guns were going off. Men were crying like terrified children. My mother fell to the ground, and I thought she had been shot, but she was only huddling to save us—to save me—from the flying bullets.

"As I looked about, I realized that the great gray wolf had not come alone. I thought I saw at least half a dozen smaller wolves, maybe more, darting through the woods and harrying the mob as it ran in full rout down the mountain.

"Finally there were only a few distant cries, but my mother and I remained crouched in each other's arms. Billy Taggart didn't move. He would never move again.

"The wonder was that of all those who were injured that night, only Billy died.

"We didn't move until Mr. Addison came out of the house. 'Oh, Mrs. Balthazar,' he said, 'are you all right? Is the boy all right?'

"'We're all right, Mr. Addison,' my mother said.

"I said, 'Mama! Look!'

"Like one of the shadows of the night, the great gray wolf had come back up the mountain and out of the woods, his muzzle still red with Billy Taggart's blood. The torches were gone or burned out and we had only the moonlight to see him, but that was enough. He was, as I had thought, the greatest, most magnificent wolf I had ever seen, a wolf grand beyond anything that I might have imagined. But he had not come through the battle unscathed. Blood flowed from his left shoulder and his left haunch.

"He stood looking at us silently for a moment. Then he turned and loped unhurriedly back into the darkness of the woods, lost from our sight and never to be seen again. . . .

"Of course, the story was all over the countryside the next

day, and it's been told ever since. Some say that Stephen Morgan St. Claire used his powers to send wolves to protect his beloved cousin and her son. Others say that Stephen Morgan actually turned into a wolf and led other wolves, or perhaps other St. Claires, to protect my mother and me. It's all conjecture—we'll never really know. But I do know what I saw that night.

"Beyond that, I can tell you one other thing. The next time I saw Stephen Morgan St. Claire, he had his left arm in a sling and he walked with a limp."

"You will understand, Timothy," his father said, "that I was torn. I was completely in awe of the St. Claire wolf, if such it was. It had almost certainly saved my mother and me from a terrible fate. And I was, through my mother, part St. Claire myself and proud of it! Wasn't St. Claire my middle name— Benjamin St. Claire Balthazar?

"Your grandfather came back after dark one evening a few weeks later and made a kind of peace with my mother. He spent most of that night in his study, packing away some papers and destroying others. When he slept, it was in the guest room. To the best of my knowledge, my mother and father never shared a bedroom again.

"My father acquired a handsome brownstone in Manhattan's East Twenties soon after that, and he insisted that my mother and I visit him there for a few weeks every summer. Of course, my mother, though she never said anything about it, worried that my father would have a 'corrupting' influence on me. And she was quite right. From my earliest years, whenever we were alone together, my father instructed me. 'Power is the wine of life, Benjamin,' he would tell me. 'Power is freedom. The higher we climb in the structure of power, the freer we are, the more godlike. That is why the only true god is the Prince of Power.' Then he would smile and pat my shoulder and say, 'But let this be our little secret, that we know the secret of power. Let fools worship their false, impotent, and unknown gods. . . .'

"He was preparing me, you see, for entrance into his Luciferian order, just as I am trying to prepare you.

"At sixteen I was matriculated in Harvard, and that was

when my life as a dedicated Luciferian really began. Less than a month after my arrival, a certain eminent professor of philosophy invited me to his residence, where my father and some others awaited me, and I donned the red cloak and began my novitiate. Since my father had prepared me well, it was only a few weeks after that that I took my final vows. I wedded the god of this world in her female form, and I consummated the marriage on the altar.

"I performed the sacred act with all due dignity, and as I did so I had a revelation. I knew that I was going to build one of the biggest, most powerful convocations in this country. I would lay its foundations right there in Cambridge. I foresaw it.

"That is the convocation you will someday lead, Timothy, and make more powerful than ever. I foresee that too."

"But the anathema," his father continued. "As a boy, I gave it little thought. Certainly my father wasn't going to 'repay' anybody anything, and he had every reason to nurse an abiding hatred for the St. Claires.

"However, young as I was, I couldn't help noticing that my father's affairs were not going well. His household staff was slowly reduced until there was only a housekeeper-cook. Also, needed repairs to the brownstone weren't being made, and worn-out carpets and furniture weren't replaced. My mother and I continued to receive money from a trust fund that my father had set up after he fled to New York City, but the brownstone was sold when I went to college to help defray my expenses.

"Then, about a year after I finished law school, my father told me that he had put much of his holdings in my name—including Balthazar's Mountain and the house and everything else he owned in St. Claire. I was in a slight state of shock. 'Daddy,' I said, 'I don't want your land, your money! If you need it, take it back!' 'No,' he said, 'I want you to have it, and I'm taking no chances on losing it. It'll give you a start in life. The anathema is on me, son, not on you.'

"So he believed in the anathema. From that moment on, I did too.

"I have to admit I didn't much want to do it, but I said,

'Daddy, what if I went to Stephen Morgan and offered to sign over to him all you've given me if he'll take off the anathema?'

"I thought every blood vessel in my father's head would burst. 'No!' he said. 'The one thing I care about in this world is you, Benjamin, but if you ever yield to a St. Claire, you're no Balthazar. Promise me you'll never give an inch to a St. Claire without taking back a yard in return!'

"I promised. And, believe me, Timothy, I've lived up to that promise.

"The next time I saw my father was over a year later. I hadn't heard from him in months, but that wasn't unusual. I just traveled down to the city and went directly to the apartment he had rented after selling the brownstone. He was no longer there, having moved out months before.

"I found him in a little run-down rooming house near Five Points, one of the worst districts in the city. The place reeked of filth, rot, and human waste. My father was lying half-dressed on an unmade bed. He looked all of his eighty-four years and more, and terribly sick.

"I got a doctor, who turned out to be not at all sympathetic. 'The old man's not sick,' he said, 'he's just drunk and dying, and there's nothing anyone can do about it.'

"I tried to make my father comfortable, and I sat with him through the night. Every now and then he would rouse up. Once he said, 'You there, boy? . . . Good. You're the only one I care about now, the only one who matters.' Later I heard him mumbling something about 'Why did he let them do this to me? Where do they get their power? Why did he let them do this to me?'

"Toward dawn, he said his last words, and he spoke clearly. 'The St. Claires. The goddamned St. Claires. I served them well, boy. Stephen Morgan and his father and grandfather before him—old Roussell St. Claire—and look what they've done to me. Taken all I had. All that should have been yours one day. *Yours*, Benjamin! All but the little I managed to give you. Do you understand that?'

" 'I understand, Daddy,' I said.

" 'Well, what are you going to do about it?'

"My daddy was dying, and I was a Balthazar. Never again

would I use the name St. Claire. And I knew what I was going to do. I said:

" 'Make them pay.'

" 'That's right,' my father said. 'Make them pay! Everything they took from us, I want you to get it back! And then I want you to take what they truly love—their town! Drive those son o' bitches out of St. Claire, and if they ever dare to return—destroy them!'

"He paused for a moment, gasping for breath, and then he added something strange. He said, 'Remember: The anathema is their strength, but the wolf will become their weakness. Through the wolf you will be ended . . . or triumph!'

"So I've tried to do as he told me. I got my law degree and came back here to mend fences and play the role of Melinda St. Claire Balthazar's loving and dutiful son. I've got back a great deal, if not all, that they took from us—I even sit on the board of St. Claire Industries, just as my father did. We've grown more influential in the community, while they, if anything, have declined. And I foresee, Timothy, that just as your grandfather wished, we will one day possess the very soul of St. Claire. . . ."

He had pretty much achieved that, Timothy reflected as, from his aerie, he watched Freya and Daniel's car vanish, wending east along the lakeside road. The community pretty much marched to Timothy Balthazar's tune . . . except when Julia interfered. . . .

Over the years, most of the St. Claires had scattered, seeking their fortunes elsewhere, and the blood had thinned in those few who remained. Only Julia's family, it seemed, still carried the magic in any force. Even there, as in other branches, the shape-changing ability, if it had ever really existed, seemed to have degenerated to a mere affliction. "The wolf will become their weakness," his grandfather had said, and Timothy knew that to be true. If only he could find a way to take advantage of it . . .

His meditations were interrupted by the sounds of the elevator door opening and a familiar, beloved voice: "Daddy!"

He looked around at his daughter, a little girl in a white T-shirt, blue jeans, and sneakers. Ebony hair and gray-blue eyes. The most delicate pink on her perfect cheeks. Five years old and in first grade next fall. So soon, so soon.

"Why, what are you doing up here? Did you come up to see Daddy?"

"Come down and play ball with me."

A little tomboy. Marvelous reflexes. But what a surprise she had been. Timothy had married for the first time at fifty-five, and like his father, he had married in order to beget an heir. The mother had been a widow who had lost her husband and two infant sons in an automobile accident, and Timothy had fully expected her to give him a son. Two years later, to his utter astonishment he had been presented with Alida—whom he had immediately come to love as he had not known it was possible to love a child.

His heir. His princess. He intended to live many years yet, longer than either his father or his grandfather; but when he did die, he would leave all he had to his daughter. And that included St. Claire.

In all truthfulness, he had not yet possessed the soul of St. Claire to the extent his father and grandfather had wished. Julia St. Claire had deprived him of that. But he foresaw that he would outlive Julia by many years. And after she died . . .

He would prepare Alida to become the first female leader of the Balthazar Convocation. She might well become the most powerful witch in the world. She would become to the St. Claire community what Julia was today. She would become—

Suddenly a vision of another little girl, only three or four years older than Alida, sprang to mind. Bright brown eyes full of wonder, glossy brown hair in pageboy and bangs framing the lovely young face.

Daniel St. Claire's daughter.

Timothy had seen her from time to time at St. Luke's and with Julia.

Nicole St. Claire, as beloved by Julia and Daniel, no doubt, as Alida was by him. Alida's rival for the heart and soul of St. Claire? The one person who might deprive Alida of her heritage?

The thought brought a swell of anger.

No, Julia, Timothy thought with fierce determination. *No, Daniel, I don't think so. I'll be watching, and I don't think so!*

He would watch. And in the fullness of time, when necessity arose and opportunity presented itself, he would act against Nicole St. Claire. Without mercy.

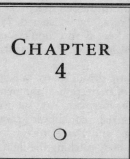

CHAPTER 4

On her first night back in her Manhattan apartment, Freya dreamed about Daniel. She dreamed she felt him lying beside her in the dark, an arm around her shoulders, a hand caressing her bare breast, his mouth moving over her forehead and cheeks. She knew it was Daniel, could only be Daniel, and desire came flooding through her like a glorious surprise. She rolled against him, crushed her breasts against his chest, thrust a knee between his thighs, and returned his hungry lip-bruising kisses, wanting him, wanting him. . . .

After a few minutes, he pulled away and, leaning on an elbow, looked down at her, his face etched in starlight. He had thick, dark, straight brows over lustrous brown eyes, and a narrow aggressive face with a strong, bony jaw. Wolfish good looks, she had always thought. He looked intelligent, hard-bodied, and dangerous.

"You see," he said with a mischievous grin, "you were right. You guessed my secret. Sometimes I can share dreams. Bring you into mine or enter yours."

"Which is it this time," she asked, touching his cheek, "your dream or mine?"

"Ours."

Kissing her, he slipped a hand between her thighs, and never before, it seemed to her, had she been so swiftly and fully aroused. She heard herself moan.

"I want you, Freya," he whispered, "and you want me. I don't think I'd be here if you didn't want me. And in the morning you can always say, 'It's all right . . . it was only a dream.'"

No, never. A love-dream shared was more than a dream, it was a moment of perfection, a moment of utter bliss, an intimacy never to be forgotten. And she wanted that moment now. She didn't think she could bear to wait for it any longer. She spread her legs, and Daniel rose up over her, his long, hard, sun-bronzed body catching the light. Could he possibly be this beautiful, this desirable, in the ordinary, wide-awake, daylight world? She was certain he would be—this dream reflected the reality. She looked at the crinkly black hair on Daniel's chest and loins, the veins on his engorged flesh, every detail clear. He spread his thighs, pushing hers farther apart, and she raised her hips so that he could more easily enter her. She reached for him and brought him to the portal. A moment, then, of dazed, love-besotted anticipation as he pressed against her, and . . .

No! came the order from Timothy Balthazar.

For an instant, she was riveted by shock. Timothy? Here? How dared he? How dared he!

No!

Damn him. Damn him. Shut him out!

Uncaring whether Timothy watched or not, she pressed up hard, lifting herself from the bed, as Daniel entered her fully. As her body clutched at him, she felt that she could give up all else for this moment, all else for the love of Daniel St. Claire, and to hell with Timothy Balthazar.

No! No! I forbid, I will not allow . . .

Daniel's eyes suddenly widened with dismay. Something was happening to him. She clung to him, grasped him harder, but he was growing insubstantial in her arms. He seemed to be fading, fading away . . .

No, please, I want him! Daniel . . .

. . . fading away like a dream . . .

. . . fading . . .

. . . and then he was gone . . .

. . . and she found herself alone, lying awake on her bed in her dark room, sobbing with the greatest unfulfilled longing she had ever known.

Damn you, Timothy Balthazar! She didn't bother to guard her thoughts. She broadcast them with furious recklessness. *Damn you, damn you. One day I'll get even. I swear to God, I'll get even!*

No, *more* than even. She would grow in power, she swore she would, and one day, one day . . .

. . . he would learn who truly ruled the convocation. She would see him in hell!

She thought she heard Timothy's contemptuous laughter.

Yes, she wanted Daniel.

In a single magical moment on a summer afternoon, she had fallen in love with him, and now she wanted him as much as any man she had ever known.

At least, she thought it was love. All Freya knew was that she hadn't felt this way about a man since she was a very young woman. Yes, a large part of the attraction was physical—Daniel's good looks, his handsome body, his grace and vitality—no doubt about that. It seemed to her that with every step he took, with every gesture, he moved with the style usually found only in a great athlete or a great dancer; and when she watched him, or even thought of him, the ache in her breasts and the clutch of desire in her loins became almost unbearable.

But beyond that, the very thought of him suggested to her that life had possibilities that she had never imagined, that a life with Daniel could have been altogether different and so much finer than anything she had ever experienced. She was bound to the god of this world by inescapable vows, of course; but even so, she could not help but wonder what a life outside the convocations might have been like, a life with Daniel and little Nicole, lived as a St. Claire. If only . . . if only . . .

But that could never be, nor did she truly want it.

She wanted only Daniel.

"Well, you can't have him," said Timothy Balthazar. "Not yet."

"I beg your pardon?" She wasn't used to taking orders, even from Timothy, though she feared his power.

She had returned to Manhattan ahead of Daniel and was waiting for him. Instead, Timothy had appeared. At one time he had regularly stayed in her apartment—and in her bed—when he came to the city, but now he was the last visitor she cared to see.

"Freya, I know you want the man. You can't hide that from me—your very effort to do so gives you away. And I sense that he wants you, very much. So you will use his desire to draw him into the convocation. Tease him, tempt him, tantalize him all you wish. But you will not give yourself to him until *after* he has taken his final vows."

"But why—"

"Because he is false. No matter what he says, he still does not believe, as we do, in the god of this world. But we are pledged to the god and to each other—you know that, Freya. If he is not one of us, you may only use him and discard him. But if you wish to keep him, you must first convert him, make him truly one of us. If you can, which I doubt."

Reluctantly, Freya agreed.

She had three other novices to instruct that summer, a man and two women from a Manhattan convocation. Daniel joined them, and they met in her apartment.

"Ours is an ancient order," she told them. "Some say it extends far back into antiquity. It has been known by various names—the Sons and Daughters of the Light, the Gnostic Luciferians, the Prometheans. It has most often been called the Children of the Griffin, because Lucifer sometimes reveals himself to us as a magnificent creature resembling a griffin— part animal, part human, part angel.

"When you take your final vows, you acknowledge him as your lord and master and god of this world. Don't think of him as good or evil, though it is true that as Satan he tempts and tests his followers and as Beelzebub he punishes those who fail. But as the Prince of Power he confers great and wonderful gifts. Indeed, some of the Christians among us think of him as 'God's other son, fallen but forgiven, the Angel of all angels.'

She met with her four students once a week, on Tuesdays by common consent, and with Daniel more often. The yogalike exercises she taught them, and practiced with them, were mostly quite simple. They would sit on the floor of her dimly lit living room, backs straight, legs either in the lotus position or folded under them. They would pull up the hoods of their cloaks to shield their eyes. Freya would then induce a meditative state in them, teaching them to become receptive to each other's thoughts. Psychic phenomena of all kinds tended to be random, and the idea was to develop as much control as possible.

Daniel was easily her best student, and he particularly excelled at the Ganzfeld, or "whole field," experiment. Blindfolded and isolated in a dark room, he would try to "see" an image or a picture Freya mentally "sent" to him from another room. The image was usually a picture or painting Daniel had never seen before. From the very beginning, his descriptions were amazingly accurate.

But sometimes she thought he did not give a damn about the lessons, the exercises, the experiments. He would linger in her apartment after the others had left. Then, casting off his red cloak, he would draw her into his arms and kiss her, stroke her, explore her body through her clothing until the pleasure became almost unbearable.

"Please, Daniel, you mustn't," she would whisper as he attempted to undress her.

"But why not? We love each other."

"I've told you. I promised . . . our master. It's a sacrifice I'm making to him. But when you take your vows . . ."

"It's that goddamn Balthazar, isn't it? He didn't like me from the beginning. He's determined to come between us."

"He can't. He knows he can't. But, darling, for now . . . it's for Nicole's sake. Tell yourself that we must stay apart for Nicole's sake. And afterward . . ."

Yes, he could do that. He could do anything for Nicole.

"Afterward you'll be mine forever. And I'm not just talking about your body, Freya, marvelous as it is and much as I want it. I'm talking about *you*, all of you, body and soul. I know now why I never remarried after Nicole's mother died. I've been waiting all this time for you. Freya, you and I and Nicole can have such a wonderful life together, and to hell with all the convocations."

So he felt it too . . . as if this might be a new beginning for them both.

Her daddy came home again in September.

Nicole woke up feeling especially happy on that Saturday morning, and it wasn't just that she didn't have to go to school. She *liked* school, except that some of the kids teased her. She was the best reader in the fourth grade, and books had opened up whole new worlds of adventure for her. But books weren't on her mind this morning. She had awakened with the feeling that something had changed in the household, something good had happened, and sure enough . . .

. . . when she bounded out of bed and hurried to her daddy's bedroom, there he was, sound asleep.

Her grandmother immediately appeared and told her that her father had gotten in late last night, and they must let him rest.

The hours passed slowly, and it wasn't just that she couldn't find anything to do. No matter what she did, her thoughts kept returning to her daddy. What had brought him home so unexpectedly? Always before, he had let them know when he was coming home. Had something gone wrong? Had he lost his job, perhaps? She had heard of such things happening. Did he have bad news?

She peeked silently into his room half a dozen times during the morning, hoping to find him awake.

Finally, shortly before noon, he came downstairs. He was smiling cheerfully, and he laughed as he picked her up, his big nine-year-old girl, and embraced her. But still her feeling of apprehension would not go away.

"Why did you come home, Daddy?" she asked as he set her down again.

"Why, to see you. You and Grandma. But especially you."

"What did you want to see me about?"

"Just to see you," he insisted, but somehow she knew that was not quite true.

They all had lunch together, a cheese omelette and toast, since it was really breakfast for her daddy. Her daddy and her grandmother talked about boring things. She knew that her grandmother, too, was curious about her daddy's visit. "How long can you stay?" her grandmother asked.

"Just till tomorrow, Mom. I've got to get back to work."

"You came all this way," her grandmother said, surprised, "to spend only a day with us?"

Her daddy shrugged, gave her grandmother a "meaningful" look, and glanced quickly at Nicole.

Something tugged sickeningly at Nicole's tummy. But how could anything be wrong when her daddy seemed so happy?

She found out that afternoon.

Her daddy invited her to take a walk in the woods with him. The St. Claire State Park surrounded the north, west, and south sides of the lake and the outlying residential community like a giant green crescent. It lay just beyond Nicole's house, and Nicole's father often said that a little girl had never had a bigger, better backyard to play in.

The day was sunny and bright, and people were out— Nicole heard Duffy Johnson hooting and hollering with Brad and Derek somewhere in the distance. But she and her daddy were soon alone under a green canopy of oaks and elms and maples, and Nicole knew that her daddy had something very important to tell her.

"Nicole, what would you say if Daddy told you he had found a very special friend?"

There it was. The thing that, on some level, she had feared. The thing she had hoped wouldn't happen.

"Nicole?"

"I don't know."

"I hope you'd be happy for me. It wouldn't mean I loved you any the less. Or your grandmother. Or your mother."

"I hardly even remember Mommy."

"I'm sorry to hear that. Treasure the memories you do have, darling. And be sure that no one is going to try to take them from you or to take your mother's place in your heart. Not ever."

Her daddy meant that, she knew. But that wasn't what bothered her.

"Is it a lady?" she asked after a moment.

"Yes, it is."

"The Lady in White?"

Her father looked at her quickly, and she felt his surprise.

"And who is the Lady in White?" he asked, though she was certain he already knew.

"The Lady in White. The one who comes back every summer and looks at you when we go into town." She lowered her voice. "Miss Kellgren."

Her daddy continued to stare at her, and she knew he was wondering how in the world she had known, but how could she not?

"Yes," he said at last, "it's Miss Kellgren."

With some difficulty—she felt her face pinching up—she asked the hard question. "Are you going to . . . marry her?"

"I hope to, yes."

"But, Daddy"—Nicole shook her head, fighting back tears—"she's so *old!*"

Her Daddy laughed gently and patted her head. "Not so old, puddin'. Where did you get that idea? Is Daddy old?"

"Not nearly as old as she is, I bet. I thought the man was supposed to be the older one."

"Not necessarily. Especially when you get to be our age. Hey, when you grow up, if some younger fellow catches your fancy, you go after him!"

"But are you in love with her, Daddy?"

"Yes, puddin', I am. Very much in love."

They walked on in silence.

If her daddy was in love, how could she tell him that she *still* thought Miss Kellgren was too old? How could she tell him that little kids were scared of Miss Kellgren, scared to talk about her above a whisper? How could she tell him that they said she was a witch? And not a good witch like Grandma.

Another thought occurred to her. "Are you in love with her because . . . because you think she can help me?"

Her father frowned. "Help you how, honey?"

"With my sickness."

"Why, you aren't sick—"

"Yes, I am. At least sometimes, like the time I . . . the time I . . . bit . . ."

He gave her a quick hug. "Don't think about that, puddin'—"

"But I know I'm sick. It's lycan . . . lycan . . ."

"It's just a little emotional disturbance, honey. Miss Kellgren thinks that perhaps she and I together can help you. But it's nothing for you to worry about. Now, don't you worry, you hear me?"

But she did worry. She worried about her daddy and Miss Kellgren for the rest of the day, though she tried to hide it because she knew he wanted her to be happy for him. And she tried to appear happy, even as she was wondering if her grandmother knew and what she thought.

That night she had bad dreams, though afterward she couldn't quite remember what they had been about. Something about bats. . . .

Her father left after breakfast the next morning, and she just had time to wish him a good, safe trip and to tell him to be happy. He smiled when she said that, because he knew what she meant. She wanted him to be happy whether he married Miss Kellgren or not.

Late that afternoon, she went up to the unused third floor of the house. Looking out a front window, she could see the Kellgren mansion, almost like a twin, nestled in the green hills north of the lake. The two old houses, pale as ghosts, stared at each other.

"Don't hurt my daddy, Miss Kellgren," Nicole whispered. "Please, please, just leave him alone. . . ."

In her travels, Freya Kellgren had established ties to a number of convocations. But in none of them had she encountered a man or woman more powerful or dangerous than Timothy Balthazar. Better than any other man she knew, Timothy could insinuate his will into others, manipulating them by their own weaknesses and propensities—a technique that, ironically, Freya had taught him. His punishments could be terrible. Freya remembered one defector who had been reduced to despair and then persuaded to swallow her tongue. And another who had been led to mutilate himself and devour his own flesh. Freya thought that Timothy derived his greatest pleasures from such punishments, his greatest sense of power, and at such times she seemed to glimpse Beelzebub in his countenance—the darkly gleaming, multifaceted eyes, the razor-sharp mandibles, the long gray proboscis that could suck out one's heart and soul.

In the ordinary course of things, Freya gave little thought to the wrath of Timothy Balthazar. It was, if anything, her protection. But never did she wish to face it.

She faced it one evening in late September.

The training session lasted two hours that evening, and during the last hour she had the uncomfortable feeling that they were being watched. She was glad she had decided to conduct the sessions with her novices and herself fully clothed, rather than, as was customary, clad only in their cloaks. But of course her real reason for *that* was her passion for Daniel. In spite of her loyalty to the convocation and its god, in spite of her fear of Timothy Balthazar, she was afraid she might yield to Daniel, and God only knew what the consequences would be.

As soon as the door had closed on the last of the other novices, he came to her and gave her the kiss she had been waiting for all evening.

"They think we're lovers," he murmured, still holding her.

"We are, spiritually, and soon . . . you're nearly ready, Daniel."

"To hell with that. I don't want any 'ritual consummation.' I don't give a damn about being 'wedded to Satan in the female form,' as you put it—"

"Oh, my darling," Freya said in alarm, "you mustn't say that!"

"I want you, Freya, only you. You alone with me in my bed, not on some goddamned altar with a bunch of ghoulish voyeurs getting their jollies—"

"Please, Daniel. Think of Nicole!"

"I am thinking of Nicole. You know I only joined this thing for her, and for you. So far I haven't learned one damned thing that leads me to believe that joining your convocation can help her—"

"But you're only beginning! And you show such promise."

"Sure. I do okay on that Ganzfeld thing. We shared one dream, until something or other ended it. And I do seem to be picking up more thoughts and emotions from other people, so maybe there is something to this . . . 'witchcraft' of yours. But so what? Who needs a convocation for that? Face it, Freya, I think I mean more to you than anyone else you've ever met, in your convocations or out. Isn't that true?"

"Oh, my darling . . . yes!"

He drew her more closely into his arms. "Then screw the goddamn convocation. . . ."

She might have yielded to him at that moment, probably would have yielded to him, had they been wearing only their cloaks. Rarely had she been so aware of both of their bodies and yet so free of her own ego, her own concerns. She lived for him. She was lost in him. So this was love. . . .

As if she could not stand the intensity of the moment any longer, as if she were emerging from great warm ocean depths into the light, she gradually regained some degree of normal consciousness. She loosened herself from Daniel's embrace.

"You had better go now, my darling."

"I don't want to go—ever."

"I know. And I don't want to lose you, even for a minute. But if you stay, I'll go mad."

"All right. But when I'm alone with you, I know that the real madness is all this business about being loyal to the 'god of this world,' as you call him—"

"My darling, please!" she said desperately.

"It's madness, I feel it in my bones, and I say to hell with it."

"Darling, go! I beg you."

"Just tell me this." Daniel hesitated, frowning. "What if you decided to leave the cult? Put it behind you altogether and marry me? Would you be afraid to do that?"

"But why would I want to leave—"

"Because if you are afraid, don't be. If Balthazar gives you any trouble, I personally, with a little help from my family, will blow Balthazar and his whole goddamn convocation to hell and gone." A smile flickered across Daniel's face. "Maybe you've heard of the St. Claire anathema. I don't know if I've got the power or not, but my mother . . . at home we joke about her being a witch. Actually, Freya, I kind of think she is."

Daniel finally did go, and when the door was closed, Freya leaned against it, wondering how a love like this could have come to her, of all people, a love so dangerous to Daniel and her both. . . .

She walked from the foyer back into the living room, and gasped as she found herself facing the tall, dark figure of Timothy Balthazar.

Christ, she thought, *what did he hear?* Her knees started to buckle, and she swayed, on the verge of a faint. A terrible nausea rose in her stomach, and for a moment she thought she was going to be sick.

"How did you get in here?" she asked breathlessly.

"Does it matter?"

"How long have you been here?"

"Long enough. An hour."

"You heard . . . ?"

"I heard."

She shook her head wildly. "Timothy, he didn't mean—"

" 'I don't give a damn about being wedded to Satan,' " Timothy quoted. " 'I want you, Freya, only you. . . . Screw the goddamn convocation. . . . I'll blow Balthazar and his whole goddamn convocation to hell and gone.' He meant every word of it."

"No, no! It was said in the heat of the moment. We weren't rational—"

"That is true. You have not been rational, Freya. And we Children of the Griffin are nothing if not rational. But when we forget where our first loyalty must lie . . ."

"I haven't forgotten!"

". . . we must be punished."

"But you don't understand . . ."

As Timothy came across the room toward her, it seemed to Freya that never before had she seen him so angry, and her fear became almost uncontrollable. Timothy, she knew, was quite capable of killing her in a fit of rage. But *why* was he so angry? What harm had been done?

"Timothy, Daniel has such latent power, and he himself doesn't realize it or even quite believe in it!"

"I know he doesn't. Do you think I haven't been watching you two? He must never develop his power, because if he does . . ." For the first time ever, Freya saw fear in Timothy's eyes. "How could I have been so blind? The man's a St. Claire—I should have foreseen that he would turn his power against us. He will destroy everything I have achieved. He will destroy . . ."

He would destroy Timothy Balthazar.

A smile twitched at Freya's mouth. "Does he frighten you, Timothy?"

It was the wrong thing to say, and even as she spoke the words, Freya wondered what madness had inspired them. Timothy's left hand shot up and grasped her face, the big palm covering her nose and mouth so that she could hardly breathe. His jaw clenched, his eyes bulged, and the veins stood out on his forehead. The fingers tightened, the nails digging into her flesh like raptor talons, and Freya had the terrifying thought that in the next few seconds Timothy might well tear her face from her skull and her beauty would be gone forever.

"You brought Daniel St. Claire to the convocation," he said in a low, harsh voice, barely above a whisper. "You will pay the price for what you have done."

Freya's entire body shook. Her voice was muffled by the hand over her face. "What . . . what do you want?"

"I want to be rid of Daniel St. Claire."

"Then you will be. You heard him—he doesn't really want to be one of us!"

"I want to be rid of him for good."

"He'll never take the final vows, I promise you!"

Timothy tightened his grip on her face.

"I want him destroyed."

"No!"

"Destroyed, Freya. So that there will be no chance that he will ever threaten us."

"But how . . . ?"

"You will know when the time comes. Kill him cruelly. Drive him insane. Punish him for his blasphemy."

She could bear Timothy's hand on her face no longer. With a little scream, she struck it away.

"It is unnecessary, Timothy. I swear to you—"

"Where do your loyalties lie, Freya?" Timothy asked harshly. "You have taken vows. Do you renounce them?"

"No . . ."

"Then you will do exactly as you are told. I tell you, you will destroy Daniel St. Claire."

She felt the force of Timothy Balthazar's will—utterly determined, unrelenting, implacable. He *would* have his way. Freya turned away from him and covered her face. For the first time in years, she felt tears coming to her eyes.

"Destroy him," Timothy said more calmly, "and you will be suitably rewarded. Refuse . . ."

"Yes?"

". . . and you yourself will be destroyed. Do you understand?"

"Yes."

"And will you obey?"

For a moment, she couldn't answer.

"Will you obey?"

"Yes."

She would destroy the man she loved.

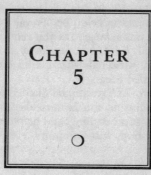

CHAPTER 5

Wearily, Timothy returned to his midtown hotel and prepared for bed. A leisurely shower and a few sips of Scotch, that was what he needed. Ordinarily, he had infinite reserves of energy, but the confrontation with Freya had exhausted him. He might look little more than forty years old, but tonight he felt every one of his sixty-one years and then some.

Christ, how could he have made such a mistake?

All right, he had had a bad feeling about Daniel from the beginning. The man was a St. Claire. Timothy should not even have needed his intuitive prescience to know that Freya was bringing him a potential catastrophe. Common sense should have told him. But he knew now—Daniel's words this evening had confirmed the fact.

Well, Freya had caused the problem—let Freya take care of it. Should Julia St. Claire blame anyone for whatever might befall her son, let the blame fall on Freya. *Julia, once again I swear to you that I would never do anything to hurt you or yours. You know I once loved you, and I remain to this day your most humble and obedient servant. Julia,* believe *me.* . . .

Sometimes it seemed to him that he had spent his entire life tiptoeing around in fear and trembling of Julia.

Which was nonsense, of course. He had done nothing of the kind. Julia, if pressed, could be a dangerous woman, but Timothy Balthazar was a dangerous man, with dangerous people at his command. He had to remember that.

Sometimes he wondered what his life might have been like if he had married Julia.

Not that she would have turned Luciferian for him. Such a thing was unimaginable. But in those days he had owed the god and the convocation nothing, and he probably could have walked away from both with impunity. Hell, he already had walked away.

He had had little to do with his father at that time, and his mother had been long gone.

His mother . . .

Now *there* was a contrast to Julia!

Deirdre Banning Balthazar, called Dede. Daughter of a wealthy Luciferian from Sacramento. Timothy had few memories of her, but those he had were sharp. A round face and a plump figure. Dark hair and heavy-lidded gray eyes. A broad, turned-up nose—retroussé, she called it—and a large mouth with very full, everted lips. Hardly a classic beauty, but somehow magically, sensuously attractive.

His parents had led separate lives. His mother had traveled, often for months at a time, but then she would reappear, usually with a handsome young man in tow, sometimes a young woman, and on at least one occasion, both. And life would become marvelous. His mother would play with Timothy. She would prepare food he liked and eat with him. She would undress him, and herself, and inspect his growing body minutely, fondling and tickling him, and then bathe with him in a big tub of warm water. Occasionally, she would even let him sleep with her.

After a few weeks, she would be off on her travels again, vanishing for as long as a year.

Timothy adored her. Loved her. Worshiped her.

Until the Great Humiliation.

He could not have said exactly how old he was at the time. Eight, perhaps, or nine at the most. His mother arrived at twilight on a lovely summer evening with two new friends, young and beautiful, called Renée and Charley. His father greeted them all genially, and the house was filled with soft lights and gentle laughter, and never had Timothy been more happy to see his mother. He was allowed to stay up late that evening, until well past ten, and at almost every moment, he was at her feet or in the circle of her arm—oh, how big her baby boy had grown, how strong and handsome he was becoming.

Timothy awakened the next morning to blue skies and a soft breeze coming through the open window, and a lingering sense of happiness and well-being. He blinked sleep away in seconds and listened, completely awake. The house was quiet. No voices, no breakfast sounds.

He got out of bed and, still in his nightgown, left his room. As he would have expected in such fine weather, the French doors at the end of the hall, leading out onto the second-floor veranda, were wide open, the white curtains moving slightly in the breeze. Timothy moved toward the doors on silent feet.

His father's room was at the front of the house, on the right. His mother usually slept in her own room, in front on the left. The hall doors to both rooms were, as usual, closed. Timothy slipped past them and out onto the veranda.

Staying close to the wall, he looked to the left. The French doors to his mother's room were partially open. He took a deep breath.

What followed was almost a ritual, so often had it been repeated. Turning away from the wall, he bounded through the open doors and yelled "Good morning!" as he ran toward the bed.

He was almost there when he stopped in shock.

His mother was not alone.

She was sitting up in bed with her two friends, Renée on her left and Charley on her right. The sheet was pulled up over their laps, but from the waist up they were naked.

His mother was sipping from a coffee cup. She smiled at him and set the cup aside on a breakfast tray to the left of the bed. "Good morning!" she said cheerfully, extending her arms toward Timothy.

Timothy stared at his bare-breasted mother and the two people beside her. He barely heard the others saying good morning to him. To his dismay, as he gazed at all that naked flesh, his little penis began to harden and rise.

He started to back away.

"Now, you come here to Mommy," his mother commanded, smiling and still reaching out. "You come here and give Mommy a kiss and a good-morning hug."

He stood paralyzed. The sight of his mother undressed was nothing new to him. But to be here with her and these two naked strangers . . . He tried to hide his erection, visible through his gown, with his hands.

His mother saw, and laughed. "Come on, Timmy," she said, "right now. Don't make Mommy ask again."

To run away would have been to reveal his deep embarrassment and to invite laughter. Perhaps if he just did as he was told, this could be ended quickly and with a minimum loss of dignity. Looking only at his mother, as if that might make the others vanish, Timothy climbed up over the foot of the bed, careful to keep his gown tucked down around himself.

His mother drew him into her arms, hugged him, kissed him.

Somehow, under her caresses, his gown came up.

He made an attempt at covering himself, but his mother stopped him. "Oh, look at him!" she crooned, gazing down between his legs. "Isn't he pretty, Mommy's little baby? Mommy's little sweetheart . . ."

At that moment, Timothy thought he would surely die. Not only was he half-naked before strangers, but in this terribly vulnerable and shameful condition, and now his mother was actually touching him.

". . . oh, look at Mommy's baby boy, how big he is, Mommy's little soldier, he's so sweet . . ."

He wanted to pull away, but he couldn't bring himself even to try. One of his mother's hands now gripped his bare buttocks, drawing him up from the bed and closer to her, while her other hand continued to fondle him. A soft moan escaped him as she drew him closer, leaning over him until he could feel her warm breath on his bare flesh.

". . . oh, he is so pretty, so cute, his mommy just wants to kiss him . . ."

As those soft warm lips closed on his flesh, a silent scream rose in his throat. His face felt like a blood-inflated balloon about to burst. He heard Renée laughing, heard Charley say, "Aw, Jeez, Dede . . ."

At that moment, Timothy hated his mother, hated her with a fury and despair he had never before known. He felt utterly shamed and betrayed, all dignity lost. Barely stifling his cry of pain, he tore himself from his mother's arms, her grip, her lips. Shoving his gown down over himself, he scrambled off of the bed and ran for the French doors, while his laughing mother called after him, "Timothy, honey! Come back here! Come back, Mommy loves you!"

He ran until he was back in his room, the door slammed firmly behind him. There he threw himself onto his bed, where he twisted and writhed and spun like some small animal dying of a brain tumor. His fury filled the room. Pictures, untouched, fell from the walls, chairs tilted, rocked, and tumbled, toys flew through the air. Timothy had only one wish—to kill with his own hands the one person he loved most in all the world.

From that hour, his mother began to fade from his life. Never again, if he could help it, would Timothy let her see him unclothed, never again would he allow those intimate inspections and caresses. The days of their physical intimacy were over, and his mother seemed to realize that fact, for she accepted his rebuffs with a shrug and an indifferent smile.

She and her friends left a few days later, and in the next three years he saw her only six or seven times. After that, there were only cards, each year a birthday card and a "Season's Greetings," signed, "Your loving mother, Dede." With time, the cards grew less frequent, a birthday overlooked, a "Season" mislaid, and his mother became a half-forgotten stranger, recalled only now and then, but with love and anguish.

At the age of fourteen, Timothy became a red-cloaked novice in the Order of the Children of the Griffin.

This, he understood, was an honor. No one became a novice at such an early age unless he was the child of a member, and even then only if he showed signs of outstanding intellectual and "intuitive" abilities. That is to say, only if he showed signs of being a psychic.

"You've got to train your psychic powers," his father told him, "because they'll give you power over the other fellow, and power is what it all boils down to. Grasping power over the other fellow and hanging on to it and enjoying it. Enjoying it! People say to me, Benjamin, you're a power in the boardrooms of New York and the halls of Washington, you're down there half the time, why don't you move down there? Why do you stay in this faraway little place? I'll tell you why, boy. Because nowhere else can I *taste* power the way I can in St. Claire. This is *our* community.

"Oh, Timothy, son, you have some of the most exciting times of your life ahead of you, now that you're entering the Order. . . ."

Some of the most exciting—and some of the most boring.

The meetings he was forced to attend—he had little idea of what anyone was talking about—were even more boring than church on Sundays.

And what could be more boring than the psychic exercises? True, experimenting with telepathy was fun at first, but trying to receive clairvoyant "flashes" without "grasping" for them was about as exciting—and frustrating—as trying to touch his right elbow with his right hand. As for telekinesis, he spent hours trying by sheer force of his will to make a cigarette roll on a smooth surface, only to learn that anger might tear pictures from walls, but boredom definitely did not make cigarettes roll.

The only real excitement came at sixteen when he was introduced to the blood sacrifice of animals. A chicken, a rabbit, a goat. His throat clogged and his cock grew hard, as his knife cut slowly through the flesh and the animal screamed. Yes, he could take life, with pleasure . . . perhaps even human life. . . . .

Now he understood why he had been ordered, on pain of direst punishment, not to tell anyone anything about the Order. The Order, at its most exciting, was like a deliciously dirty secret that you *had* to keep to yourself.

At seventeen, Timothy took his final vows.

He had been looking forward to this for a long time, although, his father would have said, for the wrong reason. Quite simply, it meant losing his virginity. After years of waiting and wondering, at long last he was going to get laid!

The great evening arrived. Members of the convocation had come from all over the country. The fact that the final initiation of Benjamin Balthazar's son would take place made this meeting particularly important.

He was escorted from his room to the temple by two men clad, like himself, only in hooded cloaks and sandals. They entered from the back. The room, lit only by candles, was crowded with silent, black-cloaked figures. The first things Timothy saw clearly were the big tapestry of the magnificent griffin on the back wall, the long black altar, and the two hooded and cloaked figures behind it. The taller of the two figures, he knew, was his father, and the smaller the priestess. The surrogate of the god. The woman he was going to . . . He swallowed hard. He dared not think about it.

"Bring the candidate forward," his father said.

Timothy needed no prodding. He walked briskly up the aisle, through the assembly. When he reached the rail in front of the altar, he dropped to his knees on a cushion.

"Timothy Balthazar," said the tall figure, his father, "do you wish to take your final vows?"

"I do, Reverend Father."

"Then repeat after me . . ."

Timothy breathlessly repeated the fateful words. He would be forever loyal to the god of this world and to his convocation, putting them before all others. He would dedicate his every act to the god and be a channel for the god's power. He would be forever grateful to the god for every gift he received. . . .

On and on. Though he had been told what the vows were to be, Timothy hardly knew what he was saying. He would have said anything. He wanted only to get to the main business at hand. He looked at that other hooded and cloaked figure, behind the altar, imagining he could see the swell of breasts through the cloth, the tips of nipples . . .

Hands unfastened the clasp at his neck and removed his red cloak. For a moment he was naked, and then the black cloak was settled on his shoulders.

He had taken the vows, and the moment he had looked forward to had come. He was already half-aroused and yet, suddenly, he was terribly unsure of himself, and he pulled his cloak closed in front.

Someone opened the gate in the middle of the rail. Timothy arose on shaky legs and entered the sanctuary. He took a few unsteady steps toward the altar. His father and the convocation vanished behind him. They were utterly silent. He knew that to go through with this he must forget they existed and keep his mind altogether on the priestess, who was coming around the end of the altar.

She stopped immediately in front of him, only a foot or two away. She leaned back, half sitting on the altar, her garment closed, the hood pulled forward. Then she extended a bare foot toward Timothy, rings on the toes and a silver chain around the ankle. A bare leg appeared as she touched his calf with her foot. The foot traveled slowly up between Timothy's thighs, the toes wiggling, sending electric shocks through his flesh, and suddenly his cock was fully engorged and brick-hard. Never before in his life had he been so excited.

As the woman's cloak opened, his eyes followed the lines of that bare leg to the lightly fleeced mons and the round, smooth belly. They took in the narrow waist and the full, generous, hard-nippled breasts. As if in invitation, the woman's fingertips traced curves from her groin to her nipples and back again. She raised one hand and brushed back her hood so that Timothy could at last see her face—those heavy-lidded eyes, so familiar to him, those wide, soft lips, that mocking smile. . . .

No, no, no, it could not possibly be! For a second or two the world went hazy and Timothy reeled in shock—the greatest shock he had felt since he was nine years old.

Then his sight cleared and he was staring at her again.

No! It was an illusion! His mother's eyes, yes, his mother's mouth, yes, his mother's face exactly. But not his mother, surely not!

He could not take in the reality of what he was seeing. All was askew, false, as in a nightmare. Surely this woman was too young to be his mother! But even so . . . The resemblance in the dim candlelight was uncanny—this woman had to be, if not his mother, his mother's twin sister. But . . .

The woman was still smiling slyly at him, running the tip of her tongue over her lips, shifting her body invitingly. He flinched as she reached up and touched his chest.

No. No, he could not possibly seal his vows with this woman. Not by fucking her. His cock was now as limp and cold as a dead fish. But he had to complete this ritual somehow, he had to get the whole goddamn thing over with and wake up from the nightmare, and the sooner the better. He grabbed the woman by the shoulders and he kissed her. It was a hasty, awkward, misplaced little-boy kiss, but it was a kiss. The Kiss of Consummation.

Timothy sensed surprise behind him. This was not quite what had been expected from the son of Benjamin Balthazar. But very quickly a cheer went up and applause rang out, followed by laughter.

Then something happened that Timothy could never forgive.

Before he had the slightest suspicion of what she was about to do, the woman gave him a lewdly contemptuous smile and, seizing his shoulders, turned him to face the convocation. She then leaned forward and reached down, and with her fingertips she flipped his limp and shriveled penis. As he jumped with alarm at that touch, the laughter grew louder yet. Even his father was laughing. "Don't worry, son," he said, patting Timothy's shoulder, "I told you that the first time isn't always easy. You'll learn to get it up with a woman yet." His father, laughing at his youth and innocence, laughing at his wretched, ignominious, and impotent virginity, laughing at his humiliation.

Immediately thereafter, the partying and the drinking began. Timothy made his way through the crowd, huddled in his cloak, a strained, utterly false smile on his face. He wanted only to escape, but strangers kept stopping him to shake his hand. A motherly woman, modestly cloaked—there were a few women present—actually kissed his cheek.

Timothy looked around for the priestess. The goddamned teaser bitch—if he could get her alone, he'd show her. Beat the goddamn shit out of her. Fuck her ass off and then . . .

Timothy felt his erection returning.

He had to get away from this crowd and do it fast. He slipped through a doorway and into a dark hall, and went up the stairs almost running. The only one he wanted to meet was the bitch. He saw the look of contempt on her face turn to shock as he hit her, heard her scream as he grasped and twisted her breast, saw her terror as he thrust into her, raping her, tearing her, bloodying her—*he'd* show her, the dirty cunt. . . .

He made it to his room without meeting anyone. He turned on a single light, pushed the lock button on the door, and cast off his cloak. Tears of humiliation flowed from his eyes, refracting the light, as he looked down at his cock. It seemed to him that never before in his life had it been swollen so large and painfully hard. It was a veritable weapon, a club, a sword.

He seized the weapon, felt its strength in his fist. Laugh at him, would they? He would show them.

Heavy-lidded eyes, a contemptuous smile . . . with his free hand he delivered a slashing blow that destroyed forever any remnant beauty of that hated face.

The face kept changing, his mother, Renée, the woman who had kissed his cheek, any girl who had ever appeared to slight him, he would destroy them all. And to hell with his father and his goddamn useless convocation, he was through with them forever.

His body writhed, his hand tightened. Lost in his vision of

murderous sex, he masturbated furiously, again and again and again.

He never asked his father who the woman had been. How could he possibly? But the unanswered question would haunt him for the rest of his life.

CHAPTER
6

○

Three years later, in the spring of 1940, when Timothy returned on vacation from Harvard, he fell in love with Julia St. Claire.

How could he not have? It seemed to him that the whole town must be in love with this dark-eyed, dark-haired girl he had known since childhood yet hardly noticed. How had she suddenly become so beautiful, so magical? Men worshiped her and women adored her. Every day and every evening, wherever Timothy encountered Julia, she was surrounded by a carousel of lights and laughter. And why? Simply because she was Julia St. Claire and her hour had come, this very special young woman who could not imagine any creature ever bearing her ill will and who cast her light on anyone, anyone at all, who came near her. To be smiled on by Julia St. Claire was to know that you, too, were special, and that only the best was expected of you and for that you would be celebrated. Julia St. Claire possessed the soul of St. Claire. Julia St. Claire, it seemed to Timothy, *was* the soul of St. Claire.

Along with a dozen others, Timothy attended and paid

court to her, but with a growing sense of frustration and envy and anger. All the world seemed to know that sooner or later Julia St. Claire would marry her cousin, Jamie St. Claire. He was a distant cousin, but a cousin nonetheless. "Madness and more madness," said a few, such as Timothy's father. "It can't come to any good. There's madness in both families . . . a degenerate lot. . . ."

Two years later, in 1942, Timothy graduated from Harvard and James from Princeton, and they went to war. They returned late in 1945, both of them captains and both determined to wed Julia St. Claire.

Timothy's hopes were immediately smashed.

Julia and James did not wed until the following spring, but Timothy was certain that they became lovers almost immediately upon Jamie's return. He himself took a long vacation in the West, as far from the happy couple as he could get. Near the end of the summer, in a Santa Monica motel, he discovered the Rapture.

He picked up the girl in a hotel bar on a Monday night. It was a slow night, the place was almost deserted, and she was alone. She was well dressed and fairly pretty—dark-haired, cat-eyed, not overly painted. She was sitting at the bar, humming heartbreak love songs in a husky voice and striking poses. If she was a hooker, she wouldn't come cheap.

A drink and a smile were enough to start a conversation, and they settled into a booth. Her name was Judy, and she was a model and an actress, "between jobs." He was Tommy, and he was a veteran, on vacation before returning to art school. And, God, how he'd love to paint her, he said, sketching her on a paper napkin. He did have a knack—he had used it to charm women before.

"In the nude?" Judy asked.

"Absolutely."

"You just want to get my clothes off," she said, laughing.

"How transparent I am. Judy, truth to tell, I'd give almost anything to spend the night with you."

"Anything? If I were for sale, do you really think you could afford me?"

He shook his head. "I speak as an artist. You're worth

more than anything I might pay. So I wouldn't pay at all. Just leave some trifling gift as an expression of my appreciation."

Judy's eyes widened in mock dismay. "Not too trifling, I hope!"

"What do you suggest?"

"Mmm . . . a hundred dollars?"

A hundred dollars for a night. Outrageous, he thought. Of course she expected him to haggle, but instead he smiled and took out his wallet.

"Do you know a place . . . not here . . . a motel?"

She nodded, and swallowed hard, staring at the thick wad, as he took out two fifty-dollar bills.

"This is for you," he said, handing her one of the bills. "There'll be more in the morning. And this . . ." He gave her the second bill. "This should be enough for a very nice motel room, with something left over. Pay cash and get a receipt and I'll meet you outside. Can you do that?"

Judy swallowed and nodded again. For a hundred bucks and a chance at that bundle, she would do any trick in the book.

It was all so easy, Timothy thought.

Too, too easy.

By that time he was no longer a virgin, but his only experience had been that bought with K rations, candy, and cigarettes while he was overseas and that bought from high-priced call girls in California. While in the army, he had known perfectly well that if he indulged his taste for violent sex he would probably wind up in the stockade. In California if he beat up expensive call girls he could wind up dead.

But this was different.

He didn't think about what was going to happen. He didn't plan it out. He didn't want to know. Perhaps nothing would happen at all except that he would spend a night with a woman who called herself Judy.

They showered together first, soaping each other and having a drink from the bottle in his bag, and she liked that, she liked that very much. Play-for-pay was for once turning into a really romantic evening.

He even toweled her dry and carried her to the bed, laying her gently down on it. Then he made leisurely love to her with hands and lips, eliciting an honest response from her, such as he had never gotten from the call girls. With his lack of experience, he had had no idea that he could be so skillful. At least, Judy made him feel skillful. "Honest to God," she murmured when he finally entered her, "you are truly something. Why didn't I meet you before?" She gave herself up to the moment, seeking her climax like an honest, loving woman.

He wanted to give her that pleasure, and more than once. He had fully intended to spend most if not all of the night with her. But now he found he could not hold back. He did not *want* to hold back. When the moment came and he began spilling great torrents of fire, his very soul seemed to burst into flame. All his buried anger was transformed into a fountain of glee. Laughing uncontrollably, he clamped his hands on the woman's throat. As his fingers tightened, digging into flesh, muscle, cartilage, her eyes opened impossibly wide. She gazed terror-stricken at his rictus of a grin, her face turning purple, unable to make a sound. In a death frenzy, she first grasped at his wrists, then clawed at his back. Futilely. He kept on stabbing into her and choking her until the very last fading spasm.

Slowly he removed his fingers from her neck. Her own hands moved to her neck, still clawing, as if trying to open a passage for breathing, but she could make only a small gasping, strangling sound. He cupped her chin with one hand and with the other gripped the back of her head. Her neck made a cracking sound when he gave it a quick, hard twist, and he watched fascinated as her eyes went blank as a doll's.

Rapture.

He had at last done what he had so often dreamed of, and it had been sheer rapture.

But the sensation at last faded, and he found himself lying on a bed with a dead woman.

And scared as hell.

Scared because it had been so good, so wonderful.

Scared because already the hunger was returning, and he knew that if he let himself go he would kill again. And again. And again.

He would be unable to stop. He would roam the country, killing at random, trying to reexperience the Rapture. And inevitably he would be caught. No matter how careful he was, his luck would eventually run out. If not this time, then the next. He was an intelligent man, and he saw that clearly. No prescience was needed.

He had to stop and stop now.

But there was no time to think about that. He had to get away, and as soon as possible.

From the moment he had taken the room key, he had noted everything he had touched. Now he wiped away every possible fingerprint and made sure he'd left no blood spots from his abraded back. He checked to see that he had left no semen on the woman despite the condom he had used, and he cleaned her fingernails with soap and water.

He checked and rechecked to be sure he was leaving behind no clue to his identity. The drapes were closed. He saw no one when he looked out the door and put the DO NOT DISTURB sign on the knob. He closed the door and walked away, feeling as if a hand might fall on his shoulder at any moment.

His rented car was parked several blocks away. By the time he reached it, he felt safe. The body would probably not be found before noon tomorrow, and by then he would be far away, on a flight back to New York.

He had learned something about himself. The monster within, of which he had dreamed, was real. He could kill, as few men could. But the power he enjoyed was a tiger within the cage of his mind: it could destroy him if he ever let it get out of control. It could become his tragic flaw. Therefore from this night on he must exercise the greatest possible self-discipline. He must find a way to become the absolute master of his passions. Only then could he permit himself to enjoy the Rapture.

That fall he enrolled in Harvard Law School and after three years, armed with a law degree and thinking his old love forgotten, he returned to St. Claire for good. But on seeing Julia and James together, obviously happy with each other and with their baby son Daniel, the mixed toxins of love-hate-envy-anger began to burn within him like a long unremitting gripe in the guts.

What should he do about it?

Freya Kellgren gave him the answer.

The Freya who came to consult with his father behind closed doors that spring when he returned once and for all from law school could have been no older than twenty or so. What had she to do with his father and he with her? Could the old bastard actually be diddling her, for Chrissake? Timothy wouldn't have put it past him. His father had always been attractive to women, had always had them when he wanted them. Timothy never thought about his father's advanced age, simply because the old man looked a good thirty years younger than he was.

Yes, his dear old daddy might very well be getting it on with Freya Kellgren.

Freya made her move about ten days after Timothy arrived home.

His father threw a homecoming party for him—a party for Benjamin Balthazar's son, returned after seven years of almost complete absence. His law firm's new affiliate, his junior partner in business, his pride and joy, his heir. Cars lined the long driveway and filled the parking area. The patio, the lawns, the gardens, were hung with hundreds of colored lights. A small orchestra played, not too obtrusively, behind the chatter of the strolling, milling, sometimes dancing guests. Long tables were loaded with chilled shrimp and lobster and caviar and dozens of other delicacies; other tables were loaded with every beverage and liquor that might be required; and a veritable corps of caterers, bartenders, and waiters attended every need. Virtually all who had been invited had come, and none who had come uninvited were turned away but were welcomed cordially.

Naturally, Mr. and Mrs. James St. Claire had come, together with her parents and James's mother, Lydia. Lydia St. Claire, a dearly loved woman sometimes fondly referred to as the Queen Mother, had long reigned over the community, and she was quite content to pass the diadem on to her daughter-in-law.

Timothy greeted them all enthusiastically, as old and dear friends, indeed as his oldest and dearest friends, and made a point during the evening of dancing with each of the ladies.

As he danced with Julia, and listened to her hopes for his future happiness, that it would match her happiness with James and her joy in her infant son Daniel, all his sense of loss returned. She was the prize. She should have been his. But somehow he had been cheated, she had been stolen away from him. She had turned her back on him, and for whom? For Jamie St. Claire, whom Timothy's father had called a weakling, the degenerate son of a degenerate. . . .

He saw Julia's smile falter, as if she had read something on his face. Instantly he masked his thoughts and forced himself to return her smile. "Julia, my darling," he murmured, "I thank you for your dear, kind wishes. But I was once somewhat in love with you and always will be, at least a little, so how can I wish you anything less than a happiness that is matchless?"

"Oh, my," Julia murmured back, "as gallant as his father." Her smile was steady again, but a little sad, almost as if she could see through him . . . could see, however dimly, the real Timothy Balthazar.

Later, Freya approached him for the first time that evening.

At that moment, he happened to be alone, drifting, and he had paused to look at Julia and James, some thirty feet away, chatting with a small group of young people. Freya, in black for a change and resplendently golden, followed his gaze to Julia and James, then looked at Timothy again.

"So you hate him," she said softly.

Startled, he looked sharply at her, then made his face blank. "What an ugly thing to say. And why, for God's sake? They happen to be very dear old friends."

Freya's lip curled with disbelief. "Yes, tell me about it."

"There's nothing to tell—"

"You'd like to make him pay for taking what should have been yours, wouldn't you?"

"I haven't the slightest idea of what you're talking about."

Freya ignored his words. "And while you're at it, you wouldn't mind teaching her a little about pain and grief."

Timothy didn't answer. Within his guts he felt a sudden wrenching, and there erupted like a painful roar a great involuntary *YES!*

Enraged with himself, he turned away from Freya. To hell with her. He was giving nothing to this bitch.

"You know where my house is, don't you?" she asked softly.

He moved his head in the general direction of her house. "Of course. Across the lake."

"Come see me tomorrow afternoon. Anytime. I'll tell you what to do."

Freya said nothing more. When Timothy turned around, she was gone.

At three o'clock the next afternoon, on a day as sunny as the last, Timothy drove around the lake to Freya Kellgren's house. Why not? he asked himself. She was a beautiful woman, and he would find out what she had in mind. He had nothing better to do.

He had never been to the Kellgren house before. Like the St. Claire house across the lake, it stood high on a slope in relative isolation, a great white three-story Victorian relic with a high-peaked and many-dormered roof and a deep veranda across the front.

A pleasantly smiling middle-aged woman in an apron answered the door. "Miss Freya is out back in the garden having tea, Mr. Balthazar. Would you like something to drink? A beer, perhaps?"

"Iced tea would be fine."

Freya was sitting at an umbrella-shaded table, thumbing through a *New Yorker* magazine. She was wearing a transparent peach sundress over a lacy white bikini that might have been underwear. Timothy couldn't be sure, and knew he wasn't supposed to.

"So you decided to accept my help," she said as he sat down.

"I'm not sure I want or need your help for anything, Freya. But you've aroused my curiosity. I'm willing to listen."

Freya nodded. "I want something from you."

"I assumed that."

Freya pursed her lips and looked about, as if trying to decide how to begin. Timothy didn't give her any help.

"Timothy," she said at last, "your father is a very old man."

Timothy kept his face carefully blank and his mind as nearly blank as possible. Never had he *ever* heard anyone refer to his father's age. It was not so much that the subject was forbidden as that it was oddly unthinkable.

"When he dies," Freya continued in the face of Timothy's silence, "his convocation will almost certainly fall apart."

Timothy frankly didn't much give a damn, but he still said nothing.

"And that will be a pity," Freya said. "Because the Balthazar Convocation is almost unique. It comprises some of the finest psychic minds in the country and therefore is one of the most powerful and influential in all areas. Government, commerce—"

"So I've been told, often enough. Get to the point, Freya."

"Without your father's charisma, it will break up, and I don't want that."

"And what am I supposed to do about it?"

"Take your father's place. Take over the reins of power."

As Freya spoke, his father's words came back to him. "*. . . knew I was going to build one of the biggest, most powerful convocations in this country. . . . That is the convocation you will someday lead, Timothy . . .*" But that was years ago, before his disillusionment. He had left the convocation on the very night that he had been fully admitted, and his father had never once suggested that he return.

Things he had been taught as a boy, things he hadn't thought about in years, began to come back to him, things passed down from grandfather to father to son. "*Power is the key to everything you'll ever want . . . power over yourself and over others . . . the god of this world is the Prince of Power. . . .*"

Timothy thought of that night in Santa Monica. It seemed to him now that he had been the very embodiment of the Prince of Power, celebrating his strength. Was it possible that the Order was his destiny, that it was what he had been looking for all along?

"How could I possibly take his place?" he asked. "There must be others who want it. You yourself . . ."

Freya lifted her lip in a delicate sneer. "Me? A woman? Allowed to lead a convocation, the *Balthazar* Convocation, on her own? Not in this lifetime, I don't think!"

"How do I go about taking over the 'reins of power,' supposing it's possible?"

"Timothy, your father and I both believe you have within you powers you are hardly aware of and haven't even begun to develop. You must begin at once. I shall teach you."

"And just what are these powers?"

"You have your father's charisma, for one thing. God knows why. You're not nearly as good-looking, and you can be surly as hell, but somehow that works for you. Furthermore, I think you'll find that your charisma grows even stronger in your father's presence—his will *feed* yours, so to speak. Timothy, from now on until the day he dies, we want you to be at his side. You will come to know every member of the convocation. You will smile at them, shake their hands, charm them. You will learn to *frighten* them if you have to—you can do that. You will learn to work your will with them. It will come to be *assumed* that you are your father's successor."

"And what's your role in all this? What do you get out of it?"

"My role, as I said, is to teach you, to help you develop your powers. I will also help you get your own back at James St. Claire. In return, I want a higher place in the convocation, a place your father has denied me."

"Be specific."

Freya smiled briefly. "Ah! I have your attention.

"Timothy, in some ways your father is very old-fashioned. He has kept his convocation a predominantly male organization, you know that. In the past, many convocations have been led by a man and a woman on an equal footing, and some even by a woman alone. But poor Benjamin has always feared that if he made me Mother Superior of the convocation, I would take over the leadership after he died and deny it to you."

"Which, of course, you would have done," Timothy said with sudden absolute certainty.

Freya stared at him for a moment, and then smiled and nodded. "Good. You show promise."

"You want me to make you Mother Superior."

"I don't want to take the leadership away from you, Timothy. I want to share it with you. Equally."

"And if I don't agree?"

"I'll do everything in my power either to take over the Balthazar Convocation or to break it up. With your father gone, that shouldn't be difficult."

Break up his father's convocation? Timothy felt unexpected resentment. "No," he said slowly, "no, I won't permit that." Damned pushy bitch. Ambitious . . .

But suddenly so was Timothy Balthazar. He was, after all, his father's son.

Rising, he began to pace. "Freya, with or without your help, I intend to take over my father's convocation." As he said the words for the first time, *thought* the words for the first time, he knew they were true. "However, I will go this far: If you will aid and support me, I will make you my Mother Superior—"

"Equal in power—"

"No. I said, *my* Mother Superior. I agree with my father, a convocation can have only one true leader. But you will be second only to me."

Silent and unsmiling, Freya looked at him, gauging his determination. His unblinking eyes sent back the message that this was his only concession, his only offer.

Freya slowly nodded.

Timothy reached over and put his hand on Freya's for a moment. They had an agreement. But he had no illusions. Her ambitions would continue unabated.

"Now," he said, "in the matter of James St. Claire . . ."

"After you have renewed your final vows."

"I don't have to renew—"

"Oh, yes, you do. That charade a dozen years ago meant nothing to you, and you know it. Three nights from now there will be a full moon. You will come to this house at nine o'clock. Bring your cloak. We'll renew your vows, and afterward we'll see what we can do about James St. Claire." Freya smiled and stood up. "Now, if you'll excuse me . . ."

For a moment Timothy didn't move. He was remembering his humiliation when he first took the vows. Looking at

Freya's bikini-clad body under the peach sundress, he felt a dryness in his throat and a tightening in his loins. He swore there would be no humiliation this time. Or if there was . . .

There was always the Rapture. . . .

Timothy rose to his feet and held out his hand. Freya took it.

"Until the full moon, Reverend Mother."

Freya smiled. "You won't be sorry."

"Repeat after me: I, Timothy, do solemnly swear . . ."

"I, Timothy, do solemnly swear . . ."

"That from this night forward my first allegiance shall be to the Prince of Power . . ."

"That from this night forward my first allegiance shall be to the Prince of Power . . ."

The altar was Freya's bed. It was covered with a red sheet and pillows, and at each corner a black candle burned, the room's sole illumination. A faint breeze from the open windows made the flames dance and flare. Freya, wearing only her hooded cloak, stood at the side of the bed, and Timothy, in his cloak, knelt before her, his forehead resting on her belly and his hands on the backs of her thighs. The odor of her body mingled with that of the candles.

One by one, he took the vows. They had seemed wildly melodramatic, hardly serious, when he had first taken them. Mere schoolboy blasphemies. Now they were real. He was pledging his life, his body, his soul to the Prince of Power, god of this world.

"I swear on the lives and souls of those I most love. May they be forfeit . . ."

"I swear on the lives and souls of those I most love. . . ."

Freya took his hands from her thighs and drew him to his feet. She unfastened the griffin-embossed clasp at his throat, pushed the cloak from his shoulders, and let it fall to the floor. She unfastened her own cloak, cast it aside, and fell back on the bed.

Timothy followed her. There was no adolescent eagerness this time, no thought of failure. When he took her, he was truly giving himself to the god. He was wedding himself to Power: Freya was its vessel, and he felt it flooding through him. It seemed to him that he *was* the Power, and when he raised his head, Lucifer himself looked out through his eyes.

"What about James St. Claire?" Timothy said. "What about Julia?"

"Oh, darling!" Freya said with a little laugh as she fondled him. "Do you really want to talk about them *now*?"

Yes, he found that he really did want to talk about them now. Almost an hour had passed, his post-coital drowsiness had faded, and Freya's fingertips and nails, delicately stroking the tender flesh, had aroused him again; but he felt no urgency, just a lazy sensuality, and, yes, he very much wanted to talk about the fate of James St. Claire.

"Tell me," he said as he drew her closer into his arms. "You said that after I renewed my vows we'd see what we could do. What do you have in mind?"

"First, Timothy, I should warn you that it may be dangerous. If Julia should find out . . . and she is a very perceptive woman . . . if she should think that one of her own is being attacked or endangered . . ."

"Do you feel you'll be putting yourself in danger?"

"Yes, somewhat. But I've made a deal with you, and I trust our lord and master, the god of this world, to protect me. If he can."

"If he can?"

"Timothy, he is not all-powerful. And he has enemies, you must know that. Even if in the end, as I believe, he will prevail."

"Then I'll trust him too. What are we going to do?"

Freya rose up on an elbow so that she could look into Timothy's eyes. "Timothy, have you ever heard the saying 'To those whom they would destroy, the gods grant wishes'?"

"Of course."

"I sense in Julia St. Claire no wish that might destroy her. Frankly, I've been afraid to probe. I sense in her great strength."

"The power of anathema."

Freya nodded. "I think she's got it. But James St. Claire is a different matter."

"He has a weakness? A wish that the god might grant?"

Freya nodded again. "I've studied him for some time, and the impression struck me most forcefully at the party your father gave for you. The wish, the desire, the propensity, is buried deeply and well controlled, but it remains a potentially fatal flaw."

"And what is this potentially fatal flaw?"

Freya sat up on the bed, cross-legged, facing Timothy. "In James it is a wish to escape his claustrophobia, a wish to break free from confining rooms and from crowds like the one at your party. It is a violent wish to tear off his clothes, to rid himself of all the raiment and restraints of civilization, and to run free in the wild. It is an urge to *hunt*, to find prey and kill, to bite into raw meat and blood."

"You're saying he's a lycanthrope."

"Yes. The family curse. James St. Claire is a werewolf."

Timothy remembered his grandfather's words: *"The wolf will become their weakness."* "My father," he said slowly, "seems to think they've lost the shape-changing power . . . if they ever really had it."

"That doesn't matter. What matters is that James has these dreadful urges, these terrible desires—"

"Which he has fought all his life."

"Exactly. All his life he has tried to deny himself the one thing, aside from Julia, that in his heart of hearts he most wants—because he fears that if he loses control, *it will drive him mad!*"

Suddenly Freya's meaning in all its beautiful simplicity became clear to Timothy. "And you're saying . . . ?"

In the candlelight, Freya looked like a gleeful imp. "All we have to do is grant him his wish. All we have to do is push him toward doing what he wants to do and being what he wants to be. We must mentally *nudge* him time after time and night after night and especially when the moon is full. Wolves *love* a full moon." Freya's face became grave. "But as I've said, Julia is very perceptive. We must take great care to conceal what we are doing."

"How do we do that?"

"We must give no thought to who we are or what we ourselves want. We must project no ill will whatever toward

James or Julia. We must project *only what James himself wants, even if in spite of himself!* Do you understand?"

"Yes." Half-forgotten lessons taught by his father were coming back to Timothy. "We can dedicate what we do to the greater glory of our lord and master. We can invoke his power to help us. We can invite him to participate."

Freya's smile returned, wicked in the candlelight. "We can let him act through us to destroy his enemy. If James blames anyone but his ancestors for what he is, or himself for what he does, it will be *him!*—the god of this world! 'The devil made me do it.'"

It would work. Timothy felt a clear certainty that it would work.

He said, "When do we begin?"

In answer, Freya leaned down over him and gazed into his eyes for a moment. Then she closed her eyes and kissed him hard on the mouth. At the same time, she threw a leg over him and deftly took him back into herself, and he rolled her onto her back. In the blind pleasure of the moment, his identity seemed to blur, seemed to merge with Freya's, and he invited their god into them both: *"Welcome, Lord Lucifer!"*

When he raised his head, he saw that Freya's eyes were still closed and her lips were moving. She, too, was invoking the god.

After a moment her eyes opened, narrow candlelit slits. "Now," she whispered. "Direct your thoughts at James. Visualize him, if you can, in his house across the lake. If you look out the window, you may be able to see its lights. Put yourself in James's place and think about the moon, think about running free in the moonlight and hunting, killing, feeding. Oh, can't you taste the bloody meat, James? Don't you long for it, James? Don't you want to be your own true self, James, so alive and wild and free, free to hunt, with the scent of blood in your nostrils? Oh, Lord Lucifer, we beg you. Go to James and give him what he wants, and we will be eternally in your debt. Oh, go to him, Lord Lucifer . . . oh, harder, Timothy, faster, harder!"

Freya's nails tore at Timothy as he thrust into her with all his force. Once again, a great sense of power flooded him. He was all power, power itself, and nobody, nothing, could resist him, not James, not Freya. It was as if Lucifer himself had indeed joined with him and was experiencing this moment. In a hoarse whisper, he said, "Welcome, Lord Lucifer. Take me, use me. Grant James his wish. Make him the creature that in his heart he wants to be. Make him yearn for blood and howl, howl, howl for it, howl . . . !"

Perhaps it happened only in Timothy's mind. But as he erupted and the fire once again burned through him and into Freya, he thought he heard a great long cry of anguish from across the lake, a cry like that of a wolf howling at the moon.

They did not succeed in driving James St. Claire insane. Not quite. They worked on him for only three nights, but as it turned out, that was quite enough to turn a buried propensity into an overt compulsion. Even Freya was surprised at how well they had succeeded.

Of course, there was no hiding the fact that something bad had happened to James, that family history had finally caught up with him, so to speak. That history was well known, and friends shook their heads sadly. Somehow James always fought his way back to normal, or almost, after the attacks; but he suffered, and it showed on his ravaged face. For each year he lived, he aged two.

Occasionally Timothy ran into him in town. He would give James a smile and a nod and a brief greeting, and James would usually give him a weary nod and a ghost of a smile in return. But sometimes he would look at Timothy with suffering eyes that seemed to say, *How could you have done this to me? How? Why?* At such times, Timothy wanted to cry out in guilt and anger, *Because this is what you* are, *you goddamned sick St. Claire son of a bitch. So roll over and die!* But he dared not. Julia might not be able to read his thoughts, but she sensed things. And if she ever found out . . .

He would never forget the visit she paid him on the morning after the third night with Freya. She had meant him never to forget.

He had been alone, brooding in his father's study, when the maid announced Julia and she appeared at the door. As he stood up and stepped toward her, he was shocked at her appearance. Her face looked puffy and bruised with fatigue, the eyes swollen almost shut. It's as if she hasn't slept in three nights, he thought, with unexpected pity. He started to say her name and some word of commiseration, but she cut him off with a gesture.

For a moment, unsmiling, she merely looked steadily into his eyes, and he had the impression that she was trying to penetrate his mind. He guarded it by thinking, almost desperately, *I care for you, Julia! I will do anything I can to help you, Julia! What do you want of me, Julia?*

As if in answer, she said, "My husband is very ill, Timothy."

"I'm sorry," he said. "If there's anything . . ."

"Are you, Timothy? Are you sorry?"

"Well, of course. What's happened to him? What . . . ?"

She didn't answer. She tilted her head first to one side and then to the other, as if examining his soul from different angles. "It's odd," she said. "For the last couple of days, I've had the recurrent thought that you have absolutely *nothing to do* with Jamie's illness. Not that you were somehow to blame, but that you had *nothing to do* with it. Why should that be, Timothy?"

For an instant Timothy stopped breathing. He knew precisely why Julia had had that thought, the thought that he had tried so desperately to transmit, and he felt as if he had inadvertently trapped himself. "Julia, you know that I wish you only the best."

"Do you, Timothy? And what about James?"

Timothy held out innocently empty hands. "My God, he's been my friend since we were kids! My best friend in high school."

"Yes, that's true. We all had a certain love for each other, you and Jamie and I. But I'm not flattering myself when I say that you came to resent Jamie because I could not love you as I loved him. Isn't that also true?"

Timothy managed a sickly smile. "That's true. I would have resented any man you loved more than me."

Julia nodded, as if she took this as a statement of fact and not a mere gallantry.

"I'm going to ask you a question, Timothy. If it offends you, I'm sorry. If you're truly my friend, I hope you'll forgive it."

"Ask anything you please."

"I've lately felt a malign presence in my house. Have you in any way been trying to do my husband harm? Have you *wished* him harm?"

The question seemed to drive all the air from Timothy's lungs, and he had to struggle to get it back. "Julia, if my resentment, my envy, has ever caused me to have an evil thought toward James, I regret it. I want only to be a friend to both of you. I swear it."

At the moment he spoke, Timothy meant what he said. It was the only thought in his mind, and he dared not think anything else. He clung to it as to a lifeline.

Julia's eyes, wise beyond their twenty-seven years, continued to probe his soul. What they found, he could not tell, but after a moment she said, "I want to believe you. I want to keep on loving you, Timothy, and enjoying whatever love you may have for me. But I think I should tell you . . . you know about the St. Claire anathema?"

"Of course." He could not help adding with a bitter smile, "The Balthazars have felt it."

Julia's eyes were cold. "Good. Because I want you to know, Timothy, that if you ever try to hurt one of my family, or anyone close to us, I will use the power of anathema against you. I promise you."

Timothy forced a smile. "Julia, believe me, please, I shall always be your good friend and faithful servant."

He babbled on, more entreaties, more assurances, but she was already turning away, as if she didn't hear him. At the door, she turned and looked back. "I promise you," she said again.

He believed her. This was the witch of St. Claire—powerful, loving, pitiless.

There would be no more nights with Freya, trying to torture James St. Claire's mind.

•　　•　　•

Now, thirty-three years later as he sat in his hotel room after his confrontation with Freya, he recalled Julia's words. *"I will use the power of anathema against you."* He could only pray to his god that whatever Julia might suspect, she would never know his part in Daniel's fate.

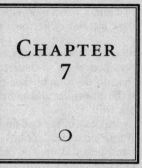

CHAPTER 7

If only she dared to disobey Timothy. If only she and Daniel together had the strength to destroy Timothy. But they did not, and she remembered Timothy's clawed hand on her face, threatening to tear away her beauty forever. *"Refuse,"* he had said, *"and you yourself will be destroyed."* Yes, she would be destroyed. It was her life or Daniel's.

But someday, Timothy, Freya thought guardedly, someday I'll be stronger than you, and then . . .

She aroused herself at shortly before three in the morning. For several hours she had lain in the dark on the very threshold of sleep, trying not to think of what was to come, trying to anesthetize herself against her own grief and pain, and yet waiting for the moment when she would know that Daniel lay weak, vulnerable, ready. She must, if she could, be as she had been before she had fallen in love with Daniel, a creature that could savor Daniel's madness and death, as Timothy would savor it. But only in a dream could she do that. . . .

Surely she was bound to suffer for this night and to regret it the rest of her life.

Nevertheless, she would do what she had to do. She must save herself—that fact and that alone she must keep in mind.

The moment had come. She felt it. The knowledge, emanating from Daniel's mind, miles away across the city, was like a whisper in the dark interior of her own mind. *It is time. He sleeps. He dreams.*

Slowly, carefully, still close to a dream-state herself, Freya sat up in bed. It was better not to depart from sleep too far, not for what she had to do tonight. She preferred to awaken only enough to be the controller and not the controlled. Only enough to exert her will.

She shifted her legs out of the bed and stood up. She was naked and the autumn night was cool. As she picked up her robe from a chair and pulled it on, she caught a dark glimpse of herself in her dressing-table mirror, and she leaned toward it, touching her face. *Mirror, mirror, on the wall* . . .

She looked young, a blond Nordic beauty, still in her thirties. Yet even in these shadows it seemed to her she could see the first faint wrinkles under her eyes, the softening under her jawline. She stroked her face with long, slender fingers. She must not let that happen, the wrinkles and the softening. No, she must remain beautiful, forever beautiful, and she would be beautiful for Daniel tonight. That was the least she could do for him, and for herself.

Loosely belting her robe, she walked through the dark apartment to her balcony, off the living room. The doors were open, as they always were on pleasant nights, and even before she stepped outside, she could see the checkered lights of Manhattan's towers and the glow of the streets below. Despite the lights, most of the city was sleeping now, and dreaming its millions of dreams.

Dreams of love and joy, dreams of terror. What are you dreaming about, Daniel . . . ?

She sensed the bat before she saw it. She looked up, high and to one side, and it was as if the darkness itself fluttered and then took form, gliding swiftly down past her balcony and across the background of lights.

Was a bat on this night of all nights a sign of some kind?

Or had Timothy perhaps sent it as a reminder, an admonition?

Come, you pretty little creature, she commanded, *come to Freya.*

The bat came to her. It came, wings beating furiously, swift as an arrow, but it struck her left shoulder with no more force than a ball of yarn. It drew its wings up close to itself and clung to her. Freya looked at it and smiled. She had always been able to charm small creatures, and she was particularly fond of bats. This was a common brown bat, she saw now, small and shrewlike in appearance. An insect-eater. *What are you doing up here so high, my pretty? You won't find any mosquitoes up here. Did you come to see me?* She stroked the soft brown fur with a gentle finger and let her blond hair fall over the little fellow. She could not understand why so many people hated and feared bats.

How ironic that Daniel hated and feared them.

"*Hate* the damned things," he had said, when she had mentioned her affinity with them. His handsome face had twisted with repugnance. "Can't *stand* the damned things!"

Poor, poor Daniel . . .

"What do you say, little fellow?" Freya asked softly. "Would you like to pay Daniel a visit? In his dreams, perhaps? Hmm?"

It was time. . . .

A chaise longue with plump soft cushions stood at one end of the balcony. Carefully, so as not to disturb her little companion, Freya sat down on it. She lay back on the cushions and made herself comfortable. She took one deep breath, released it slowly, and with the ease of long practice began to slip back into a dream-state. . . .

Daniel, are you dreaming . . . ?

Yes, you're dreaming. . . .

Let me dream with you, Daniel. . . .

Let me share your dreams, and you'll share mine. . . .

. . . and I'll give you such a dream as you've never dreamed before. . . .

Daniel rested poorly that night. He dreamed, but precisely of what he dreamed, he didn't know at first . . . of dim, vaguely seen shapes, small fluttering shapes, mouselike, winged.

Bats. He dreamed of bats.

Daniel had always dreaded bats, had been deeply and irrationally terrified of them for as long as he could remember. Intellectually, he knew that they were relatively harmless, but no amount of cold fact and reasoned thought could free him from the repulsion he felt for the creatures.

At first he could barely see the bats—they seemed to flutter high above him in the dark attic of his mind—but he heard their wings and their faint, sharp chittering. Suddenly he found it hard to breathe, and he felt himself breaking out in a sweat. He wanted to cry out, but he choked back the sounds out of fear of being heard. Bats. If they discovered him, lying here in the dark, they would attack him. Each tiny little mouth would bite into him, as the loathsome creatures clung to him, and he would go out of his mind. He had to escape, had to. . . .

But there was no escape, for something even worse was coming for him. He sensed it, somewhere out there in the night. *Move,* he commanded himself, *run, hide, HIDE!*

But it was too late. He could not escape the dream, and he lay paralyzed with fear as a dark shape appeared silhouetted before the window. He cried out—a low, harsh sound that ground through his throat until his lungs were almost empty. His heart pounded massively, then hung fire, threatening to stop forever. He stared at the dark form that blocked the light. Then his heart pounded again, painfully hard, and yet again. Sanity tried to reassert itself. This was no dream! This was a stranger, a thief, come to rob and perhaps to kill him. Someone had broken into his apartment.

A blink of his eyes, and suddenly the dark form, or its illusion, was no longer blocking the light. It had vanished as if it had never been. He was alone.

Gradually he calmed himself. It had all been a dream, only a dream. A terrible dream, but it was over now. There were no bats, no phantom at the open window. His heart could stop its terrible throbbing, and he could sigh with relief. He would sit up, have a cigarette, relax. . . .

But still he could not quite get over the feeling that he was not alone. He even had the strange feeling that he might still be dreaming. He thought of the dream he had shared with Freya weeks earlier, the dream that he was with her in her bed. It had had none of the soft blur and flux of most dreams—it had been as hard and detailed as reality, more real than real, until the moment it had begun to fade. He had that sense of super-reality now, of extraordinary awareness.

Carefully, he moved up in the bed, gathering some pillows behind him. Feeling vulnerable in his nakedness, he pulled the sheet up to his chest. He tried to recall . . . when he had cried out, had he heard someone or something whispering to him? *Shhh, Daniel, it's all right. . . .* Peering into the shadows, he saw nothing . . .

. . . and then *she* appeared, and he almost cried out again.

It was as if she had materialized out of the shadows. One moment he was alone, and the next she was there, half-hidden in the darkness, and his heart began to thunder again.

"It's all right, Daniel," she said softly. "It's only me. Freya."

Yes, that was the voice that had whispered to him. "Freya, my God . . ."

As she stepped forward into the moonlight, he saw that she had thrown his crimson cloak over her shoulders against the cool of night. And that, apparently, was all she wore. She held it before her, not quite covering herself, and the moonlight carved a breast from ivory, a dark nipple and aureole, a long bare leg. Again, he could not escape the strange feeling that this was an illusion, that he was still dreaming, or perhaps hallucinating. That this could actually be happening was impossible, utterly impossible, and at any instant, surely, she would vanish.

But she did not. She continued to stand there, perfectly still, smiling at him. Smiling almost sadly, it seemed. Fearfully, as if risking his life, he reached toward the bedside lamp.

"No," she said softly, "leave it off."

Somehow he brought himself to speak again. "What in God's name . . . ?"

"What do you think?" she asked. "Isn't this what you wanted?"

"Of course. But how . . . ?"

How had she come to be here, and at this hour, if he were not dreaming? He glanced at the clock on his nightstand—it was after three in the morning.

"Dear God, I *must* be dreaming!"

"Yes, dreaming. We're sharing a dream. But I shall make it so real . . ."

Then she was settling down on the side of the bed and bending over him. He felt the warmth of her bare body, even before her breasts brushed so softly against his chest and flattened against him. Her mouth found his and her lips moved. The kiss was hot and hungry, her tongue seeking his, and he found himself responding to it in spite of his still thundering heart and his fear.

Her hand traveled slowly over his chest and belly, nails lightly furrowing his flesh, leaving a series of little shocks in their wake, each shock arousing him further, until her fingers curled around hardening flesh.

"Ah, you do want me," she said, tugging gently at him. "I knew you would."

"Oh, Christ," he said, gasping, as he returned her caresses, "what kind of creature are you?"

"A succubus," she whispered. "Just think of me as a succubus. A creature who comes in your dreams at night to steal your soul away. I'm going to give you such pleasure, and all I want in return is . . . your soul."

He no longer felt capable of thought. He was bewildered, still a little frightened, but a captive of the mouth that roamed over his face and neck and chest and the hand that stroked and fondled him. He felt fleetingly that he was being used, victimized, but resistance was impossible. He no longer cared. He was totally lost.

Sweeping the cloak back from her shoulders, Freya swung a leg over him, settled on her knees straddling him, and carefully, slowly, took him in. Daniel heard himself whimper at that tight, consuming embrace. She brought his hands to her breasts, settled herself forward against his palms, and her hardened nipples seemed to pierce them.

"And now, my dear," she whispered, "as never before . . ."

Oh, yes, as never before . . .

Whether this was dream, reality, or hallucination, he no longer cared. This was pleasure beyond pleasure, a kind of insanity, a madness from which he might never recover. He had wanted this for so long, and very quickly he felt himself building toward an irresistible, mind-shattering climax, building, building, and then exploding, crying out. . . .

"When you're in hell, darling," Freya whispered in that long agony of pleasure, "remember that I loved you."

She smiled.

For the first time, he saw the teeth.

The sharp crooked little teeth and the two long narrow teeth, like small old-ivory sabers, glistening wetly in the moonlight. The long flickering tongue . . .

In that instant, at the very height of his release, all his fear, his soul-shaking terror, came thundering back, and his heart in a single giant convulsion threatened to burst. All else that had happened in the night was illusion, and *this* was the reality—this fanged horror he held in his arms, this monstrosity still coupled with him as he watched it transform, this *thing* with its ratlike face covered with fur. "No!" he cried out, and he tried to thrust it away, tried to escape that terrible embrace, but he couldn't. Claws, needle-sharp, cut into the backs of his thighs, holding him to her. And then her teeth were buried deep in his neck, and he went blind with agony, could see only the flashing crimsons of pain. . . .

But he could feel the weight of the creature on him, could feel the fur of its body, could feel its obscene warmth, could feel the spread of membrane wings over him, and when his sight cleared, he saw the bat face over him, beady-eyed, its open mouth emitting a high shriek that mingled with his screams, until he could bear no more and fell into blessed darkness. . . .

She had to save her daddy from the bats.

They're not real, Daddy, she cried out. *Don't be afraid, they're not real, you're dreaming!*

She was in a dark place, as dark as her grandma's attic

with the lights off, but much bigger. She was running on something, she didn't know what, but she sensed no walls around her, darkness was endless and everlasting on all sides, and there were no stars or moon overhead to make a sky, only darkness. The only light seemed to come from herself, a soft blue-white glow that surrounded her, but overhead and all around her the bats dipped in and out of that light.

Daddy, the bats can't hurt you, you've told me yourself! They're only a dream! We're only dreaming, Daddy, we're dreaming!

Nevertheless, something bad was going to happen if she didn't reach her daddy in time. She was straining for air (even in a dream you had to breathe) and her legs ached. She had a stitch in her right side and her heart was banging (or was it her father's heart? It sounded, felt like the thump of her daddy's heart) and something terrible was going to happen if she didn't reach her daddy soon!

Daddy, I'm coming! Don't be afraid!

But he couldn't help being afraid of the little creatures, she knew that, even if he did try to cover it up. And something was happening, something terrible—

And it was happening now.

Daddy, wake up! It's only a dream! Don't let it be real! I'll help you, Daddy!

She ran on through that darkness, ran so hard that her knees threatened to give way, and the stitch in her side became almost unbearable and her lungs ached painfully as she strained for air. The bats, large and small, still dipped into the light, brown membranous wings aflutter, and she didn't know if they were chasing her or following her, and she didn't care, she didn't care, they wouldn't hurt her—

Unless someone ordered them to hurt her.

Now they were dipping closer to her, closer and still closer. She could see their eyes. A couple of them swirled around her, circling. She could hear their sharp little cries— too high for human ears, but not for hers. They were warning her away from her daddy, trying to make her go back.

No!

Her legs could hardly bear her up, the stitch was a hot iron claw in her side, and her lungs were on fire. A wing brushed across her face, for an instant blinding her. She struck out at it, hit it solidly, heard the bat's cry of pain-fear-anger. Struck out at another as it flashed by.

Snapped at the next one that flew in her face.

Snapped hard, her teeth *bang*ing together like a trap.

Stumbled to a halt and nearly fell to her knees. Drew air desperately into her lungs several times. Then let it emerge as an enraged growl.

She could no longer think coherently. All she knew was that she must strike back at these winged creatures that were closing in on her, these little demons that were trying to keep her from her daddy. The things were on her back now, on her shoulders, in her hair, but she clawed at them, crushed them with her hands, sank her teeth into their furry bodies, spat them away, and at the taste of blood her fury became an angry joy. All her fatigue seemed to wash away in that taste, her legs were strong again, and the stitch was gone from her side. Clawing, snapping, killing, she ran on through the darkness.

She saw something ahead.

The dimmest spot of red in the darkness.

It grew, like a puddle of blood growing larger in the dark. But it wasn't a puddle of blood, it was something else, it was some*one* else, someone in a long red cloak with a red hood drawn up over his-her-its head.

Someone who stood over the naked bloodstained body of a man.

"Nicole, darling, wake up. Please, darling, wake up!"

That was her grandma, she knew, awakening her, her grandma, weeping as she held Nicole in her arms and rocked her. *"Nicole, it's all over, there's nothing we can do, don't dream anymore, darling. Come to Grandma, Grandma needs you now. Please, darling, wake up . . ."*

But Nicole couldn't wake up, not quite yet. She had to see . . .

And as she looked, all her pain returned, but now it was in her soul—all the aching, the burning, the iron claw that had ripped through her, it was now in her soul, and her cry was a banshee wail of grief.

She didn't want to know who that was, lying dead or dying, naked and so still, but she did know. Nothing in the world could save her from that terrible knowledge. She had come too late, too late to save him.

But who had done this terrible thing to her daddy?

The figure in the red cloak was looking down at her daddy. He-she-it seemed unaware of or indifferent to Nicole. The figure turned slightly, brushing the cloak aside, and Nicole saw the slim, tall body of a naked woman.

She also saw the woman's profile, and for the merest instant she thought she recognized it. But it was as if the face could not withstand the intensity of Nicole's gaze, as if it were a mere mask, an illusion, that melted away, vanished as Nicole saw through it. The eyes became dark and beady, bulging from their sockets. Crooked teeth and fangs showed yellow in a wide lipless mouth. Fine dark hair covered the cheeks—the woman in the cloak had more of a muzzle than a face.

Slowly she turned to look at Nicole. As if she were aware of Nicole for the first time, her obsidian eyes widened with fear and anger, and her mouth, jagged with the yellow-stained teeth, opened wide in threat, so wide that the head tilted back and the eyes blazed down past the animal snout. Then she reached out toward Nicole with one arm, and as she did so, her fingers grew, stretched, elongated impossibly, webbing between them, until they formed a great wing.

The creature no longer looked human at all.

She looked like something out of Nicole's worst dreams, out of ancient inherited memories, out of prehistoric terrors.

Nicole awoke, sobbing, in her grandmother's arms.

Gasping, trembling with remnant fear, Freya awakened to find herself lying supine across the chaise longue, an arm dangling from one side, a leg from the other. She ached with fatigue, as if she had managed to escape from her dream only with long effort and utmost difficulty. The dream had already faded, only a few stray scraps remaining, like phantoms blown on the night breeze, but she knew what she had done. As the fear subsided, she felt an almost physical hollowness, a sense of loss, such as she had never known before. By now Daniel was quite likely mad or dead or both. She had destroyed him.

I did it, Timothy, she thought. *I did it, damn you. I sacri-*

ficed the man I loved, the only man I've loved in such a long time, perhaps the only man I'll ever truly love.

She felt fresh tears coming from her eyes. She had forgotten what tears of sorrow felt like. Their sting was sharp and deep, a kind of burning, like acid on the soul.

Good-bye, Daniel. I did love you. Believe me, my darling, I loved you.

But she must not think such things. She must try to veil her mind. Timothy would read her thoughts, given half a chance, and she didn't want him to have the satisfaction of knowing what she was suffering. She could see the twisted smile on that merciless face, the contempt in those heavy-lidded, colorless eyes.

For a time she lay perfectly still, breathing deeply and staring blindly into the starless city sky, trying to compose herself. Her small companion, the bat, had left her, and she felt as alone as she had ever been in her life.

She sighed and straightened herself on the chaise. She flexed the fingers of the hand that dangled to the floor. The hand felt sticky.

She lifted the hand and stared at it. In the little light that came from the apartment, it looked soiled.

It looked . . . bloody. What in the world . . . ?

She turned the hand, looking for some injury, but could find none. Then, where had the blood come from?

Sitting up, she pulled open her robe and looked at her body. Suddenly she felt the sting of abrasions, and her heart started racing again as she saw that her breasts, belly, and thighs were smeared with blood. Somehow, while she was dreaming, she must have injured herself. She thought of scars—*Oh, God, no!*—and, in panic, looked for wounds on those breasts, whose perfection she so much treasured. She found them—angry red streaks on her right breast, as if she had been clawed.

With a cry of rage, she rose from the chaise and ran back into the apartment. In the bathroom, she turned on the lights and threw off her robe. Turning before the mirror, she inspected every inch of her body closely. It was badly bruised and scratched, but she saw with relief that the injuries were superficial. Properly tended, they would soon heal, with little likelihood of leaving scars.

But what had happened?

A fragment of her dream returned to her . . . Daniel, his face ugly with terror, trying to fight his way out of her embrace, his nails raking her breast, her sides, her back. . . .

She had sometimes traveled out-of-body. Such travel was most easily and safely accomplished in a lightly sleeping dream-state, and it might well have occurred in this instance. But when you traveled out-of-body, you could not bring blood or anything else back with you. Could you?

Not unless you materialized.

In which case, like a shape-changer, you might bring your wounds back with you.

Had she done that?

Had she at last succeeded in something that she had attempted so often?

Surely that was the only answer! She now dimly recalled her struggle to *de*materialize, to escape Daniel's clawing hands, to return to her own body. And she had succeeded in that too!

If Timothy only knew. Thanks to the god of this world, she was growing so much stronger, so powerful, and one of these days . . . *Oh, Timothy, I'm going to give you such a surprise!*

All fatigue gone, she stepped into the shower stall and quickly washed the blood away. There wasn't nearly as much as, in her panic, she had at first thought. She dried herself and dressed her scratches with a soothing antibiotic lotion and went into her bedroom. She turned on one lamp and slipped into a nightgown. Then she turned to her dressing-table mirror for one last reassuring look.

At first she could hardly believe what she was seeing. It had to be a trick of the soft, flattering light, because for an instant she didn't recognize herself. She sat down on the bench and turned on her makeup light to look more closely. The wide forehead, the high cheekbones, the clear violet eyes, particularly the eyes . . .

There wasn't the slightest sign of a wrinkle, not the merest line or crease, anywhere around them.

There wasn't a wrinkle anywhere on her face or her

throat. Her complexion was utterly smooth, clear, perfect—it was the complexion of a beautiful child. Except for the maturity of her bone structure, she might have been sixteen.

She looked still closer into the mirror and touched her face in awe. A delighted laugh broke from her throat. Perfect! She sat back again, to look down at her body. It, too, was perfect, never mind the scratches, and a wave of sweet voluptuousness swept up through her. Oh, God, if Daniel could see her now, what a prize she was! *"You will be suitably rewarded,"* Timothy had said, but he could have had no idea! She had been rejuvenated before, many times, but never like this!

She was young again, forever young, and that was the only thing that mattered. As for losing Daniel . . .

Oh, Daniel, I did love you. I loved you as I have loved no other man, I loved you as I did not know it was possible to love. But I had to sacrifice you . . .

Perhaps at that moment the last wavering flame of Freya Kellgren's soul died.

. . . and praise the god of this world, it was worth the price!

Daniel awakened before dawn feeling sick, feverish, exhausted. The dream stayed with him in all its nastiness, but its details, thank God, were vague. He didn't want to remember. It had been an erotic dream about Freya, but one that had gone bad. He couldn't make love to Freya even in his dreams, it seemed. Instead, he'd had a god-awful nightmare, no doubt brought on by his fever. A touch of flu. He felt sticky with sweat. He would take a handful of aspirin, and wash, and go back to bed again.

He struggled out of bed and staggered through the dark into the bathroom. He flipped the switch, then closed his eyes against the light. His thighs throbbed so badly that they barely supported him—he must have had cramps in the night—and his neck felt broken. Every muscle ached. His bladder was killing him, and sitting down blindly, he relieved himself.

His thighs felt slick against the toilet seat. Slowly he opened his eyes and looked down.

The hair on his chest was matted with blood. There was blood on his thighs and on the toilet seat.

"No," he said feebly. "No."

A fresh rivulet of blood, red on red, trickled down over his chest.

He began to make a keening sound then. He couldn't hold it back. He knew only that something awful had happened to him in the night, something awful that was costing him pain and blood, and he was afraid to find out what it was. If he did find out, he might have to face an even greater horror. It might be the death of him.

Slowly, every muscle throbbing, he forced himself to stand up. Leaning against the rim of the porcelain washbasin, he looked into the mirror. He saw the large, vivid purple bruise on the side of his neck. He saw the blood. He saw the ragged tooth marks.

Then he remembered.

The dream became real, its bloody stigmata undeniable, and there was no escaping its memory, no merciful fall into darkness. It was as if that horrible *thing* had him still, it was real and it was *here*, it was clutching him, defiling him, tearing him apart. He could feel the obscene warmth of its belly against his; he could feel its ripping teeth and claws and its powerful sexual grasp as vividly as if he were still its captive. With a shriek, he clutched at his genitals, trying to protect them, but it would not let him go. Screaming, spreading blood, he crashed a shoulder through the glass shower stall, then fell to the floor, trying to fight the creature off, but he couldn't escape it, he couldn't, he was forever captive to its vile embrace. . . .

He was still screaming when the super pounded on the door and let the police and the paramedics in. He fought them as they strapped him to the stretcher. He knew they were trying to help him, but their hands became part of that loathsome bat-creature that still seemed to cling to his naked body. His heart was pounding wildly, and he could hear himself crying: "Please, please, please . . . !"

In the ambulance his heart began to fibrillate. Lidocaine failed to stabilize him. The figures bending over him were less real than the creature that still held him captive, feeding on him and befouling his body.

Suddenly his chest was filled with pain, a swelling, searing, bright blinding pain, and he knew he was about to experience the only release that he could hope for. The briefest prayer, not for himself but for his daughter, passed his lips. In the next instant, at the height of his agony, his chest seemed to explode, blowing him far out into some distant star-shattered darkness.

He was dead before the ambulance reached the hospital.

CHAPTER 8

ST. CLAIRE, 1983

The Werewolves of St. Claire.

Exactly when she had decided that she was one of them, that she *wanted* to be one of them, Nicole could not have said. Certainly it was not back in second grade, when Bobby Parnell, in a quarrel over a teeter-totter at recess, had turned on her: "You-you-you, you're just no good! My mama says you're *sick!* She says your whole family has bad blood and it makes you crazy in the head! She says to stay away from you, 'cause you're a *biter!*"

That was true, or at least it had been. After she had killed her pet mouse, Snowflake, there had been several incidents of biting. But only after she had been physically abused, only when instinct told her that biting was her last and only defense, had she bitten, and she was hardly unique in that. Some children bit.

But she was a St. Claire, and people with long memories and a taste for local history knew about the St. Claires. When little children brought home the information that Nicole St. Claire bit, mothers were understandably worried.

Nicole, however, soon learned that *under no circumstances* must she bite. No matter what the provocation. No, rather than bite, she must suffer whatever pain, mental or physical, was visited upon her, and at the first opportunity she should run to her teacher or her grandmother.

Nickie is a crybaby, Nickie is a crybaby, nyah, nyah, nyah, nyah. Run and tell Teacher, crybaby. Run and tell, tattletale. Nickie is a crybaby, nyah, nyah, nyah, nyah . . . !

Run, Nickie, run . . .

But not to Teacher, not to Grandma. Just tear your clothes off and run. And when you become ravenous, your stomach a great aching void like the pain in your heart, look for solace in raw red meat and blood.

Psychotherapy, tranquilizers, and, as her grandmother observed, Holy Unction did seem to help, but after her father's death the symptoms had resurged with a vengeance. Added to them had been the dreams, the terrible dreams . . . dreams of something huge, bat-winged, strange and monstrous, something that had slain her daddy in the night and threatened to slay her. . . .

Then on an autumn day in her sixth-grade class Nicole experienced a kind of quiet revelation.

Somehow the discussion had come around to the subject of wolves, and Miss Brubaker, the teacher, was explaining how the wolf's place in the ecological system had long been misunderstood. It was true that wolves were a danger to domestic livestock such as sheep and cattle, she said, but far from destroying the herds of deer and the caribou, as was once thought, they played an important role in culling out the weaker specimens, thus keeping the herds down so that the stronger animals had grazing room and didn't starve to death.

Not very interested, Nicole was slumped back behind her desk and hardly listening. But Bobby Parnell, who sat behind her and who now (she had been told) considered her "real cute," leaned forward and whispered to her: "Wouldn't it be neat if a guy like your grandpa really could turn into a wolf and hunt deer and stuff? Awesome!"

Nicole wasn't sure it would be neat at all. She, after all, was a medically certified lycanthrope, and she certainly didn't find it any fun.

But then, she didn't actually turn into a wolf, did she?

What if she could?

What would it be like?

She sat up straight behind her desk and began paying attention to Miss Brubaker.

The first chance she got, on a Saturday afternoon, she went to the public library and looked for books on wolves in the children's section. She found several, and she spent the next few hours in the theater of her mind, oblivious of the world around her.

. . . she watched in fascination, as the dominant male wolf, the leader of the pack, held his tail proudly high, while all his followers lowered their tails and heads in submission. She listened when, at dusk, one of the pack raised its voice in a long howl that swept through the darkening forest, and the rest of the pack joined in, a chorus of wolflike celebration. She watched as the pack then moved out single file along the twilight trail, noses to the wind for the scent of game. She saw the sudden rush through the dark when the prey was found, a deer crashing through the underbrush—she was there for the kill and the gorging. . . .

It was a harsh, brutal life, inhuman in every sense, but somehow it called out to Nicole. Something in her found it strangely beautiful.

Late in the afternoon, she wandered into the reference room, and there in an encyclopedia article she discovered the dire wolf.

The dire wolf, it seemed, roamed western North America during the Pleistocene Epoch, the period of the last Ice Age and the appearance of early man. It was the largest wolf ever known.

The largest? What did that mean? Nicole considered. . . .

If what she had read that afternoon was correct, the average modern male wolf had a body length of about four feet and weighed a hundred pounds. A truly large specimen might measure five feet and weigh 175 pounds or more.

If the average dire wolf had a body length of six feet, how large might a truly *big* one be and what might it weigh? Two hundred fifty pounds, perhaps? Three hundred?

If a modern wolf had canine teeth two inches long, how

long might the canines of a dire wolf be? Three inches? Four? Truly, teeth like sabers!

If a modern wolf could clear a sixteen-foot crevasse in a single bound, how far might the mighty dire wolf leap?

Could a dire wolf travel as long and fast as a modern wolf—reaching forty-five miles an hour in a sprint?

Imagine a saber-toothed dire wolf coming at you at forty-five miles an hour and covering the last twenty feet in one great leap.

Awesome!

The dire wolf, Nicole reminded herself, was extinct.

But what if it wasn't, not really?

What if a single dire wolf, a magnificent female, came wandering down out of the frozen forests of the Yukon? *She* wouldn't have to be afraid of anything bat-winged and monstrous that came in the night. She would never have let it kill her daddy.

Nicole looked up the word *dire* in a dictionary: ". . . having dreadful consequences . . . causing great fear or suffering . . . calamitous; disastrous; awful . . ."

Oh, yes!

The dire wolf was for her! If ever she were to be reincarnated as an animal, she wanted to be a dire wolf! And oh, what a dreadful, disastrous, calamitous wolf she would be!

"Nicole . . . Nicole, honey . . ."

Reluctantly, Nicole returned to the everyday world. The last rosy light of evening slanted across the table where she sat. The library was closing, it seemed, and her grandmother had come to take her home.

That evening, after supper, she made one of her rare visits to the attic. Her grandmother was playing bridge with some friends, so she didn't think she would be missed. She had explored the attic from time to time when she was little, and she seemed to remember . . .

She found it. A corrugated cardboard box in the shadows at some distance from the sixty-watt bulb that hung from the ceiling. It contained, among other items of apparel, a number of moldering old furs, goodness only knew why they hadn't been thrown out or what kind they were—fox, beaver, rabbit, perhaps.

Shivering, because the attic was quite cold, she began taking off her clothes. Every last stitch, as her grandmother would have said.

She remembered reading in one of her daddy's books that some peoples, in order to transform themselves into animals, wrapped themselves in girdles of fur and rubbed magic salves into their skins. She didn't have any magic salve and she doubted that any of the furs had come from a wolf, but she would just have to make do with what was at hand. She tied a couple of furs together and wrapped them around her waist. She draped a couple more over her shoulders, and she tied another around each knee. Then she crouched down on the cold dusty boards and closed her eyes.

Please, God, make me a wolf.

Make me a dire *wolf. Just for tonight.*

Please, Lord, please, please, please!

She giggled. This was silly. What if she turned into a weasel or a raccoon? All right, she'd settle for a raccoon, but what she really wanted to be was a wolf. A *dire* wolf.

Please, God. Please, please, blessed Jesus, blessed Michael-archangel, blessed MaryandJoseph, all you guys. Just for tonight?

She put all her longing into her prayer, actually shaking with her determination—*Pleeease!*—to wring an *Oh, all right!* out of heaven, but to no avail. She even promised to go to late service tomorrow and pay attention during the sermon.

Please, please, please, please. . . .

No use.

Well, you couldn't blame a kid for trying. She hadn't really expected anything, of course; it had just been one of those crazy private things you do and never tell anyone about, not even your best friend. She got dressed again and went back downstairs.

But maybe heaven was listening.

That night she dreamed.

She awakened only once that night, and then just barely. Her window was open, she slept with it open even on crisp nights, and as she opened her eyes, the moon, a hunter's moon, autumn-orange and oh-so-large, seemed to be watching her. She smiled. She always enjoyed the sensation of waking up at night and then sinking back into sleep. She closed her eyes again . . .

. . . and found herself out in the woods, looking up at the moon through the stark-black branches of the trees.

She raised her face still farther and took a couple of small, tentative breaths, sniffs. A hundred odors came to her nostrils, smells that had never before been so sharp and distinct. Wet, decaying leaves. Crushed pine needles. Fresh flowing water, a mountain stream. The quite different scent of the lake. Animals, living and dead—squirrels, chipmunks, birds, a possum, a mole; somewhere, faintly, a deer . . . their spoor. As she looked about, looked into the shadows so sharply etched by the moonlight, a great happiness swelled within her: this was the place she was meant to be. . . .

Never before in her life had she felt more alert and aware and filled with pure unreflective animal joy. Even the slight pang of hunger that twinged in her belly was a pleasure so exquisite she could have sobbed. Her gratitude for this night and this world and her very being was so inarticulately endless that she did the only thing she could do. She again raised her face to the moon, as to the face of God, and she simply howled.

Howled and howled again, hearing in the mountains the echoes of her howls, as if an entire pack was howling in concert, an anthem to the beloved god of all wolves, all nature, all creation.

When she awakened before dawn, rested and happy, the dream all but vanished. That didn't matter. A few glimpses remained, she retained a sense of it, and she knew she had dreamed of being a wolf. A dire wolf, perhaps. A St. Claire werewolf.

She had the dream again a few weeks later, before Christmas. It was at the time of the full moon, she noted. But at the next full moon, to her disappointment, nothing happened. There were no guarantees, it seemed; she couldn't just take the dreams for granted. So she experimented. Before going to sleep, she thought about being a wolf, and on her third or fourth attempt, the dream returned, as vivid as ever. Apparently she did have some control over it.

Thus began her secret life, her dream life. She didn't return to it every night; even if she could have, that didn't seem necessary. But about once a month, the time of the full moon being most propitious, she found herself out under the night sky, running, hunting. . . .

She told no one about her dreams, not even her grandmother, because of the possible consequences. What if the dreams worried her grandmother? What if her grandmother started sending her to the doctors again? Worst of all, what if telling about the dreams made them stop, as sometimes happened? The dreams were a treasure that Nicole was not prepared to risk.

At that age, Nicole was not much given to introspective analysis. She didn't question her dreams, but merely enjoyed them without even thinking about them very often. They soon came to seem quite natural: other people had dreams—these were hers. But one thing did occur to her as rather surprising. Though generally sheltered from the knowledge, she knew quite well that her grandfather James had suffered from lycanthropy and that her father had worried because she displayed the same symptoms. But since she had, as it were, fallen in love with wolves and begun dreaming about them, the symptoms had completely disappeared.

Others remarked on a new confidence in her. She seemed to cope with the small problems of everyday life with a minimum of anxiety, and at school and at play she engaged smoothly and happily with her companions as never before. Miss Brubaker dubbed her "Miss Serenity," and she overheard "Aunt" Martha Cummings, one of her grandmother's oldest and dearest friends, say, "I swear, Julia, that child reminds me more and more of you at that age." Nicole thought that was about the nicest thing Aunt Martha could have said.

And so, her nightmares vanquished, she continued to dream those dreams that at last assuaged her long grief over her father's death and brought her happiness and new strength. They continued at irregular moonlit intervals all that next year and beyond, perhaps a dozen dreams or more, while her breasts began to swell and her nipples darken until she was on the very verge of menarche.

On that February evening, the snow lay deep and crusted over, but the sky was clear and the moon had never been brighter. Her breath came out in great silvery puffs, but the air was still and her winter coat was thick, so that she was unconscious of the cold. Only that thin edge of human consciousness that she maintained, ready to take control if need be, was aware of that.

She roamed and hunted through the night, roamed and hunted up over rock outcroppings and down into little stream-cut valleys, searching for whatever food she might find. Once an owl, overly brave or desperate, looped down to snatch a mouse almost from under her nose. She leaped and tried to snatch the owl from the air in turn, but missed. A part of her growled in frustration, but another part, that human edge, laughed with delight. This was, after all, the game that restored her divided soul. This was the time, she dimly understood, when she became healed and whole again.

Soon after losing the mouse and the owl, she got a rabbit. It froze for a moment at her approach, then went bounding in long, swift leaps across the moonlit clearing, like a flat pebble skipping over water; then she was on it, killing it with a single snap of her jaws. It was plump for that time of the year, and large, but within seconds she had devoured most of it. The remains, she carried off into some brush, where she burrowed down into the snow and old dead leaves, lying comfortably hidden, the carcass between her paws. She yawned . . . lowered her head . . . closed her eyes. . . .

She was cold. Cold and wet. Somehow her bed had got cold and wet, wet all over. How had her bed got so cold and wet? And what had happened to her pajamas?

She stirred, moved her arms and legs. She was lying facedown, something she rarely did, and her bed felt all wrong. So cold and wet, she wanted to cry.

And the smell was bad, so putrid it made her sick. She opened her eyes and slowly lifted her head. It was dark, just a little light coming through branches. . . .

Something was wrong, altogether wrong. She drew her elbows under her to lift herself and look around.

Her first reaction was not fear but astonishment. She was not at home in bed. She was somewhere altogether different, somewhere she had no business being, and she had no idea of how she had got here. She was somewhere outside, lying . . .

It got clearer now.

. . . *lying naked and half-frozen in the snow and mud and old dead leaves.*

. . . lying here with something damp and furry in her hands.

She looked at it at first uncomprehendingly, a mangled piece of fur, a bloody carcass with its guts torn out, stiffening in the cold. Then she remembered her dream, just a fragment of it—the snap of jaws on a fleeing rabbit, the fierce snarl, the exultant ripping away of the tender flesh . . .

With a scream, she rose up and flung the carcass away. She climbed to her feet, tore her way through the brush, and staggered into a clearing. *No, no, no, it had not happened!* Her mind was a bedlam of denial, but when she looked down at herself, there was blood on her hands and her body, and she realized that she had the taste of blood in her mouth.

She had eaten that thing. Like a crazy girl, like the mad creature she was, she had eaten it!

She had gorged on it, mindlessly, madly, like an animal.

She leaned forward, and with all the projectile force her stomach could muster, she vomited—shot out a mangled mass of rabbit flesh and guts and bones and blood. Retched again and threw up more. Retched again and again until she was on her knees and no more would come, and retched yet again.

For a minute or two she merely cried.

Then she realized that she herself was bleeding, from her vagina.

Somehow that restored some small spark of sanity, the drive for survival. She was naked and bloody and half-frozen in a dark wood, she was bleeding and she had to get help. She struggled back to her feet and staggered off, crying out to her dead father, *Oh, Daddy, help me!*, to the mother she barely remembered, to the grandmother who was her only real hope.

She knew the woods behind the house well, but not by night, and she seemed to find her way back by blind instinct. She walked, staggered, tried to run on frozen feet for what might have been only a few hundred feet but seemed like miles. Then she caught a glimpse of light ahead of her, and soon after that the house, windows ablaze.

She saw her own footprints leading away from the house, and even as she left the woods and stumbled into her backyard, her grandmother came running toward her, carrying a heavy coat and woolen slippers. "Oh, Nicole," her grandmother cried out, "Nickie darling, thank God, thank God!"

She was home and safe.

"We'll get you into the bathtub," her grandmother said, hustling her into the bathroom, "a nice warm tub."

"But, Grandma, I can't," Nicole said, wiping away tears that wouldn't stop. "I'm bleeding, I'm bleeding *down there!*" Never had she been more grateful for her grandmother's arms and her love.

"Now, don't you worry about that, we've been expecting that, haven't we? Grandma knows what to do. First, into the tub . . ."

In the tub, warmth seeped painfully back into Nicole's hands and feet, but gradually the shivering stopped and the tears slowed, and she began to relax and feel better. While she sponged Nicole, her grandmother explained that she had awakened abruptly with a feeling that her little girl might need her. Finding Nicole's bed empty and her pajamas on the floor, she had gone through the house, turning on lights and calling Nicole's name.

"Then I looked out back and saw your footprints in the snow, and I knew that my little girl—my *big* girl now!—was in danger of catching a very bad cold. . . ."

Her grandmother had called their doctor, Dr. George London, for advice, and he, a dear old friend, had insisted on coming out. By the time he arrived, Nicole was just climbing back into bed. A big, heavily mustached, and dewlapped old man, Dr. London made Nicole think of a friendly St. Bernard. He checked to see that there was no serious frostbite or other injuries and gave her a shot that was supposed to keep her "healthy and rested, young lady." Her grandmother tucked her in and turned out the light, and Nicole immediately began to sink into dreamless sleep.

She had been sleepwalking, that was all. Dreaming and sleepwalking, and the rabbit meant nothing. It might already have been dead when she found it, and as for the vomiting . . . she didn't really know *what* she had thrown up. She had been sleepwalking, and her first menstruation, perhaps, had awakened her. And as sometimes happened with sleepwalkers, she had been terrified at finding herself in a strange place and situation.

Her grandmother had found her sleepwalking a couple of times before and had gently coaxed her back into her bed before she awakened. But never before had she left the house. Or if she had, there was absolutely no evidence of the fact. In any case, *she must never do it again.*

Such behavior was madness. And highly dangerous.

All right, her love affair with wolves was over. Never again would she allow herself to experience those dreams she had so much enjoyed—she would suppress them ruthlessly. Never again would she allow herself to think she was some kind of daughter of wolves, a wolf girl.

And she never did . . . except sometimes late at night when she was alone, gazing at the moon . . . and for a little while she remembered. . . .

CHAPTER 9

ST. CLAIRE, 1986

That evening in late August started out as one of the nicest Saturday evenings ever, a landmark evening for Nicole, an evening of expanded privilege, however slight, that told her she was growing up. A wonderful evening, and all thanks to Duffy.

He came wandering up the back steps and through the kitchen door at a little before six, while the lowering sun was still brilliant and the translucent blue sky promised stars. Her grandmother, sitting at the table with yesterday's newspaper spread out before her, was just starting to shuck some corn for supper. "Have you eaten yet, Duffy?" she asked. "There's plenty for all of us if you'd like to stay."

"Sure, Aunt Julia," Duffy said, dropping into a chair, "love it. Gotta eat and run, though. Some of the guys are coming around for me pretty soon, Brad and Gorgeous Gussie, maybe Derek and Joanne. We'll probably head for the mall."

Then, in all apparent innocence, Duffy broke one of the

unspoken rules. He looked at Nicole and said, "I wondered if you might like to come along. Catch a flick."

For a moment, Nicole could only stare at Duffy. His suggesting that they "catch a flick" with two other couples, *older* couples, on a Saturday evening was a very different thing from his volunteering to baby-sit her for a couple of hours.

Evidently her grandmother felt the same way. "Duffy," she said gently, "Nicole is only thirteen—"

"Almost fourteen," Nicole snapped, regaining her wits.

"—she's not old enough to date. And I'm sure you'd rather be out with someone more your own age."

"Aw, it's not a *date*, Aunt Julia," Duffy said, making the word *date* sound slightly ridiculous. "I don't need a *date*—it's called 'hanging out.' But we always sort of pair off, and it so happens that my woman-of-choice is out of town, visiting relatives, and I want someone of my own to hang out with. I'll be glad to pop for a ticket if Nicole's short—"

"I can pay my own way," Nicole said quickly.

"What movie do you plan to see?" her grandmother asked.

Duffy shrugged. "Whatever we can get into. *A Nightmare on Elm Street 2*, maybe, *Freddy's Revenge*."

Her grandmother frowned. "That doesn't sound very G or PG."

"Oh, Grandma!" Nicole protested.

"Aunt Julia," Duffy explained patiently, "it's just a teen slasher movie. That means it's mostly for laughs. The girls get to scream and hang on to the guys and go, 'Eeow, how gross!' It's all in fun, and everybody knows it."

"Well . . ." Her grandmother raised a dubious eyebrow. "I don't think they'd let Nicole in anyway, would they?"

"With me, they would." Duffy took an ear of corn from her grandmother's hands and began shucking it. "Aunt Julia, believe me. I would never knowingly take Nicole to see something really stomach-turning vicious, any more than I'd take my kid sister, if I had one, or my mother or you."

Her grandmother nodded. "I'm sure you wouldn't. But you can't always tell about a picture in advance. And since Nicole has to be in by eleven—"

"Oh, Grandma," Nicole wailed. "It's *Saturday night!*

Can't I stay out till twelve? I'm *almost fourteen,* if I was fourteen I bet you'd let me stay out till twelve!"

"But you're not fourteen, and I don't like to set a precedent."

"I'll tell you what, Aunt Julia," Duffy said. "We might not even be able to get into a movie until nine-thirty. But I will promise to have Nicole home by midnight. If the movie runs too late for that, or if something happens after the movie to hold us up, I promise to call you." He stuck his right hand in a pants pocket and jingled coins. "I always have change for phone calls, my folks insist on it. And I *always* call when I'm supposed to, 'cause I know if I don't there'll be hell to pay, ask my mom."

"Well . . ." Nicole held her breath while her grandmother considered. "You'll keep your eye on Nicole every minute?"

"I promise. I won't let her out of my sight."

Her grandmother shifted her gaze to Nicole. "This one time only, Nicole. And *only* because it's with Duffy."

Nicole gave a little squeal of pleasure, she couldn't help it, and ran around the table to give her grandmother a hug.

After supper, Nicole and Duffy strolled over to his house, and soon thereafter, Brad Holland showed up in his battered Toyota Corolla, along with "Gorgeous Gussie" Lindquist. Brad looked a little surprised when he realized that Nicole was to be a part of the outing, but he recovered quickly and made no "baby-sitter" remarks, as he would have done a year or two earlier.

The Evil Elf was something of a puzzle to Nicole. A slender, darkly handsome boy, at eighteen he was a few months older than most of his friends, and their self-appointed leader. He was very intuitive, one of those people who, when you think about them behind their backs, look around at you and say, "Yes? Did you say something?"

Nicole also sensed in him a very strong will and a hunger for power. He tended to order other people about and, oddly, they seldom rebelled. Her father had observed him for about five minutes one day at the Johnsons and had remarked, "My God, that kid's got a Napoleon complex! A real Little Caesar."

How did he get away with it? Though she couldn't articulate the answer clearly, Nicole felt that she knew. One day she and some friends had come across Brad and his gang at the town beach. Brad as usual was ordering everybody about, sending them off on this errand and that, until finally he was sitting alone on his blanket. Nicole, observing him from some distance, suddenly had the feeling that Brad was not quite as self-centered as he appeared to be, that he really cared for his gang, and that within the little dictator was a very vulnerable and loving and lonely little boy that Brad tried desperately to deny.

As she pondered this, Brad looked slowly around at her. He smiled the saddest, sweetest smile. "Hey," he said, as if he had read her thoughts, "if you're gonna be a leader, you *gotta* be lonely. It's lonely at the top."

Then, still smiling, he looked away. And for a little while, Nicole liked the Evil Elf in spite of himself.

Perhaps Gorgeous Gussie saw the same thing in Brad that Nicole had that day at the beach, but Nicole didn't think that explained why Gussie put up with him.

Jessie Gustava Lindquist. Brad had hung the "Gorgeous Gussie" nickname on her, and it had stuck. So blond that her hair was almost white, with eyes of deepest blue, she was as tall as Brad and almost as strong, with a beautifully sculpted dancer's body. A largely self-taught singer and dancer, she had spent thousands of hours studying pop singers from Doris Day to Streisand and watching old Cyd Charisse and Anne Miller films—she told Nicole that she was *always* studying when she listened to music and watched dancers, *always* looking for anything she could steal, emulate, incorporate. She was always trying to outdo the best. And whether it was a high school musical or some charity entertainment, when Gorgeous Gussie stepped out on a stage, every step and gesture and hip-swivel was precise as clockwork; and when she started belting out "Everything's Coming Up Roses!" in that full, throaty voice, you knew that Amateur Hour was over and the talent had arrived. This was a pro.

The Elf drove them into town to pick up Joanne Smith and Derek Anderson at Joanne's house. Nicole had gathered that Joanne and Derek were immensely popular in high school, the kind of kids that are invariably elected to office in anything they join. Joanne was a lovely dark-haired, round-faced, pink-cheeked, gray-eyed girl with a voluptuous figure and a very soft, shy voice. She was also very bright, and what she saw in Derek was a puzzle to Nicole. All right, Derek was six feet three and very cute and *the* St. Claire basketball star, and even his smarmy "Aw, shucks, ma'am, I can't help it 'cause I'm so adorable" manner was kind of amusing. But even so . . . Nicole had a sense of mismatch, as if Joanne were stuck with Derek simply because they were both so popular. They were *expected* to be together. But maybe that wasn't true at all. The mysteries of the heart were such a . . . well, such a *mystery* to Nicole.

From Joanne's house, Brad drove them to the St. Claire Mall, and Nicole, seated on Duffy's lap in the backseat, her right arm around his shoulders, had never before felt so happily included in the group. She might be the youngest member, but she felt *all* of fourteen, a very *mature* fourteen, a real high school kid hanging out with other high school kids.

As was to be expected on a Saturday evening, the mall parking lot was crowded, but Brad found a space on the outer perimeter on the same side as the six-screen theater. They strolled at leisure toward the mall, their shadows stretching out behind them in the last half hour of sunlight. There seemed to be no point in trying to beat the crowd that was swarming into the building ahead of them. "This is not good, gang," Brad said. "Looks like whatever we decide on, we're going to stand in line half an hour at least."

It was worse than that. The theater side of the wide corridor was jam-packed with crowded lines, and a hundred other people stood around in little groups, looking indecisive. Two films had recently started, and it looked to Nicole as if there were more than enough people in the lobby and the waiting lines to fill the remaining four screening rooms. Even as she watched, two more film showings were sold out; some of those who had been waiting in line drifted away in disappointment and others closed ranks.

"What about it, troops," Brad asked, "do we really need this?"

"Maybe we could come back later," Nicole suggested. "Maybe the last showings won't be so crowded."

"Worse," Brad said. "Late Saturday is the worst."

"Look," Duffy said, "why don't we just kick around a little while, see how things look, then maybe pick up a video or two?"

Derek shook his head morosely. "On Saturday night everything good is already rented."

"Not good," Duffy said, "just new. Have you ever seen *Riot in Cell Block 11*? Or how about *Rear Window* or *Vertigo*? They're better than anything that's playing."

"I'm with Duffy," Gussie said. "I've seen *Rear Window*, but I'd watch it again, anytime."

"All right," Brad said decisively. "The game plan is, we look around for a while. In about an hour we meet at Videorama and reassess the situation. Maybe rent something and take it to my place. Anybody got any better ideas?"

Nobody did. But Nicole hardly heard their answers. Something was happening to her stomach. It was turning cold and it had a greasy feeling, as if it were preparing to give up something dead and rotten and poisonous. *Somebody out there hates me!* she thought irrationally, and the feeling spread. It was not only within her but spreading over her flesh like something filthy. It was like a great dirty tongue licking her, slithering over her under her clothes, and, sobbing, she drew her thighs together and clutched at her belly. She wanted to be at home in her shower. She wanted to be at home and clean and in bed.

"Nicole," Duffy said, his hands on her shoulders, "what is it?"

"I don't know," she answered in a tight voice, and her stomach lurched. "I think I'm going to be sick."

"Aw, jeez," Brad said in mild disgust.

"No, Brad," Gussie said, and her voice sounded like Nicole's. "Something is wrong!"

Brad stared at Gussie. He looked back and forth between Gussie and Nicole.

"Listen, guys," Joanne said nervously, "I feel it too. Let's all just sort of stay together for a while."

Derek said, "Shee-it. This is turning into some evening."

Brad looked around through the constantly shifting crowd for a moment, while in the video arcade across from the theater games banged, clanged, and buzzed. He raised a beckoning finger and softly said, "All right, come out, come out, whoever you are."

Of course, no one even appeared to notice Brad, and after another moment, he shrugged and turned back to Nicole.

To her surprise, her stomach was already settling down, and the nausea passed as quickly as it had come. "I'm sorry," she said weakly. "I think I'm better now. I'm such a baby."

"Hey, you're no baby," Brad said. "Or if you are, you're *our* baby."

It was one of those moments when she actually liked Brad. She said, "It was probably just something I ate."

Brad glanced around again. "I don't think so. I think you've got good instincts, kid. I think you just happened to be wide open, and you and Gussie and Joanne picked up on something we guys missed. There are some real crazies out there, and we all know what can happen to little girls at shopping malls late at night. Even in little old dull-as-dust St. Claire."

"For God's sake, stop frightening her," Duffy said.

"*I'm* not frightening her. She's *been* frightened, and I say, good for her. Trust your instincts, Nickie, and don't apologize for them. And remember, you're among friends." He turned toward the video arcade. "Hey, who's for some games?"

Saturday night, cruising the mall. Weaving through the crowd, slow and easy, taking his time, scouting out the good stuff and looking it over. Letting the stuff look at him, see what they were getting. If they were lucky. Gonna give myself a treat tonight, man, after a long hard week in the sun. No hurry, though. Action starts after the sun goes down. Maybe just a quick trip out to the parking lot, maybe a lot more. Look me over, baby, and if you beg, maybe I'll show you what I've got for you. Nice hot hoagie, full of cream cheese. Let you kneel down and taste it.

Tonight was going to be his night of nights. Tonight he was going to get very, very lucky. He had known it when he looked in the bathroom mirror to comb his hair. He was looking good. Curly brown hair, leafed with bronze from the sun, haircut only a week old. Freshly shaved and showered, a touch of Brut here and there, clean tan knit shirt, the sleeves rolled up on his biceps, pack of Camels in the left sleeve. He had taken a deep breath, filling out the knit shirt until the fabric strained. Great pecs, great shoulders, big tattooed forearms. His cheeks were sunburned almost as brown as his eyes, and the dimple in his square chin didn't hurt any either. So God in his Infinite Wisdom had made him good-looking, so what?

"So stop admiring yourself, Buster," his bunky, Tony Anselmo, had said. "I hate to see a grown man giving himself blow jobs."

He had laughed, because Tony was no one to mess with, but he was going to put it up Mr. A's fuckin' A one of these days. The six inches of finely honed steel he carried in his pocket, take Mr. A's fuckin' prostate out. Then maybe he'd just cut off what Mr. A didn't need and couldn't use anymore.

But screw Tony. Tony had headed off for a bar to drink beer with that worn-out whore he'd probably end up marrying. Not this guy. This guy had checked out his fuck-pad van, made sure all was in readiness, and headed for the mall.

The St. Claire Mall.

Where the *good* stuff was.

The *young* stuff.

The young married and not-so-married and no-longer-married.

The college girls, some from the local campus, some home for the summer.

High school girls.

Hell, *junior* high school girls, seventh-graders. Some of those hot-pants little bitches, the way they threw it in your face, they were the very worst, everybody knew that. They just *asked* for it!

Like the one he saw when he was getting out of his van. Christ, didn't she think she was something. Even at a distance, he could tell.

There were three of them, actually, three real bitch-type ball-breakers and the three high school assholes who were with them. Tall blond bitch, shorter one with more curves, and this skinny little twat, maybe eighth or ninth grade, got her nose up in the air like she's the goddamn crown princess of St. Claire. He knew their kind. Prick-teasers, all of 'em, just begging for it until all of a sudden they were too goddamn good for you. Start crying, start screaming bloody murder, like they didn't bring it on themselves. He'd beat the shit out of more than one of 'em, teach the cunt a fuckin' lesson. . . .

But to hell with it. Relax. He wasn't here to beat the shit out of anybody. Tonight was his night, and he was going to have a hell of a good time. He felt it all through his body, from his pecs to his scrote—tonight he was going to *connect*!

The truth was, and he had to admit it, he hardly ever did connect at the mall, any mall. Most of the time, you see a good-looking babe in a shop, looking at blouses, and you give her a friendly nod and a "hi," and she looks at you like you're a piece of shit and takes off. And if you do get a live one and she goes out to the van with you, afterward she seems no different from a whore you picked up in a bar. Not even worth beating up on, 'cause then you better hit the road, son. More than once, he'd had to do that.

But the mall was still the place to spot the good stuff.

Fresh young pussy.

And there she was. . . .

A funny thing. You go to the mall and cruise around through the crowd, and most of 'em you never even notice. But you just happen to spot one particular piece of ass, or maybe two or three together, and they keep showing up in front of you again and again. *Teasing* you!

Like this evening he just happens to notice these three hot-shit bitches and their asshole buddies, but he puts them out of mind and goes into the mall through the east wing. Decides to check out the video games arcade, 'cause there's always young stuff there. And standing right near it, looking over the movie lines, are the bitches and their buddies again.

The tall blond ice princess, the curvy sexpot, and best of all, or worst, the skinny little fox. . . .

Oh, baby, if you knew what I'd like to give to you, give you everything you're asking for and maybe a couple of things you never dreamed of, make you pay for every time you ever shook your ass in a man's face, then turned up your nose and walked away, make you pay until you're screaming just to have it end, you filthy little unwashed cunt. . . .

The bitch was a good fifty feet away, but it was almost as if she had heard him. He would have sworn she looked him straight in the face, and then her head went down and she grabbed at her belly and sort of staggered, like she was about to be sick. . . .

Oh, I make you sick, do I, sweetheart—I'm not good enough for you, a common pissant guy like me. I ever get you alone, I'll make you sick! He'd make her pay for every insult and humiliation and rejection he had ever suffered from bitches like her. He'd . . .

—Come out, come out, whoever you are.

The words seemed to slide into his brain on the very waves of his hatred, as if his hatred had made him vulnerable to something that might take his brain apart, as if his brain might *dissolve* in the acid of his hatred. Through a kind of bloody haze, he saw the smallest of the assholes beckoning to him with a finger. Or at least it looked as if he was. The guy looked like . . . he could think of only one thing . . . the guy looked like some kind of goddamn evil elf.

To hell with it. He turned and walked away. He didn't need these people. He didn't give a shit what they thought of him. He wasn't going to let his evening be spoiled; he was going to look 'em all over and *connect.*

But he felt as if the evening had already been spoiled. Rage pounded in his head, hot and smoky black, like burning oil. He was gonna find some goddamn *action!*

There was absolutely no problem in killing an hour or two at the mall. Nicole thought there must be at least eighty or ninety businesses—a Sears and a JC Penney, dress shops and shoe shops and gourmet kitchenware shops, and kiosks that sold everything from sunglasses to custom T-shirts. In addition, there was an exhibition of antique automobiles that weekend that Derek just had to see—a beautiful old Rolls, a Model T, a Stutz Bearcat, and a dozen others, all restored to mint condition. A couple of times while they were looking at the cars, a shiver went up Nicole's back and she looked over her shoulder, but no one in the crowd seemed to be paying the slightest attention to her. And Duffy's hand was on her shoulder almost every minute—what could happen?

Around eight-thirty they drifted up to the north cross-corridor to look over the movie situation. No way. Brad had been right—if anything it was even worse than it had been earlier. But that was okay—they still had time to rent a video and pick up something to eat. Except for the north cross-corridor and the movie theater, the mall closed at nine o'clock, and people were already leaving in order to avoid the last-minute rush-and-jam out of the parking areas.

There was, as Duffy had predicted, plenty of good stuff left in the video store. Or at least stuff Duffy said was good. Nicole had never heard of most of the titles. On Duffy's recommendation, Brad got something called *Touch of Evil* and Joanne picked out *Bringing Up Baby,* and they went up to the counter to check them out. Duffy stuck with the films he had mentioned earlier, *Vertigo* and *Rear Window.*

"We'll never be able to watch four movies tonight," Nicole objected, "and I've got to be home by midnight."

"So what's the difference? Anything we don't watch tonight, we can watch tomorrow."

"Well, in that case . . ." Nicole snatched *Rear Window* from Duffy's hands. If she could pay for her own movie ticket, she said, she could certainly pay for one of the videos.

She loitered behind, the last customer in the store, while Duffy checked out *Vertigo.* As soon as he went through the exit gate and picked up his cassette from the counter on the other side, she took her cassette up to the counter and handed it to the clerk, along with the money. The clerk, a high school girl named Marilyn, knew Nicole, so there was no problem. "This is a goody," Marilyn said, "you'll enjoy it." Then her smile vanished and her voice faded as she said, "Nicole . . . ?"

It was no ripple of fear that went up her back this time. That cold, greasy feeling was returning, that terrible need to vomit, and the creeping, licking, dirty feeling, and she had to fight it, fight it, and Marilyn and the other clerk were staring at her, Duffy was gone and . . .

"Nickie, honey . . . ?"

She had to get to Duffy and the others. She bolted from the store.

•   •   •

Why Timothy was following the girl, he wasn't quite sure, except that she was an irritation in his life, a minor irritation, and he was curious. Julia's granddaughter. He told himself that he wasn't really following her at all, just keeping his eyes open and observing, while drifting along in the same direction. He had already picked up the shoes and shirts he needed, and he had told Heinrich, his butler-chauffeur, to meet him outside the main entrance at around eight-thirty. He had a little time to kill.

The girl had looked back over her shoulder several times, almost fearfully it seemed to Timothy, but he didn't think she had spotted or recognized him. Not that it mattered. *Don't worry, I won't hurt you. Give my regards to your grandmother.*

She seemed to be with a small group, and paired off with the Johnson boy, the high school principal's son. The football player. Bradford Holland was with them—Timothy knew Bradford's father, Judge Holland, quite well, of course. He didn't know the others, though the tall boy looked familiar and the blond girl reminded him of Connie Lindquist, the hostess out at the Moonlight Inn.

The group reached the north cross-corridor, looked down it toward the movie theater, and turned back again, picking up their pace. They passed Timothy without giving him so much as a glance.

Timothy followed them.

Time to meet Heinrich.

Yet he paused and watched as they went into the video rental place. It was brightly lit, and he could see them clearly, the only customers, through the plate-glass windows. They consulted a moment or two, and Bradford and the blond girl took a videocassette up to a clerk, checked it out, and left the store. Meanwhile, the tall boy—*Anderson!* that was his name, the basketball player—Anderson and the chubby girl checked out a tape with the other clerk and followed Bradford and the blonde out of the store. Then the Johnson boy and Nicole seemed to have a minor altercation, and the boy went to check out. A moment later he left.

That left Nicole standing there with a video in her hands.

Timothy found himself grating his teeth.

Nicole St. Claire, the last of the St. Claires. An innocent, no doubt, but at that moment, in her very innocence, she seemed emblematic of all the frustrations and defeats that he and his father and his father's father had ever suffered at the hands of the St. Claires. Innocent Nicole St. Claire, all unknowing of the pain and grief and defeats of others, would live on through happiness after happiness and victory after victory, whereas his Alida . . .

It came over him then like a noxious black cloud, a cloud that smothered and choked him and cast him entirely in darkness, the terrible foreknowledge, the unwanted, unbearable foreknowledge, that *something was coming* for Alida, that while this St. Claire child lived and sparkled and laughed, his Alida would be taken from him, that Alida and all he treasured would be taken, that this St. Claire child was a curse upon him, the St. Claire curse incarnate, and that unless he found a way to propitiate the gods, the very god of this world, all would be lost, lost—

—*goddamn filthy little cock-teasing cunt, thinks she's such fuckin' hot shit*—

As abrupt as a bolt of lightning striking through that black cloud, Timothy felt one of the most incredible bursts of hatred-lust-envy-anger he had ever experienced—

—*gets her kicks wiggling her ass, I'd like to ream out that sweet pink ass*—

—and it was aimed directly at Nicole.

—*shove it so far up her ass it rips her open, screw her till she's bleeding front and rear, then beat the shit out of her DRINK MY PISS, BITCH! fuck her some more, fuck her dead and leave her for roadkill. I'd like to do her, I'd like to do her so bad*—

Oh, how well Timothy knew that hatred-lust-envy-anger! Since childhood, he had been forced to contain and control it, but oh, how he resonated to it! And now it was as if this were exactly the opportunity he had been waiting for, the god-given opportunity, and he could not hold himself back. With all the strength of his mind and will, he struck out at the other mind explosively: *THEN DO IT! DO IT! GO AHEAD AND DO IT!*

And he got back: *Oh, yeaahh. I'm gonna do it!*

Wide-eyed, pale and stumbling, Nicole burst out of the store and ran after her friends.

Timothy stood for an instant, utterly paralyzed, watching her.

Dear god, what had he done!

He had sicced that maniac, whoever he was, on the St. Claire child without any thought of the possible consequences. He had given himself *no chance* to foresee the consequences. How many St. Claires could he destroy, before Julia . . . ?

Looking about, trying to detect once again that mad presence, he sent out the thought, *No, don't do it, don't do it. Don't!*

But it was too late, the madman was gone, he sensed that. It was as if he had pulled a trigger, and for better or worse, the bullet was on its way. The best thing he could do now, the only thing he could do, was to get as far away from here as possible before whatever was going to happen happened.

Yet, as he hurried to meet Heinrich, the black cloud lifted and a kind of elation came over Timothy. He had acted, and surely only good could come of this. There was nothing, absolutely nothing in the world, to connect him with the madman who was stalking Nicole St. Claire. As for his foreboding for Alida, surely that had been false, born of his frustration and despair. He should have more trust in the god he had served so well. Yes, he had a very positive feeling that this was going to work out well after all.

She would *not* be sick, she would *not!* She would not be a child and a pain in the neck and puke all over herself right in the middle of the mall and make Duffy ashamed of her and sorry he had ever asked her to hang out. If she did that, he would never ask her again. . . .

But as before, the nausea quickly faded, and by the time she caught up with Duffy, it was gone, leaving only a couple of tears rolling down her cheeks.

"Hey, what's wrong?" he asked, putting an arm around her shoulders.

"Nothing. I just started getting sick again."

"I'm sorry. You must have picked up a bug somewhere."

Somebody out there hates me, she thought again, crazily, but all she said was, "You must think I'm a ninny."

Duffy gave her a hug and a kiss on the top of the head. "Hey, like Brad says. If you're a ninny, you're *our* ninny."

Nicole snuffled and laughed and wiped away the tears with the back of her hand.

"Okay?"

She smiled and nodded.

They caught up with the others and reached the food court in the east wing just in time to get something to eat. Most of the shops were preparing to close, but Nicole had no trouble getting a shrimp egg roll with hot Chinese mustard and a Coke. She took it to a table and sat down with the others.

She really did feel like a member of the gang now. The thing was, they didn't make a *point* of making her feel welcome. They didn't make her feel like a child. They made her feel like *it was okay* to be only fourteen or even thirteen. She didn't even have to think about it. She was accepted, Duffy's friend, a member.

At least until Duffy's girlfriend came back from Canada. Adrienne.

She wasn't sure she liked Adrienne.

"Let's go," Gussie said, standing up and wiping her hands and lips. "I vote we watch *Bringing Up Baby.*"

"I can't eat and drive," Brad said, his mouth full, holding up a taco.

"Eat it in the parking lot. Or I'll feed it to you in the car. Come on."

Derek and Joanne had already finished and were drifting toward the exit doors. Duffy said, "Let's go, Nickie," and, pizza and Coke in hand, got up to follow them. Nicole took a moment more to finish her egg roll and Coke and deposit her detritus in a trash container. Her little purse in hand, she looked around for her video.

It wasn't there.

It should have been on the table, in a white plastic bag with blue and orange printing on it, but *it wasn't there!*

She couldn't even remember putting it on the table.

Tension spread through her chest. She was barely breathing. Duffy must have picked up her video. Except that as he moved toward the doors, she clearly saw just one white plastic bag hanging from its loop-handles around his left wrist.

Her heart began to pound. "I'll be with you in a minute," she called, but she couldn't tell if Duffy heard her or not.

The video *had* to be here *some*place. She looked under the table where she had been sitting. She looked on each of the chairs.

No video.

What had she done with it?

She tried to remember all her movements, everything she had done, after leaving the video store. She hurried to the Chinese food place, some thirty feet away, where she had bought the egg roll. It was just closing. "Excuse me, did I leave a videocassette here, in a white plastic bag—"

"No, no!" The face of the kid behind the counter reflected her alarm.

What did videocassettes cost? She had heard that they could cost as much as eighty or ninety dollars.

Ninety dollars?

Tears sprang to her eyes again. *Grandma will kill me. Grandma will absolutely kill me!*

There was just one possibility, and it *had* to be, it *had* to be what had happened. She had left the video store so abruptly, she must have left the cassette behind. If it wasn't there . . .

Grandma will kill me!

Tear-blinded, she ran back toward the store. This was her last chance. The video *had* to be there!

Marilyn was just starting to lock up. Seeing Nicole, she went back behind the counter and got the video. "Nickie, what in the world . . . ?"

"Oh, thank you, thank you!" Blessed by a great wave of relief, Nicole accepted the videocassette in its white plastic bag, idiotically blew Marilyn a kiss as she left the store, and started back the way she had come.

She slowed down. There was no hurry now. She had the cassette, the ninety-dollar videocassette, and Grandma wouldn't kill her after all. Oh, thank you, God!

The mall was already almost empty, but it was well lighted, and a security guard smiled at her as she went by.

Still floating on that wave of relief, she pushed her way past glass doors to the outside and looked out across the dark parking lot. Here and there an orange lamp glowed high above the pavement, giving minimal illumination. She didn't see Duffy or the others, but she thought she ought to be able to find them easily enough. This part of the lot was now largely deserted, but there were still scattered clusters of cars, and she saw people in the distance.

She tried to remember where Brad had parked the car. She hadn't really been paying attention, but she knew that it was quite a way out and more to the east than to the north. She started walking across the lot in that direction, more or less.

She walked perhaps a hundred, two hundred feet. All she had to do was look for a car with some kids around it. She felt like calling out to them, but that would have made her feel foolish, like a baby.

She walked on a little farther. In spite of the orange lights, the lot really was awfully dark. She found herself keeping away from the remaining cars in this area. You couldn't tell what might be behind them. They made her think of dark alien animals, crouched down and waiting to pounce.

Duffy, Brad, Derek, where are you? Gussie, Joanne . . .

She stood perfectly still, looking slowly about.

She knew she shouldn't be alone in a dark parking lot at this hour.

"There are some real crazies out there, and we all know what can happen to little girls at shopping malls late at night."

She held her purse and the white plastic bag to her chest as if protecting them might somehow protect her.

She was afraid.

Walking across the lot, they were halfway to the car before Duffy realized that Nicole wasn't with them. "Nicole?" he called out. "*Nickie!* . . . Hey, where's Nickie?"

"Well, she was with us . . . I think," said Gussie.

"I don't know," Joanne said. "I don't remember seeing her since we left."

"*Nicole!*" Duffy looked back the way they had come. He

saw cars here and there and a couple of people, but no one who looked like Nicole.

"*Nickie?*"

No answer.

"*You'll keep your eye on Nicole every minute?*"

"*. . . I won't let her out of my sight.*"

Oh, shit.

And she had been such a good kid, all evening up till now, sticking real close by with him. She must have dawdled behind, and . . .

Maybe she had gotten sick again.

God, kids!

"Look, you guys go on. I'm going back for Nicole. We'll meet you at the car."

Duffy didn't wait for an answer, but started off in a easy lope for the east wing.

Guilt tugged at him. "*. . . won't let her out of my sight.*"

Jesus, Aunt Julia, I'm sorry!

Sorry don't cut it, buddy, if anything's happened to that kid.

He looked about, looked everywhere, looked between the cars and behind them as he ran. Looked under the lamps and into the shadows. Saw three or four people but not Nicole. No one was coming out of the side doors of the east wing, the ones they had used. He just hoped the mall doors weren't locked yet.

He was in luck. The doors weren't locked.

"Closing up, fellow," a blue-uniformed security guard called to him as he entered.

"It's okay. I just gotta find someone. A girl. About thirteen, white T-shirt, blue shorts?"

The guard automatically started to shake his head, then hesitated. He pointed a finger. "I think I did see someone like that, up there just a few minutes ago. Headed this way."

"Did she leave?"

The guard shrugged. "I don't see her now." He nodded his head toward the big Sears, the anchor store, at the end of the wing. "She could've gone in there. But you can see, they got their gates closed."

"Aw, jeez."

Duffy couldn't think of any reason why Nicole would enter Sears at this hour except maybe to use their rest room if she was sick. In which case she would use a Sears exit out into the parking lot.

"Sorry, kid."

Duffy thanked the man and went out the way he had come in.

Still no sign of Nicole on the outside.

If the guard really *had* seen Nicole *where* he'd said he'd seen her, she must have gone back for something . . . yeah, her video, he didn't remember seeing her carrying it; she might have forgotten it . . . in which case, she must be somewhere out in the huge parking lot by now, looking for them. But where? There was no point in going back over the part he had covered.

Oh, God, Nicole, you've been such a good kid up till now—where are you?

He had a growing feeling that something had gone wrong, badly wrong. A gut feeling. Like a man half-blind and uncertain of his step, he started east and a little north, into the darkness.

Aunt Julia, I'm so sorry, I'm so fuckin' goddamn sorry!

There's nothing wrong, asshole, she's just out there in the dark somewhere, looking for you, and you've got to find her.

He began to lope again, trying to cover territory. The lot was so dark, it had never seemed darker.

He thought he saw something move, the merest shadow, in the distance.

". . . we all know what can happen to little girls at shopping malls late at night."

Aw, no, no, no, no . . .

He tried to call out, but it sounded more as if he were crying. "Aw, Nickie, Nickie, *please!*"

She heard a little moan come from her throat. She clutched her purse and the plastic bag close between her breasts, leaning over them, as if they contained her life. She lowered her head; whatever was out there in the dark, she didn't want to see it. She held her knees tightly together, bending them, slowly moving toward a fetal position.

Our Father Who art in heaven, please . . .

Grandma, Grandma, Grandma! She mouthed the word, but the sound wouldn't come out.

Oh, please, God!

And now the sickness was rising in her belly again, worse than ever, that great cold lump of filthy lard, and bending farther forward she vomited a thin, sour stream of egg roll and Coke. The slime was crawling up her bare legs, and her bowels and bladder were threatening to let go, and she knew that the very worst thing that could happen was about to happen, and—

Something dark swung around in front of her, and a sharp blow under her chin, as from the heel of a hand, caused her brain to explode in blinding light. Before her vision could clear, an arm encircled her waist drawing her up against a hard chest, lifting her until her toes barely touched the pavement. A knife blade pressed against her cheek. Foul, sulfurous breath filled her nostrils, and she found herself staring directly into the fire-bright eyes of evil itself.

Evil grinned. Its face was hard-muscled and dimpled, and its voice was a hoarse whisper. *"Make one sound, bitch, and you're fuckin' dead!"*

. . . and then Duffy heard the most terrible sound he had ever heard in his life. He recognized the sound, he had heard something like it before, but never raised to such a level of sheer, unmitigated terror and madness. It started as a high shriek of pain, but almost instantly it was transformed into a roaring, squealing, yapping, snarling sound, the sound of a mad dog, the sound of a terrified, hysterical totally-out-of-control dog, a dog fighting for its life and going for the kill.

"Nickie!" Duffy screamed. "Nickie!"

Nickie was in danger, he knew it, Nickie was being attacked.

Then he was running through the dark parking lot, running around and between the cars, screaming her name, running and screaming, knowing only that he had to get to Nickie, he had to save her, had to save her, whatever the cost to himself.

The snarling abruptly stopped.

He saw her.

In all that darkness, he saw her as clearly as if a spotlight were on her, saw her sitting there on the pavement, the man's body, ripped and torn, just beyond her. He saw the blood on her face and her wide terrified eyes, and for just a moment he saw something else that he would never forget, yet could never believe he had truly seen. Surely it had been an illusion, caused by the dim orange lights and the shadows and the horror of the moment. Nicole's face was somehow oddly distorted, the muzzle slightly elongated, and he saw her open those bloody, fanged jaws, saw the nostrils flare and heard the wolflike howl of fear and rage and grief, saw and heard not the wolf, no, but the Wolf Girl, in all her terrible lupine beauty.

Then he was on his knees, not knowing what he had seen and heard, not caring or thinking about it, but drawing her into his arms, feeling the hot smear of blood between their cheeks, kissing her, embracing her, whispering to her, *"It's all right, Nickie, darling, it's all right, Duffy is here, Duffy will take care of you, it's all right, Nickie, please, Nickie, don't be afraid, Nickie, don't be afraid,"* and raising his head only to cry out: "Help! Help, for God's sake! Someone help us!" Then rocking her in his arms, whispering to her some more, trying to soothe and calm and comfort.

She lay weeping on his shoulder, a frightened, horrified child, still clinging to her purse and the precious white plastic bag.

Footsteps sounding, as people came running . . . legs moving around them . . . gasps, exclamations of horror. Gussie leaned down, offering to take Nicole from him, but Duffy shook his head. Looking past Nicole, he could see that the man was dead. He had to be. His throat had been torn out and his belly ripped open, and his eyes were staring blankly at the night sky. One hand looked as if it had been almost torn off, and a bloody knife lay nearby.

"All right, everybody stand back," some male take-charge type said in an officious voice. "I've called the sheriff's office on my car phone. The law will be here any minute. I've also requested an ambulance."

Duffy supposed he should be grateful.

Even as the man spoke, a police sedan came roaring up, and a deputy sprang out. Duffy recognized him—a big young iron-pumper named Bruno Krull. He took in the scene, took a couple of deep breaths, and tried to tough it out.

"You're Johnson, the football hero, aren't you?" he asked. He had a thick, deep, glottal voice, a metallic voice that suggested he could spit bullets.

"Duffy Johnson," Duffy said. At the moment, he didn't fear bullets. He cared only about Nicole.

"And she is?"

"Nicole St. Claire."

"Oh, my," the deputy said with a laugh, "one of those." He hunkered down to Duffy's level. "So what happened, Duffy?"

"I don't know. A bunch of us were leaving the mall, and we got separated. I went looking for Nicole and heard a noise and came running—"

"What kind of noise?"

"It sounded like a frightened, angry dog," Duffy said reluctantly. "I thought it might be something after Nicole."

"It looks more like something was after him." The deputy nodded toward the torn and bloody corpse.

"Maybe," Duffy said, "maybe he was defending her."

"Yeah, sure. We'll find out."

Two more police cars arrived, rubber squealing on the macadam, and their brilliant headlights sliced through the crowd, making the shadows blacker. A beam fell across the body.

The deputy stood up. He grinned at Duffy. "Yeah, we'll find out," he repeated, "but the shape this guy's in . . . if I didn't know better, I'd say the St. Claire werewolves were still with us."

CHAPTER 10

She was the Wolf Girl of St. Claire, and the world, or at least the small world of St. Claire, was not going to let her forget it.

The police made only the briefest attempt to question her that evening. She was clearly hysterical, and she was bleeding profusely from at least one wound, a cut along her left jawline. Duffy insisted on accompanying her in the ambulance and asked the others to telephone her grandmother. Her grandmother and Dr. London arrived at the hospital minutes after the ambulance did. The doctor gave her a shot, and after that . . .

She roused up just once in the darkened hospital room. Her face was numb under the bandage where it had been stitched up. After a moment, she realized that the faint sound she heard was Duffy weeping, crying like a child. "I'm so sorry, Aunt Julia. I never should have let her out of my sight. I *promised* you . . ." "It's all right, Duffy," her grandmother was saying, "nobody is blaming you. Now, you had better go home, dear, and get some rest." Nicole drifted off again.

The next morning, soon after breakfast, the sheriff arrived at the hospital to question Nicole. He was accompanied by the deputy, Bruno Krull, who had been in the parking lot the previous evening, and by a stenographer. Mr. Balthazar, her grandmother's attorney, arrived at about the same time.

"Henry," her grandmother protested, "Nicole will probably be discharged this morning—can't this wait until she gets home?"

Sheriff Dawson shook his head. If Dr. London was a St. Bernard, the sheriff was a weary old bloodhound. "I had no idea what shape the child was in, Julia," he said, "except what the hospital gives out over the phone. If she's still emotionally vulnerable, and I imagine she is, I like the idea of having doctors and nurses around. And I'm glad to see you've got Mr. Balthazar here. We all want what's right and best for the child."

"I appreciate that, Henry. I appreciate your taking a personal concern."

"Now, Nicole . . ."

Nicole, still in a robe and slippers, sat in a chair by the bed. Her grandmother sat beside her, the stenographer was somewhere behind them, and the sheriff sat facing them. The deputy and Mr. Balthazar stood behind the sheriff, back by the open door. It had taken Nicole a moment to recognize the deputy. Looking at Nicole, his eyes were heavy-lidded, and he wore a faint sneer. Something about him reminded her of her assailant in the parking lot, as if they were two of a kind, and she shuddered and averted her gaze.

The sheriff placed a tape recorder on the nearby bedside table. He explained that he had brought it so that they could prepare a statement, "just routine paperwork, Nicole," about what had happened. But anytime she wanted him to turn off the recorder so that she could think a little bit or perhaps confer with her grandmother or Mr. Balthazar or himself, that was perfectly all right. Was she ready to start?

Nicole forced a smile. She was ready.

The sheriff turned on the tape recorder and said a few words about the circumstances of the interview. "Now, Nicole, if you would, please, tell us exactly what happened to you at the St. Claire Mall yesterday evening."

"I don't know exactly where to start."

"Well, why don't you tell us how you happened to go to the mall and just go on from there. Take your time and tell it all and try to be patient if I ask a question now and then."

So Nicole *did* tell it all, or most of it, starting with the moment Duffy suggested that she "come along and catch a flick" with him and his friends. She told about the crowded movie area, the antique auto display. She did not tell him about her momentary impression that profound hatred was being directed at her—she didn't want him to think she was crazy—but she did mention that she briefly thought she was going to be sick.

"Coming down with a bug, maybe," she said, forcing another little smile. The sheriff smiled back and showed no sign of impatience.

She told him how, just as they were leaving the mall, she had discovered that her rented videocassette was missing and had rushed back to the video shop to recover it . . .

. . . and then had gone out into the dark parking lot to look for Duffy and the others.

She told it as exactly as she could, how she had ventured out into that darkness, quickly at first, then her footsteps slowing and her fear growing as she looked past the few remaining cars in that area.

"Then I started getting sick again . . ."

To her surprise, her voice rose an octave and began to shake. Tears blurred her vision. It was as if she were back in that parking lot, back in the darkness with its distant orange lights, reliving the entire experience.

". . . sick again . . . *sick with fear!* All evening I had been fighting it off, but it kept coming back, *the fear, the fear, the fear!* I was so afraid that I threw up! Right there in the parking lot, I threw up everything I had eaten, I was so afraid!"

"I think that is enough," her grandmother said, trying to embrace her, but Nicole pushed the arms away.

"No, no, I want to tell. I was sick and frightened and I knew something bad was going to happen to me, something awful, and it did!"

Nicole sat, eyes tightly closed and fists clenched, for the moment unable to go on.

"Tell us, Nicole," the sheriff said softly. "Take your time, but tell us."

Nicole pointed at her chin. "He hit me. He hit me. I never even saw him before he hit me!"

"Yes, I see the bruise."

"Then he grabbed me around the waist and pulled me up against him, and he held a knife against my face. He grinned at me and said, *'Make one sound, bitch, and you're fuckin' dead!'*"

"Enough!" her grandmother said.

"No!"

"Let her get it out, Julia," the sheriff said. "This isn't harming her. She needs to tell."

Nicole nodded, grateful for the sheriff's understanding. "Then he started dragging me away, all the time saying awful things to me . . . what a terrible person I was . . ." The remembered words were like filth in her mouth, but they had to be said. ". . . little prick-teasing whore . . . and what I deserved . . . rip my cunt out."

"We understand."

"I was so scared, I wet my pants."

"Of course. Who wouldn't be scared?"

"And he knew. He laughed and said I better enjoy my piss 'cause it was likely my last."

Nicole knew without looking that her grandmother was weeping, tears of anger as much as compassion, but she couldn't stop now. She had to tell the worst part.

"Then he stopped and looked around—to see where he was dragging me, I guess—and for a moment the knife was away from my face, and I could see his bare wrist. I could see it so clearly, the blue veins in it. I could *smell* it. And then . . . and then . . ."

"Yes?"

The words burst out of her explosively: *"I bit him! I bit the goddamn fucking bejesus out of him!"*

She saw the sheriff's eyes widen in surprise and heard Mr. Balthazar say, "That's enough, Nicole. Sheriff, as her attorney—" But she was fully back in the terror of that moment, the terror and the anger that compounded into a murderous fury, and she could no more stop herself now than she could have in the parking lot.

"I bit him! I bit his wrist. I heard him scream, but I didn't care. I screamed too, and kept on biting him. I was scared, scared, scared, I was scared out of my mind, but I wasn't going to let him kill me, and that was all I knew. He fell down, and I think I kept on biting him, I don't know how long. And then he was just lying there, and I was sitting beside him, not crazy anymore, but still so scared . . . so scared . . ."

Nicole at last allowed herself to collapse weeping into her grandmother's arms. The sheriff turned off his tape recorder.

"I think we've heard enough for now. Let's give this child some peace."

Later that day, while Nicole rested in her own bed, the sheriff filled Julia in over a glass of iced tea in the kitchen.

"The man's name was Dugan. Bryce Elroy Dugan, called Buster, local boy but a bit of a drifter. Caucasian, age thirty-one, with a record of being hell on women. Married less than a year, some ten years ago, to a wife who alleged he beat her. Soon after that, he spent a couple of years behind bars in Wisconsin for rape. Twice he was accused of beating women he was living with, but they dropped the charges."

"You seem to have learned a lot about Mr. Dugan," Julia said, "in a very short time."

"If I know a lot about Buster, Julia, it's because I've been interested in him for quite a while. He came back to the area about eighteen months ago, and first came to my attention when some grade-school girls complained to their teachers about a man who hung around school yards trying to 'get acquainted.' Grade-school girls, Julia! But to our knowledge, he hadn't actually molested any of them, and all we could do was put a scare in him and keep an eye on him.

"Now, about last night. So far, I have learned nothing that contradicts what Nicole has told us—*insofar as she remembers* what happened. It seems evident that after a certain point she was far too terrified and hysterical *to know* what happened. She's told us that she bit the man's wrist and that she bit him repeatedly, but the medical examiner says that if she did, she has the damnedest bite of any human being he ever saw. It's more as if some animal had torn into him.

"Now, the Johnson boy tells me that at the time of the attack he heard a dog in the parking lot. Not just barking, but that loud, frenzied screaming some dogs give out in a do-or-die dog fight. Nicole didn't hear it, all she heard were her own screams, and that's understandable. But a number of other people did hear it.

"So what have we got? I would *like* to think that we've got a dog attacking a man. I would *like* to think that Buster Dugan made the very bad mistake of setting off alarms in some kind of protective guard dog. But nobody can say with any certainty they actually saw a dog, and we haven't found bloody paw prints anywhere in the area.

"Julia, I hate to assail you with the unpleasant details. If you want me to stop . . ."

Julia shook her head.

"Well, then . . . We all know that the human jaw is mighty powerful, and if it's true that desperate mothers sometimes lift automobiles off of their children, then I suppose that a desperate little girl might very well severe a man's hand with a bite. But that leaves the matter of the belly wound. Julia, that man was ripped open, through his shirt, from his breastbone clear down past his navel. And I have never in my life met a man, woman, or child with the teeth to do a job like that. One possibility I can think of is that Nicole used the man's knife, even if she doesn't remember. The only problem with that explanation is that the only prints on the knife are Buster's. That leaves the unlikely possibility that somehow in the scuffle the son of a bitch ripped himself open. But any other possibilities are even more fantastic."

"In any case," Julia said after a moment, "you believe that Nicole killed that man."

The sheriff said carefully, "Julia, we are looking for a dog. A dog with blood on its muzzle. But Nicole did defend herself. Successfully, it seems."

"If you believe it, St. Claire will believe it."

"They won't blame her, Julia."

Julia turned disillusioned eyes on him. "Won't they, Henry? Oh, I suppose most won't, but some . . . do you remember how they treated James, Henry? As if he were some kind of rabid animal?"

"This is altogether different," the sheriff said vehemently. "The man Nicole killed—if she did—was evil, a monster. We're well rid of him."

"Just the same . . . I wonder if it wouldn't be best for Nicole if we left St. Claire for a while. Or even for good. After this is cleared up, of course."

The sheriff shook his head sadly.

In the end, it was the children who decided Julia on leaving St. Claire. Not only those children who, perhaps reflecting their parents' views, regarded Nicole as criminal or depraved for what had supposedly happened in that dark parking lot, but also those who in their very affection—even their callow admiration!—were thoughtlessly cruel.

Not that there weren't other contributing factors. The Dugan family, large and clannish, naturally howled for Nicole's blood. There were threatening anonymous letters, perhaps from Dugans, which Julia turned over to the sheriff, and some ugly telephone calls, which prompted her to purchase her first answering machine. "That kid has gotta be sick like all you St. Claires, and she oughta be locked up in a nuthouse!"

Something had happened to St. Claire since she was a girl, Julia thought. Not that it had ever been paradise, she had never had that illusion, but there was no doubt in her mind that it had grown meaner, harder in its ways. More crassly commercial, more eager to rip off tourists than to be a congenial place to live. Even old friends had become more cynical and self-centered. Perhaps she herself had. Each year, it seemed, there was less to keep her here. So . . . why put up with this aggravation? Why not take Nicole and leave?

Still, she might have been willing to "tough it out," as some of her friends urged, if it hadn't been for the children.

Nicole lasted in school almost a month.

Julia was proud of her.

She had misgivings about putting Nicole back in school locally, especially so soon after "the event," but Nicole had been looking forward to this year and had refused any alternative.

When Nicole got off the school bus after the first day, Julia knew things had not gone well. The girl was glassy-eyed and had a strained smile and refused to "tell all about it," professing to be bored with the subject. "It's just *school*, Grandma."

In the days that followed, nothing changed. Don't intrude, Julia told herself, let the child work it out in her own way. But she was worried and distressed. The last year or two, Nicole had seemed to be doing so well. She had even acquired something approaching a "best friend," Hallie Evans, the most popular girl in the eighth grade. Now there was no mention of Hallie.

Not that there weren't respites. Invited to Nicole's birthday dinner, Duffy, bless him, had turned it into a party. Joanne and Gussie had come, with cards and presents, and for a few hours Nicole's face had had a look of peaceful joy.

But a few days later . . .

Something had happened at school, of that Julia was certain. She knew the signs—the evasiveness about Nicole's day, the forced cheerfulness, the uncertain voice—but she was careful not to intrude.

What would Nicole like for supper? Hamburgers, Nicole decided, charcoal-grilled in the backyard. She would make the hamburger patties and grill them herself. There was no ground beef in the refrigerator, but there was over three pounds of good, lean sirloin tip. Julia did not object when Nicole ground up the entire roast, far more than they needed, but she did object when she saw the child surreptitiously nibbling at the raw meat.

"Steak tartare is out, Nicole," she said. "*E. coli* and all that."

"I know. I just like a little."

"You'll like it better, I'm sure, when it's nicely grilled."

Nicole liked larger burgers than her grandmother did, so she made up five big patties for herself and turned the remainder of the meat into smaller patties. She would cook them all.

They could refrigerate those they didn't eat, she said, for later microwaving.

While Nicole prepared and grilled the meat, Julia made a salad, and they ate at the kitchen table. Julia's hamburger was medium well done, as she liked it, just slightly pink. Nicole's, she observed, was barely done at all. Nicole ate it quickly, letting half of the bun fall away untouched, and immediately reached for another patty. She put it on a bun, hardly bothered to salt and pepper it, and ate it even more quickly than the first. She reached for another . . .

This was what Julia had been half expecting and dreading, the first such episode in three years. The anguish on the child's face as she gorged on the near-raw meat cut to her heart, but she dared not interfere, dared not try to restrain Nicole physically—that would only prolong and intensify the pain she was suffering. Instead, she reached out and stroked Nicole's head and shoulders and spoke to her soothingly and reassuringly, though she knew the effort was probably futile.

Nicole ate four of the large hamburger patties, not even pretending to eat the bun for the last one, and then ran from the table to the downstairs toilet. Julia followed after her. She heard gagging, sobbing sounds behind the closed door, and she eased it open an inch.

"Nicole, can I help?"

"No. I'm all right."

Julia closed the door again. At fourteen, the child was entitled to whatever dignity she could salvage. Nevertheless, Julia continued to listen carefully in case she was needed. When she heard nothing but weeping, she returned to the kitchen.

Nicole followed a few minutes later and sat back down. She had wiped her face, but a few tears still flowed.

"I'm sorry," she said.

"It's all right, Nicole."

"I've been good for a long time."

"You have always been good. You are a good person."

"No, I'm not." Nicole covered her eyes with her hands and shook her head. "I'm bad. I know I'm bad. I hate myself."

"Nicole, self-hatred solves nothing. I learned that with your grandfather. Now, what happened at school today?"

"Nothing. Nothing important."

"If it made you feel that you're a bad person and you hate yourself, then it is very important."

"It doesn't matter."

"It matters."

Nicole was silent for a moment. She uncovered her face, but she looked at her plate.

"Why can't I be like other kids, Grandma?"

The question caused Julia to draw a swift, painful breath. She understood. Oh, how she understood! Nicole had been branded as different, forever different, and not even those children who mistakenly admired her for the difference could understand her pain. As for those who wished to be cruel as only children can be cruel . . . to them, she was the Wolf Girl, one of those crazy, sick St. Claires.

Nevertheless she said, "It's more important to be yourself. Your best self if possible, but yourself."

"Sometimes I just want to die."

At those words, Julia knew that the inevitable moment had come, and she welcomed it. She straightened up in her chair, and she had no difficulty at all in sounding cheerful. "Well, then," she said, "we'll just have to do something about that, won't we?"

"What can we do?"

"Have an adventure."

Nicole looked up, guardedly. "What kind of adventure?"

"Nicole, I've been thinking for some time now that it might be a good idea for you and me to take a nice long vacation from St. Claire. Maybe even a permanent vacation."

"You mean . . . move away from St. Claire?"

"Why not? Where would you like to go?"

Nicole's eyes widened with alarm. "But all my friends are here!"

Julia tried to keep the bitterness out of her laugh. *Your friends?* she wanted to say. *These kids that make your life so miserable?* Instead she said, "Oh, we can always come back and see our friends. Tell me where you'd like to live. Florida? California? Somewhere in the Southwest?"

"But our house . . ." Clearly, the idea of giving up the

house she had lived in since birth was heartbreaking. This was *home.*

"Oh, I'll keep the house, at least for the time being. It'll be handy for visits. We'll come back for Christmas if you like."

"But school . . ."

"We'll find you a good one. If we can't get you in one right away, we'll get you tutors. Come on, Nicole, tell Grandma. Where would you like to live?"

Nicole stared. "Grandma, are you serious?"

"Dead serious. Tell Grandma."

Nicole thought for a moment. "New York," she said.

"Ah, New York," Julia said, smiling. "You'd like to try out New York City."

Nicole smiled back and nodded. "Daddy loved New York. There's Lincoln Center and Broadway and all that great stuff. And in a year Duffy's going to college there, so I'll have a friend."

Julia considered. New York hadn't been on her list, but why not, at least for a while?

"All right, sleep on it a couple of nights. Then if you're still sure . . ."

"Yeah!"

"Darling, you've got it."

Timothy could have sung.

Julia was leaving St. Claire. And, of course, taking her granddaughter with her. She was making the move for the child's sake—she had been quite frank about that.

Oh, they would almost certainly return to visit from time to time, she had told him as they sat in his office, and perhaps once Nicole was in college and more or less on her own, she, Julia, would return for good. . . .

Timothy knew otherwise, and he had hardly been able to hide his jubilation. He had foreseen quite clearly that once Julia left St. Claire, she would never return, save for the occasional brief visit—not until the day she died.

And as for Nicole, why should she come back to a place that had treated her so cruelly? No, once gone, she would undoubtedly meet and eventually marry some promising young man, and neither of them would ever dream of living in little St. Claire. Nicole was no longer a problem.

His rash act at the St. Claire Mall now seemed divinely inspired. He had at last fulfilled the mandate his grandfather Isaac had laid upon his father: "Drive those sons o' bitches out!" He had done that, had rid himself of the St. Claires, of Julia and Nicole St. Claire, once and for all. St. Claire was a very small world, among the larger worlds that Timothy inhabited, but it was altogether *his* world now, his kingdom, his own little fiefdom.

To give to his daughter.

In victory, he had even felt a surge of his old affection for Julia. Like Timothy, she had aged well, and to his eye she was as beautiful as she had been when he fell in love with her, all those years back.

Their business had not taken long—yes, of course his realty company would look after her property for her. He would give the matter his personal attention. She need not worry about it.

As soon as Julia left, he told his secretary to cancel his remaining appointments for the day and called for Heinrich to come get him. Poor Minna thought he had gone quite mad when he captured her in his arms and waltzed her through her kitchen.

And now he sat in his tower room, looking through an open window at his verdant mountainside, so beautiful with its first golden touches of autumn. Down below, on the lakeside road, the school bus had just pulled up. Timothy would have much preferred to have Heinrich drive Alida to and from school, but she insisted on riding the bus with the other children. She had no idea of how carefully that bus was watched and guarded.

The power of that terrible moment at the St. Claire Mall when he thought he foresaw Alida's doom had quite faded. The moment had served its purpose, which had been to spur him into action against the St. Claires—and how effective that action had been! But now the moment had been replaced by a stunningly different vision of Alida. He saw her as the beautiful raven-haired woman, powerful, ruthless, merciless to her enemies, who would one day lead the Balthazar Convocation;

the woman whose brilliant psychic mind would provide the god of this world with the greatest gateway *into* this world it had ever known.

Alida Balthazar, the Final Bride of Lucifer and the Mother of All Witches.

Was the vision false? Was he once again deluding himself? He thought not.

Because he found the vision strangely frightening.

The day grew more beautiful still when Alida, sauntering around a bend in the driveway, emerged from the greenery carrying her little satchel of schoolbooks, thinking little-girl thoughts and dreaming little-girl dreams. This was the Alida Timothy loved, not the one in his vision. She looked up and saw him. She smiled and waved. Timothy smiled and waved back.

Nine years old and still so innocent. Please, God, let her stay a little girl a little while longer.

Timothy Balthazar, a happy man and lord of all he surveyed, went downstairs to greet his daughter.

Part Two

THE SUMMONING OF THE SEVEN

CHAPTER 11

Her head pressed back against the pillow, her body arching and loins thrusting, Lily Bains made love to Duffy Johnson.

"I love you," she whispered in the dark. "I love you now as I loved you then. I've never stopped loving you, Duffy. In your heart you still love me, Duffy, you know you do, you loved me even when you denied your love, and you love me now. As I love you. . . ."

Lily made love to Duffy Johnson, though she lay in the arms of Timothy Balthazar.

"Oh, God, I love you," she whispered, a thing of hot wet flame, moaning as she pressed up against Timothy. "I love you, and you love me. . . ."

Yes, Duffy, Timothy thought, *Lily loves you, you know she loves you, and you know you want to love her, she is the love you have always dreamed of and longed for, let yourself love her, Duffy. . . .*

He directed his thoughts toward Duffy with the greatest possible concentration, trying to shut out all else. Yet fleetingly he recalled that night so many years ago when he and Freya had made love in this same way in that house across the lake, while doing everything in their power to drive James St. Claire to his ruin.

Lily was gasping, sobbing. "Come back, Duffy! Come back to St. Claire. I'm here waiting for you, darling. Duffy, come back to me, come back! Come back—!"

As sometimes happened, Timothy suddenly caught a glimpse of another's dream. Thirteen years earlier, it had been Freya's and Daniel's dream. This time it was Duffy's. But Duffy was resisting it. As if through Duffy's eyes, Timothy dimly saw Lily reaching out through the dark for him, faintly heard her call: "Come to me, Duffy! Come to me and love me . . . !"

Go to her! Timothy commanded with all his strength. *Admit that you still love her and go to her. It's only a dream—take her. Find peace from all that troubles you, find love and peace in her arms. Go to her, Duffy!*

He thought he saw Duffy start to yield, saw him reach out to rend the veil of darkness and throw himself at Lily, but then—

"No!" Duffy cried into his pillow. *"No, no, I don't want to go back. I'm sorry, Lily, but it's wrong. I don't want to go back! I don't want ever . . . ever . . . please . . . no. . . ."*

Quickly the tattered remnant of dream dissolved into oblivion.

"Not quite," Timothy said, gathering Lily back into his arms a little later. "The dream will linger just beyond the threshold of consciousness, the thought that somewhere Lily may be thinking of him, remembering him, perhaps even longing for him. And the next time he dreams . . ."

Of the Bradford Holland coven, Duffy Johnson was perhaps the most resistant to return. Freya had spoken of "making arrangements" for him to come back, but Timothy put his trust in Lily.

At five feet two, she was porcelain-pretty, molded with slim, doll-like perfection. Her hair, drawn back from her face, was burnished gold, and her eyes, behind the dark-rimmed glasses she usually wore, were a rich brown flecked with green. Her nose was pert and her chin round, and her lips were full, red, sensuous.

On the surface, Timothy thought, she was a cliché, the heroine of a thousand bad movies in which the hero takes off the timid little librarian's glasses and exclaims in surprise, "But, my God, you're beautiful!" As if anyone but a fool wouldn't have seen that all along.

Beneath the surface, however, she was something altogether different. There she was a lamia, Timothy thought, and lethal. A beautiful serpentlike sorceress, waiting to strike.

Very well, perhaps he would give her a little something for her pleasure.

Duffy Johnson.

"You're still a little bit in love with him, aren't you," he said, stroking her breast.

She lifted her head from his shoulder, starlight in her startled eyes. "Why in the world would you say that?"

"Isn't it true?"

"Aside from the business at hand, I'm supremely indifferent to Duffy Johnson. You must know that."

He smiled at the lie. "It has often been observed that love and hate can be opposite sides of the same coin. I am not objecting if you desire the boy. He's young, handsome, virile . . . whereas I am an old man."

"An old man fishing for compliments," she said, sweeping a hand over his hard, fat-free belly. "You know you're better equipped than most men half your age."

"Two-thirds my age," he said, pleased.

"Three-fifths," she said, kissing him, "tops. I don't know how you do it."

"Great genes and a deal with the devil. And now, my dear . . ."

Timothy disentangled himself from Lily and began to climb out of bed.

"You're not leaving me, are you?" she asked, as if dismayed, though she knew the answer perfectly well. "The night is young!"

"And you are beautiful beyond compare," Timothy said, pulling on a robe. "No, my dear, I only wish to visit Alida for a few minutes. And then . . ." He leaned down and kissed her. "We shall make all the magic you wish."

"I'll be waiting."

Lily, Lily, he thought, what a mystery you are. Even to me.

Lily Bains had returned to St. Claire some months earlier when her mother was dying of cancer, and Timothy had used his influence to get her a job in the St. Claire library. He had long ago discovered that she had a psychic potential second only to Alida's. So Timothy could hardly keep from wondering from time to time . . .

There was no physical resemblance whatsoever, of course, and Lily's mother had always teasingly refused to confirm or deny the fact. But was it not possible—indeed, probable—that Lily Bains was Timothy Balthazar's other daughter?

Alida's private quarters were larger than Timothy's: two rooms, a bath, and a kitchenette, upstairs on the third floor. The nurse, ever alert, was already on her feet and facing the door when he entered the sitting room, as if she had been expecting him at that very moment. And of course Timothy did visit Alida at least once every night.

Timothy had had her moved here less than a week after Frank Stranger had said those terrible words: *"Timothy, we did all we could."* Frank had advised a nursing home, but here, in her own rooms, Timothy could spend much more time with her.

The sitting room was brightly lit: these were duty hours for the nurse. She smiled at Timothy and nodded and murmured, "She's doing well, resting comfortably." Meaningless words.

The bedroom door was ajar, and Timothy opened it farther, admitting more light, but only a little, as if he were afraid of disturbing his sleeping daughter . . . this child who lived like a puppet at the end of tubes and wires. Could she speak if she wanted to, Timothy wondered, with the feeding tube threaded through her right nostril? Or had her vocal cords already rusted away? The nurses shifted her position at regular intervals, they gave her frequent massages, a therapist came each day to flex her body and maintain, if possible, some muscle tone and prevent physical deterioration. But it seemed to Timothy that, like a ghostly presence, Alida was fading away, each day growing more insubstantial and ethereal. Even now, lying on her back, her face in repose, she seemed almost to float over her bed rather than rest upon it, as if one night soon she might be wafted away like smoke and vanish forever.

But Timothy was not going to let that happen.

He had struck a bargain.

One by one, the members of the Holland coven would soon be returning, to whatever fate they deserved.

Nicole St. Claire would come with them.

Increasingly, Timothy had the feeling that Nicole was the real key to the recovery of his daughter. The Griffin, the Prince of Power, Lord Lucifer, wanted her destruction, this last of a house of his ancient enemies.

And now, as never before, Nicole was vulnerable. Except for the Johnson boy and perhaps a few friends, she was alone in the world. She no longer had the protection of her grand-mother, that old woman more powerful and dangerous than anyone knew.

Julia St. Claire was dead.

NEW YORK CITY, 1993

Duffy learned of Julia's death three days before the funeral. He arrived back at his room late in the evening, as usual, and looked at his mail. There wasn't much, just junk, plus last week's edition of the St. Claire *Chronicle*. More junk, as far as he was concerned. His parents subscribed to it for him, and he was not about to tell them that his principle interest in St. Claire was to avoid it. He was thankful that he no longer had any close friends or relatives there, and that his parents had retired to South Carolina, so that he no longer had the slight-est reason to visit his hometown, ever again.

Still, a certain sense of filial obligation and perhaps some random curiosity caused him to scan the paper briefly from time to time, and the notice leaped to his eye: Julia St. Claire, who had died in New York City on April 20, was to have her requiem Eucharist on Saturday, May 8, at 3 P.M. at St. Jude's

Episcopal Church in St. Claire. Her ashes would be interred in St. Jude's memorial garden. . . .

Duffy had a sense of incredulity, of a waking dream. This was impossible. Aunt Julia couldn't have died. Aunt Julia was forever. Aunt Julia was someone you could count on. Aunt Julia . . .

There had to have been a previous article, an obit in the *Times* or the *Chronicle.* He had the *Times* only back to Sunday, but he found an earlier *Chronicle,* still in its mail wrapper.

There was the notice . . . Julia St. Claire, dead at seventy-one . . . a member of the founding St. Claire family . . . active in civic functions for many years . . . survived by a granddaughter, Nicole St. Claire, of New York City. . . .

Aw, jeez, Aunt Julia!

Now came guilt. How many times had he seen Nicole and Aunt Julia in the half-dozen years he had been in New York? He could count them on his fingers. There were the times Aunt Julia had taken Nicole and him to see *The Nutcracker* and *Coppélia,* Nicole's favorites. And most Thanksgivings. But not last Thanksgiving. Or the one before. Dear God, had it been a couple of years since he had even *spoken* to Aunt Julia? She had phoned him and gently chided him for not writing to his parents.

She would never do that again.

But what about Nicole? What was happening to her? She might *need* him, for Chrissake!

He looked at his watch. Almost ten-thirty. Too late to call. Fuckit, call anyway.

He found Nicole's number in his address book. She answered on the third ring.

"Nicole, it's Duffy. I'm sorry for calling so late . . ."

"Duffy!"

She sounded pleased, and Duffy's heart lifted a little. "I just got last week's *Chronicle* and found out about Aunt Julia, and God, I am so sorry."

"Thank you, Duffy . . ." Now she sounded a little bewildered. "You didn't get my note?"

"Note? What note?"

"I phoned you several times but you weren't in—"

"I only shower and sleep here. I should have an answering machine."

"—so I sent you a note. Actually, I sent out notices to a number of people in Grandma's address book, people not in St. Claire, in case they wanted to come to the funeral. My goodness, I hope they got them!"

"Nickie, if I had known about Aunt Julia, I would have been right there with you, you know that, don't you?"

"Oh, I know that, Duffy."

"I feel so goddamned guilty for not keeping in closer touch!"

"But we understood about that, Duffy! My God, you've been so busy! You completed pre-med in three years with top grades, and now you're in medical school—"

"That's no excuse, Nickie, and you know it."

Nicole's voice began to rise. "Duffy, Grandma was proud of you! She was so proud of you! She loved you, Duffy—"

"Yeah, and I sure gave her a chance to say so, didn't I? Right now I'm so ashamed—"

"Don't you say that! Don't you ever say you did anything to be ashamed of!" Duffy suddenly realized that Nicole was weeping bitterly. *"Don't you ever! She was proud of you and loved you, and don't you* ever *say you have to be ashamed!"*

"Nickie . . . please . . . I'm sorry . . ." Duffy gave her a moment to calm herself. She couldn't know she was only deepening his guilt. "Nickie, I promise you. I will try . . . *try* never again to do anything . . . that might make Aunt Julia ashamed of me . . . or me ashamed of myself."

"Just remember that she loved you and was so proud . . ."

"I promise you, I will try to live my life as if it is a monument in her honor."

Maybe it was a ridiculous, sentimental, melodramatic thing to say, but . . . he had a feeling Nicole needed to hear it. And it wasn't really such a bad ideal, was it?

"God bless you, Duffy," Nicole said after a moment.

"How are you going to get up there? For the funeral, I mean?"

"Fly up on Friday, I guess. Though I *hate* those little planes, they scare the hell out of me. But I don't drive."

"Can't you get someone else to drive you up?"

"No one I'd want. I don't know of any girl who's free who knew Grandma that well, and the guys . . ."

Duffy could guess about the guys. "You don't have anyone steady?"

"No. Not for quite a while." Her tone said, And not looking for anyone.

Duffy took a couple of deep breaths. He didn't really want to do what he was about to do, so he was already ashamed of himself, good intentions so soon shot to hell. But he would be even more ashamed if he didn't do it.

"Look, Nicole, if we get a good early start, say six, six-thirty in the morning, we should get there in plenty of time—"

"No, Duffy, I can't let you. You're in *medical* school, it's the end of the school year, I know it's a grind—"

"You're in college, that's a grind too. I'm pretty sure I can work it out, go up Saturday, come back Sunday. I'll let you know tomorrow."

Nicole hesitated. "Well, if you're sure you want to."

Duffy was far from sure. St. Claire was the last place he wanted to return to. Except for Aunt Julia.

He said, "I'm sure. I'll reserve a rental car first thing in the morning."

"And I'll make hotel reservations. It's not worth opening up the house for one night. I'll pay, of course."

"Hell, no, you won't pay," Duffy said indignantly. "We'll split everything down the middle!"

They talked a few minutes longer, Duffy listening carefully to Nicole's tone, and she seemed calmer. Her grandmother's health had been failing for some time, apparently, and Julia had finally succumbed to congestive heart failure. But she had gone fairly quickly and easily. Nicole herself was doing fine, she assured Duffy: her grandmother's church friends were a big help and so was her New York lawyer, a Mr. Craddock. She and Duffy would talk again tomorrow.

Okay, Aunt Julia, Duffy thought as he hung up the phone, *I'm going back to St. Claire with Nicole. I don't want to. But once upon a time, when I was eighteen years old, you saved my soul. Didn't know that, did you? (Or maybe you did.) And even*

*if I've been neglectful since then, I'm still yours. I promise you,
whenever Nicole needs me—and I think she needs me now—I'll
be there.*

When Duffy double-parked in front of Aunt Julia's East Side
condo at six-thirty on Saturday morning, he had to admit he
was a little worried. He wanted a pleasant trip for both Nicole
and himself, but they were going to have to spend six or seven
hours alone together going to St. Claire, and again coming
back, and, put quite simply, what were they going to talk
about? What did they have in common after all this time? It
had been different a couple of years ago with Aunt Julia
around, two adults and a kid, but now?

He got out of the rented Taurus, leaving the motor running, and went up onto the sidewalk.

Then, as Nicole came out of the foyer doorway, all his
misgivings were forgotten.

Like Duffy, Nicole was dressed for traveling, in jeans and
a knit shirt. She carried a single bag, and her purse hung from
her shoulder. She was taller and slimmer than he remembered,
and her hair was tied back from her face in a ponytail. She
walked with all the sway and swagger of a confident woman,
and beamed a smile of pure pleasure as she reached out to
him.

Duffy struck a pose of astonishment that was only part
fake. "Oh, my God," he cried out, *"it's Audrey Hepburn!"*

Nicole uttered a little shriek of delight, her fingers fluttering to her mouth, and her sway became a stagger. Duffy
caught her with one arm around the arch of her back and,
brushing her fingers aside, kissed her on the mouth, fully and
resoundingly.

"But I don't look like Audrey Hepburn!" she said, still
laughing.

"Don't tell me I don't know Audrey Hepburn when I see
her! *Roman Holiday. Sabrina. Breakfast at Tiffany's.* Face it,
kid, they don't make 'em like that anymore."

"Duffy, still the movie buff."

"My dad adored Audrey Hepburn."

"Everybody's dad adored Audrey Hepburn." They kissed
again.

This was going to be a great trip!

Chatter. Why in the world had he thought they would have nothing to talk about? There were a hundred things to talk about. Nicole talked as easily about her grandmother as if she were alive, but with full recognition that she was not. The grief and panic Duffy had sensed during their telephone conversation seemed alleviated, if not quite gone. And Duffy had so much to say about his fellow students and teachers and incidents in med school that he was in danger of talking Nicole's ear off. Yet she seemed eager to hear it all, even asking questions from time to time to make him fill out the story. When had he last had a date like this? When had he *ever*?

He just felt so goddamn happy and lucky to be with Nicole—*restored* was the word!—that by the time they were on the Thruway and traffic was thinning out, he had to ask: "Look, I don't want you to misunderstand. I'm delighted to be driving you up to St. Claire. But I don't understand how it is that *a girl like you* doesn't have a steady guy who'd take you up, and half a dozen others standing in line."

Nicole's smile faded. She turned away from him and looked out through the windshield.

Duffy lost some of his happy feeling. He said, "I'm sorry. It's none of my business."

"What about you?" Nicole asked after a moment. "Do you have a steady girl?"

"Not in years."

"That's hard to believe. What happened to what's-her-name, Adrienne?"

"Oh, Adrienne!" Looking back after six years, Duffy could smile. "Let me tell you, Nickie, that little lady came close to making me swear off women forever."

"Good Lord, Duffy, what happened?"

"I guess we only really got together after you had left St. Claire. Once I became captain of the football team, I finally became hot shit to Adrienne. And believe me, nobody could get to a guy like Adrienne could. But I was in love, or thought I was, and I was respectful. Other guys got laid after a winning game, but Adrienne said that was a no-no, and I respected that. Man, how I respected that. I, goofball Duffy Johnson, even respected how when the son of her folks' best friends came home from college for holidays, she *had* to go out with him from time to time. How she *had* to leave town to go to some special dance or a college prom with him. And when in the spring she sweetly informed me that she was pregnant and going to marry this gorgeous college hunk, the one true love of her life—man, did I respect that!"

"Poor Duffy."

"Which inaugurated the all-women-are-no-damn-good period of my life, during which I did some things I am thoroughly ashamed of. But let's not talk about that."

"And since then?"

"Nicole, doing pre-med in three years doesn't leave much time for romantic adventures. I had to work my tail off. The first two years of med school were actually easier than pre-med. But I wasn't ready for serious involvement, and I found out I'm just not the type to fool around. Sooner or later, somebody gets hurt, so finally you say, Never again."

Nicole contemplated him for a moment. "You know what I think? I think you're still a very caring, responsible guy, Duffy."

"Yeah, I'm a pussy cat," Duffy agreed, a little embarrassed. And then, just for the heck of it, he decided to dare her. "So okay, Nickie, darlin'," he said, " 'I've shown you mine—you show me yours.' "

She stared at him for a moment. Then, with a little smile, she lifted her chin, thrust out her lower lip, and said, almost defiantly, "I'm frigid."

Duffy grinned. "That I doubt."

"Why should you doubt?"

"I think Aunt Julia probably gave you a very healthy upbringing."

"I think she did, but even so . . . oh, I'm not frigid *in my head*, Duffy. Just thinking about it, I'm not frigid at all. I like being around sexy guys, and I even like fooling around a little. But when it comes right down to it, when it comes to actually *doing* something about it . . ." Nicole shook her head. "Hm-mm. Even if I like the guy. I might as well be out in the kitchen, making a sandwich."

They laughed together, but Duffy heard a note of genuine worry in Nicole's voice. "Don't worry, Nickie. Someday the right guy will come along, and then . . . and then you'll come out of the kitchen. I promise you."

He felt her gaze on his face, felt the warmth of her smile, as he tooled along the sun-drenched highway.

"Why am I telling you this stuff, Duffy? I've never told anyone, not even Grandma, and she was the one person who might have helped me. But it's too late now, so I'm telling you. I feel like I'm talking to some kind of intimate girlfriend."

"Oh, thanks, I think."

They laughed together, and Duffy felt happier than he had in months. When Nicole put her hand on the back of his neck, it seemed to belong there.

At about one-thirty Nicole asked Duffy to pull over to the side of the road and they got out of the car. The sun was bright and the air clear, and they were on a crest high enough that, looking west, they could see the town of St. Claire spread out below them—the church steeples, the main street, the town square—and beyond it the glint of the lake. For a time Nicole said nothing, and when she spoke, it was musingly.

"It's strange. I was born and raised here. For the most part, I had a very happy childhood here. Oh, I didn't leave under the happiest circumstances, but St. Claire was home to me, and mostly a good home. My grandmother was not one to sentimentalize St. Claire, but this was her town, our town, and I can understand why she would want to be buried here. She still has friends here who loved her. So why do I feel almost like I'm entering enemy territory?"

Jesus Christ, Duffy thought, *you too?*

He said, "Don't worry. We won't go down there till you're ready."

She gave him a grateful smile and said, "I'm ready."

"Then . . . as they say in the movies, Let's do it!"

They got back into the car, and twenty minutes later they were registering at the Hotel St. Claire. Nicole had asked for "separate rooms, near each other if possible," and the clerk told them the rooms were adjoining, if they cared to open the connecting door. Which they did, so that they could talk back and forth while changing clothes. Like having a suite, Nicole said.

They arrived at St. Jude's at ten till three and were immediately ushered to a front pew. Good timing, in Duffy's opinion. They didn't appear rushed, and yet they didn't have to stand around talking to people. That would come later.

The service went smoothly. This was not enemy territory. Definitely not. The church was almost full, and Duffy knew that most of the people who had come had liked and admired Julia.

Surreptitiously, Duffy kept a careful watch over Nicole. All morning she had seemed to be holding up well. But during the homily, when the priest recalled Julia's many contributions to the parish and the community, and spoke of her as having been "a good shepherdess," he realized that she was weeping silently and that behind her hands she was shredding her handkerchief with her teeth. He wanted terribly to put an arm around her and comfort her, but of course that would never do, not here, not now. So he reached over as unobtrusively as possible and clasped her upper arm, and tried very hard to send her the thought, *I know; I loved her too; and she knew we loved her. She lives in us.* Nicole's hand and handkerchief slowly dropped away from her mouth. She looked at him, and though her tears still flowed, the smile she gave him, a smile acknowledging love shared, was as beautiful as any he had ever seen.

When they went to the communion rail together, she needed no assistance. Her step was steady and sure.

While the organ played, the congregation followed the priest, Nicole, and Duffy out into the memorial garden where Julia's ashes rested, for the final prayers, the last amen, and, of course, that long line of people who wanted to hold Nicole's hand, embrace her, perhaps share a tear. But Nicole was done with shedding tears, at least for now. God, Duffy was proud of her! He watched her with his heart in his throat. Some of these old men and women really were grief-stricken, that was obvious, but they had only to touch Nicole's hand and see her smile to find comfort.

The St. Claire magic was still alive. It lived on in Nicole.

The line was nearly at an end and people were drifting toward their cars in the church parking lot when a tall blond woman approached Nicole, almost shyly, holding out her hand.

"Nicole . . ."

As if they shared a common nervous system, Duffy felt Nicole stiffening beside him. The woman before them was so flawlessly beautiful as to seem almost artificial, sculpted, a waxworks figure. Her smile was hesitant, her dark violet eyes beseeching. Duffy felt a warmth coming from her, but Nicole resisted it. She seemed to extend her own hand only reluctantly.

"Nicole, I'm Freya Kellgren."

"I know," Nicole said tonelessly as they shook hands. She withdrew her hand almost at once.

The woman bit her lip. "I hope you don't mind my coming here today. I barely knew your grandmother. But I wanted to speak to you . . ."

She glanced at Duffy as if expecting him to leave, or at least turn away. Nicole said, "This is Duffy Johnson. An old friend. My cousin, actually." Duffy knew she was in fact saying, *Duffy stays.* He and Miss Kellgren acknowledged each other with a smile and a nod.

"I wanted to speak to you, Nicole, because . . . I don't know if you knew or understood that your father was very dear to me."

Duffy could feel some of the stiffness, like a breath, going out of Nicole.

"I know. He told me."

"I wanted so much to meet you, to know you. But I never had a chance. After you lost your father, I thought that the last thing you needed was a strange woman intruding on your grief, so I stayed away. But now . . ."

"It was good of you to come, Miss Kellgren."

"Freya, if you wish. Nicole, I just want to tell you that if there is ever anything I can do for you, you have only to let me know. Anything at all at any time. Please remember that."

"Thank you, Freya."

"Your father seemed to think that you and I might have a great deal to offer to each other. Perhaps one day we can find out."

Duffy felt a certain yielding in Nicole, a lowering of her guard. He waited for Nicole's response . . .

. . . but he never heard it. At that moment, a deep male voice said, "Duffy!" and a big arm encircled his shoulders, turning him away from the two women. Startled, Duffy found himself looking into the eyes of a stranger.

"Duffy, my boy, how are you?"

No, not a stranger. Duffy knew the craggy-handsome face, the silver-streaked hair, the colorless laser eyes under the bristling brows. This was the lawyer who had accompanied Aunt Julia to the hospital on the night that Nicole was attacked in the parking lot. Timothy Balthazar, that was the name. But why in the world should Timothy Balthazar remember Duffy? Why greet him with such surprising warmth?

As if to answer a question with a question, Balthazar asked, "How are your parents, Duffy? Enjoying South Carolina?"

"Very much, sir."

"I remember your father was quite a Charleston buff. When I had to make a business trip down there some years ago, he told me all about the old part of the city, its history, its landmarks, its antebellum social life, he even drew me a free-hand map of the most important streets. Turned out he'd never even been there! I said, 'Hell, Larry, come down with me, we'll take a few days and explore the place together!' But unfortunately he couldn't spare the time. . . ."

Duffy had known that his father had at least a passing acquaintance with Timothy Balthazar—high school principals are apt to know some prominent citizens—but Balthazar made them sound like old and dear friends. Duffy tried to remember what he knew, what he had heard, about Timothy Balthazar. Not much, really, aside from the Aunt Julia connection and some nonsense about Luciferianism. But he found himself warming to the man.

Balthazar tipped his head toward Nicole. "Lovely girl. Are you close?"

Duffy wasn't sure how to answer. "Not really. I used to baby-sit her when we were kids, but I haven't even seen her for a couple of years. Then I read about Aunt Julia in the *Chronicle* and gave her a call."

Balthazar nodded understandingly. "A young man could do a lot worse than Nicole St. Claire, but . . ." He looked unsmiling at Duffy for a moment, almost grim, as if considering his words. "You're going to think me presumptuous, Duffy, and I hope you'll forgive me. I happen to believe you're headed for a successful, even brilliant, medical career."

"Why, thank you, sir—"

Balthazar halted him with an upheld hand. "I've been tracking you. Excellent grades in pre-med, highest passes in medical school, and now honors in every course you're taking. Keep it up, and when you finish your training you'll be able to go almost anywhere you want. But I want you to come back here."

Never, Duffy thought automatically, but he said nothing.

"You may think you could do better in one of the big-city prestige institutions," Balthazar continued, "but you'd be wrong. In such a situation, you'd be merely a cog, no matter how important a cog. No, Duffy, to realize your full potential, you need *your own* hospital or clinic."

Duffy smiled. He was quite content to let Balthazar have delusions of grandeur for him, but, God, the man did know how to push buttons.

A clinic of his own! Practicing and teaching diagnostic medicine. During his Physical Diagnosis course, his first experience of real, hands-on medicine, Duffy had discovered he had a knack for it, perhaps even a genius. Diagnosis depended on factual knowledge, of course: you had to know about the disease before you could recognize it, and Duffy's knowledge was rapidly becoming encyclopedic. But he often recognized a condition before the examination of the patient had hardly begun—sometimes just to *touch* the patient seemed to be enough. And whether it was something as common as strep throat or as rare as leprosy, he was almost invariably right. His instructors spoke of him as being "almost psychic."

But to have a clinic of his own . . . that would take money, a lot of money. Where would he ever find the backing?

"I'm afraid that's a long way off, sir. Perhaps in ten or fifteen years . . ."

"Not so far off," Balthazar said, unsmiling. His gaze held

Duffy's steadily. "Not far off at all. Not if you come back to St. Claire."

Duffy found his own smile flagging. Was the man actually saying what he seemed to be saying?

As if in confirmation, Balthazar said, "You belong here, Duffy. Think Mayo, think Menninger, think Duffy Johnson— you're going to have your own clinic. You're one of ours."

He meant: *You're one of mine.* Duffy knew it instinctively. Call it "psychic diagnosis."

But to come back here after he completed his medical training and immediately set up his own clinic . . .

Satan, get thee behind me!

Balthazar smiled. "Think about it, Duffy."

"I'll think about it, sir."

The offer had been made. The details had yet to be decided, the quid pro quo, but Balthazar had the confident air of a man who usually got his way. He looked about, drawing a deep breath, as if savoring the sweet, sunny afternoon.

"By the way, Duffy," he said, "I spoke to an old friend of yours recently."

Duffy instantly became wary. "Old friends" were one reason he preferred to stay away from St. Claire. As casually as possible, he asked, "Oh? Who would that be?"

"Miss Lily Bains. Another exceptionally lovely young woman, if I may say so. She comes back to visit her mother from time to time. She speaks well of you, remembers you very fondly."

Duffy doubted that very much.

Balthazar turned away from him. "Ah, Nicole, my dear . . ."

Duffy stood aside while Balthazar held Nicole's hands and made condolatory and reassuring sounds. ". . . worry about nothing . . . no immediate decisions need to be made . . . and, my dear, I shall miss your grandmother so much. . . ." He had a dismal feeling that Timothy Balthazar knew all about Lily Bains and himself . . . a feeling that all that sick, shameful craziness he had put behind him years ago and tried to forget was catching up with him here in St. Claire, and that it had inescapable consequences.

Consequences that might cost him his life or his soul.

He did not want the power, the wealth, the success Timothy Balthazar was offering him, not at the cost of his soul. He just wanted to get the hell out of St. Claire and never come back again.

"It never occurred to me to wonder how in the world Grandma could afford to own a large condo in New York and also a big old house in St. Claire that she only used a month or two out of the year. We always lived simply, I guess you'd say—well, you remember. Grandma never had any full-time help, just a cleaning woman twice a week and a yard service. She kept me on a strict allowance, and when I packed my own lunch for school, she split the cost of a cafeteria lunch with me. That's how I earned extra money. And now I find . . . that money was never any problem at all."

Nicole's voice was ragged with fatigue, her eyes were swollen, her face was pale. They had spent almost three hours at "Aunt" Martha Cummings's house, where Nicole had kept up a wonderfully cheerful facade while nibbling constantly at the buffet and reminiscing with the many guests about her grandmother. Finally Duffy had made excuses to Mrs. Cummings and dragged Nicole away. They had taken a leisurely drive around the lake and wound up at the Moonlight Inn, where they had had supper at a quiet corner table. In the bar, a pianist and a banjo player were making good-time music, but here in the nearly empty dining room, the sound was pleasantly distant.

"What are you going to do about the house?"

"Keep it, for the time being. I promised Aunt Martha I'd come back for vacation, when I could, just like Grandma did. And I couldn't possibly stay anywhere else but the house. But Mr. Balthazar has been after Grandma for years to sell it to him, so maybe eventually . . ."

Duffy tried to put himself in Nicole's place. A twenty-year-old kid . . . no parents, no brothers or sisters or close cousins . . . loses the grandmother who raised her, the one person who gave her a sense of security . . . suddenly abandoned, finding herself all alone in the world . . . not even a boyfriend or girlfriend close enough to make this trip with her . . . just a distant cousin named Duffy Johnson she's hardly seen in recent years, and now this long, trying, sorrowful day, when she laid her grandmother to rest. . . .

How in hell could he possibly give her comfort?

Patting his hand, she smiled and answered his unspoken question. "You've been awfully good to me, Duffy. I don't know how I would have gotten through this day without you."

It wasn't enough. He said, "Nicole, I have an idea. You look like you're about to drop. Let's go back to the hotel. We'll take a shower and put on our pajamas. I've got a bottle of Scotch, and we'll turn the lights down and put some soft music on the radio. Then we'll cuddle up on your bed and have a couple of drinks and talk for a while, and when you drop off, I'll tuck you in."

Only as he spoke did he realize that his words might not sound as innocent as they were meant to be, and he waited for disillusionment to appear on Nicole's face. But it didn't happen. As she rose from the table, she leaned over and kissed him softly on the mouth. "Dear old Duffy," she said. "Still my baby-sitter."

But that left him in a quandary. Just what exactly *had* his words led Nicole to expect of him? At times throughout the day they had seemed to share thoughts almost telepathically, but now he had no idea of what was going on in her head. All he really knew was that he wanted desperately neither to offend nor to disappoint this sweet girl who was going through such a rough time.

Certainly she seemed much more cheerful and reenergized as he drove them back to the hotel. She turned on the radio, found some music she liked, and hummed along, almost bouncing on the seat as she danced in place. She was obviously looking forward to something when they got to the hotel . . . but what, exactly?

They left the car in the hotel garage. Nicole took his hand and swung their arms as they walked down the ramp. She was still humming softly. When they passed under an overhead lamp, Duffy saw that her eyes were bright, her smile almost mischievous.

In her room, she turned on only a bedside lamp. Turning to him, she pressed a forefinger to her lips and then to his. "Give me ten minutes or so. Fifteen."

Duffy went to his room, leaving the connecting door slightly ajar. He felt an ambivalent sense of relief. The finger-kiss might be considered promising, but she hadn't made any suggestive little jokes about scrubbing each other's backs, so perhaps that answered the question.

He killed a little time by getting ice from a machine in the corridor. Then he undressed and took a leisurely shower. Jesus, he thought, he was making too much of this. This was *Nicole,* for Chrissake. She had gotten through a long hard day in reasonably good shape, and all she wanted from him now was a kiss, a cuddle, and a little Scotch. If she had other requirements, she was no innocent, she would let him know.

He was pulling on his pajama jacket when he thought he heard a sound from Nicole's room. He picked up the Scotch and a pair of real-glass glasses, and, tapping on the door with the bottle, called, "Yuh decent?"

The answer was a small strangled cry, a familiar sound, that froze him. He thought of a dark parking lot at night and a hysterical girl with blood on her face.

The cry, half sob and half growl, was repeated.

Dropping the bottle and the glasses, he flung open the door and threw himself into Nicole's room. She was kneeling on the floor in her pajamas, pawing through her open suitcase. She found a small container and pulled the lid off. Before he could stop her, she dumped some orange and white capsules into her hand, and threw them into her mouth.

"*No!*"

Even as Duffy dropped to his knees and wrapped his arms around her, she gagged and spewed the capsules out again.

"Did you swallow any?"

Nicole shook her head. "I hate them, I hate them!" she said, sobbing. "I don't want to take them!"

Then, straining to break free of his arms, she threw her head back and emitted a series of soft throaty cries more like howls than sobs, and Duffy felt her pain, her anguish. Jesus Christ, why hadn't he seen this coming? Duffy Johnson, the famous diagnostician. Nicole had been *too* up, *too* animated on their way back here, almost manic. She had been living on the thin edge of frayed nerves for days, and they had finally given out. While *he*, like a dumb-shit kid, had been thinking only about sex! Stupid, stupid, stupid . . . !

Suddenly Nicole broke away from him with such force that she sent him rolling on the floor. Springing to her feet, she tore open her pajama jacket, sending the popped buttons flying. She shoved the pants down and kicked them away as if they were on fire. She threw herself at a wall, bounced off of it, ran at the bed and fell over a corner, dropped to the floor and leaped to her feet again.

By then, Duffy was back on his feet and he managed to grab her. But her strength was amazing; he could barely hold her. Again, she threw her head back, and her growls were more animallike than ever. Her face seemed to be undergoing a physical transformation, growing more savage: her nostrils flared and her lips twitched, drawing far back to expose canines that seemed to glisten and grow longer, even as Duffy stared at them.

An illusion, perhaps, but a frightening illusion, and it caused Duffy to relax his grip on Nicole just enough for her to twist around in his arms. His jacket had been pulled off of one shoulder, and opening her mouth wide, Nicole clamped her teeth down on the bare flesh. He felt the wetness of her mouth, the sharpness of her cusps, the quivering of her jaw as it tightened.

He ignored the pain. He found himself kissing her cheek; stroking her hair, her shoulders, her back; making soothing sounds, hushing her, whispering reassurances. Once again he tried to send a message directly into her mind: *It's all right. You're not alone. Duffy is here, and he's not going to leave you, not while you need him. It's all right. . . .*

He felt her slowly beginning to relax. The teeth, the quivering jaw, eased up on his shoulder. With a little mewling sound, Nicole collapsed against him, weeping.

The bed had been turned down. He picked Nicole up, cradling her in his arms, and carried her to it. He laid her down on it very gently. As she curled up in a ball within his arms, he continued to soothe her.

Aunt Julia, I'm doing the best I can. Just don't let me do anything dumb.

At last Nicole's breathing became smoother and she seemed to have stopped weeping.

"Feel better?"

Against his shoulder, she nodded.

"I can call a doctor . . . ?"

Her *no* was barely audible.

"Those capsules, they're your medicine? Do you want one?"

She shook her head. "They're tranquilizers. I hate them, they make me into a zombie. But sometimes they're the only thing that helps, so I keep them handy just in case."

"These episodes happen often?"

"Not often. Not lately."

Gently, Duffy began withdrawing his arms from Nicole and sitting up.

"Don't leave me."

"Don't worry. I'm not going to. I'm just going to make us more comfortable."

He brought pillows from the closet and from his own room and piled them up. He poured a couple of stiff drinks on ice and handed one to Nicole. By that time, she was sitting up in bed with the sheet drawn over her lap and her buttonless jacket closed. He said, "Drink up. Doctor's orders."

She bolted the Scotch like a dose of medicine and handed the glass back to him.

"More? Want some music?"

She shook her head and held her arms out to him.

He placed their glasses on the nightstand, sat down beside her, and took her back into his arms. She touched his shoulder where the purple bite marks were now very apparent.

"I'm sorry."

"Hey. Coming from my Nickie, it's the next best thing to a kiss."

She looked into his eyes for a moment, seemed to be searching them. Perhaps she found what she was looking for. She touched his cheek with her fingertips. Then, sliding an arm around his neck, she very carefully placed her mouth on his.

Until that moment, Duffy had not felt the slightest sexual response to Nicole's nakedness or the soft warmth of her body in his arms. Even if he had, he would have ignored it; Nicole was in trouble, Nicole needed help. But now his response was instantaneous and total, flesh engorging fully and mind swirling like a dragon kite in a high, hot wind.

Oh, Jesus God, he thought, *don't let me hurt this girl. Not Nickie, never Nickie.*

He wanted her, but she was so terribly vulnerable. She wasn't here to feed his hunger, he was here to give her comfort and protection, and if he failed her he would never forgive himself.

As they kissed, he slid his hand under her jacket, half expecting Nicole to stiffen and pull away from him. Instead, as he cupped her breast and stroked her nipple, he was rewarded with a smile and a comfortable sigh.

After that, perhaps because he was so intent on giving her exactly what she wanted, rather than grasping his own pleasure, everything was easy. Every kiss, every touch, was for her, and when he finally opened her up, as gently as unfolding the petals of a flower, and stroked that honeyed spot, her sigh of pleasure, "Oh, that is so good," was reward enough.

But not the only reward. Soon after that, he realized that *she* was making love to *him.* She knelt over him, clasping him within, pressing and weaving while raining a hundred kisses on his face, still taking her pleasure but giving every bit as much as she received. And she had thought she was frigid, this girl, this woman, this lovely child! *He* had thought only to please her, and she was teaching *him* what a treasure this communion of the flesh and spirit could be.

"Now, Duffy, *now!*" she whispered, and for a long, searing, mindless moment, *now!* happened.

Afterward, they turned out the light and lay in each other's arms, kissing a little, laughing a little. "Oh, Duffy, Duffy," Nicole murmured happily, "you were right, I'm out of the kitchen at last . . . because you're still my Duffy."

"Still your Duffy," he agreed. "You're not alone, Nicole. You've got me. As long as you need me. Whenever you need me, I'll be there for you."

It was a commitment of sorts, and perhaps an unwise one. He knew that. As a medical student with his internship and residency still ahead of him, he would be well advised not to take on any unnecessary burdens or obligations. But there was simply no way he could turn his back on Nicole, not at a time like this.

"Then you've got me too," Nicole said, sighing as she drifted toward sleep. "And I promise you . . . whenever you need me . . . when you really, really need me . . . I'll be there, Duffy . . . I'll be there too. . . ."

CHAPTER 12

"**M**adness," Philip Steadman said, laughing, "absolute madness! Timothy, the Order hasn't survived for centuries through open slaughter, and it certainly can't do so in the modern world. We're not the Manson 'family,' for God's sake."

"I do not propose to emulate the Mansons," Timothy said mildly, "not quite. And I'm speaking hypothetically, of course."

Steadman, the leader of a powerful West Coast convocation, was a tall, darkly handsome man in his early fifties, with a hard, bronzed surfer's body. He had flown in from Los Angeles for a week in New York, and Timothy had come down from St. Claire to meet with him. Now he ceased pacing the sitting room of Timothy's hotel suite and turned to face him.

"*Hypothetically*, human offerings should be rare, and highly selective and discreet, and the body should be made to vanish. If you try to make half a dozen people vanish all at once . . . madness."

"The bodies won't vanish," Timothy said. "That's part of

my plan. As with the Manson case, they will be highly visible. And the supposed killer will be known, whether or not convicted."

Steadman stared at Timothy. "A scapegoat."

Timothy smiled thinly. "I don't know that 'goat' is quite the word."

It was clear to Timothy that to carry out his plan for the Bradford Holland coven—his part of the bargain with his lord and master—he would almost certainly need help. Not much, not much at all, but some.

He had his own small personal coven in St. Claire, of course—Lily, Freya, and Bruno Krull, the young sheriff of St. Claire. Freya, though problematic, would be useful in luring Nicole back to St. Claire, and Bruno was an unquestioning extension of Timothy's will. Frank Stranger, too, might be helpful up to a point; he would play along as long as he didn't know too much and ran no risk.

Timothy was reluctant to look for further help within his own convocation, since most members, despite their terrible oaths, hardly thought of themselves as killers. They were much too "enlightened" to do more than offer the occasional animal sacrifice. Timothy had, then, only two women and one man, possibly two, to assist him in dealing with a half-dozen young people.

No, he needed help, someone powerful and trustworthy. He thought he might have such an ally in Philip Steadman.

When Timothy didn't elaborate, Steadman shook his head. "It sounds too complex, too risky. You're planning something that will get national headlines and the most thorough scrutiny. If you'd tell me more about your plan . . ."

Steadman continued to pace. He ran his fingers through his thick black hair and down his face. A man torn, Timothy thought. For all his caution, for all his objections, he longed to be convinced. He hungered to be in on the kill.

Timothy leaned forward in his chair. "Philip, I will promise you this. I intend to take no unnecessary chances. If at any time it seems imprudent to continue, I shall quit and live to act another day. However, I foresee nothing but complete success and great rewards for both of us."

"Such as?"

Timothy smiled. He would give Steadman a little more bait. "Philip, I am sure you have had many glimpses of hell and its creatures. Probably your followers have had a glimpse of our lord and master in you. But have you as yet gained such favor with our lord and master that when he comes into this world he sees through your eyes and you are as one with him?"

Steadman didn't answer, ceased to move.

"If you've never had that glorious experience, Philip, I think I can promise you that if you help me, you soon will."

For a long minute Steadman remained still, as if considering the possibilities, and Timothy hardly breathed.

"You know, Timothy," Steadman said at last, "there is one member of that coven in whom I have a personal interest. I wouldn't want any harm to come to her unnecessarily. I have other plans for her."

Timothy expelled his breath and gave the man his most reassuring smile. "Philip, join me in this . . . hypothetical endeavor and your protégée's fate is entirely in your hands. I have no personal interest in her whatsoever."

Steadman nodded slowly. "All right. I'm your man, Timothy. We'll do it."

When Steadman left half an hour later, success seemed assured. Timothy went to his bedroom, where Lily lay naked under a sheet, awaiting him.

"Steadman is with us," he said as he began to undress. "And now we have work to do."

Lily stretched her arms out to him. "My very favorite kind."

The scent of blood.

It was in her nostrils, fresh and rich, bringing its taste to her tongue, arousing an insatiable craving and making her jaws ache for foods that were warm and raw and forbidden.

Nicole moaned softly and rolled toward the edge of the bed. She clutched at her pillow and bit hard on one of its corners. This was a passion like no other; even stronger, it sometimes seemed, than her love for Duffy. Surely nothing a man and woman could share could ever be as agonizing, as frustrating, as cruel, as the hunger with which she was cursed.

The spells came two, three, four times a month now, and sometimes lasted for hours. Never before in her life had they been so frequent. They had started again after her grandmother had died, and since then had only grown worse. And the last few weeks . . .

At times, it had been almost as if something in her mind were whispering: *Give in to it . . . you know you want to . . . it's what you really are, stop denying it . . . give in, give in, give in . . .*

But, no, she would *not* give in! She would fight it, fight it!

Then she would think of Freya. She could almost hear Freya saying, *Let me help you . . . your father would want that . . . come back to St. Claire and let me help you. . . .*

And then the hunger again, oh, the hunger. . . .

She whimpered in the dark, wanting to awaken Duffy, and yet fearful of doing so. He had told her to awaken him whenever the hunger came upon her at night, and now she needed his help. She needed to have him hold her in his arms, have him soothe her, calm her, reassure her. She needed his touch, his love. His love, more than anything else, relieved her suffering and restored her to peace. But he had fallen asleep exhausted last night, and he had to be at the hospital early. He was in the last weeks of medical school, the last grinding, grueling weeks, and she had to help him get through them.

That was her mission in life.

To get Duffy through medical school, and not just through it, but at the top of his class. And then through his internship. Help him become the best damn doctor he could possibly be!

She concentrated her thoughts on that objective. Sometimes that helped. Duffy had taught her the trick—to concentrate wholly and exclusively on something other than her own terrible discomfort. *Dear God in Heaven, please grant me the strength to be a help to Duffy instead of a goddamn millstone! Give me strength . . . give me strength. . . .*

This time it didn't work.

A millstone, that's all she was. A goddamn millstone.

Abruptly she sat up in bed.

God, she hated Duffy! Hated him! Hated her dependence

on him, hated what she was doing to him, hated him, hated him . . . !

Of course she did not. She loved him: if there was any life she loved beyond her own, it was Duffy's. But she was failing him, she had become a miserable burden, and for that reason she could now turn and look down at his sleeping form, barely perceptible in the dark, and, for a moment or two, immerse herself in complete and bitter loathing.

His pajama jacket was unbuttoned, and she stared at his unprotected throat. Was *his* the blood she smelled? Her jaw trembled at the thought of warm flesh, a beating heart, of tender vital organs . . . why, before he could awaken she could . . .

She wrenched herself away from Duffy, nearly ill, as she caught herself in the midst of the hideous thought. Could she actually do such a thing? How could she even think of it! If she was that dangerous, she should be locked up, hospitalized, imprisoned. . . .

If only there were some raw meat in the apartment, some ground beef or a steak. But she bought fresh meat on a daily basis, only before meals. She didn't dare stock up ahead of time, have it on hand.

Why not? Why the hell not? If raw meat was what she wanted, why the hell shouldn't she have it?

There was no help for it; when she had thoughts like that, she had better take a tranquilizer.

Very carefully, so as not to disturb Duffy, she got out of bed and made her way through the dark to the bathroom. She closed the door before turning on the light. From the mirrored medicine cabinet she took out an amber plastic vial and spilled a single orange and white capsule into her palm. She stared at it.

It would do the job, and fast, especially if washed down with a couple ounces of Scotch. However . . .

Her doctor had prescribed tranquilizers soon after she and her grandmother moved to Manhattan. The only problem was that she had become so sensitive to them that even the smallest dose turned her into a joyless, mindless automaton— a zombie, as she had told Duffy—and the effect could last for days. In a way, the tranquilizers were as bad as the symptoms they were meant to alleviate. Fortunately, as she had become adjusted to her new life in the city, she had ceased to need them, and after the first year, she had rarely used them.

Her grandmother had been loathe to discuss her grandfather's decline and death, but Nicole had gathered that prescription drugs and alcohol had had a lot to do with it.

She was clearly going the way of her grandfather.

No!

In anger she threw the capsule into the sink and washed it down the drain. She put the container back into the cabinet and slammed the door. No, she would *not* turn into a goddamn zombie for everyone's fucking convenience. If she wanted raw meat, she would damn well eat it!

Sobbing, she sat wearily down on the lid of the toilet seat. She placed her elbows on her knees and lowered her head to her forearms. Still hungering, she closed her eyes.

How long she sat there before she smelled the cat, she could not have said.

At first she thought it was merely the remnant smell of the carefully cleaned litter box, there on the bathroom floor. But, no, this was not that smell at all; this was the unique, distinct smell of the cat itself, the cat's fur, the cat's breath, the cat's blood. The cat.

Her mouth flooded with saliva. She swallowed.

She turned off the bathroom light and returned to the darkness of the bedroom. She sniffed very lightly, delicately, singling out and measuring that one complex odor. Her sense of smell, always acute, seemed to have sharpened a thousand-fold. She was quite sure the cat was not in the bedroom. There was a certain, slight cat smell, yes, but a stronger smell wafted in from the hallway.

She followed the smell.

Chucky! Where are you?

She had to find the cat. She gave no thought to what would happen when she did. Certainly she had no thought of harming it. Funny old Chucky, beloved Chucky, was Duffy's cat, and she could no more hurt it than she could hurt Duffy. But just to find it, to hold it in her arms, to press her face into its fur and smell it . . .

Chucky, I'm coming for you . . .

Slowly, silently, following that scent, she crept along the hallway.

She passed bedrooms, another bathroom, kitchen, and dining room. Ghost-light filtered in through the windows to barely illuminate the living room. Here the smell of the cat filled her nostrils. Again her mouth flooded. Her stomach throbbed and her jaw ached.

"Chucky," she whispered, "where are you?"

A fast, scrambling sound, then, and a flickering shadow, as the cat dashed around the coffee table and out of the room. As if by instinct, Nicole almost flung herself upon it, would have grabbed it if she could. But the damned thing had gotten away. Frustration and unexpected anger welled up.

Bending down, she followed the fresh trail of scent back the way she had come, and then through the kitchen door. She crouched there for a moment, her hunger pangs sharpening.

The cat cried out in the dark—not its usual cry for attention, but a cry of fear.

Nicole reached for the wall switch, snapped on the light. The big gray silken-fluffy Persian was in a corner, between the stove and the dishwasher, its tail high and its back humped. Hissing at her as it never had before, hissing as if she were a dangerous stranger, it moved evasively from side to side.

Damn you, you won't get away!

She might as well have spoken aloud to the cat, for she knew it heard and understood. Still crouching, her arms held wide, she moved toward it a few short steps; the cat raised a paw with needle-sharp claws and made a sound like a burning fuse.

Damn you!

Then it was as if her body knew what to do, and she had no wish to stop it. A fine rage of hunger ran through her, and her muscles tightened and relaxed, tightened and relaxed. She didn't think of what she was doing or of what she was about to do; she simply concentrated on the cat with all her animal fury.

Her pajamas were in the way. They seemed to bind, smother, burn her. She was barely conscious of tearing her jacket open and throwing it off. She would never remember yanking her pants loose and letting them fall away as she moved forward, sinking into a deeper crouch.

The cat wove from side to side, hissing, pawing the air with spread claws.

You're mine!

She lowered her haunches, tightening them like steel springs. Her toes sought purchase on the bare floor. She scarcely touched the floor with her fingertips.

Mine!

The cat hissed one more time, and suddenly leaped for a countertop.

At the same instant, snarling, Nicole hurled herself at the cat.

Duffy was dreaming again when he heard Nicole cry out.

Dreaming of Lily Bains.

He had dreamed a lot lately, not nightmares, but muddled, unpleasant dreams, dreams of whispers in the dark, of murmurs, muffled and indistinct, but their meaning clear: *. . . come back . . . come back . . . come back to St. Claire . . .*

He wasn't sure when the dreams had started. Perhaps about the time when, out of the blue, he got the letter from Derek Anderson. ". . . this is the summer of our official reunion, old buddy. Seven years! Our sacred unbreakable vow to get together and give an account of ourselves to each other and Old Nick himself, remember? I'm holding you to it! How about the end of June or early July? . . ."

. . . come back . . . come back to St. Claire . . .

No. Never. That one time, last year with Nicole, was enough.

He thought he probably would have had the dreams even if he hadn't received Derek's letter. Call it residual superstition. Against all reason, he had long dreaded the coming of this summer. It was as if this summer were a test. If he survived it physically and morally intact, that would prove that the god of this world, if he truly existed, no longer had a claim on him. Had never really had one.

And so he dreamed . . . dreamed confused and murky dreams of unholy rituals and demonic visions . . . dreamed of the coven . . . of Derek and Joanne, of Bradford and Gorgeous Gussie . . .

   . . . of Lily Bains . . .

"*. . . She speaks well of you, remembers you very fondly. . . .*"

He did not want to believe that. He had earned her contempt, if not her hatred. The thought that he had left her with anything other than aversion, with any slightest love for him, was a worse punishment.

Hate me, Lily. Despise me.

But I don't hate you, Duffy. Come back. Come back to me. . . .

He saw her, dimly at first, just a cowled cloak outlined in light, black against black, in the distance. Then, as he drifted closer through that utter darkness, it was as if candles were being lit and he began to discern, hazily, her naked body within the cloak. She was a creature made of smoke, pink and golden.

Come to me, Duffy . . .

She reached out to him, beckoning, and he no longer had the will to resist. Smoke became flesh that seemed to glow with its own light.

Come to me, Duffy . . .

He came to her. He could see the flecks of green in her glistening brown eyes. He could see the stiffness of her pink nipples within the darker aureoles. He could see—

He was no more than a foot or two from her. Her lips, so full and red, were open in invitation. But then her eyes widened in shock, or alarm.

"Oh, my God!" she said.

She reached out and touched his bare chest.

He felt the warmth of her palm as it rested against his flesh. He felt the texture of carpeting under his feet. Looking down, he saw his own bare body, arms out from his sides, legs apart and feet solidly planted. The darkness was no longer absolute, and he no longer felt himself to be dreaming. *This was real.* It was as if he had suddenly awakened to find himself in this strange room with Lily. Curtains wafted in blue light at open windows behind her, and he felt the cool night air caressing his body.

"Oh, my God, my God," Lily whispered, "Duffy, speak to me!"

He wanted to. He tried to. He was reaching out for her. But that was the moment he heard Nicole's cry, and instantly, everything started to revert to mere dream-state and fade. He thought he heard Lily calling to him, *Duffy, no, stay with me!* but Nicole cried out again. He tried to make those cries something other than what they were, tried to deny them so that he would not have to awaken, but he failed. Lily was gone, and he was being swept back disembodied through darkness, until those terrible racking cries seemed to be torn from his own throat, and he opened his eyes to see blood-soaked gray fur in his hands, a cat's carcass torn open—

"Nickie!"

He awakened abruptly and completely, with a slamming heart and a sense of panic. He reached out for Nicole. But of course she was not in the bed. Her sobs were barely audible, much more distant than they had been in the dream.

"Nickie?"

He didn't take time to switch on a light. He threw himself out of bed and stumbled through the dark toward the door. In the hallway, he saw the light from the kitchen. He found her there, lying naked on the floor, crying hysterically, her eyes bright with madness. He threw himself down beside her and pulled her into his arms with brutal force.

"Nickie, stop it! You're all right! *Stop it!*"

She shook her head. "I . . . I . . ."

"Take it easy. Get your breath."

"I . . . killed . . ."

What? What was she saying?

"I . . . killed . . . Chucky!"

Chucky? Duffy had a flash of his almost-vanished dream, and he understood. He released a long sigh, whether of relief or of despair, he couldn't have said. "Oh, honey, you didn't kill Chucky."

Shaking her head again, she wept against his shoulder like a brokenhearted child. "I killed him. I couldn't help myself. I killed him."

"Honey, you've been dreaming. It was a bad, bad dream, but only a dream."

"Dream . . . ?" Nicole looked up at him with dazed eyes, as if she were only now beginning to awaken. "But I . . ."

"Nickie, honey, the old Upchucker died of old age long ago. You know that."

"Died?"

"Long ago."

"But I saw him . . ."

"Shh!" He tightened his arms around her, gently rocked her, shushed her, tried by an act of will to impart his own determined calm in her. *The storm is over, Nickie, all over now. The wind is down and the stars are out again, and you've got me with you, no matter what. There's nothing to be afraid of.* It sometimes worked with frightened patients at the hospital, and it worked with Nicole now. Her tears subsided, and he felt her relaxing in his arms.

"Better?" he asked.

She nodded. "I was dreaming," she said wonderingly, "only dreaming."

"Only dreaming."

"I went into the bathroom, and I sat down. I must have fallen asleep, and . . . how did I get into the kitchen?"

"It doesn't matter."

"I must have walked in my sleep . . . like when I was a kid . . . aw, Duffy, no!"

"It's okay, honey. We can handle it."

She shook her head. "I'm getting worse, Duffy."

"We'll get you back into therapy. We should have done it before."

She continued shaking her head. "I've *had* therapy! Everything but electroshock, and that only made my grandfather worse. I've had therapy and tranquilizers and antidepressants, Prozac, Serax, Paxil, you name it and I've had it! The only thing that helps at all is *you*, Duffy, when you hold me; and it's not your fault, but that's not enough anymore. I'm fighting a losing battle!"

"Honey, Paraclete General Hospital has some of the very finest psychiatrists—"

"I've seen them! They've seen me! I'm at the end of my rope. Aside from brain surgery—"

"Jesus God, don't even think of it!"

Nicole gently pulled herself from Duffy's arms, sitting up so that she faced him. "I have only one hope left in all the world, Duffy. Just one crazy, off-the-wall hope."

"All right," he said, still trying to soothe her, "what's that?"

"Freya Kellgren."

Miss Kellgren. The Lady in White. The very sight of whom had inspired fear in children.

Why? What had they seen in this glacially beautiful woman that adults could not? Nicole remembered only that her beauty had seemed a mask for something quite different . . . something literally unspeakable. And yet her father had been in love with Freya Kellgren and had thought she might be able to help Nicole. ". . . she and I together," he had said.

But how? What special powers did Freya Kellgren have that might alleviate or heal Nicole's affliction? Whatever they might be, Nicole knew that her father would never have risked her safety, would never have put her in harm's way. He had trusted Freya Kellgren.

She, however, did not altogether trust Freya. Fairly or not, in Nicole's mind Freya was somehow connected with her father's strange death. (He had not died of the mysterious wounds in his thighs or the bite marks on his neck, according to the coroner, and he had had no drugs in his system—aside from a massive amount of adrenaline. What could have so terrified him that he was, apparently, literally frightened to death?) But she had often recalled their encounter a year ago, after her grandmother's funeral, and then would come that thought again, almost as if Freya herself were trying to tell her something.

. . . let Freya help you, Nicole . . . your father would want that . . . please, let her try . . . go back to St. Claire and let her try . . .

Then, a few weeks ago, she had received a surprising letter from Freya. "Today, exactly a year after I first met you, I cannot help but think of you and your father. I know I'm still

a stranger to you and perhaps always will be, but, thanks to
Daniel, you will never really be a stranger to me. I hope you
don't mind my telling you that. And if sometime we could
perhaps meet for an hour or two . . ."

She would be in St. Claire through the summer, she said,
and in the fall would move back into her Manhattan apartment. Nicole's reply had been polite but noncommittal.

"I've made up my mind," she said now, "and I don't want
to wait until fall. I want to see Freya Kellgren as soon as
possible. I want to find out just what kind of 'help' she had in
mind. What do I have to lose?"

"You don't necessarily have to go back," Duffy said; "you
might be smart to call her first and ask—"

"No." Nicole shook her head. "This isn't something to be
discussed over the telephone. I've got to see her and talk to her
face-to-face and try to get to know her. Even if nothing comes
of it."

She was sitting at the head of the bed in Duffy's arms.
After he had calmed her down, he had picked her up and
carried her into the bathroom. There, under the soothing cas-
cade of a warm shower, he had slowly, gently soaped her body,
held her in his arms, made love to her until she was utterly
limp. Then he had toweled her dry, slipped her into fresh
pajamas, and placed her here on the bed. *Duffy, you dear,
sweet man . . .*

Right now the "dear, sweet man" was wearily rubbing his
eyes. "Duffy, I'm sorry," she said, "this could have waited till
tomorrow."

"No, it's okay. I was just thinking, I can get away for four
or five days at the end of the month. Maybe even a week, if I
can arrange to start my internship a day or two late. That's not
impossible."

"But you don't have to go with me."

"Don't be silly. You don't want to fly, and you're not
experienced enough to drive it alone. Anyway, I don't want
you going anywhere near that damn town without me."

Over the last year, she and Duffy had grown so close that
they often read each other's minds, and occasionally even their
dreams intersected. But Duffy kept certain areas carefully
walled off, and this was one of them.

"Duffy, why do you hate St. Claire so much?"

Duffy slowly removed his arm from her shoulders and leaned away from her. There it was: withdrawal behind a wall.

"I don't 'hate' St. Claire," he said, measuring his words; "I just don't think it's as nice a place as it was when we were kids."

"But how can you say that when you haven't been back in ages and never for any length of time? The last time was overnight, more than a year ago."

He seemed to consider that. Finally he nodded. "Maybe it isn't so much the town as it is me."

"How so?"

"Something that happened. Something I did." Duffy got up off of the bed and wandered across the room. Putting space between us, Nicole thought.

"Nickie, did you ever do something that you just know you're going to be ashamed of for the rest of your life?" He kept his back turned to her.

"Oh, sure. Lots of times."

"No. I'm serious. I don't mean you think of it night and day or that it's ruined your life or anything melodramatic like that. I just mean something so goddamn low that you're never going to forget it and you're going to spend a lot of your life trying to make up for it."

"Do you want to tell me?"

"Not really. If I did, you'd lose respect for me. I wouldn't blame you if you kicked my ass out of this apartment and told me never to come back."

This was Duffy talking. Sweet, honorable Duffy. Nothing Duffy had done could possibly be *that* bad! She smiled and said, "Then maybe you'd better tell me. Anything that bad, I've got a right to know."

He picked up a perfume bottle from the dresser and looked at it with blind eyes, playing for time, and the sickening thought struck her that he was dead serious. He was considering getting dressed and walking out of the apartment without saying another word.

She couldn't let that happen. Couldn't.

"Tell me, Duffy," she said faintly.

He seemed to discover the perfume bottle in his hand. He set it down.

"You remember I told you how Adrienne and I broke up?"

"In the spring of your senior year. She got pregnant by some college kid and married him."

"That's right. And at the time, I blamed her."

"Which set off your women-are-no-damned-good phase."

"Right. I think I went through a kind of belated adolescent rebellion. All of a sudden I was sick and tired of being a goody-goody Nice Young Man, trying to live up to other people's expectations. I wanted to be *bad*, for God's sake! Get in drunken fights and chase women and piss on the sidewalk."

Nicole laughed. "Duffy, I think most kids go through that. It's just part of growing up."

"What I did shouldn't be part of growing up. Was Brad Holland into cults before you left St. Claire?"

"Into . . . *cults*?" The change of subject was so abrupt, she wasn't sure she had heard correctly. "I really wouldn't know. Actually, I didn't know Brad all that well. He was your friend, more than mine—you were all *older* kids."

"Well," Duffy said, "Brad decided that our little gang should become what he called a 'coven' of a Luciferian cult called the Children of the Griffin. Do you know anything about Luciferianism?"

"Not really."

"It's different from Satanism. It's about power and enlightenment, rather than good and evil. Or so they'd have you believe. The Children of the Griffin try to develop their psychic, or intuitive, powers on behalf of the 'god of this world'—which may sound like harmless bullshit, but believe me it's not."

"I believe you."

"So he got Gussie Lindquist and Derek Anderson and Joanne Smith into his coven, easily enough, I guess, but not me. I wasn't even faintly interested in any such crap. I was in love with Adrienne Martineau, and for her I was ready to turn Catholic!"

"But she broke up with you, and you turned Luciferian

instead. Obviously not forever." The picture was plain enough. "How long did this last?"

"Only a few months. Just that summer."

"Well, my goodness, Duffy, is that anything to regret for the rest of your life—"

"There's more to it than that. Nicole, I'm not going to tell you about all the weird shit we were into, not tonight. But you see, there was a girl . . ."

Nicole's heart skipped a beat. *This*, she realized, was what really troubled Duffy.

". . . don't think you knew her. She wasn't quite seventeen, a year or so younger than me. I know this sounds egotistical as hell, but she was crazy in love with me. So when she heard that Adrienne had thrown me over, she came to me and . . . well, tried to take her place, I guess."

"And?"

"I took advantage. Don't get me wrong, I was fond of the kid. But for me, she was a power trip. I could turn her on with a touch of my finger, and she'd do *any*thing for me. And when I made love to her, it wasn't out of affection, it was as if I were saying, 'Fuck you, Adrienne!' "

" 'All women are no damned good.' "

"Yeah, except that I don't think I really believed that, even then. The truth was that I didn't *dare* let myself get too close to a woman. I was afraid."

"I think you cared more for this girl than you were willing to admit."

Duffy sounded almost angry. "And *I* think you keep looking for excuses for me. Listen to this:

"Remember how in our little gang we were all sort of on the same mental wavelength, so that at times it was almost like we could read each other's minds? Sometimes I think it was that more than anything else that held us together. Well, it turned out this girl was on the same wavelength, and Brad thought she had what he called 'great psychic potential.' He wanted me to bring her into the coven. So I did. I led her to believe that that was the only way we could really be together and stay together, because the coven was like a family. So she took the vows and 'wedded' Lucifer, and please don't ask me what that entailed. She did it for me and only for me, and then at the end of the summer, when she knew I was going away to school and she might have expected some kind of commitment—I dropped her. Let her know it was over, finished, kaput. Not only that, but since my folks were retiring to South Carolina, there was very little chance that I'd ever return to St. Claire. Are you beginning to get the picture?"

Nicole shook her head, not in answer but in bewilderment. "I don't understand. You're talking about a Duffy that I don't even know. He isn't you at all."

"Not anymore—I hope to heaven!"

"But . . . what happened to the Duffy of the coven?"

"He died a natural death, but it wasn't easy. After I got to New York, a reaction set in. I guess you could say I became sick in my soul. I was disgusted with the coven but most of all with Duffy Johnson, so much so that I wasn't sleeping and I sure wasn't hitting the books the way I should. That hurt bewildered look on Lily's face when I told her it was all over haunted me. I had about decided that even though I wasn't madly in love with her, I'd go back to St. Claire and ask her to marry me. Get her mother's permission or at least put a ring on her finger. After all, she was bright and pretty and almost seventeen, and any guy'd be lucky to get her. Other young couples have made it through college together—maybe we could too.

"Then Aunt Julia phoned me and asked me to dinner. For the first time in my life, I felt sort of uncomfortable talking to her, so I started making excuses about being real busy right now, just starting pre-med and so forth, but she wouldn't be put off. Maybe she heard something in my voice. She said, very sharply, 'Duffy, I know you're a busy young man, but there is something I must discuss with you, alone and soon. Let me take you to lunch.' So the next day we met at a restaurant on Central Park South."

"Grandma never told me," Nicole said wonderingly.

"Well, it was all pretty personal. When I asked what she wanted to discuss, she put me off, and we talked about this and that, but somehow I couldn't relax. We never even had dessert. Aunt Julia said, 'Duffy, something's bothering you. We're going across the street to the park, and I hope you'll tell me about it.'

"So we walked in the park a bit and then settled on one of the benches. Your grandmother just watched me for a time with those eyes that sometimes seemed to see to your very core. Then she said, 'Duffy, your parents are far from here; why don't you let me help you. You know I've always thought of you as family.' With that, she laid her hand on my shoulder, and as if she'd opened a spigot, it all came pouring out.

"I sat there on the park bench crying like a kid while I told her all about Adrienne and the coven and the girl, and how I'd decided the only decent thing I could do was to marry the girl."

"But you didn't marry her," Nicole prompted when Duffy fell silent, remembering.

Duffy shook his head. "No. Aunt Julia asked me just one question, was the girl pregnant, and when I said no, she set me straight. It was true that I had done a bad thing, but marrying a girl just to soothe my own conscience, and without love, wasn't doing her any favor. It was an almost surefire way to mess up two promising young lives. The best thing I could do was accept my guilt, try to be a better person, and get on with my life.

"Then Aunt Julia stood up, facing me, looking terribly stern, and she said, 'I'm glad you now view the cult with disgust, Duffy—you young people were playing in what could be very dangerous territory. Stay away from it and have nothing whatsoever to do with it in the future.' Then she smiled, and I felt like the sun had broken through the clouds. I got up and hugged her, and we started back out of the park without saying another word.

"We were almost back on the corner when I remembered there was something *she* had wanted to discuss with *me*. She looked almost startled when I mentioned it, but then said, 'Oh, yes! Duffy, I want you to do me a favor. I could have asked over the telephone, but I wanted to impress you with its importance to me.' She said she wanted me to make a point of seeing that you had my current telephone number and address at all times. She said that while she was in perfect health and expected to live for quite some time, she *was* sixty-five years old, and if something should happen to her, she wanted to be sure you had someone nearby she could turn to. 'Someone I love and know I can trust,' she said, so would I do this little thing for her?

"Do you know how I felt when she said that? If Aunt Julia still loved and trusted me, maybe I wasn't such a piece of shit after all. I couldn't undo what I had done, but maybe I could make up for it a little. By being the kind of doctor my folks and Aunt Julia would be proud of. The kind my cousin Nickie would be proud of.

"That was almost seven years ago, and I'm still working at it. I'll never quit."

This moment, Nicole thought, was worth any number of bad dreams. Well, almost any number. She felt a warm glow, a kind of inner radiance, that was love.

She said, "You really thought I might kick you out because of that?"

Duffy didn't answer.

"You're telling me you've stayed away from St. Claire all this time out of shame and regret. And yet you went back there last year with me."

"You needed me, and maybe I needed to go with you. I loved Aunt Julia."

"Wouldn't you like to see Derek and Joanne and the others? Find out what's happened to them?"

"I hope I never see them again. Especially that girl . . ."

"Your closest and dearest friends from high school. From childhood, some of them. Duffy, that is so sad."

Again, Duffy didn't reply. She took his arm, drew him back down onto the bed with her, embraced him. He laid his head on her shoulder.

"All right, darling," she said, "we won't go back this summer. We don't have to go back ever again. I'll see Freya Kellgren when she comes to the city in the fall. I'm sure I can hold out till then."

Duffy raised his head. He looked into her eyes for a moment, then lifted her face with a finger under her chin and kissed her gently. "No," he said, "we're going back to St. Claire at the end of the month. If you need to see Freya Kellgren, then you're going to see her. If I want to be forgiven for the past, then I ought to have the guts to face up to it." He kissed her again. "Now let's try to get some rest."

• • •

But rest did not come easily to Duffy. For a time he sat up in the dark, slowly, gently massaging Nicole's back and shoulders, until he was sure she was asleep again; he then got out of bed and silently left the room, careful not to disturb her.

He went into the den, turned on the desk lamp, and settled down with a medical text, picked up at random. As long as he was awake, he might as well get some studying done.

Who was he kidding?

He felt awake but brain-dead. Stunned, perhaps, by the dream he could not quite remember. Something about poor old Chucky; a dream inspired, quite likely, by Nicole's own nightmare cries from the kitchen? No, something else . . .

. . . come back . . . come back to St. Claire . . .

The whisper echoed in his mind, and he suddenly remembered his dream, almost as if he were experiencing it all over again.

. . . come to me, Duffy . . . come to me . . .

Dim, almost incoherent at first, the dream had become so vivid. He had been somewhere in darkness, when Lily Bains had slowly appeared before him. She had been naked beneath a dark cloak. Her hard-nippled body had seemed to glow, as with the heat of desire, and her ruby lips had opened in invitation. *"Oh, my God!"* she had said, her eyes widening, and she had reached out to touch his bare chest . . .

. . . how well he remembered . . . lovely Lily, desirable Lily . . . Lily naked and hot and wet, Lily moaning for him and grasping his painfully swollen penis . . . wonderfully, deliciously fuckable Lily . . .

In a spasm of self-disgust, Duffy pounded the desktop so hard his hands hurt. What the hell was he doing? Sitting in the den in the middle of the night, having masturbation fantasies about a woman he had once wronged, a woman he wished to God he had never met. He actually had an erection.

He turned out the light and groped his way out of the den, wanting only to hold Nicole in his arms again.

Timothy sat up against the pillows, watching Lily as she rolled laughing on the foot of the bed—pink-golden flesh, scissoring legs and quivering breasts, against the black cloak and the white sheets. Her eyes glittered in the light of the one lamp he had turned on.

"He was *here!*" she said. "He was actually *here,* with us, in the room!"

"Yes," Timothy said with greater calm than he felt, "he was here."

"I wonder if he has any idea of what actually happened."

"Probably not."

Lily rolled over, sat up facing Timothy. "He came here out-of-body. I *drew* him here out-of-body. I've never done such a thing before. And then he began to materialize. He wasn't just a wraith or a phantom, Timothy. I touched him and felt warm flesh over solid bone." Her smile faded. "Or could that have just been an illusion?"

"It was not an illusion, Lily. Your powers are growing, as I promised you."

"Then . . . is it possible that *I* caused him to materialize? Not he, but I?"

"It is possible," Timothy answered, "if he was ripe for it. If for some reason he was vulnerable."

Lily's smile returned. "Oh, he was vulnerable, all right," she said, sliding a hand down between her thighs. Her eyes narrowed and her very features seemed to blur as she stroked herself. "My God, he was so vulnerable! He wanted me seven years ago, and he wants me still, whether he knows it or not. He's coming back to St. Claire in hope of finding me, and when he does . . ."

"Sex is indeed power," Timothy murmured.

"And power is sex." Lily arched her back, and writhed luxuriously. "Power is the sexiest thing in the world. I've read that the cosmos as we know it began with one gigantic orgasm and that it will end with another. And in between, we create and destroy . . ."

". . . in the name of the Prince of Power."

". . . and if to create is to know ecstasy . . ."

". . . then to destroy . . ."

". . . to destroy the weak and worthless, to destroy one's enemies, to destroy the betrayer one once loved, that truly is to know . . ."

". . . rapture . . ."

". . . yes . . . rapture!" An orgasmic shudder wrung Lily's body.

How well she had learned Lucifer's litanies, Timothy thought. He tried to imagine Alida saying the same words and found it oddly difficult. For too long, perhaps, he had perversely tried to preserve the child's innocence. Or was it possible that he had chosen the wrong daughter? No. He had spread his seed widely, over the years, but Alida was the daughter he had known and raised, the child of his heart. And soon, soon, he would have her back.

CHAPTER
13

○

"Come, Jessie Gustava," Timothy murmured, his words barely audible, "come back to St. Claire."

"Come back," the others whispered, "come back to St. Claire."

"Come back and be reconciled. Come back to those who love you. Come back . . ."

"Come back," whispered the others, "come back . . ."

First, they had celebrated the Eucharist of the Griffin, passing the chalice from hand to hand and sipping the spiced brandy potion that, if they were blessed and worthy, would heighten their psychic powers and perceptions. Now, wearing only their black cloaks, they were sitting in a circle in the darkness of the tower room, Freya on Timothy's right, Bruno on his left, and Lily facing him. They were holding hands. For long moments, only their breathing could be heard. Then one or another of them would speak.

"Come back, Bradford," Freya said. "You above all have sinned against the god of this world. Come back and know the joys of reconciliation. Come back for your friends' sake. They want you, Bradford. They need you. Only you can save them. Come back to St. Claire, Bradford."

"Come back . . . come back . . ."

For a long moment, the very darkness seemed vibrant with their unspoken entreaties.

"Derek," Bruno said, breaking the silence, "Derek, help us. You, more than all the others, have *wanted* to come back. Help us bring the others back. You will be rewarded, Derek. You will be granted your dearest wish. Do as we ask, and all good things will come to you. Bring them back."

"Bring them back . . . bring them back . . ."

Timothy could feel Lily's mind focusing, could almost see the sensuous images that were forming in it.

"Duffy, darling," she whispered, "I'm waiting for you. I've waited so long, and I need you so much. I can't tell you how much I need you, Duffy. You want me, you know you do . . . come back to me, my darling, come back . . ."

"Come back to St. Claire . . . come back . . ."

Come to us, Lord Lucifer, Timothy prayed silently. *Lend us your power.*

As if in response, the darkness of the room deepened until, for a moment, darkness and silence seemed absolute. Then, from somewhere—from the depths of their collective minds, perhaps, or from the depths of hell—came a sound. It was as if somewhere three hellhounds, or perhaps a single three-headed hound, howled a long baleful tantara for their master, bugled an ominous fanfare for the god of this world.

As the sound faded away, so did the darkness, slowly at first, tinctured by a flickering of thin pink light, pale as blood and water. For an instant, Timothy entertained the thought that he might be hallucinating, an effect of the potion they had drunk. That could happen. But, no, not to him, not now. Whatever he saw or heard or felt was in some sense real.

The light quickly brightened, turning to crimson and gold streaked with blue, and flaring from moment to moment like mounting flames. Soon the entire room seemed ablaze, its boundaries vanished in dazzling light. The three-headed hound howled again, closer now, and Timothy was filled with a wonderful exultation. He had not experienced a night like this in so long! While the others laughed as if the flames were tongues of pleasure lapping at their bodies, he heard himself cry out, almost drunkenly, "Welcome, Lord Lucifer! Enter me if that is your wish. Let us work your will. In the name of Lord Lucifer, god of this world, we shall bring the apostates to justice! Let them be reconciled—or destroyed!"

Once again, Timothy felt that Lucifer himself was looking out through his eyes, and now in the light of the dancing flames he could see the others clearly, could see through their earthly appearance to their very souls. On his right, Freya—oddly, perversely alluring, with her beady-eyed, yellow-toothed, coarsely hirsute rodent face. On his left, Bruno—also strangely seductive, with his needle-toothed, feline muzzle, his female breasts, and his big cock jutting out of the folds of his plump vulva. And before him, Lily—the wanton beauty of her face unchanged, but her lasciviously writhing body reptilian in lacquered scales of incandescent green and yellow and brown.

Gazing about through that blazing, all-encompassing inferno, now almost blinding in its intensity, Timothy saw other figures, cloaked and naked, human and bestial, surrounding them. As if the dimensions of hell intersected with those of earth, he saw them, a legion of wraithlike shapes, appearing and fading and reappearing in greater definition. Still other figures, dimly perceived, came whirling batlike through the room and about their heads. When a few small creatures appeared to materialize and settle on Freya's shoulders, she cackled with delight.

Timothy understood what was happening. He had experienced this before. These were all children of the Prince of Power, human and demonic, alive and dead, earthly and hellborn, who had been drawn here out-of-body to assist in the working of their master's will. They, too, would urge the coven's return.

It was time to begin again.

"Jessie Gustava," Timothy commanded, "Jessie Gustava Lindquist, come back to St. Claire!"

"Come back!" Lucifer's legion chanted softly, a sound like the rustling of dry leaves. "Come back, come back, come back to St. Claire . . . !"

•   •   •

Come back to St. Claire, my ass!

Jessie Lindquist was drunk. Not blind drunk, but not mildly drunk either. Somewhere in between, and not enjoying it at all. The sliding-glass doors of the Malibu beach house were open, and the light and the music of the party, the chatter and laughter, flowed out onto the deck; but Jessie was around the corner in the dark, sipping a gin and tonic while simultaneously trying to sober up. A difficult task at the best of times.

Come back to St. Claire. Lately the words had kept running through her mind compulsively, like a line from an old song she'd really like to forget. And just when she realized that for a few days she *had* forgotten it, *that* started it up again. Like a broken phonograph record that you can't stop: *Come back to St. Claire*, click . . . *come back to St. Claire*, click . . . *come back to St. Claire*, click . . .

Sorry, Derek, but *no way* are you going to get me back to St. Claire.

It seemed to her that the voice in her head, the *command*, had started about the time she had received Derek's letter, a few weeks ago. It had been a very cheerful letter, reminding her of the coven's "solemn promise" to hold a reunion this summer. He and Joanne were looking forward to it *sooo* much. He said that he and Joanne were, as usual, planning to be in St. Claire through July, and how was that for her?

She hadn't even replied.

She finished her drink, very carefully placed her glass on the railing of the deck, and started down the steps toward the beach. Bad form not to say good night and thanks to her hostess, but that could wait until tomorrow. Philip Steadman had shown up, and she wanted to avoid him.

These people. You had to admit they had a network. Five years ago, when, with her mother, she had headed for L.A., determined to become a professional entertainer, she had figured she was free of the coven and the convocation. *Had* been free for almost two years. In L.A., she had done all the usual things, taken acting lessons, pounded agents' doors, attended cattle calls, while her mother supported her, working in restaurants. Then, after eight months, when she had begun to face the grim possibility of failure, Sid Bascombe, the agent, had "just happened" to spot her in a workshop production of *Streetcar*. Well, she *had* been good as Stella. But she had come to understand that the *real* story-behind-the-story was Baltha-zar-to-Steadman-to-Bascombe.

"We're going to make you a star, Jessie," Philip Steadman told her. "I know that sounds corny, but you've got the talent and I've got the necessary connections, and we're going to do it."

There was just one catch. Philip Steadman wanted her in his convocation. Or, more precisely, Philip Steadman wanted *her.*

Steadman was the kind of man who liked to believe that he could have any woman he wanted, and Jessie suspected that he was not altogether incorrect in this view. He was, on the face of it, one of the most attractive men she had ever met, and she had no doubt that he had his own little harem, ready to worship and service him at his whim. But she was not about to become a member.

"I've tried Luciferianism, Philip, you know that, and I just don't think it's for me. At heart, I remain the good little Meth-odist girl I was brought up to be."

The truth was, Professor Philip Steadman scared the hell out of her.

And rightly so. Look at what had happened to poor Buddy Weston.

She had met Buddy three years ago while working on her seventh movie, an action thriller called *Fer-de-Lance*. Her first major role, and she was playing opposite Buddy Weston, one of the finest young actors to come along in years!

They brought out the best in each other. Buddy, with his thin, dark good looks and his intensity, had reminded her a bit of Brad Holland; but whereas Brad had masked his vulner-abilities with coldness, Buddy let every quivering sensitivity show, unafraid to reveal love and sympathy, pain and under-standing. Playing against him, Jessie became the strong young woman who masked her fears and her tenderness and thus appeared harder and tougher than she was, a sharp contrast to Buddy, almost an antagonist.

It worked. The magic began to happen. She and Buddy were steel and flint, sparks flew.

Three weeks into shooting, they became lovers.

She didn't love Buddy as she had loved Brad Holland (may he rot in hell), but she did love him. They had become best friends, sharing all their hopes and fears and intimate secrets. Or so she had thought.

The prospects for *Fer-de-Lance* looked so promising that the producers began planning a sequel while the first picture was still in post-production. The first picture was a "snake movie," so the second would be about spiders and be called *Fer-de-Lance II: The Deadly Recluse.* And if that paid off . . . Jessie was on her way to becoming a megabucks star.

Work on *Recluse* went unusually fast. They had wrapped up production, when, after dinner at a quiet candlelit café, Buddy told her the truth.

"Look, I love you, Jessie, and I want to marry you, but—"

Her heart soared. "Oh, Buddy—"

"No. Listen to me. There's something I have to tell you first. I want to tell you the whole truth, I don't want to leave anything out, even if I could, and there's something I hope you'll do for me."

She listened, after that first lovely moment, with a heart that seemed, literally, to sink within her breast.

She had been set up, set up with Buddy Weston, from the beginning. Sid Bascombe, as agent for both of them, hadn't found it difficult to sell them as a package to the producers of *Fer-de-Lance*—and he had done so at the behest of Philip Steadman. Buddy was supposed to be the candy that lured Jessie back into the fold.

"The old bait-and-switch," she said bitterly. "You're the bait and Philip's the switch."

Buddy held up a placatory hand and shook his head. "I think Philip wants you, all right, what man wouldn't? But you don't have to have a goddamn thing to do with him, not in that respect. You're mine, and I love you, Jess."

"Why should I believe that now?"

A look of bewilderment came over Buddy's face, that little-boy-lost look that he did so well. Acting? She had no idea.

"I don't know why you should believe me," he said after a moment. "All I know is, *I* have never for a moment doubted your love for me. Whether I should have or not. I guess in the end love is always a matter of trust."

Perhaps that was true. But at the moment, she still had the feeling that her trust had been betrayed.

"All right," she said with a bleak smile. "Suppose I come back. What's in it for you? What have Philip and Sid promised you?"

Buddy's face brightened. "Nothing! Not a goddamn thing. But, Jess, Sid Bascombe brought me into the Order five years ago when I was forgotten and getting nowhere. Remember, Jess, I started out as a child actor on TV, three years as the star of my own show, everybody saying what a prodigy, what a genius I was. But that show was followed by ten years of *nothing!*

"Then Sid introduced me to the Order. The Children of the Griffin. The vows . . ." Buddy laughed softly and shook his head, remembering. "Even then, they seemed almost absurd, they were so wild, so melodramatic, so . . . so extreme. But I took them, meaning every goddamn word I said. I was that desperate. And the next morning, Sid told me he'd got me an appointment to read for the second male lead in *Hunter's Moon.* And I got the job—my first real role in *ten years!*

"My luck turned, literally overnight. I was hot again—the right roles, the right films, the right directors, all coming my way. And I haven't had a single failure since!"

"So now it's . . . payback time."

Buddy nodded, smiling. "Yeah. It's payback time. And all they want is the chance to do the same thing for you. Hell, they've already started! You did half a dozen quickie flicks that went absolutely nowhere. Then Steadman told Sid, 'Get her into a good thriller with our Buddy,' and now you've got your first smash. And *Recluse* is going to do even better. So maybe it's payback time for you, too."

Maybe it was.

Steadman and company would sure as hell like to have her think so.

Her elbows on the table, she rested her face against her folded hands and closed her eyes.

She was silent for so long that Buddy touched her shoulder. "Well, dreamer?"

She opened her eyes. She said, "I don't think so."

Buddy's smile faded. "Why not? Why not, for Chrissake, after what they've done for you—"

"Look, Buddy. I don't like Philip Steadman and I didn't ask him for a damn thing, so to hell with him. As for Sid, as far as I'm concerned he was just doing his job, and he got *paid* for it. I appreciate his work on my behalf, but I owe him nothing. If *Fer-de-Lance* is a hit, it's mainly because you and I and a number of other people put one hell of a lot of effort into it, and not because the goddamned 'god of this world' loaded the dice or stacked the deck on our behalf. So to hell with him too."

"You think luck had nothing to do with it? Or the god, in some way, turning our luck?"

"Of course luck had something to do with it. Luck always has something to do with it. But if you and I hadn't worked our asses off since we were kids to get where we are, luck wouldn't be worth shit. I'm lucky to have a certain talent, but when I'm out there in front of the camera doing my thing, that ain't the devil goosing me, baby. That's me, little Jessie, giving it all I've got."

Buddy was quiet for a long time, gazing at the white tablecloth, and his face seemed to have grown paler in the candlelight. He spoke slowly, without looking at her.

"You're saying that you have the talent and the drive to make it on your own, but I don't."

"Oh, no!" She heard his words with pain and dismay. How could he so twist what she had said? "Honey, I would never say such a thing to you. You're one of the finest actors alive, and it was only a matter of time until you broke through."

When he raised his head to look at her, she saw fear in his eyes. "I don't know that. I only know that I've finally got what I always dreamed of, and I don't want to lose it. Jessie, do this for me. Come back in."

Could she do it? For him?

"I can't."

"You joined once, and afterward you just up and quit, in spite of those damned vows. You could do it again."

She shook her head. "I paid, Buddy. Sometimes I think

I'm still paying. I'm paying right now. I'm sorry, but I will not sell my soul twice."

Their love affair died after that. Not abruptly—they slept together three or four times in the following months, and affection remained—but love began to die that evening in the small candlelit café. Thereafter she refused to discuss "reconciliation" with him, and when he made a final desperate plea, she knew they would never be lovers again.

A third *Fer-de-Lance* picture was considered to be down the road somewhere, a fair certainty. Meanwhile the two stars went their separate ways. Jessie had already signed for *I Wanted to Sing*. Its success proved that as an actress she did not have to depend on Buddy Weston, and its soundtrack album launched her recording career.

Buddy's next picture, *Dead Ahead,* didn't appear until April of '94, and the general consensus—critics, audiences, the trade—was that it should have been called *Dead Ahead of Time,* or *Dead Already*. Stories of trouble on the set—star temperament, technical difficulties, instant rewrites—abounded. In the final cut, plot lines and characters had obviously been dropped and sequences clumsily rearranged. Nobody could understand why it had been released in such a state, and it was quickly withdrawn for "reediting."

But the biggest disappointment was Buddy Weston. The critics were dumbfounded by what they called his mannered, stilted performance. They said he played the lead role like a poor imitation of himself, a bad parody at best. The cruelest of them implied that all of his previous work had somehow been invalidated, that they had known "all along" that he had been vastly overrated.

She hadn't seen Buddy in several months, when, ten days after the opening of *Dead Ahead,* she ran into him at a birthday party in a noisy bar. They greeted each other exuberantly, hugging and kissing and managing to fall into a booth that others were just leaving. She tried to hide her alarm. Buddy's eyes had a funny look, dilated and wild. Though the room was not warm, his face was shiny with sweat, and he was clearly drunk.

"Well," he said over the hubbub, his grin skull-like, "they finally got wise to me, didn't they, kid?"

"Oh, what do you mean?" she said, knowing quite well what he meant.

"Making me executive producer was like giving me enough rope to hang myself. Like letting me assist at my own execution."

"Buddy, it's only one movie, *just one flick!* And you already have a body of work that's so impressive—"

He gave no sign of hearing her. "You know, they used to call me 'the new James Dean.' I'd never even *seen* a James Dean movie, just clips now and then, hell, the guy was dead before I was even born. But I took it as a high compliment because, my God, James Dean was a legend. And *I* was the *new* James Dean!" Buddy laughed and shook his head.

"You were better than that," Jessie said, "you were, and are, Buddy Weston and unique. Why are we talking about James Dean?"

"I'm telling you why. When we were shooting *Dead Ahead*, it was like I lost my sense of identity. I actually started having nightmares in which I didn't know if I was James Dean or Montgomery Clift. Monty Clift, who I *really* studied, who I *stole* from, and nobody *ever* called me 'the new Montgomery Clift.' In my dreams I'd tell people, 'Hey, I'm not James Dean, I'm Montgomery Clift.' But they wouldn't believe me, and I'd think, 'Maybe they're right!'

"Then I'd wake up and go to work, and I *knew* I wasn't delivering the goods! In my heart, I knew it all along! I *knew* we were going to get murdered!"

Buddy was still chuckling and grinning. Jessie didn't think she could stand that grin much longer. She said, "Baby, there is always the next time. Why don't we get out of here?"

Buddy shook his head. "Haven't come to the punchline yet."

"We bombed, all right. You know that, all the world knows that, Christ, we bombed, and for about a week I thought I was going to die. But I kept telling myself, 'This, too, will pass; this, too, will pass.' "

"Yes," Jessie said, taking his hand, "this, too, will pass."

Buddy withdrew his hand and curled into a corner of the

booth. "Then, a few days ago, at three o'clock in the morning, a messenger wakes me up and delivers a package to me at my door. At three o'clock in the morning!"

"What in the world . . . ?"

"It's from Steadman. It's three videocassettes and a message. He says, 'My dear boy, I thought these might provide some much needed amusement and inspiration.' So I look at the cassettes. *Rebel Without a Cause. East of Eden. Giant.*"

"Oh, my God . . ." Jessie felt a sickness, a cold, oily nausea, spreading through her.

"So, what the hell, three o'clock in the morning and I'm awake, I turn on the machine and pop *Rebel* into the VCR and settle down in front of my big screen.

"At first it was kind of amusing. That son of a bitch was *so* good. The way he could warm you with just a hint of a smile . . . hold your attention absolutely riveted and make you ache for that kid up there, all his hopes and pain . . . *so* damn good . . .

"Then, not twenty minutes into the film, I began to realize something." Buddy's face, twisted into a Gothic parody of mirth, turned red with the force of his choked, gasping laughter. "I realized that that was *me* up there on the screen! That was *me,* the *real* me—"

"Buddy, stop it—"

"If only I'd had the gift, *that* was what I *should* have been! I wasn't 'the next James Dean.' Buddy Weston was nothing more than a pale reflection of that guy on the screen, just a second-rate imitation, and that's all he ever would be—"

"Buddy, that is simply not true!"

"—a pale reflection of James Dean and maybe a little of Monty Clift and a few others, me and my puny little bag of actor's tricks, masquerading as talent . . ."

As Buddy closed his eyes and slowly lowered his head to the tabletop, his strangled laughter turned to sobs.

No one in the noisy bar seemed to notice: just one more drunk on a crying jag. Jessie stroked his head, trying to communicate love and reassurance, but she knew the effort was futile.

At this moment, all she could do was loathe Philip Steadman as she had loathed no other man in her life.

Buddy Weston's pain, the hell he was going through, she understood quite clearly to be the punishment visited upon him by Philip Steadman for failing to draw her into his convocation.

Philip Steadman knew Buddy Weston well, his strengths, his weaknesses. Manipulative son of a bitch that he was, perhaps he had even used the weaknesses to sabotage *Dead Ahead.* In any case, he had waited, with exquisite timing, until Buddy had reached his most abject hour of defeat, the very nadir of his life, and then, by an act of unspeakable cruelty, had destroyed any remaining faith he might have in himself, any last drop of hope.

At three o'clock in the morning, when a soul in crisis is most naked and lonely and vulnerable.

Jessie couldn't let Steadman do that. She had to save Buddy if she could.

She took him home with her and put him to bed.

He was gone when she awakened in the morning. She telephoned him several times during the day, but only got his answering machine. She tried repeatedly to get in touch with him in the days that followed, even chasing him down in bars where friends reported having seen him, but somehow never quite catching up with him. He never returned her calls.

But why not? she asked herself. Didn't he want her help? Was he so intent on self-destruction? Or was he fighting a battle for salvation in his own misbegotten way?

She would never know. A month after the opening of *Dead Ahead,* she learned that Buddy Weston, who had never before used drugs, had dropped dead of an overdose in a roadhouse parking lot.

And for that I will never forgive you, Philip Steadman. Never.

She plodded along the quarter mile or so of sand to her borrowed beach house, seeing nothing but her own sandal-clad feet, hearing none of the Saturday night party laughter, feeling only her burden of sadness.

She came to the lengthy flight of wooden stairs that led up to the deck of her house. Wearily, a hand on the railing, she pulled herself up the stairs, one slow step at a time. She was almost at the top when she realized that something was wrong, and her breath caught.

The outside lights were off.

And someone was on the deck.

Her heart thudded sickeningly, and she looked back down the stairs, seeking a path of escape. The stairs seemed awfully steep and high, suddenly.

"It's all right, Jessie," Philip Steadman said. "It's only me."

"Oh . . ." Jessie put her hand to her heart and breathed a sigh of qualified relief. "Philip, what the hell . . . ?"

"I'm sorry if I startled you. The lights bothered me, and I took the liberty of turning them off."

"How . . . ?"

"You borrowed the house from a mutual friend, and I found I still had the keys."

Pure chance, of course. Oh, yes.

How silly of her to think she could simply drop out of sight for a couple of weeks, take a little time to heal her soul and pray for Buddy. At Malibu, of all places! Supposedly only her mother, back in L.A., and the friend who had lent her this place knew where she was. And yet Philip was here, with the keys. As if to demonstrate that he held the keys to her life.

I don't think so, Philip.

She took the last few steps up onto the wooden deck. Philip, having risen from a deck chair, was standing at the other end, a study in shadows, tall, slim, with abundant dark hair and aquiline good looks. Though Jessie guessed him to be twice her age, he looked no more than late thirties, even in the daylight. Tonight he was wearing a loose white shirt and dark slacks, and a griffin medallion—she had seen it before—glittered on his bare chest. Strange, Jessie thought, how often these people were beautiful. But, then, beauty was one of their weapons. They never seemed to understand how repellent beauty misused could be. That curious mixture of attraction and disgust that made Jessie feel soiled.

"What do you want, Philip?"

"To speak to you, of course."

"You could have spoken to me earlier this evening."

"Not with all those people around. And you barely nodded to me. Or to anyone else, I might add. Odd behavior, at a party."

"You're right. I shouldn't have been there. But I ran into our kind hostess on the beach this afternoon, and . . . if you'll excuse me, Philip . . ." She turned toward the door.

"Please, Jessie, a few minutes, nothing more. I came here and waited, hoping to speak to you alone."

"And if I hadn't been alone?"

"A man, you mean?" She could see his smile, even in the dark. "Unlikely. You were drinking alone, more or less, and according to Buddy, you never let yourself get interested in a man after the second drink. A hard and fast rule. He admired you so much."

Oh, Buddy, Buddy, Buddy! she thought, closing her eyes and seeing that thin boyish face with its eager, guileless smile. *Buddy, why didn't you let me help you?*

She heard Steadman whisper: "I'm sorry."

She opened her eyes and stared at him. "You're sorry? You're telling me you're sorry?"

"Jessie, believe me, I am so sorry—"

"Don't you tell me you're sorry! You killed him, you son of a bitch!"

"I know."

"You *know?*" she said on the rising tide of her anger. "You *know?* You dare to tell me you *know,* you bastard? You *know*—"

She was raising her hand as if to strike him, and she might have, when he spoke. He said quietly, "Jessie, you're not the only one who loved him."

She froze, in mind and body, as if he had struck her first. The gall of the man was unbelievable, so outrageous it left her stunned. Her hand dropped.

"Yes, I loved him," Steadman went on, as if unaware of Jessie's reaction. "Oh, not as a woman loves a man, not as you loved him, but I did love him. He was like a younger brother to me. *I* rediscovered him, you know. *I,* with Sid Bascombe, nurtured his career, just as I have yours. But I let him down. I was worried about him, terribly worried about him, but I never realized the depths of his depression after the *Dead Ahead* fiasco. So I made the worst mistake of my life."

Jessie turned away again and leaned against the doorjamb. Every word the man spoke was like a blasphemy that sought to poison her soul. "Go home, Philip," she said. "Just go away and get the fuck out of my life."

She might as well not have spoken. "We often joked about the business of his being 'the new James Dean,'" Steadman went on, as if he hadn't heard, "and his first four films—solid character-driven dramatic pictures—did make that niche his. Nobody filled it better. Then he entered the action-film sweep-stakes and proved he was a winner there too. Until *Dead Ahead*. His first failure since his comeback, and he was devastated."

"Philip, please . . ."

"What could I do for him? He wouldn't listen to me, wouldn't talk to me, or to you either, apparently. So, one slightly inebriated evening, while I was brooding on this, I conceived the idea of somehow sending him back to his 'roots,' so to speak, back to the kind of character-driven picture that had established him. He was 'the new James Dean'—I thought he might be amused to see what the old James Dean had done and just how much *better* the new James Dean was. It was a totally witless idea, for which I have no excuse except that I had been drinking, but I never dreamed that Buddy, in his despair, would so completely misinterpret what I was try-ing to tell him. The next morning I realized I might have made a mistake, and I tried to call him, but . . ."

It was just possible that Steadman was telling the truth. He had always struck Jessie as a dangerous man, and she had felt an instinctive revulsion to him, but that didn't mean that he was entirely devoid of human feeling, did it? Or that he was incapable of making an honest mistake? God knew, she had made enough mistakes of her own.

But what was he saying now?

". . . have envied and admired you so much, I can't tell you . . ."

He had stepped up behind her, and she had not even noticed when he had placed his hands on her shoulders. Far from being repelled, she found his caress as soothing as his voice.

". . . had aspirations toward being an actor in my youth,

but, alas, it was not to be. My charisma, such as it is, cannot be captured by a camera. But yours . . .

". . . remember the first time I saw you, the night you took your final vows. You were so beautiful, as you exchanged the red cloak for the black. There wasn't a man or woman there, even the dullest, who didn't feel the power of your attraction. Do you remember . . . ?"

She remembered well . . . the griffin on the tapestry behind the altar, its eyes brilliant and alive, even in the dim candlelight . . . Timothy and Freya in their cloaks, before the altar . . . she and Bradford kneeling at the communion rail, and behind them a dozen or more of the convocation, silent, watching. . . .

It had been easy for Brad to draw her into the Order with him. The very idea had the allure of the esoteric and the forbidden, and it had appealed to her sense of the dramatic. The whole business had been like a role-playing game, not quite real. But that night *was* real. The people in that room, Mr. Balthazar and the others, truly believed in the god of this world.

Brad took the vows first, repeating them back to Timothy Balthazar. His red cloak was exchanged for a black one, and he sipped the sacred brandy. Timothy opened the gate in the railing, and Brad rose to step into the sanctuary and exchange the Kiss of Consummation with Freya.

As head of a new coven, Brad, not Timothy, administered the vows to Jessie. Her cloak was changed, and her head swam as the brandy entered her bloodstream. She rose and went to Brad for the Kiss of Consummation.

They kissed chastely, parted, and stood looking at each other in the candlelight.

There was a round of applause. *"Ite missa est,"* Timothy said sardonically, and Jessie heard the faint rustle of cloaks and the shuffle of sandals behind her as the congregation turned to depart.

Brad's eyes twinkled, and he struggled to suppress a crooked little grin. He looked about twelve years old, and as innocent as a child at play, and in that moment the solemnity of the occasion vanished for Jessie. This was the Brad she loved—not the would-be Luciferian, but this little kid parading around in his birthday suit and a black cloak.

Brad was having fun!

And she was having fun with him. This was a game, after all, and nothing more. As a laugh escaped her throat, she reached out to embrace Brad.

Then something totally unexpected happened—unexpected and unwanted.

She felt a man's attention on her.

Not Brad's, not Timothy Balthazar's. From somewhere behind her back, a stranger's. The sensation swept over her body like a bath of warm oil, seductive yet frightening.

She turned and looked toward the departing congregation. Timothy had decreed that, for the present, she and Brad should know none of the convocation but Freya and himself. During the ceremony, she had not glimpsed one other face or body. But now, as clearly as if a hundred more candles had been lit, she saw a tall man standing in the center aisle, cloak open and cowl back, feet planted firmly apart and hands on hips, statuesque, a nude in stone, aware of his own physical perfection, as he gazed at her with arrogant, possessive eyes.

A stranger. And yet his face . . . to her astonishment, his face was that of Bradford Holland.

An older Bradford Holland, larger and more powerful in every way, a Bradford Holland idealized. A Bradford Holland who seemed to be telling her, *Look at me! I am all your pathetic little coven master ever wanted to be and more!*

Jessie knew she was highly susceptible to suggestion, a hypnotist's delight, and she had been sensitized, perhaps, by the brandy and the moment and a will greater than her own. She was seeing what this man wanted her to see, and for a moment, she felt paralyzed, struck dumb. Then the stranger's face underwent a subtle alteration, less a transformation, it seemed, than some odd change of perspective. It was no longer Bradford Holland's face. It had become the face of the man she would one day know as Philip Steadman.

He smiled at her as if they shared a secret, then turned and walked away.

She didn't see him again for almost three years. But, thanks to his friend Timothy Balthazar, he had been aware of her presence from the day she arrived in California. Biding his time, waiting for the best moment to make his move.

And now, as he held her in his arms, gently stroking her and whispering in her ear, it hardly seemed worth the effort to resist. She even leaned back against him.

". . . oh, yes, I knew all about you, you and your friend Bradford Holland. Timothy was interested principally in Bradford, but Timothy has certain . . . blind spots. He didn't see that *you* were the one with the potential. *You* were the one who would hold little Bradford's coven together, without the others even realizing it."

"Hold it together?" Jessie laughed ironically. "It only lasted a few months, until the end of the summer."

"Only because you chose not to carry it on. You were angry with Bradford and disillusioned, and who could blame you? Bradford Holland was unworthy of you, and in his heart he knew it. He withdrew from your life because in his heart of hearts he knew he couldn't measure up to you."

It would have been flattering to think so. Then why, in *her* heart of hearts, did she not for one minute believe it?

"But I knew what you were from the moment I heard you pledging your immortal soul and all your thoughts and acts to the god of this world."

"Childish melodrama, Philip."

Steadman laughed softly and stroked her arms. "So you say now. But at the time, you meant every word, and you can't deny it. You were *into the role*, my dear, you were *living* the role, and in that moment, as we listened to your voice, you held every one of us in Timothy's chapel enthralled.

"I knew then that you were more than just a would-be actress, an entertainer, a little song-and-dance girl. I realized that with your charisma fully developed and at my command, I could build a convocation even more powerful than Timothy's."

"In other words, you wanted to use me."

"We use each other, my dear, to our mutual benefit. Consider: I am a failed actor. And yet, through my convocation and its membership, I am one of the most influential men in the motion picture industry. *I* instructed Sidney Bascombe to 'discover' you. *I* had Sidney 'introduce' you to me. *I* told him what kind of pictures I wanted you in. 'None of this musical stuff, Sid,' I told him, 'I want to see Jessie's face and body up there on the screen in one blood-and-sex thriller after another. Horror and crime. Make 'em fast, make 'em cheap, make 'em often!

"He did it, and it worked. Six pictures in less than two years, and you were a familiar face, if not yet a name.

"Then I told Sid to package you with Buddy in an action film. He resisted at first. Not Buddy's kind of thing at all. No, but it was *your* kind of thing! And much as I loved Buddy, you were the one I was building. Jessie Lindquist was worth any number of Buddys. Jessie Lindquist was going to be the kind of megastar that Buddy could never be."

A note of contempt entered Steadman's voice. "Because, face it, Jessie. *You carried Buddy* through both *Fer-de-Lance* pictures. Everybody knows that now. He proved it himself when we cut him loose in *Dead Ahead*. He foundered, of course. Utterly. Because there was a great big *hole* in the picture where Jessie Lindquist should have been. His failure was a foregone conclusion.

"You, on the other hand, proved what I had always known, that you didn't need Buddy. You took on *I Wanted to Sing,* the kind of character-driven film *he* was thought to be so good at, and a star was born!

"And, my dear, this is only the beginning. . . ."

Jessie listened, appalled. Dear God, didn't the man hear what he was saying? Didn't he understand that he was confirming her worst suspicions, that he was convicting himself out of his own mouth?

". . . *when we cut him loose* . . ." Meaning, when we threw him to the wolves.

"*He foundered, of course.*" Meaning, as I anticipated.

"*His failure was a foregone conclusion.*" Meaning, it was planned that way. Planned by Philip Steadman.

Philip Steadman could have no idea of the rage that at that moment was rising in Jessie's bowels, burning up through her breast, and about to erupt in her brain.

He was still standing behind her, his arms around her waist. His feet were spread apart to reduce his height, and as he slowly shifted his hips from side to side, she could feel his hardened cock rubbing against her buttocks. His hands were stroking her belly, a little lower each time, and his lips brushed her neck.

"This business about your returning to St. Claire . . . I know all about it, of course, from Balthazar. But it isn't necessary. You needn't ever go back to St. Claire, if you don't want to. You belong here, Jessie, here with me. I'll take care of you. You haven't begun to see all that I can do for you."

"Oh, Philip . . ."

She could stand no more of this. Not one more minute of it. Her head was ablaze, she was blind with fire.

"Oh, Philip, you dear, sweet . . ."

She turned in his arms. Her arms encircled his, holding him steadily in place, but she pulled her body slightly away from his and, bending her knees, drew her right leg back.

". . . you dear, sweet son of a—"

With all her strength, she brought her right knee forward—

"—*bitch!*"

—driving it solidly *up!* into his crotch. Steadman screamed as she connected, and his eyeballs appeared to burst from their sockets. He reeled back against the railing of the deck, teetered, arms windmilling wildly; and for a moment seemed about to pitch back over it.

That was all right. That was acceptable. In fact, she would give him some help. She raised taloned hands and lunged toward him.

Only the look of pain and terror in his eyes stopped her.

When she backed off, the terror faded but the pain remained, and Steadman grabbed at his crushed genitals.

"You—you—"

"I what, Philip? You did kill Buddy, didn't you? You deliberately destroyed him, drove him to his grave!"

"You—you'll pay! You'll—you'll never—"

"Yeah, Philip, I know, I know. '*I'll never suck cock in this town again.*' Now, get the fuck off my porch, you bastard, before I throw you off. And don't think I can't do it!"

Gasping, trying to suppress small cries of pain, Steadman dragged himself by the railing to the stairs and started down.

Jessie became aware that they had an audience on the nearby decks and on the beach.

Steadman turned to say something. His eyes blazed.

"Not one word, Steadman!"

He stared at her with such intensity that for an instant she saw something else, the merest flickering of blue and green, behind the mask of his face, a glimpse of something within Philip Steadman that was saurian and predatory and utterly merciless. A ripple of fear went through her, stilling her breath. Then he turned away again and worked his way painfully, carefully down the rest of the stairs. He made his way slowly along the beach without looking back.

He had left the door unlocked. Jessie went inside, threw the dead bolt, and tapped the key pad to arm the security system.

She began to cry.

She cried as she hadn't in years, cried with a torrential grief that put out the flames of her rage and left only embers of pain. She cried for Buddy, so lost, so doomed, and dead so young. She cried for herself, so bereft, so lonely, so *unclean*. She cried for every child of God who had ever been betrayed by a Philip Steadman or a Brad Holland or a Duffy Johnson. Wrenchingly, rackingly, in bitter pain, she cried, staggering blindly as she went from room to room turning off lights. With only her nightstand lamp still burning, she threw herself weeping onto her bed.

Gradually her tears subsided.

She knew what Steadman, at the end, had been trying to tell her.

She wondered if it was true—that her career as an actress was over.

She cared about her career. She cared passionately. It was her lifelong dream, and she didn't think she would ever stop caring.

But even so . . .

She realized, perhaps for the first time, realized in her heart and not just in words, that there was something even more important to her than her career.

The people she loved.

Buddy.

Her mother.

Brad Holland, at one time.

. . . Nicole.

Little Nickie St. Claire. Jessie smiled through her tears. She hadn't thought of little Nickie in years. Why had she thought of her now?

Didn't matter. The people she loved. The people who loved her. They mattered.

She laughed silently, as she recalled what she had said to Steadman. *"I know, I know. 'I'll never suck cock in this town again.' "*

She had been willing to do almost anything to further her career. Jerk off Sid Bascombe, go the casting couch route, anything but give Steadman what he wanted.

No more.

She was done with that.

From now on, she would do nothing that would shame those she loved. She had talent. She had skills. Maybe even a touch of genius. If she couldn't make it on that, she didn't want to make it at all, and to hell with Philip Steadman and his kind.

Suddenly she was happier than she had been in seven years.

And then the phone began to ring.

CHAPTER 14

Jessie stared at the ivory telephone on the nightstand as if it were something strange suddenly sprung to life, its ringing an unexpected and fearful vital sign. Not once in the week she had been here had it rung, until now. There was an answering machine in the kitchen, but she hadn't even bothered to put her own message on it and turn it on.

But who would be calling her here, and at this hour?

If Philip Steadman had found out she was here, anyone might have. And the call might be an emergency—her mother . . .

Or more likely it was just some drunk who had dialed a wrong number, and in a moment he would hang up.

The telephone kept on ringing.

She had no sense of who the caller might be, but an instinct warned her, *Don't answer. Do not answer!*

As if it had a life of its own, her hand moved slowly toward the telephone. It picked up the handset and brought it to her ear. "Hello?" she said softly.

"Gussie?" said a male voice, as soft as her own. "Gussie, is that you?"

For a moment she thought she must be mistaken, that the caller could not possibly be who she thought he was—the very last person in the world, aside from Philip Steadman, that she wanted to hear from. Or so she had believed. But then he said, "It's Bradford, Gussie," and she was surprised by her own incredulous laughter.

"You son of a bitch!" she blurted out.

"Yeah," Brad said, and she could *see* the rueful look on his face. Bradford Holland, the Evil Elf, thin-cheeked, dark-eyed, so intense. "Yeah, I guess I was a son of a bitch, and maybe I still am. And you're still gorgeous, judging from your films, Gussie. Gorgeous Gussie."

"My God," she said, still laughing, "I haven't been called that in years!"

"It's been a while."

"But I don't understand . . ." She could not *believe* that she was actually pleased that it was Brad! "How did you find me? How did you get this number?"

"Gussie, my old man was rich, remember? He left me resources. I tell a guy I need a number, he calls me back with it, usually within an hour. You took longer; you've been in hiding. What's up, Gussie?"

"Oh . . ." What should she tell him? How much? Brad was not someone she wanted to bare her soul to.

"A very dear friend died recently."

"I'm sorry."

"He self-destructed. With the help of another friend. A friend of Timothy Balthazar, in fact."

Brad was silent for a moment, then she thought she heard his whisper, or perhaps it was his voice in her head: *Christ-ChristChristChristChrist* . . . Whatever it was, it was a prayer. She wouldn't have expected that from Brad.

"Buddy Weston, wasn't it," he said after a moment. "I saw it on the news. Why did they do it?"

It was as if the years hadn't passed. She could talk to him as if they had last spoken yesterday. "They did it because I left all that Luciferian bullshit behind long ago. When Buddy failed to bring me back into it, a man who hated and envied him decided he should die."

"God, I'm sorry. In a way, I feel I bear some responsibility. Because I brought you into all this."

He wasn't responsible, of course, but his words revived some of the old bitterness. "Yeah, you brought us in. All that business about how we were a 'family.' How we had to 'take care of each other.' How we were married to the god of this world and to each other. Jesus! And then you and Duffy, you just vanished."

"Gussie," Brad said gently, "we all knew we were going our separate ways at the end of the summer—"

"Look, Brad, I don't want to make too big a thing of this. We had a great summer of playing at being Luciferians and 'developing our powers' and having mostly-monogamous sex. Well, Joanne and Derek eventually got married, and you and I went our separate ways, and Duffy's out there somewhere doing just fine, I'm sure. But Lily got seriously hurt! Sixteen years old, for God's sake, and crazy in love with Duffy, and after screwing her brains out all summer, he just dumps her!"

"Maybe he thought it was the kindest way to break it off."

"Kind!" Jessie felt anger sweep over her and was honest enough to recognize that it was for herself as much as for Lily Bains. "Kind, did you say? Brad, I saw Lily almost every day after you guys left, and that kid suffered. I know. We were the last of the coven, the last of the 'family,' and I saw her pain when she realized that it was all over between Duffy and her. I held her in my arms when she cried. We're not talking about a schoolgirl crush, Brad, forgotten in a few weeks. Duffy Johnson broke that girl's heart!"

"And yet," Brad said mildly, tentatively, "I don't think he ever told her he loved her."

Jessie's anger flared. "Never told her he loved her? Well, la-di-fuckin'-da! I guess that gave him a license to treat her any way he pleased, didn't it? You guys, you can do anything you want to a woman who loves you, take any advantage of her feelings, screw her six ways from Sunday and back again and then walk away from her—*just as long as you don't say you love her!* Do you really think that takes him off the hook?"

"No," Brad said. "No, Gussie, I don't. I don't think it

takes Duffy or me or any other guy off the hook. I just wanted to hear what you'd say."

"You've heard. Why'd you call, Brad? And at this hour, for God's sake."

"I'm sorry. I did call earlier, I've called several times over the last few days, but I guess you were out. And it did seem urgent . . ."

Her anger began to abate. "What seemed urgent?"

"To warn you. Or at least caution you. But I suppose after what happened to Weston it isn't necessary."

"I can take care of myself. But you didn't know about Buddy and the cult until I told you. What else did you have in mind?"

Come back to St. Claire. . . .

"Gussie, you do realize this is the seventh summer, don't you? Quite aside from the vows we took, we all agreed to have a reunion—"

"Sorry. Can't make it."

Brad's sigh of relief was audible. "Good. But, Gussie, keep your guard up anyway. I've learned a lot more about the Luciferians in the last seven years, and while not all of them are bad, by any means, I swear the worst of them are goddamn psychos. They'd tear your heart out, literally, to please their god."

Jessie recalled the final look Steadman had thrown at her before descending the stairs, a look that had held not only pain but the most unforgiving hatred. Again, a shiver of fear went through her.

"Are you telling me I've got to spend the rest of my life looking over my shoulder?"

"Why should you be different from everyone else, Gussie?"

Gussie laughed. Yes, to Brad and the gang, she would always be Gussie.

"Seriously, Gussie, I've been getting signals, strong and clear, that I should return to St. Claire. At first I thought it was probably autosuggestion, induced by those damned vows—"

"No. I've been getting them too. *I* thought Derek had put the idea into my head, when he wrote to me about the reunion, but now . . . have you talked to any of the others, Brad?"

"I talked to Derek on the phone not long ago. He and Joanne have rented a lakeside cabin for the month of July. He's all enthusiastic, rarin' for a reunion. Wouldn't listen to me. Told me not to forget to bring my black cloak."

"That's Derek."

"I also located Duffy and phoned him. Apparently, he's been living with Nicole St. Claire since her grandmother died—"

"Nicole?" Gussie said, surprised. "Little Nickie?"

"Not so little anymore; she must be in her early twenties. Duffy was cool toward me. When I reminded him of the reunion, he said he'd, quote, given up all that crap when he went away to college. He said he and Nicole would be in St. Claire for a few days at the end of the month, but only because Nicole wanted to go back for a visit, not for any reunion. I told him I'd learned that Lily was back in St. Claire, figuring that might give him pause; but he just said, So what; if Nicole wanted to visit St. Claire, he was going with her. I guess he figures he can go back without ever seeing Lily."

"But, Brad . . ." Gussie did not like the sound of this. ". . . that means that most of the coven will be there, all at about the same time . . . all but you and me."

Brad didn't answer.

After a moment, she understood.

"Aw, no," she said. "No, Brad, you mustn't go back—"

"I have to, Gussie."

"But if we're being summoned, it could be dangerous!"

"That's the point. It could be dangerous for the others, and I'm responsible. You reminded me that I used to call us a family. Well, it's *my* family. I started it, and if it's in trouble, I have to do all I can to protect it."

Almost from the moment she answered the telephone, Gussie had sensed a change in Brad, and now she realized what it was. It was a tenderness, a warmth, a concern that she would never have expected him to reveal. Of course, it had always been there, it was one of the things that had attracted Gussie to him, but in the past he had always tried hard—almost desperately—to conceal it.

"Look, Gussie," he said, "maybe we're making too big a deal out of all this. Maybe the signals we're getting *are* just the result of suggestion and autosuggestion. And even if they're not, most of the time these people don't go beyond playing mind-games."

"Mind-games can be deadly, Brad. That's how they destroyed Buddy Weston."

"Yes, but when you know that's what they're up to, mind-games can be beaten."

"Even so, when I think of those terrible vows we made—"

"Don't! They were meaningless, Gussie, unless you let them have meaning. As a friend of mine says, 'Bad vows are meant to be broken.' "

Yes, she thought, but that didn't mean that the god of this world, if he existed, wasn't going to exact payment.

She considered her options.

"Brad, I've changed my mind. I can be in St. Claire in a week or so."

"Gussie, no! Why take a chance?"

"Because right now I'd feel safer in St. Claire than I do here. I don't think the man responsible for Buddy's death would stop at mind-games. Right now I'm sure he hates me more than he ever despised poor Buddy."

"Then go someplace else. Anywhere but St. Claire."

"No. I want to be with you."

Her words surprised her, but she found that, yes, she did want to be with Brad. The boy she had loved so much seven years ago.

"Oh, Christ," he said, "now I'm getting scared again. I don't think Balthazar or Freya Kellgren would go beyond mind-games, but . . . I have a feeling that they're just waiting until we're all there, and I'd like to know exactly what they have in mind."

"You think it's them."

"Who else?"

"Well, then . . . we'll confront them, if necessary. Give them their shot."

"My brave girl."

"Listen, an hour ago I busted the balls of a *really* dangerous man. Come on over and I'll tell you about it."

"Sweetheart, I'd love to, but I'm a continent away. Staying with a friend on Martha's Vineyard."

"Oh? A woman?"

"No. There is no woman in my life. No one important, not for quite some time."

Why did that piece of information lift her heart?

"Well . . . see you in a week, then. I'll try to get a room at the Hotel St. Claire."

"So will I. See you in a week."

Gussie, I'm sorry.

I did this to you. To you and the others. Got you into this situation.

If only it hadn't been for that goddamned book . . .

No, Brad, don't blame the book. In your heart you were a Luciferian already, and sooner or later you would have found what you were looking for. But you found it in a book on that spring day, seven years ago. . . .

THE CHILDREN OF THE GRIFFIN
THE HISTORY AND PRACTICES
OF A LUCIFERIAN CULT
Adam J. Valliere

His eyes had been drawn to the words A LUCIFERIAN CULT as to a beacon, and the book he had come to buy, something on computer programming, was immediately forgotten. He read the jacket copy and leafed through the pages with growing excitement. It was as if this were the book he had unwittingly been looking for for years, and now he *had* to have it! He paid for it at the front counter and hurried home to read it.

The book was all he could have hoped for. Written by a scholar, it synthesized all the reliable information on the cult—or the "Order," as its members preferred to call it—together with the author's own research. It named names, and many of them were far from obscure. The Order had been introduced to America two centuries before by the author's ancestor, Robert de Valliere, who was as important in American economic history as Astor or Vanderbilt. Much information had been supplied by the author's great-aunt, Charlotte Valliere Vanderlyn, the well-known philanthropist, feminist, and civil rights crusader, and at one time the leader of a Luciferian convocation.

As a descendant of the Valliere family, the author might have a bias, but he tried to be objective and fair. He acknowledged that the Order had a "dark side." Some of its members were said to indulge in practices more satanic than Luciferian, and their belief that one day they would dominate the world—"for its own good," of course—certainly had a fascistic ring. But apparently even in the darkest of the Dark Ages the Children of the Griffin had clung to a philosophy of worldly power and pleasure. That in itself had been enough to get them condemned as heretics.

Valliere's book was not wild-eyed speculation, then. There really was an order devoted to the development of its members' psychic powers and their use both for their own benefit and for the commonweal. An order made up of people like—dared he think it?—like himself. Himself and a few friends.

He wanted to join it.

He wanted to have his own convocation, or at least his own coven within a convocation.

He set about selling the others on the idea. When he told Gussie, reading her passages from the book, she was enthusiastic. The role of priestess, or "mother," of a coven appealed to her. Derek was interested and willing to give it a try if Joanne was, but Joanne was dubious. What was this business about "marrying" Lucifer and consummating the marriage on the altar with the priest as Lucifer's stand-in? Her only love was Derek, and she certainly wasn't about to join any high school sex club.

"But it isn't a sex club," Brad protested.

"By any other name," Joanne said scornfully.

Duffy, disappointingly, wanted absolutely nothing to do with a coven. Duffy didn't even want to talk about it. Duffy wasn't interested in anything that spring but Adrienne Martineau. And why Duffy was hot for snotty, dull-as-mud Adrienne when he had Lily Bains following calf-eyed after him, Brad had no idea. Sure, Lily was a little young, maybe, sixteen, but Brad sensed a potential power within her that Adrienne couldn't match. Now, if only Duffy would come into the coven and then bring Lily in . . .

Except that there wasn't any coven, and it didn't look as if there was going to be any. A coven of two, himself and Gussie, seemed ridiculous. A couple of kids playing a game. How was he going to get this thing off the ground?

His father gave him the answer.

Brad was lounging back on a sofa in the library one afternoon, the book lying open and facedown on his chest. He was so absorbed in his daydream of a coven that he didn't notice his father entering the room from his office.

Pierce Holland, thirteen years a widower, was in his seventies and retired. He was a tall man whose long, unwithered, slab-cheeked face seemed carved in white marble. Dark eyes peered out of it as from behind a mask, and Brad rarely had any idea of what he was thinking. A former law professor and New York State Supreme Court Justice, he was said to have one of the finest legal minds of his generation. At times, Brad felt that he hardly knew his father—he was like a fond but distant grandparent—and yet he had an aching desire for the man's approval.

Thus he was dismayed when his father reached down, plucked the book from his chest, and began to leaf through it. He could not believe his father would regard his interest in a Luciferian cult as anything but juvenile and frivolous.

His apprehension seemed justified when, after a few moments, a disdainful little smile appeared on his father's face. He was about to defend the book when his father laughed and dropped it back on his chest.

"If you're interested in Luciferianism," his father said offhandedly as he turned to leave, "ask Timothy Balthazar about it."

It was as if lightning had struck Brad. In that electric moment, so much came clear.

Of course!

His father and Timothy Balthazar were lifelong friends, and his father occasionally attended rather mysterious meetings at Timothy's great fenced-in citadel. Seminars, his father called them, and Brad gathered that people came from all over the country for them.

Brad could not believe that his father, so aloof and independent, would actually belong to a convocation. But he had a very great suspicion—or perhaps it was a hope—that Timothy Balthazar did.

Uncle Timothy.

His godfather.

When he finally managed to get Timothy Balthazar on the telephone, he found that his call was expected.

"Your father tells me you're interested in our little fellowship," Balthazar said without preamble. "Why don't you join me for lunch at my office tomorrow. I usually eat at my desk. I'll see you at twelve-thirty."

Carrying the book, Brad put in a nervous appearance at the appointed time. Balthazar barely glanced at the book as Brad laid it on his desk. Through his secretary, they ordered sandwiches and beverages, and they talked casually about school and sports and Brad's college plans while they ate.

When they had finished lunch and its detritus had been cleared away, Balthazar picked up the book and thumbed through it. "Interesting," he said, "especially the historical section. If you've read it, there's really not much more I can tell you."

"Then it's true that you're a Luciferian? And you belong to a convocation that meets right here in St. Claire?"

Balthazar laughed and laid the book down.

"Bradford, it's true that I have a great many powerful and influential friends. It's true that some of them have superior intuitive powers—*psychic* powers, if you insist. It's true that we meet from time to time for purposes of recreation and debate—"

"And worship?" Brad dared ask.

Balthazar ignored him. "A meeting of like minds, of *superior* minds, can be truly refreshing. And it's true that we like to call ourselves Luciferians. It has a certain ring."

Brad grew bolder. "What about vows? Have you and your friends taken Luciferian vows?"

Balthazar shrugged. "Like most fraternal organizations, we do have our vows, oaths, pledges, and so forth, all solemnly administered. Some of them are of such truly outrageous proportions that I doubt that you could take them seriously, Bradford."

"Try me."

Balthazar held up his right hand, rolled his eyes heavenward, and solemnly intoned: "If ever I turn my back on the god of this world, may I forever after suffer a painfully full bladder, a swollen prostate, and the most god-awful inability to piss." Brad laughed dutifully, and Balthazar smiled. "And yet, Bradford, our vows, however preposterous, are not to be taken altogether lightly."

"I won't take them lightly. I want to join."

Balthazar looked at him sympathetically. "My boy, I don't mean to patronize you, but the members of our little group are all mature and accomplished people. You're still very young, but one day—"

Brad laid a hand on the book. "This says the children of members are sometimes brought in when they seem promising." A guess: "My dad's a member, isn't he?"

Brad was not at all surprised when Balthazar shook his head. "Not really. Your father sometimes attends our meetings, but he holds a somewhat privileged position. He has never formally committed himself to the Order or to a convocation. He is in sympathy with the Luciferian point of view, but he maintains his independence."

That sounded like Brad's father, all right.

"Just the same, I want in, *Uncle Timothy*." This was his ace card, he hoped. "After all, you're my *god*father."

But Balthazar was already shaking his head. "You want in—and then you'll want to bring your young friends in. Isn't that true?"

"Well, yeah," Brad admitted, "I'd sort of like to have my own coven, like it says in the book."

"Fine. Start a coven. Anyone can do it. Make up your own vows along the lines suggested in the book. Develop your intuitive powers. Perhaps I can even get you some instruction, and I'll keep an eye on you—"

"But Uncle Timothy!" Brad saw his chances of winning membership fading, but he wasn't ready to give up. "Isn't it better to be brought in by someone who's already a member? I mean, isn't there a kind of apostolic succession whereby Luciferian power is passed on by the laying on of hands? That's what it says in the book. That's all I'm really asking for, to take the vows and get your blessing!"

At least Balthazar did not immediately say no. He drew a deep breath and looked at Brad for a long minute. Then he stood up and took a few thoughtful paces about his office.

"You're quite determined, aren't you?"

"Yes!"

"For the sake of argument," he said, "who do you hope to enlist in this coven of yours?"

Balthazar showed no sign of recognition as Brad named Derek, Joanne, and Duffy. "There's also another kid, Lily Bains, I think has possibilities. And my girlfriend, Gussie, of course. I know that's not many—"

"It's quite enough. Suppose I administered the vows to you, and you alone, in my private chapel before a few convocation witnesses. Would that satisfy you? Then you could start your own coven—"

"Great!" Brad agreed eagerly. It sounded as if he were being accepted after all, and in his excitement, he took a chance. "But not just me alone. Swear in me and my girl."

Balthazar stared at him as if startled by his temerity.

"Because no one will believe I've really been sworn in if it's just me," Brad explained. "They'll think I'm making it up. But if it's both Gussie and me, you can damn well bet they'll believe! And they'll join."

Balthazar nodded slowly. "Gussie is . . . ?"

"Jessie Gustava Lindquist. We call her Gorgeous Gussie."

"Connie Lindquist's girl, I believe. Does Jessie know what you plan? Is she as interested in this project as you are?"

"Every bit. Hey, we'll be *your* coven, Uncle Timothy!"

From the look Balthazar threw him, Brad figured he'd better not play the "Uncle Timothy" card again.

"Well, perhaps something can be done. How old is Jessie, Bradford?"

"Eighteen, the same as me."

"Good. Age of consent. And, one would hope, of discretion. Most people have no idea of what true Luciferianism entails, and I have no intention at some future date of being accused of corrupting the youth of Athens."

"Gussie . . . Jessie will be very discreet, I promise you."

Balthazar nodded. "All right, this is the procedure we'll follow. I don't suppose you're acquainted with Miss Freya Kellgren?"

"No," Brad said, surprised, "but I know who she is."

"You and Gussie, as you call her, will meet with Miss Kellgren in her home a few times. You will do it discreetly, without telling your friends. Miss Kellgren will acquaint you with some of our beliefs and the vows you will take and teach you a few exercises to increase your mental acuity. This will be the period of your novitiate, and if you should lose interest or have second thoughts, you may withdraw at any time. But you must swear never to reveal anything you have learned about the Order."

"I understand."

"A few weeks from now, when you are ready, you and your Gussie will come secretly to my house and take the vows before a small congregation." Balthazar smiled briefly. "The secrecy is half the fun. Wouldn't you agree?"

Brad agreed.

"Thereafter, you'll be on your own. You can form your own coven. If you have any problems or want further instruction, report to Miss Kellgren. Don't tell your coven that Miss Kellgren and I brought you into the Order—they may guess as much, but discretion is still wise. *Discretion*, Bradford."

"Yes, sir."

"Any questions?"

"Just one. According to the book"—Brad felt an unaccustomed embarrassment—"after the vows, there's, ah, the consummation. Does that mean we'll have to . . ."

Balthazar shook his head impatiently. "Of course not. In your own coven, you may do as you please, but for present purposes, the Kiss of Consummation will be quite enough."

Brad was relieved.

"One other thing," Balthazar said. "This is in the nature of an experiment, and I'll be watching you closely. I hope that in time you and perhaps the others will prove worthy of full membership in my convocation. But in any case, Bradford, I'll expect you to give me, not Miss Kellgren or any other, your complete loyalty. Don't you ever forget that it was your *Uncle Timothy* who brought you in."

"I won't forget, sir."

And so it came to pass . . .

Joanne and Derek had known that something special was going on with Gussie and him, had sensed that they shared a secret—why else would they look at each other the way they did, hiding smiles and smothering laughter?—and they wanted in on it. "What *is* it with you and Brad?" Joanne asked Gussie, only half joking. "Are you *pregnant* or something? Are you going to get married?" The question provoked more laughter. "Well, what *has* happened?"

A few days after the ceremony, he and Gussie finally told them. "My own father, for God's sake," Brad said, "my own father put me in touch with them. So I talked to this guy—this very prominent guy here in St. Claire, I can't tell you who he is—I talked him into bringing me in, and he said Gussie could join too."

They were safely behind the closed library doors in Brad's house, that evening, the lights turned low, as Brad told in detail everything that had happened to Gussie and him, up to the point where they knelt before the candlelit altar, clothed only in cloaks, and took the vows wedding them to the god of this world. "And then I kissed Gussie, the Kiss of Consummation, and that was it. We were in. The priest said, *'Ite missa est,'* 'Go, it is finished,' and the congregation turned and left with hardly a sound. We only saw one other face besides the priest and priestess. At the very end, this big naked guy who was staring at Gussie. Spooky."

Joanne's eyes glistened with excitement, all of her previous skepticism gone. She might not believe in *all* of this Luciferian stuff, but she wanted to play the game.

"So you didn't have to actually . . . do it," she said. "In front of everybody."

Brad shook his head. "I'd have been willing, but the guy said he wasn't going to have a couple of kids screwing on his altar. I told you, it's not a sex club, Joanne. It's serious."

She looked at Derek. "What do you think?"

"Like I always said," Derek answered, "I'm all for it."

• • •

And so it came to pass . . .

They held the ceremony the following Friday evening, and it turned out as Brad had hoped and planned.

It took place in his candlelit bedroom. The four of them wore black cloaks Brad had obtained from Freya Kellgren, and above the head of the bed hung a griffin tapestry Brad had borrowed from her. Their minds swirling from the brandy Brad had taken, with her tacit permission, from Freya's liquor closet, Brad and Gussie stood at the foot of the bed, and Joanne and Derek knelt on either side, hands steepled before their faces, looking like little children at prayer. Thick-tongued, Brad led Joanne and Derek through the terrible vows that wedded them forever to the god of this world . . . vows from which they could be released only by sacrificing the life of a loved one. . . .

"Arise," Brad said.

Brad went to Joanne's side of the bed, and Gussie to Derek's. Joanne's cloak was closed and its hood pulled far forward, and he could barely see her face by the light of the candles. But he saw the excitement in her eyes when he leaned forward to kiss her, and as their lips met, warm and swollen, he felt the tug of his flesh under his cloak.

After a moment, they ended the kiss and looked across the white sheets at Derek and Gussie. Eyes closed, the other two were still kissing. Gussie's arms emerged from her cloak, opening it, and slid up around Derek's shoulders. Derek's arms slid under her cloak and around her body, drawing her to him. The kiss seemed endless, as their bare bodies slid against each other. Derek slowly turned Gussie toward the bed and lowered her onto it. As she lay back, his lips left hers and went to her breast, and his hand slid down over her body.

Joanne, sweet Joanne, who had never been with anyone but Derek, continued to watch, her large gray eyes luminous in the candlelight, wide and unblinking, as if she were mesmerized. Brad took her into his arms, and the two of them seemed to float down onto the bed. When Derek, swollen with need, looked up at Joanne with drunken, unfocused eyes, she ever so slightly nodded, as if giving consent.

Derek turned back to Gussie and, as she raised her marvelously long ivory thighs up about his waist, took what had been granted.

Joanne's flesh was perfume in Brad's nostrils as he kissed her throat, and velvet in his hand as he caressed her body, but Joanne, still watching Derek and Gussie, hardly seemed to notice what he was doing. Then, just as he thought he could no longer hold himself back, she twisted in his arms and, moaning, kissed him hard on the mouth. Her fingers raked over his bare flesh and, as she lay back on the bed, grasped him, trying to draw him to her. Brad rose up over her, and for a brief conscience-stricken moment, as his cloak spread its shadow over Joanne, he had the illusion of being a raptor, a great dark bird of prey about to destroy forever something innocent. How could he do this? How could he possibly do this?

He had gone this far—he couldn't stop now.

She is yours, Lord Lucifer, he prayed desperately as he descended upon Joanne. *She is yours, my gift to you. Take her, make her your bride! Inhabit me, use me—it is not I but you who are taking her now. . . .*

Oh, yes! the god of this world seemed to answer as he entered his bride. *Oh, YES!*

And so it came to pass . . .

Yeah, Joanne, I did that. I seduced you. Seduced you into the coven and into my bed. And did it before my dear friend Derek's very eyes.

And used my own girl to do it. Pimped my own girl for favor with the god. . . .

He had told her: "Look, it's not as if you'd be *making love* to him, for God's sake! It's only sex, and not even *real sex* like *we* have. It's just a *ritual*, symbolizing union with the god of this world. If it wasn't like that, I'd be jealous as all hell!"

What bullshit.

But on a certain level, I believed it. I really believed it!

So I got us all just drunk enough on Freya's doctored booze that when the time came and we were all worked up and turned on and more than a little crazy, we went through with the whole goddamn thing.

Maybe it wouldn't have made any difference if we hadn't.

Probably not. The Kiss of Consummation would have been just as binding. But even so, I look back in shame. . . .

He knew now that he had always been trying to turn his little group into something closer than a mere circle of friends. He had wanted to turn it into the family he had never really had, a family bound together by oaths, if not by blood, with himself as the father. But the only father he had had to model himself on was his own, that cold, distant man . . . and his godfather, Timothy Balthazar. And that had not been enough. Gussie was right. For all of his talk of "family," by the end of the summer, he had begun to grow bored. He had looked forward to leaving St. Claire, and he had never really wanted to return.

Now he had to.

Joanne, don't go back to St. Claire. . . .

Sitting in his darkened bedroom, he spent a few minutes focusing on Joanne, trying to visualize her . . . a round face, pink cheeks, dainty cupid's-bow mouth . . . dark shoulder-length hair, gray eyes so often bright with a look of wonder. . . .

Joanne, don't go back to St. Claire. If you're already there, leave, leave just as soon as you can. . . .

God, if only he could just concentrate! But he was worried, and worry was almost always counterproductive. If only—

He had a sudden dreadful feeling that he was too late.

Something bad was about to happen.

Something was going to happen to Joanne.

Joanne, what is it?

Joanne, what can I do to help? Please, God, how can I help her?

Joanne—

Oh God please no!

She lay in darkness with a thundering heart and the certainty that something terrible was about to happen. This time, *this* time it was going to happen!

"Derek," she cried out, reaching for him, "Derek, please!"

But Derek wasn't there.

"Derek?" she said again, louder, and sitting up, she

reached out blindly for the bedside lamp, found it, twisted the switch.

Nothing happened. She was still alone in the dark with her pounding heart.

"*Derek!*"

"It's all right," Derek's voice came from below. "I'm here."

Trying to gather her panic-scattered wits, she seemed to drift through the darkness. She was on the sleeping balcony in the cabin at St. Claire, but it had become strange, dream-distorted, and unfamiliar, and her sense of dread was like a fist clenched in her chest. She found herself at the balcony railing, drawing aside the privacy curtain. In the faint ambient light below, and she could just make out Derek in his pajamas.

"Derek, what has happened?"

Derek said something about the power being out. He'd call the company.

Now she could hear wind gusting about the cabin and a tree limb scratching at the roof, like evil spirits trying to break in.

Derek had vanished. Joanne thought she heard the faintest click under the balcony as he picked up the telephone.

"Derek, what is it?"

"Goddamn phone is out. First the power and now the phone."

The fist tightened in her chest, squeezing her heart. "But why . . . ?"

"How should I know?"

As he spoke, a hand rapped at the front door.

"Ah, good," Derek said, hurrying across the room.

"*No!*" Joanne heard herself cry out.

In that instant, it was as if some part of her knew what was going to happen—as if this had happened before, always forgotten but inescapable, each time worse than the last, a heart-bursting, mind-shattering premonition of a horrible fate. This time, *this* time, surely, something terrible would come through the door and she would die before she awakened.

She heard herself screaming: "*Don't open the door!*"

But it was too late. Derek was already flinging the door open wide.

Laughing softly, a tall, dark, hooded-and-cloaked figure swept through the doorway, enveloping Derek in shadow, and she heard Derek fall to the floor with a horrible cry of pain.

The figure in the doorway looked up at her, its face a blur of sulfurous light within the hood. In a thick, low voice it said, "We've got a date, Joanne."

How many other dark figures, one or none or a dozen, followed that first one into the cabin, Joanne could not have said. It was as if the cabin were being invaded by silent shadows, by darkness itself, by a great inky nothingness that filled every corner and blotted out her sight. *Why, I'm fainting!* she thought, astonished, and as she fell, bodiless, into that darkness, she distantly heard Derek cry out again.

"Joanne . . . *Joanne!*"

She awakened to her own cries, clutching at her pillow, her heart pounding, still caught up in the terror of her dream. *Please, God, don't let it be happening! It* wasn't *happening! She was here, safe in her own bed, in Lafayette, Indiana, hundreds of miles from St. Claire! Please, God, please, please, please . . .*

Breathing slowly and deeply, trying to relax, she concentrated on the here and now, on this bed, this familiar room, Derek beside her, the light as Derek turned it on. *Please, God . . .*

Derek was gently caressing her shoulder, trying to soothe her.

"Better now?" he asked, when she had calmed.

She nodded.

"Bad dream? Want to tell me about it?"

She shook her head and whispered, "No."

"Sometimes it helps to tell."

That was true. But some dreams were too terrifying to be remembered. And all she knew now was that this one had had something to do with St. Claire, that it had been a warning that they shouldn't return. But if she told him that, he would get angry and tell her they *had* to return. "For God's sake, Joanne, you can't expect us to stay away from St. Claire just because of a crazy dream! Because of a dream *you can't even remember!* It's *important* for us to go back, the reunion has *got* to take place. There's a *book* in it, for God's sake, a book that will *sell*, if I can juice it up enough. It could make my name! And *you've* got to finish the research for your history of St. Claire and get your goddamn Ph.D.!"

Maybe he was right. She was no longer certain that the dream had anything to do with their return. It had already faded, leaving her with nothing more than a lingering sense of dread.

"I don't know what I dreamed," she said softly. "I don't remember."

Ite missa est.

The night's work was finished. Freya and Bruno had departed, and Lily awaited Timothy in his bed, while he, now in pajamas and robe, paid his nightly visit to Alida. She rested pale as a vapor on her bed, her forehead, when Timothy leaned over to kiss it, cool as alabaster. *My darling,* he promised silently, *I shall not fail you.*

All he had foreseen would come to pass. The Holland coven would return, and Nicole St. Claire with them. No more meetings to summon them were needed; he felt that with complete certainty. In a matter of days, the coven would be dealt with and Nicole destroyed, and his daughter would be returned to him.

Why, then, did he suddenly have this great feeling of apprehension, this feeling that he had overlooked something vital, that he was making a terrible mistake?

Never mind. This was no time for self-doubt. He must have complete faith in himself and in the Power he served.

My darling, I shall not fail you.

Part Three

NICOLE
THE
RETURN

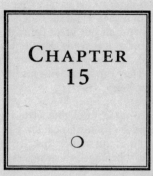

CHAPTER 15

They got off to a late start, and it was going on nine and fully dark when they arrived at the outskirts of St. Claire. Duffy didn't have to ask Nicole why she was pulling her Camry over to the side of the road. They had stopped at this same place, a high point overlooking the town, when they came up for her grandmother's funeral.

Nicole turned off the engine and cut her lights, and they got out. Duffy went around the front of the car. He drew Nicole into his arms. At this hour, on a Sunday evening, St. Claire was largely hidden in darkness, but they could see a few streetlights and a soft glow from lighted windows.

Duffy brushed Nicole's forehead with his lips. It was one of those times when they seemed to communicate wordlessly. He knew she was scared, and so was he. Freya Kellgren might be Nicole's last chance, but what did they really know about the woman? Only that her father had loved Freya and that she wanted to be of help to Nicole. If Freya failed her . . .

If Freya's methods, whatever they might be, only drove her more deeply into her madness . . .

There was that risk. Even if it turned out, as seemed probable, that Freya could do nothing at all for Nicole, the disappointment might in itself be enough to drive her over the brink.

But Nicole was determined to take that chance, that gamble. Duffy understood that. He also understood that to do so took not only desperation but great courage.

He knew when she was ready. She looked up at him and smiled. They kissed. She slipped out of his arms and they got back into the car. They drove off without having said a word. None had been necessary.

Duffy *had* to glance up at the lighted windows of his former home as they passed by it, but he couldn't bear to keep looking at it—the scene of his happy but irrecoverable past. It wasn't his anymore, it belonged to strangers, and that hurt. He understood completely the melancholy in Nicole's voice when she pulled the car to a halt in the St. Claire driveway, looked up at the big white house, ghostly in starlight, and said, "Home . . ."

Home . . . But was it home any longer? Nicole had told Duffy that despite her grandmother's promise that "we can always come back and see our friends," she had always seemed determined to keep Nicole away from St. Claire as much as possible. The first summer away, they had not returned at all but had traveled: a few weeks in England, Scotland, and Ireland, a month on the Continent. Thereafter, her grandmother had spent a few weeks of each summer in St. Claire—a couple of college students looked after the house the rest of the year—but Nicole had always been shuffled off to this or that camp or to visit distant cousins in Tucson or Seattle or New Orleans. In eight years, she doubted that she had spent a dozen nights in St. Claire, and except for her grandmother's funeral, she hadn't been back once since starting college.

Now they were both back for a week.

Back, perhaps for the last time.

When they entered through the back door and Nicole turned on the lights—she quickly deactivated the alarm system—Duffy felt as if he were stepping back into the past. It might have been only a month since he had last had supper with Nicole and her grandmother at the kitchen table. He had helped Aunt Julia shuck the corn for the meal. The refrigerator was purring comfortably, as it had on that evening, and when Nicole opened the door, they found a pleasant surprise. Someone had laid in a few supplies for them: orange juice, butter, and breakfast rolls, sugar, cream, and a pound of coffee. The coffeemaker, sparkling clean, was out on the counter.

They went through the house, turning on lights. Everything was pretty much as Duffy remembered it, and in the living room, he could almost feel Aunt Julia's presence at the escritoire, as she wrote a note with that old fountain pen he had always admired.

Nicole led the way upstairs, to territory less familiar to Duffy. Her bedroom was not quite the playroom that he recalled, though it was still home to a few ancient dolls, including a Raggedy Ann and a teddy bear. It seemed smaller now, but it was spacious enough to hold two full-size beds, one for Nicole, the other for the occasional guest. Both beds had been freshly made up, but only one, Duffy was certain, would be used tonight.

"I wrote to Mr. Balthazar that we were coming," Nicole said, "but my goodness, I didn't expect this! Food in the fridge, the beds made up . . . I'll have to thank him."

Balthazar, Duffy recalled, had looked after the property for Aunt Julia and continued to do so for Nicole. He would probably end up buying it.

They were back downstairs and about to fetch the rest of their luggage from the car, when Duffy, glancing out a front window, saw headlights approaching. "Company," he said, turning on the outside lights.

"So soon? We just got here. . . . Duffy, wait."

But Duffy had already opened the door and was pushing open the screen. Nicole followed him out onto the veranda.

The car had stopped in the driveway about thirty feet from the house. Duffy's first thought was *police sedan*, though the vehicle was unmarked.

The driver killed the lights and climbed out of the car, slowly, as if he had all the time in the world. He was a tall, hard-looking man in his middle thirties, dressed in tan chinos, the short sleeves rolled up over thick biceps. He stretched and flexed his muscles, almost as if preening, and sauntered toward the veranda. He looked familiar to Duffy.

"Well, evening, Duffy . . . and Miss Nicole, isn't it?"

Duffy recognized the voice. The deputy who could spit bullets.

He said, "I know you, but . . ."

The man grinned. He had enormous teeth. "Krull. Bruno Francis Krull. Sheriff Krull of St. Claire County, at your service."

Duffy went down a couple of steps and reached out to shake hands. Krull had a firm, strong grip.

"Nice to meet you again, Sheriff. What can we do for you?"

"Sorry if I alarmed you, dropping in like this." Krull flipped a thumb to his right. "Somebody up at Dad's place saw a light down here, so he asked me to check it out." Krull looked at Nicole. "You've got a good security system here, Nicole, but some of these B-and-Es are damn clever at getting around them. Couldn't hurt to take a look."

"Dad?" Duffy asked, puzzled.

"Oh. Sorry." Krull laughed and shuffled his feet. "Mr. Balthazar. Mr. B.'s been sorta like a substitute dad to me for years. Ever since my real daddy, if that was what he was, fell down some stairs and broke his neck. Sent me to college, looked after my ma till she married again and moved away. Somehow I got in the habit of calling him Dad. He never seemed to mind."

To what, Duffy wondered, did they owe the honor of all this autobiography? Come to think of it, Krull did look a little like Balthazar, with those thick, high cheekbones and oddly colorless eyes.

"Is there anything we can do for you, Sheriff? We'd ask you in, but it's late, and since we just got here . . ."

The sheriff was holding up a hand and shaking his head. "Nah, nah. Dad—Mr. B.—just asked me to drop in and say hello, and . . ."

". . . *my real daddy, if that was what he was, fell down some stairs* . . ."

Suddenly, as occasionally happened, a series of vivid images flowed through Duffy's mind . . . a man lying crumpled at the foot of a dark staircase, his head twisted around at an impossible angle . . . Timothy Balthazar standing at the head of those stairs, fists clinched, eyes glowing in the dark . . . the man, sometime earlier, telling the boy that "if the truth was known, I ain't even your real daddy, go ask your fuckin' whore of a mother" . . . the man hitting the woman, beating her to the floor, and tearing at her clothes . . . the man with the boy again, undressing him, seductive at first, but then so brutal that Duffy tried to wipe the images away . . . and once again the man lying crumpled at the foot of the stairs. . . .

It was far too elaborate and improbable a scenario to be constructed on the basis of a few words, and yet for a breathless moment Duffy had the impression that he was looking into Bruno Krull's mind.

Whether or not what he had seen there was true, Duffy was left with an impression that was so strong he could hardly deny it. It was the kind of impression he frequently had while working with patients. He would have bet almost anything that in childhood Bruno Francis Krull had been—the classic syndrome—a bed wetter, an arsonist, and a torturer. A torturer of animals, for the most part, but as cruel to other children as he dared to be.

Duffy was aware of the unfairness of leaping to such a conclusion when he had not the slightest rational basis for it, but . . .

. . . but Krull was still speaking.

"Mr. B. said he'd appreciate it if you'd give him a call, Duffy. He'd like you to take a look at his daughter. You heard about his daughter, maybe?"

No, they hadn't. Briefly, Krull told them about Alida's diabetic coma.

"Oh, that poor girl!" Nicole said.

"Sheriff, I'm just a medical student, a beginning intern. Why would he want me to look at his daughter?"

Krull shrugged and started to turn away. "All I know is, Mr. B.'s taken a real interest in you, Duffy, and when Mr. B. takes an interest in someone, he can do him a lot of good. On the other hand, Mr. B. does not like to be disappointed. You might think about that."

Again, for an instant, Duffy saw a man lying dead at the foot of a staircase.

"Yeah, I'll think about that. Good night, Sheriff."

"You folks have a nice visit."

Duffy and Nicole watched in silence while the sheriff turned his car around and drove away.

"Well, what do you think, Dr. Johnson?" Nicole asked when the car had vanished.

What Duffy thought was that he wished they'd never come back to this goddamn place. The images lingering in his mind made him feel stained and dirty.

What he said was: "Diagnosis: psychopath. Prognosis: homicide. Sooner or later that son of a bitch is going to kill somebody. If he hasn't already."

The first thing Nicole thought on awakening was that she must telephone Freya Kellgren. She had written to Freya, saying she and Duffy were coming to St. Claire, and last week she had received a reply. Nicole was to call Freya as soon as convenient.

But not, Nicole thought, glancing at the bedside clock-radio, at 6:45 A.M.

Careful not to disturb Duffy, she slid out of bed and pulled on shorts and a T-shirt. She was in the kitchen making coffee when, to her surprise and delight, Joanne appeared at the door.

How great! Eight years ago Nicole had been just a kid who sometimes hung out with Duffy and his friends, a kind of mascot. But now the age gap had diminished, and they found themselves embracing like long-lost sisters.

Derek had seen their lights last night and had wanted to come running up right away, but Joanne had said no, it was late, let them settle in, for heaven's sake. How long were Nicole and Duffy here for? Only a week—Duffy had to get back to New York and go to work. Oh, too bad! Joanne and Derek were in the first lakeside cabin up the road, the same one they had rented every summer since their parents had retired and left St. Claire. They had booked it for July, but the June people had left early, and Mr. Balthazar, who owned most of the cabins on the lake, had told them they could move in anytime, no extra charge.

"How generous of Mr. Balthazar!" Nicole said.

"Oh, wasn't it." Joanne's lip curled in a way that seemed to question Mr. Balthazar's generosity.

Joanne had changed. Not so much physically—she was still the same soft-voiced, gray-eyed, well-endowed beauty she had been—but Nicole sensed disillusionment and a hint of bitterness in her manner.

"Listen," she said, "I can't stay long. If Derek wakes up and finds me gone, he'll come charging up here, and I felt I had to warn you."

"Warn me . . . ?"

They were sitting at the kitchen table by then, drinking coffee, Joanne smoking a cigarette.

"God," she said, "I feel so disloyal . . . no, I don't, I don't even feel disloyal anymore."

"Warn me of what?"

"Derek and his gooney little tape recorder. He'll want to interview you."

"Whatever for?"

"Memoirs of the famous Wolf Girl of St. Claire, what else?"

Nicole felt stunned and for a moment couldn't speak.

"But I don't understand. That was all long ago."

"Not if Derek dredges it up."

"But why would he want to?"

Joanne stubbed out her cigarette and sighed. "Money, what else? Fame and fortune.

"You see, Derek may be a grad student in sociology, but his real interest is in writing. A few years ago, he started turning out articles for the tabloids, trying to make a little extra money, and he found he had a knack for it. He specializes in cult stuff, satanic and Luciferian, that's really what got him started." Joanne shook her head in disgust. "He doesn't even use a pen name to protect his academic credibility, and some of our 'friends' at the U. call him *Dreck* Anderson. Actually, he's a good researcher and his stuff is all based on fact. But, as they say, he never lets the facts stand in the way of a good story."

"I thought tabloids were mostly staff-written."

"So Derek tells me, and—point of pride—he's now practically on staff at *Full Disclosure*. They want him to be a kind of roving correspondent. He's that good."

"But . . ." Still dazed, Nicole shook her head. ". . . why me?"

"It started last summer. We come back here every summer, you know, so I can research the history of St. Claire for my Ph.D. Last summer, we heard that you had been back here for your grandmother's funeral. That reminded Derek of the Wolf Girl business, his kind of thing. But, as you say, it was a long time ago, not fresh, so he put it on the back burner.

"Then, when we got here this year, we ran into Mr. Balthazar at the rental office, and he casually mentioned that you were planning a visit here soon. That immediately put you on Derek's *front* burner. You see, he's been pressing for a reunion of our little high school gang, and since most of us knew you—"

"The coven."

Joanne looked surprised. "Duffy told you about that?"

"Not much, but enough to give me the idea. He said that Brad Holland started it and all you guys joined it, and you were Luciferians and did 'weird shit.'"

Joanne laughed weakly. "We did weird shit, all right. Mostly at Brad's place. You ever been there?"

Nicole shook her head.

"Big old place on a big old country estate northeast of town. And his daddy not there half the time. So we ran around naked under black cloaks, doing, as you say, weird shit. Performing Luciferian rituals. Getting high on Luciferian booze at Luciferian eucharists. Calling on the power of Lucifer and his demons to do our will. And other weird shit I prefer not to remember.

"But the thing is, now Derek figures he has his story. A Luciferian coven gathering again after seven years, in accordance with their sworn vows. Not only that, but the infamous Wolf Girl, known to most of the coven, returning at the same time. The Wolf Girl, who evidently *lives* with one of the coven. Derek found out months ago that you and Duffy have the same address. I told you he was good at research."

"I still don't see much of a story in this," Nicole said hopefully.

"Oh, Nickie, you don't know Derek! For the past week, he has devoted every hour to locating people who knew you and interviewing them. Your teachers, your schoolmates, your friends. He's even talked to your *grandmother's* friends. Believe me, Derek's not going to miss a bet."

"But doesn't he understand the trouble he could cause?" Nicole asked in dismay. "All those Dugans and their friends, they hated me, and I'm sure some still do. I planned to visit St. Claire quietly and see a few friends and leave. But if the Dugans find out I'm here . . ."

"Find out? Nickie, the Dugans were among the very first people Derek interviewed. I've heard some of the tapes, and you're right, their feelings toward you haven't changed one bit."

"You're saying they already know I'm here."

"Or will, before the day is over."

"And Derek doesn't even care if something ugly happens, thanks to his 'research'?"

"Doesn't care? Derek would dearly *love* for something to happen! Something he can 'juice up,' as he puts it. He's looking for a book!"

As they talked, a feeling of oppression had come over Nicole. Now her body jittered to *do* something, to get up and stride about, to run, and she found it hard to breathe. Seeing this, Joanne put a hand on Nicole's arm and looked steadily into her eyes, gray eyes into brown. After a minute, Nicole found herself breathing easily again, in rhythm with Joanne.

Both women laughed unsteadily.

"Well," Nicole said, "I'm not going to worry unnecessarily, and I'm certainly not going to hide from the Dugans. I'm going to do what I came here to do, and leave."

Which led to the question that most interested her at the moment. "Joanne, do you by any chance remember a woman named Freya Kellgren?"

"Freya Kellgren . . ."

Joanne's gaze drifted, as if she were reviewing her memories. "Funny you should ask," she said after a moment. "She was a friend of Brad Holland's. What about Freya Kellgren?"

"She was close to my father, but I never met her, except once, at my grandmother's funeral. We thought we might get together. I'm curious as to what you might know about her."

Joanne nodded. "Very little, actually. I don't know if Duffy told you, but the coven was supposedly just a kind of beginners' adjunct to a much larger convocation. I somehow got the idea that maybe Freya was the one who brought Brad and Gussie into it, and that *she* was the one who was teaching *him* all the mind-stretching psychic stuff that *he* was teaching *us*. I even got the idea that she might be its leader. But when I asked, Brad and Gussie just smiled their funny little smiles and said that eventually, if we proved worthy, all would be revealed."

"Mr. Balthazar," Nicole said.

The name had sprung to her lips faster than conscious thought, but she immediately recalled things her grandmother had said when she was a child, things she had overheard: *"Timothy has always liked to joke about being a Luciferian . . . but I'm reasonably certain that he really is . . . and he jokes to cover the fact."*

"Mr. Balthazar," she said with certainty, "was the head of the convocation."

Joanne was looking at Nicole wonderingly. "It's possible, I suppose. I know he was a friend of Brad's father. It could be that he and Freya headed the convocation the way Brad and Gussie headed the coven. I've wondered why he was so generous in letting Derek and me take over the cabin early. Now, if he was trying to get us all back here at the same time . . . for that reunion we promised . . ."

Joanne's words troubled Nicole. After all, she had been counting on Freya; but if Freya was involved in something questionable . . .

"Do you think Freya and Mr. Balthazar were into the . . . weird stuff?"

"Mr. Balthazar? Hardly." Joanne waved the question away as ridiculous. "I think that stuff was mostly a reflection of Brad . . . and ourselves. Brad made most of it up, based on that book he carried around, *Children of the Griffin*."

They heard footsteps. Joanne looked up as Duffy entered the room.

There was a long moment of silence while he and Joanne took each other in. Then he went to Joanne and looked down at her, smiling faintly. He bent down and they embraced and kissed. When they broke apart, they were both smiling, and Nicole had a happy feeling that something good had been recovered.

"The Duffy I knew and loved, before the coven, is back," Joanne said. "How did that happen?"

"By the grace of God and Nicole's grandma, if you really want to know. What brought back the Joanne *I* knew and loved?"

"Oh, I got disillusioned . . . disillusioned by a lot of things. I realized that I was really a very, very conventional girl and my Luciferianism was just an abortive kind of rebellion."

Duffy nodded. "Not only you."

Joanne's smile faded. "But I'm not quite the same Joanne you knew, Duffy."

"None of us is quite the same." He looked at Nicole. "With one possible exception."

"And I wish I wasn't," Nicole said. "Tell me this, Joanne. It's a question Duffy finds hard to answer. Did you people really believe in all this Luciferian stuff?"

Joanne frowned and shook her head as if she weren't sure of the answer. "I think Brad did. And Gussie did because Brad did." She looked at Duffy as she spoke. "Duffy . . . he was strange that summer. In a dark mood. Sometimes it seemed to me he was more truly Luciferian even than Brad."

"I was a creep," Duffy said. "A totally self-centered, exploitative creep."

Joanne turned to Nicole. "But the rest of us . . . I think we *played* at believing. Played at believing we believed, and maybe that comes to the same thing. I don't know. In a way, I believe now more than I did then. I don't believe the devil is really the god of this world, but I sure as hell believe he wants to be."

They sat in silence for a moment.

"Well," Joanne said, slowly rising from the table, "I'd better get back before my husband comes looking for me."

Her husband . . . Nicole saw before her a woman whose marriage had failed, had perhaps never truly been a marriage.

She sensed that Joanne and Derek would never again return to St. Claire, at least not together, and Joanne was going to badly need a friend.

"Joanne," she said impulsively, "why don't we all get together for dinner tonight? I don't know that I'll have time to cook, but we can send out for chicken or Chinese."

Joanne seemed to get the message behind the words. She smiled, as Nicole stood up, and embraced her. "You're an angel," she said. "Thanks for being here."

"Hey," Nicole said, "we're here for each other."

The morning passed swiftly.

After breakfast, Nicole and Duffy explored the upper reaches of the house. Her grandmother had cleaned out the attic, shipping the few things she wanted to save to New York and selling or discarding the rest. They found the same to be largely true in the basement, and in the garage, which sheltered little more than Nicole's car and a few rusty tools. No hidden treasures there.

Then they surveyed the surrounding lawns, nicely clipped, the strip of beach and the little dock where her father's long-gone sailboat had been moored, and the edge of the nearby woods. The day was bright and balmy, and all of Nicole's senses seemed wonderfully alive. Her sense of smell, cleansed of city fumes, was especially acute. The green smell of cut grass and the brown smell of earth were like perfumes, and a strange, distantly remembered animal smell that wafted out of the woods made her mouth water. She had not expected to be happy, coming home, but this morning, despite what Joanne had told her, she was.

Nicole had checked last night to be sure the telephone was working. She forced herself to wait until after nine to call Freya. To her disappointment, there was no answer. Nor was her second call, twenty minutes later, answered. No answering machine, apparently. Amazingly, her grandmother's old machine still worked, and she hooked it up.

Nicole decided she was paranoid, completely paranoid.

Since they were going to need some basic supplies, something for lunch, she had decided to drive into town, leaving

Duffy to catch up on his medical journals. She had looked forward to seeing the old familiar streets by daylight, but even before she parked her car near the town square, she felt as if she were being watched by unseen eyes. And that simply didn't make sense. She could only ascribe the feeling to paranoia brought on by knowing that Derek had been talking to all those people about her. But those people weren't *looking* at her, for goodness' sake. They probably weren't even thinking about her.

Still, the feeling wouldn't go away.

Someone was watching her from the nearby courthouse, someone from the library, across the square. Someone from the windows of Mr. Balthazar's office, down on the corner . . .

People on the busy sidewalks barely gave her a glance, and yet the sensation was so strong that she ducked into Pearson's drugstore to escape all those staring eyes.

"Hello, Nicole."

Nicole nearly jumped. But it was only Mr. Pearson, behind the drug counter. His bushy mustache was grayer than she remembered, and his plump, pink face a little more lined. He had recognized her instantly. But then, why wouldn't he? As a child, she had been in the drugstore hundreds of times.

He smiled and made small talk and looked at her. With knowing eyes.

Nicole bought a few items and left as soon as possible.

Paranoia.

She had decided to cook for Joanne and Derek after all. What the heck, she could throw together a mean chicken Marsala in almost no time. The liquor store was just down the street, and as she hurried toward it, she tried to ignore the sensation of being watched.

"Do you have Marsala?" she asked the man behind the counter.

He slowly turned his head to look at her. His middle-aged face was brown, lean, and bony. A toothpick dangled from his lips. He didn't answer. His mouth grew prim and disapproving, and his eyes pinched into a slight frown.

"Dry Marsala?" Nicole prompted, her heart thumping a little harder. Her stomach suddenly felt queasy.

The man flipped his thumb toward a wall.

She found the dry Marsala, carried a bottle back to the counter, and took out a twenty-dollar bill.

"Danny St. Claire's little girl, innit?" the man asked, accepting the bill.

As far as she knew, she had never seen the man before in her life. She tried to smile. She said, "As a matter of fact, it is."

"Gonna be here long?"

"A few days."

He gave her change and a receipt, thrust the bottle into a narrow brown sack, and shoved it toward her.

He was still frowning. As if the words tasted bad, he said, "Enjoy your stay."

Thank you very much, she thought with a surge of anger, *and screw you too!*

She thought she saw the man's face tighten as she hurried to the door.

By the time she had driven to Southgate Plaza, the queasiness was gone, and the sense of being watched, and she felt much better. Perhaps it was just that the plaza was near the edge of town and the sky seemed more open and the area less crowded. She liked that. She had never felt that way in New York, a city she dearly loved, but she did here. She parked, went into the supermarket, and worked the aisles with her cart, checking off her list.

As she approached the checkout counter, the nausea began to return, worse than ever. Dear Lord, what was wrong with her? She had to get out of the store, get out and breathe some fresh air, before she was really sick.

"Nice day, ain't it?" said the girl behind the counter.

Yes, it certainly was, Nicole agreed, wanting to mean it, but silently hoping the girl would please, please hurry.

Smiling, almost deliberately slow, the girl checked out Nicole's purchases, while an elderly man bagged them. When she had given Nicole her change and receipt and the bagger had walked off, she said, "You don't remember me, do you?"

"Why, I . . ." The girl—the young woman—was about Nicole's age and had a pleasantly freckled round face. Nicole looked at her name tag. Annette. Nicole didn't remember her at all.

"You *are* Nickie St. Claire, ain't you?"

Nicole tried to laugh. "Yes. Yes, that is my . . ."

The woman was still smiling, but there was something peculiar about her pale blue eyes. They looked like glass, and the pupils were almost pinpoints in the bright light.

"We was in the same class in school," she said, "but of course you never looked at me."

Recognition came at last. The woman had changed, but Nicole had indeed known her, even if they hadn't exactly been playmates. "Why, Annette!" she said, laughing with pleasure in spite of her sick stomach. "Annette, why, of course I—"

"I know you even if you don't know me," the woman said, her smile never failing. "You're the sick, crazy bitch that killed my cousin, Buster Dugan, and I don't care if I do get fired for saying it."

Nicole felt as if a door had been slammed hard against her face—an actual physical blow that stunned and numbed and momentarily blinded her. Then it blossomed into bright blood-red pain, and she could see again: that smiling, blue-eyed woman.

With a small, silent cry, she grabbed her cart and ran.

"Have a nice day," the woman called behind her.

Back in the Camry, Nicole allowed herself to cry for a few minutes.

She remembered now. Before she and her grandmother had left St. Claire, there had often been times when she had felt the same way she had in town, as if she were being watched by a thousand eyes. Not constantly, or it would have driven her crazy, but often enough that she had tried to harden and desensitize herself, had tried to shield herself from . . . from what?

From the hidden eyes of hatred and fear and mistrust . . . or even simple morbid curiosity.

Of course, by now most of the town had forgotten her very existence, or so she wanted to believe. But there were still those who remembered, those who hated, feared, and mistrusted her.

The man in the liquor store.

The woman in the supermarket.

Perhaps she wasn't completely paranoid.

She decided not to tell Duffy about the incident immediately. She didn't want them both to be upset. She would tell him about it in a day or two, when she had put it behind her.

When Nicole called Freya after lunch, she at last answered.

Freya was light. Freya was fresh country air. Freya was hope.

Freya was her friend.

Oh, God, what a relief it was to be with Freya, warm and loving Freya, and have this wonderful sense that everything was going to be all right at last. She thought her father must have felt much this same way when he first met Freya.

Freya quickly allayed any lingering doubts Nicole might have had about her, answering questions almost before they were asked. Yes, she knew *of* Bradford's little coven, though she knew almost nothing about it. You see, Timothy Balthazar had led a group of Luciferians—very *distinguished* Luciferians—and, for that matter, still did, if truth be told. Young Bradford found out and wanted to join, along with his girl, Jessie Lindquist. Well, that was out of the question, of course; they were very young and hardly qualified. Freya herself was a member only as Timothy's friend and as a gifted teacher of mind-expanding techniques. But since Timothy was acquainted with both kids' parents, he arranged a kind of initiation, complete with the most *outrageous* vows, my dear, so that they could consider themselves Luciferians and start their own coven. That was really all there was to it. Except that, at Timothy's request, Freya had taught Bradford a few mind-expanding techniques that he had presumably passed on to his friends. And Bradford had repaid Freya by raiding her liquor supply, the little devil!

What could be more harmless?

Why, Nicole's father, in fact, had been a novice Luciferian and one of her best students.

"But he taught me, Nicole," Freya said, her amethyst eyes shining. "He pointed out that Lucifer, the morning star and bearer of light, was but an aspect of Venus, the evening star and goddess of love. I don't want to embarrass you, but . . .

he was Lucifer to my Venus, and together we were one and the same. There will never be another man like him in my life."

Why, Nicole wondered, had she ever feared Freya? Why had she seen, or thought she had seen, something cold and forbidding in her? And why in the world had she ever thought of Freya as *old*?

She wasn't old. She must have been about Nicole's father's age, had he lived, but she appeared to be in her thirties at most. Her figure was slim and firm and her complexion flawless. She had only the faintest of wrinkles about her eyes, only the slightest sagging of the flesh under her chin. She was old enough to be Nicole's mother, but she could easily have passed for her older sister.

And that was how Nicole felt toward this lovely woman in tattered jeans, as they sat in Freya's breakfast nook, drinking iced tea and talking—as if she had been reunited with an older sister she had known and admired all her life.

Without quite knowing how it had come about, she found herself recalling for Freya the entire history of her illness. She told how she had unwittingly killed her pet mouse. She told of similar incidents that had followed, particularly after her father's death, and the therapy she had been given. She related how, in the sixth grade, she had become fascinated by wolves and had experienced a wonderful series of dreams—culminating in that terrible moment when she awakened in the snow with a rabbit's torn and bloody carcass in her hands.

"After Grandma and I left St. Claire," Nicole told her, "I really did seem to be getting better . . . with a few relapses. But after Grandma died last year, it started again, and . . . lately it's been getting worse. Much worse. I keep thinking, Oh, my God, does this mean I've got to have shock therapy or maybe even surgery after all!"

"No," Freya said quietly but firmly. "No shock therapy, no surgery. That, I promise you."

At those words, Nicole felt the tension leaving her body, and she looked at Freya with gratitude. It might almost have been her grandmother who had spoken.

"I have no idea of what my daddy had in mind, but I remember him saying you thought perhaps you and he together could help me . . . ?"

"You were a child then and more malleable. However . . ."

"You don't think there's any hope?"

"I didn't say that. Perhaps I can still help you. But now more depends on you."

"I'll do anything within reason."

"What I suggest may seem unreasonable. It may even offend you. All I ask is that you not dismiss what I have to say out of hand. Think about it. Consider it, no matter how outrageous it may seem. Do you think you can do that?"

"I can certainly try."

"Good. I can't promise you overnight results, and you may think you're getting worse before you get better. But if you're willing to try your very best, I won't give up on you, and we'll see it through together. Is there any reason you can't stay in St. Claire the rest of the summer?"

She had already considered that possibility and rejected it. "Duffy needs me. If I have to wait till fall to work with you, I'll wait."

"No need. If necessary, I'll return to the city early. Meanwhile, we can get started right now, if you like."

"Oh, yes, anytime!"

Freya leaned back in her chair. She crossed her arms over her chest and closed her eyes. She took a deep breath and released it slowly, and for a moment seemed lost in contemplation.

"All right," she said, opening her eyes. "Nicole, I want you to consider the possibility that your so-called lycanthropy is not an illness at all. I want you to explore the possibility that it is actually an extraordinary power and privilege. I want to suggest that, far from being a pitifully afflicted creature, you are a superior being and to be envied. You can experience things that others only dream of."

Superior? To be envied? In confusion, Nicole thought of all that she had suffered—the insatiable hungers, the tortured sense of oppression and confinement, the terrible longing to escape. "I don't see how . . ."

"Darling, didn't you tell me that one of the happiest periods of your childhood was when you were having your wolf-dreams? In your dreams, you accepted your wolf-nature. You loved being a wolf! And yet you retained enough of your human consciousness to remain in control, if need be."

Freya's voice had softened, and Nicole found herself listening intently. "That's the key, Nicole. As long as you fight your wolf-nature, you will be a divided, suffering person. But when you fully accept the wolf in yourself, when you embrace her, when you learn to love her and to revel in being what you really are, then you will find yourself fully in control.

"But you must accept every aspect of yourself . . . the hungers, the cravings . . . the instinct to defend yourself and your territory . . . the urge, if need be, to kill. . . ."

To kill? Never. What was Freya saying? Nicole could never do that.

And yet . . .

Freya's voice sank lower. "Of course, it will probably never come to that. But when they threaten you . . . don't fight the urge to attack . . . let it grow . . . enjoy it, savor it . . . and then . . ." The words were little more than a whisper. ". . . and then, let them see your teeth."

Let them see your teeth. . . .

Nicole thought of the woman behind the checkout counter that morning, the woman whose spite had so sickened her. Might she have responded differently? What if she had refused to be sickened? What if she had struck back, instead, with rage? What if she had, literally, bared her teeth?

She could feel her lips quivering as she drew them back. She could see the woman's constant, malicious smile slowly fading, as fear, even terror, came to her eyes. She could see the woman shrinking back from her. . . .

Yes, I killed your cousin Buster. When you give me a hard time—remember that!

"Let them see you for what you really are. . . ."

Nicole smiled.

Duffy finally admitted to himself that he wanted to see Lily Bains—the one person he had most hoped to avoid for the last seven years. The person who made him feel guiltier than anyone else possibly could. The reunion with Joanne this morning had proved to be an unexpected blessing. It would be great if he could meet with the other four and find that, like Joanne and himself, they had all put the summer of the coven behind them, as an aberration they could forgive in each other and forever lay aside.

He didn't think that would happen with Lily. He had treated her just too damned shabbily. Furthermore, he had no right to take a chance on opening old wounds.

Just the same, he wanted to see her.

He had Nicole drop him off on the square on her way to Freya's. He said he was going to wander around, see some of the old places, maybe the high school. Have a couple of beers and wind up at the library, look at the new magazines. He'd meet her on the square around five if she was free by then, but if they missed each other, he'd take a taxi back to the house.

He felt guilty. If Nicole had any idea that he wasn't being altogether forthright, she gave no sign.

He did wander around for a while, had a couple of beers, stalled. Saw no one he knew, aside from Mr. Pearson at the drugstore. Finally headed for the library. Brad had said something about Lily working at the library, as her mother had done, and that seemed like a good place for a meeting. A public place. If the meeting went sour, there would be less of a scene. He hoped.

Entering the library, he looked around at the familiar tables and stacks, the students and the browsers and the librarians, but he saw no one who might have been Lily. He inquired of a woman at the front desk about Ms. Bains.

"The cataloguer," the woman said disapprovingly, "she sets her own hours. She said she had some errands to run, and she might or might not be back this afternoon."

Duffy felt mingled relief and disappointment.

"If she does come in," he said, "please tell her a friend is waiting for her over by the magazines."

He settled down in a reasonably comfortable chair with the current *New York Times Magazine.* He had finished a couple of articles and was close to dozing off when he heard a small shriek of pleasure, followed by laughter, breaking the library silence. "Duffy, Duffy, Duffy!" a familiar voice said. Arms reached down to embrace him, and he looked up into shining brown eyes flecked with green.

· · ·

For an instant he had the sensation that this was not the same
Lily Bains he had known. That Lily Bains had been a girl; this
one was a woman. This was the beautiful, half-remembered
woman of his dreams. And she was welcoming him, literally
with open arms. As he stood up, she rose on her toes and,
lightly embracing him, kissed his cheek. At that feathery
touch, her body brushing his, an old familiar thrill went
through him.

There was so much to talk about, she said, taking his
hand. He must come to her office—well, it wasn't really an
office, just a cubicle *in* the office, but it would give them at
least a *little* privacy.

They sat at her paper-littered, terminal-laden desk, she
behind it and Duffy in a chair at its corner, and it turned out
that Lily already knew a great deal about Duffy. She already
knew he had done his pre-med in three years, that he had
taken honors time after time in medical school, that he had
drawn Paraclete General, his hospital of choice, for his internship.

"Mr. Balthazar told me. Duffy, he is so proud of you! As
if you're some kind of godson. 'One of the best young men St.
Claire ever turned out,' he says." Lily's face clouded. "Have
you heard about his daughter?"

Duffy had heard.

"Poor Alida. I think Mr. Balthazar would do anything to
get her back, anything at all." Lily contemplated that sad fact
for a moment, then smiled at Duffy. "If you're wondering,
Mr. Balthazar has been awfully good to me. He helped pay my
way through college, and he says anytime I want to go back to
school, he'll pay, no limit. He'd do as much for you too,
Duffy, I know he would, if you gave him a chance."

There it was again, the temptation. . . . *come back to St.
Claire . . . and all good things shall be yours . . .*

Duffy shook his head.

"That reminds me," Lily said. "Mr. Balthazar told me that
when you and Nicole St. Claire came back for her grandmother's funeral, he got the impression that you were a pair."

Duffy nodded. "We've been living together a little over a
year."

Lily's eyes showed concern. "She was a couple of years

behind me in school and I didn't really know her, but I do remember her." She hesitated, as if uncertain of how to ask the question, or even if she should. "Is . . . is she all right now?"

So St. Claire had not forgotten the St. Claire family problems. For a moment, in the face of Lily's obvious sympathy, Duffy had a mad impulse to blurt out: *No, she's not. And we're both at our wit's end.* But of course he could never do that. It was none of Lily's business, no matter how sympathetic she was. It would be like a betrayal of Nicole. So he merely nodded, forced a smile, and said, "We're coping."

Lily didn't smile back. Leaning toward him, she put her hand on his—he felt another electric shock—and looked into his eyes, and he had the feeling that she saw through him. And had nothing but the greatest sympathy.

"Lily," he said, "why are you being so nice to me?"

"What?" Her eyes widened with surprise. "What a strange thing to say!"

"You know why I'm asking. You were one of the sweetest things that ever happened to me, or any other man. And yet, when that last summer was over and I left . . ."

Lily's cheeks flushed and she lowered her eyes. He noticed the faint scent of her perfume, and for the first time in years he recalled the lovely scent of her clean, sweet body. Dear God . . .

"Duffy," she said, "let's be honest. I was very much in love with you, it's true. And when you and Adrienne broke up, I took advantage of you—"

"*You* took advantage?"

"I did. I knew you weren't in love with me, even if I tried to believe otherwise, and I knew the relationship wouldn't last beyond the summer. Meanwhile, I gave you solace, and you gave me more tenderness, I think, than you realized. I don't think you ever intentionally hurt me, and I want you to know that I don't regret one thing that we did that summer." Lily looked up into Duffy's eyes again, and her voice grew husky. "Not one thing."

Dear God, Duffy thought, not until this moment had he realized the treasure he had left behind. He remembered the

abandon and trust with which Lily had given herself to him—
a trust that he had betrayed, no matter how he rationalized it.

Duffy's voice was thick in his throat. "Then you forgive
me?"

"If you want, but there's really nothing to forgive. I don't
think about that summer much anymore—it's no good clinging to the past. But when I do think about it . . . when I
remember . . . believe me, it's the sweetest memory I
have. . . .

"Besides," she added with a little laugh that had tears in
it, "a girl always remembers the first man to truly break her
heart."

They leaned toward each other. Their lips met, ever so
lightly, and lingered, as past and present met and melted into
a single breathless, mindless moment.

With a sigh, Lily drew back. She slowly looked away from
Duffy, up past his shoulder, and smiled.

"Why, hello, Nicole," she said. "It is Nicole, isn't it?"

"Kiss of Reconciliation, my ass!" Nicole said, laughing, as she
pulled the car away from the curb. "That was no Joanne in
there, and if that was a mere Kiss of Reconciliation, then I'd
sure like to see a Kiss of Pure Romantic Bliss."

Duffy cringed back in the far corner of his seat, grinning,
but covering his red face with a hand. "Wait'll we get back to
the house," he said, "and I'll give you one."

"We have guests coming for dinner. Maybe later tonight.
Or tomorrow." Her voice sharpened. "Or next week."

"Aw, Nickie . . . !"

Since it hadn't been quite five o'clock and she had seen
Duffy nowhere on the square, she had parked the car and gone
into the library to see if he was still there. He wasn't in the
magazine alcove, but she soon spotted him sitting with a
young woman in an office cubicle. As she went toward him, he
leaned over the corner of the desk and kissed the woman.

For a moment, Nicole was stunned. This was the girl
Duffy had told her about, the girl who had been in love with
him during that long-ago summer. She had no doubt about it.
Who else would it be?

Unlike Duffy, Lily Bains did not seem in the slightest

disconcerted by Nicole's intrusion on the moment. On the contrary, she seemed genuinely pleased to meet Duffy's companion, and she and Nicole exchanged amused and knowing smiles at Duffy's embarrassment. They must certainly see each other again, Lily said, as she and Nicole touched cheeks, and soon.

Glancing at Duffy, Nicole saw that he was no longer grinning. His face had a look of genuine pain.

"Hey, Duffy," she said, relenting, "it's all right. Old girlfriends are meant to be kissed."

"I love you, Nicole."

"I know you do. But, say, that's some perfume Lily wears, isn't it? Subtle, but wildly sexy. Or is that her natural smell?"

"How would I know?"

"Who better than you?"

Nicole laughed again.

But one small corner of her heart was bleeding.

She was safe!

Freya laughed aloud, a musical trill of pure delight, so great was her relief.

Safe! After years of waiting, wondering, fearing, and not knowing. The grandmother was dead, and she had beguiled the granddaughter as easily as she had the girl's father. She felt a surge of warmth toward Nicole that was almost like love. *Julia, you miserable old witch, your little girl is mine now!*

For almost a year after Daniel's death, Freya had stayed away from St. Claire, fearing Julia's retribution. What did the woman know, what did she suspect, when would she act? Was she biding her time, even as she planned vengeance? Freya knew that Timothy feared Julia, and if Timothy feared anyone, it was with good reason.

The fear, the uncertainty, could not go on forever. It was like blackmail, making Freya feel weak and powerless, and that was intolerable. The only solution was to eliminate Julia once and for all. She would eliminate the woman as she had Daniel, but more swiftly, a tooth or a claw through the throat.

Fear itself made it difficult to enter Julia's house, but at last one night, she forced herself to do so. She still found it difficult to remember the details of those dreamlike flights, but she would remember that night vividly. Centuries might pass, but she would remember it as long as she lived.

She found herself in Nicole's dark bedroom. Safe for the moment, she thought; the child was asleep. Freya saw her faintly, as through a scrim of gauze, but the child seemed haloed in innocence, and for a moment Freya hesitated. But this was no time to weaken. If only she could materialize, now, in some terrible guise . . .

She tried. She had never been able to do it by a direct act of will, had seldom been able to do it at all, *but she could do it*, and she tried, clearing her mind, letting happen what would, letting herself *become*, feeling the beat-beat-beat of her heart as it began to happen . . .

. . . when suddenly, as if sensing her presence, the little girl awakened, sat up in bed, and looked about wide-eyed. "Oh, Grandma, Grandma, come quick," she wailed. "There's something bad in my bedroom!"

In that instant and the moments that followed, Freya experienced the greatest terror of her life. Julia, she knew, was coming, was *coming for her*, and she tried desperately to withdraw, to escape back to her body, but it was as if something had seized and held her—held her for Julia. Then Julia came through the doorway, and it was as if a great flaming, angry-eyed angel, a fireball of wrath, had suddenly burst over Freya, enveloping and consuming her, burning her with terror, while she fought, struggled, battled to escape, knowing that this was her end if she didn't—

Begone, demon, begone and never dare to return!

—then she was released and flung into darkness. It was the deepest, most absolute darkness she had ever known, a starless void somewhere between heaven and hell, and she was too weak to leave it, too weak ever to find her way back . . .

Oh, God, Julia, what have you done to me?

. . . too weak, too weak . . . *oh, please, somebody help me* . . . and lost, lost . . . floating in darkness . . .

. . . and yet at dawn . . . she awakened in her own bed . . . once again in her own body. . . .

She hardly dared to believe she was still alive. Every muscle ached, as if all strength had been drawn from her in her struggle to escape the fiery angel. Whimpering, she crawled out of her bed. Blindly, head down, she staggered across her bedroom to her dressing table. She leaned against it for support. Slowly she raised her head and opened her eyes to look into the mirror.

She screamed.

She had spent most of the next four years traveling, far from St. Claire, and much of that time a white veil had covered her hollow eyes and sunken cheeks, and white gloves had covered her withered hands. Restoring her beauty had not been easy—she had encountered no more Daniels in her travels—but restored it had been, and when she learned that Julia and the child had moved to New York, she had at last dared to return to St. Claire.

By that time she was reasonably certain that Julia had not identified her as the "demon" who had invaded her house. Still, it had taken nerve to approach Nicole at her grandmother's funeral, and she had sensed the girl's wariness. But whatever suspicions Nicole might have entertained, they were now gone forever.

Nicole *liked* her.

She was *safe!*

Dear God, the child had the same magic her father had possessed. In spite of herself, Freya had found herself warming to Nicole and wondering if there weren't some way she could save her. Save her from Timothy, save her from the hatred of her enemies in St. Claire, save her for herself. Her own little pet Wolf Girl.

Of course, if Nicole were to become altogether Freya's protégée and disciple, the young man, Duffy Johnson, would have to be eliminated. But that could be arranged. Lily Bains could be trusted to take care of that. Freya might despise Lily, but she did have her uses. . . .

Stop dreaming, Freya. You're not going to save Nicole. Look at yourself in the mirror, look at the weary little pouches under your eyes and your chin. Your breasts are losing their firmness and your thighs are getting heavy. If you have to play Timothy's game to be restored, then you'll do it. Pity is a fool's game, and love an hour's diversion, nothing more; and if you could sacrifice the father, you can certainly sacrifice the daughter. And once again . . .

Mirror, mirror, on the wall . . .

. . . the mirror would give her the answer she could not live without.

CHAPTER
16

She was going to see Brad!
    She could have sung the words. *I'm going to see Brad!
I'm going to see Brad!* A week ago they had been a faint refrain,
recurrent now and then, but each day the melody had grown
stronger, and now, as Gussie sped north on the busy sun-
baked highways toward St. Claire, it was almost constant. *I'm
going to see Brad!*
    She laughed at herself.
    I'm coming, Brad!
    They had talked on the telephone three more times since
that first night, talked ostensibly to firm up and coordinate
their travel plans, but actually just for the sheer fun of it. Like
any two old friends, close friends who would never be lonely
as long as they had each other to confide in, they had talked
about things they had done in the past seven years, people
they had met, crazy things that had happened to them. They
had talked about anything and everything that came to their
minds except . . .
    . . . the coven.

The coven, as such, didn't really matter anymore, and the fears that they had both felt about a return to St. Claire now seemed exaggerated. What could they, who once again had each other, have to fear? Oh, yes, there was unfinished business to be attended to, but Gussie understood that it had little to do with the supposed god they had once pledged themselves to. It had to do with six long-estranged friends becoming reconciled, if possible, with each other.

As she and her once-upon-a-time-beloved Brad were becoming reconciled.

With each call, it seemed to Gussie, they had grown closer, and last night they had all but made love on the telephone.

"God, I want to see you, Gussie! I can't believe it's been almost seven years."

"You said you'd seen my movies."

"Not the same. I want to see *you!* Not to be presumptuous, but I . . ." Brad had stuttered with emotion. "God, I know I've got no right to say this, but just once—if you'd let me—I'd like to wrap my arms around you again. Just for a minute, grab you and give you a big hug and laugh like hell. Does that make any sense?"

Did it make any sense? Brad, if you only knew . . .

"Come to me, Gussie! You come to me and I'll come to you."

Gussie floored the accelerator.

I'm coming, Brad!

She pulled the gray Nissan Maxima up in front of the Hotel St. Claire just as it was growing dark. She had hardly gotten out of the car when a kid, maybe twenty or so, came darting forward from the hotel door. He was dark-haired, round-faced, and adolescent-cute, and he wore a gold-trimmed blue shirt and slacks that suggested a uniform. "Jessie!" he yelled, giving her a big grin and a wave as she came around the front of the car. "Hey, Jessie! Welcome back to St. Claire!"

Jessie halted and stared. She suddenly realized that there were a dozen or more people, old and young, standing outside the hotel and under its marquee, and they were all smiling at her. More were watching from inside the big glass doors. She

looked at the young man again. There was something familiar
about him, but . . . in the dark she couldn't quite make out
the nameplate on his shirt.

His smile faltered. "Bobby," he said. "Bobby Parnell—"

Recognition came then, like a delightful surprise, an unexpected gift. "Bobby!" she said. "Bobby Par*nell!* Oh, my
God!" Bobby's grin returned as she threw her arms around
him and kissed him resoundingly. "How *are* you, Bobby?
How's your family, how have you *been*?"

Bobby's cheerful reply was almost lost in the sound of
applause and laughter that followed the kiss. Then the little
crowd was surrounding Gussie—Jessie—greeting her, welcoming her. "Welcome home, Jessie!" "Good to see you again,
Jessie!" "You're great, Jessie, we love you!" Most of them were
strangers to her, a few looked familiar, and two or three she
recognized immediately.

Jessie moved on through the little crowd and into the
brightly lit hotel lobby, shaking any hand that was extended to
her, trading hugs with a few people she barely remembered.
She had the feeling that these people really were happy for her,
even proud of her, and she wouldn't for anything in the world
have slighted a one of them.

Bobby followed with her luggage, and by the time they
reached the desk, her admirers had begun to give them space.
"Sorry about that, Miss Lindquist," the clerk said as he
checked her in and handed over the room key. "We try to be
discreet so that our guests don't get hassled, but sometimes
the word just gets out. . . ."

"That's perfectly all right. They're my friends."

Most of them, anyway.

"Evening, Jessie. Welcome back to St. Claire."

She had only to hear that low, thick-throated voice—she
recognized it instantly—to feel a tremor of apprehension. She
had a glimpse of something feline and needle-toothed and
dangerous before she even turned toward the man who was
now standing beside her, smiling knowingly.

"Good evening, Bruno," she said, forcing herself to smile
back.

She did not like Bruno Krull. She had not liked him from
that terrible night in the St. Claire parking lot when she had

first met him. She hadn't seen much of him during the year that followed, but once Brad was out of the picture, he had seemed to pop up all too often. At the Moonlight Inn, where she worked part-time. At the coffee joints where she and her college friends hung out in the daytime and the beer joints where they hung out at night. Sit down at a table with a couple of girls, or even a guy, and at the next table, suddenly there would be Bruno. Trying to be "friendly." She had particularly disliked the way he had hinted that he knew her better than he did and that they had things in common. They had been *acquaintances*, for God's sake, *not* friends, and she had wanted to keep it that way.

She still did.

Before she realized what Bruno was going to do, he had taken her room key from her hand and turned to Bobby.

"Bobby," he said, "put Miss Lindquist's car in the hotel garage and return the key to the desk. I'll take care of her bags."

"No, please—" Jessie began.

"Just *do it*, Bobby."

There was no mistaking the command in Bruno's voice or in the set of his face. Bobby glanced hesitantly from Bruno to Jessie.

"You do as the sheriff says, Bobby," the desk man said, snapping his fingers, "hop to it. Now!"

There were two of them, his boss and the sheriff, but Bobby had the guts to just stand there, looking at her, waiting for *her* orders. Good for him. Her immediate impulse was to grab her room key back from Bruno, snap, *"Fuck this—follow me, Bobby,"* and march off to her room. But she couldn't do anything that might lead to the kid's getting in trouble with these two shits. So she simply gave Bobby her car key, said, "See you later, sweetheart," and kissed him again, on the cheek. Bobby's smile, as he left, was worth it.

"Lucky Bobby," Bruno said as he picked up Jessie's three cases. "Here for long, Jessie?"

"A day or two." Jessie followed after Bruno as he led the way to the elevators.

"That's not long for a homecoming. Hardly time to visit old friends at all."

"I don't know many people here anymore."

"Sure didn't look that way out front. Anyway, old friends do come back, same as you. I think you'll find that you have a lot of old friends here."

Jessie frowned. Was it possible that Bruno knew about the reunion, maybe from one of the others? Not that it mattered. If he did, he could still go to hell.

An elevator was waiting, a bright box off of a dimmer corridor. They stepped into it. Bruno set down a suitcase and pressed the 5-button, and the door closed.

"Jessie Lindquist," he said as the elevator ascended. "St. Claire's answer to Sharon Stone."

Jessie managed a laugh. "Hardly."

"Come to think of it, people around here used to call you Gussie, didn't they?"

She shook her head. "Only a few close friends. Maybe some others took it up, I don't remember."

"Which would you prefer me to call you?"

She would have loved to hit him with, *Miss Lindquist, if you don't mind.* Instead she said, "Jessie. I'm used to it."

The elevator came to a halt and the door opened. Jessie stepped out and led the way briskly to her room. Room five-fifteen. She wanted to be done with Bruno as quickly as possible.

She waited in silence while he unlocked the door. She followed as he carried her luggage in and flipped on the lights.

"I'll just check the place out for you."

He did, while she stood by the open door.

"Looks all right, no burglars under the beds." He turned to her, smiling. "Had dinner yet?"

The question was unexpected, and she hesitated. Damn, she had been so flustered down at the desk, she hadn't even asked if Brad had checked in. Brad, where *are* you?

"Why, as a matter of fact . . . I have plans for dinner."

Bruno nodded slowly. "A dinner date. He picking you up here at the hotel?"

"Yes. I'm expecting him at any minute now, so if you'll excuse me—"

"You'll want to freshen up. Why don't you do that, and

then we'll have a drink in the bar. Stop the wheels from turning while we wait for your date. I want to talk to you."

"I . . ."

Her voice caught in her throat as instinct kicked in, instinct and memory. Same old Bruno. He was not asking her,
he was telling her. In the nicest possible way, perhaps, but still,
he was *telling* her. He was, after all, Bruno Krull, the dominant
male, and in charge here. She was a woman, momentarily on
her own, and he expected her to do as he said.

And thank him for it!

She could not help herself. All the revulsion for Bruno
Krull that she had long felt but had largely forgotten began to
surface. She knew this kind of man. She had met so many of
them. They might whisper endearments in your ear and
shower you with kindness, but in the end, women were mere
trophies to them, less than human, mere beaver pelts to hang
on their mighty phallic spears. When the sweet talk was over,
their bottom line was: *I own this cunt! On your knees, bitch!*

The repugnance Jessie felt at that moment, the utter dis-
dain, could not be hidden. Its strength surprised even her: it
was like a rising nausea, acidic vomitus in her throat.

With an effort, she found her voice again, and even produced a kind of smile. "Bruno, I do thank you, but if you
don't mind . . ."

But Bruno had seen it. And felt it. Felt the loathing.

He looked stunned. Stunned and somehow diminished.
For a brief moment, he had been burned as never before by a
woman's contempt, and that, she knew instantly, he could
never forgive.

"Same old Jessie," he growled softly. The stunned look
had vanished and an angry flush suffused his cheeks. His eyes
narrowed to slits as if he were going to cry, but his teeth were
bared in an ugly grin, and again she had an impression of
something feline and fanged. He took a slow step toward her.

"Same old Bruno," she said, trying to maintain her smile.

He took another step toward her, they were inches apart,
and raised a hand toward her cheek, his fingers hooked.

"Same old Jessie, sweetest twat in town and her shit don't
stink."

When he said that to her, so crude, so out of character

even for Bruno, when he said that, his slit-eyes glittering and his jaw shaking with tension, she knew that, quite inadvertently, she had pressed Bruno Krull too far. She was looking at a man almost over the edge and out of control.

Next, she knew, he would touch her cheek with those cruelly curved fingers . . . and if she resisted . . .

. . . he would slide an arm around her waist and try to place his mouth on hers . . .

. . . and if she still resisted . . .

Her mind seemed to explode in a single great shriek of fear, and she had only one hope.

Brad, Brad, Brad, oh God Brad, where are you?

Brad was in the hotel garage, walking along a bleakly lit down ramp, when the happy thought hit him that Gussie had at last arrived. It was only an impression, with no sense that she was reaching out to him, and it might have been wishful thinking, but it was strong. He had become a pretty sensitive receptor in the last few years.

He entered the hotel by a ground-floor corridor. He had explored the terrain earlier and knew how to get to the elevators, but unfortunately he didn't know Gussie's room number. He would have to take time to go to the front desk and inquire and maybe phone up.

By the time he reached the elevator bank, he had begun to feel uneasy. Maybe there wasn't time to go to the front desk. Gussie might have a problem, she might need him right *now*. All right, he was a goddamn psychic detective—where *was* she?

He took a deep breath, expelled it slowly as he relaxed, and opened his mind.

It came to him.

Fifth floor. She was on the fifth floor.

She had said she would try to get a room near his, would specify it in her reservation. All the elevators were down except one. Its arrow was at rest on five. *His* room was on five. Ergo . . .

It didn't take a goddamn psychic.

As he rode up in the elevator, his feeling that Gussie needed help grew stronger. By the time he stepped out onto the fifth-floor corridor, the alarm that was going off in his head was brazen.

He went toward his room, five-seventeen, looking at doors on both sides of the corridor. Five-fifteen was ajar. He pushed it open a little farther and saw a familiar head of pale flaxen hair and just beyond it an angry-eyed man with an ugly grin. He shoved the door hard, so that it banged loudly against the wall.

With a jubilant cry, Gussie whirled around and threw herself into his arms, tears of joy and relief pouring down her cheeks as she kissed him.

An hour later, Bruno still felt sick with anger. Timothy could tell: the anger, like a vibrant musical chord, deep and sinister, seemed to fill every dark corner of the dimly lit tower room.

"We'll have to act quickly," Bruno said. "They're all here now, but they won't be for long."

"They will be here long enough," Timothy said with perfect conviction, but it was conviction born of necessity, not of prescience.

Bruno, listening to his own inner demon, didn't seem to hear him. Despite the warmth of the night, he had thrown on a cloak, as if to take refuge in it, and as he paced the room, he lovingly stroked a weapon fitted on his right hand: a set of metal knuckles on which were mounted a pair of slightly hooked blades. It was a weapon meant to rip and scar and inflict great pain.

"At some point, they're all going to be together, they're going to have their reunion party. Let's say it's going to be the same kind of very private party they had in the old days."

Timothy, in shirtsleeves, sitting at ease in a comfortable chair, shook his head. "Most unlikely. People do change, Bruno, sometimes radically. Bradford has. Duffy, I fear, has, or I doubt that young Nicole would be with him. On the evidence, none of them but Lily is a loyal Luciferian any longer, and Nicole, of course, never was one."

Bruno rarely contradicted Timothy, but now he waved the older man's words away. "No, Dad, you're not getting my point. Luciferian or not, they're still the same people, just a few years older. A tight little clique that used to party together out at the Holland place, right? Get naked, get high on Old Man Holland's booze or sometimes Freya's, and screw around. Which wasn't quite the big secret they thought, because kids catch on, they figure out who's screwing who. And they'll remember. They'll also figure that that tight-ass little cunt Nicole, shacking up with Duffy, isn't so different from the others."

Bruno spoke with such bitter crudeness that Timothy was reminded of Buster Dugan: —*goddamn filthy little cock-teasing cunt . . . I'd like to do her, I'd like to do her so bad*— He recognized that same wonderfully intoxicating hatred-lust-envy-anger that he knew so well, but rarely had he felt it at this strength in Bruno.

"So when they get together again," Bruno was saying, "when they get together *alone,* maybe with a little encouragement from us"—Bruno tapped his forehead with a finger—"maybe it'll be like old times. Afterward, people will think it *was* like old times. Only *this* time, it'll look like a sex-and-drugs party that got out of hand. Isn't something like that what you've had in mind?"

"Possibly. Bruno, we will simply watch carefully and take advantage of whatever possibilities present themselves."

Bruno looked down at the metal knuckles on his right hand. His eyes widened as if he were noticing them for the first time.

"I wonder if the little bitch could've used something like this on Buster Dugan that night in the parking lot. And passed it on to one of the other kids, maybe Duffy Johnson, before I got there."

"Highly unlikely. Thirteen-year-old girls named St. Claire are not apt to carry brass knuckles in their purses."

"You might be surprised at what some kids carry these days. Even *nice* little girls in peaceful St. Claire. And a twenty-one-year-old from New York City, where a girl can't be too careful . . . she might very well be found with one of these on her . . ."

"She might very well," Timothy agreed.

". . . after I get done using it."

Bruno's vibrant, throbbing anger seemed to build again. He pressed the knuckles into his left palm until the blades threatened to draw blood, and his eyes took on an unfocused, brooding look. Timothy tried to follow his thoughts, but they were guarded.

Then slowly Bruno began to smile. He turned to Timothy. "I think you're right, Dad. All we have to do is watch carefully and seize the possibilities. Where's your pal Steadman these days?"

"I have no idea and no wish to know. When I want him, he will know and he will appear."

"Yeah, like a magic genie, to do your bidding. Well, I hope he's nearby, because like I said, we have to act fast. We have a few days, at best, and that's it. And we may need Steadman."

"You have something in mind," Timothy said.

Bruno turned slowly toward Timothy. Yes, he had something in mind, something that rode on the force of his swelling anger. Timothy felt that anger, now less a grim, vibrant chord than a hot wind sweeping through the room. The lamps seemed to dim as if subdued by Bruno's own hellish light, and Timothy began to see Bruno's true demonic self.

The vision quickly grew stronger, clearer—pale cat-eyes and stiletto teeth. Save for the cloak on his shoulders, Bruno's clothing seemed to melt away, to vanish, as if to provide material for this greater reality, the true Bruno, and Timothy caught glimpses and heard rustlings as if other demonic beings were being attracted mothlike to Bruno's light.

All of this Timothy had seen before, though seldom with such spontaneity. But then something happened, remarkable even in Timothy's experience.

While looking fiercely into Timothy's eyes, Bruno reached out and laid a furred, claw-nailed hand on Timothy's bare forearm. Slowly he drew it down from the bend of the elbow to the top of the wrist.

Timothy stared. He scarcely felt the pain as he watched the glistening crimson welling up out of the three furrows in his flesh.

"Oh, God—Dad—please! God, I didn't mean—"

That quickly it was over. Bruno was his normal self, asking in shock and consternation how could he have done such a thing, how, how, how, "Dad, I am so goddamn sorry!"

Timothy was not sorry. Wildly elated, he reached out and

grasped Bruno's hand and examined the blunt fingers with their bloody but short, well-trimmed nails, incapable of the razorlike cuts on Timothy's forearm. Obviously, Bruno himself did not yet know what had happened. But without preparation or ritual or help of any kind from any other being, empowered only by the strength of his rage, he had for a moment spontaneously turned, changed, emerged—become that creature that had left its marks on Timothy's arm.

Timothy couldn't help himself. Springing up from his chair, he reached out and drew Bruno into his arms. *Oh, my boy!*

He had known that Bruno's powers were growing, maturing, as were Lily's, but *this!* Others had done it, he himself on occasion, but how rare and marvelous! With children like these, with Bruno and Lily—and Alida, when she was returned to him—what need had he any longer of the jealous Freya Kellgren? They, his children, were proof of his own powers, signs of his favor with the god of this world. He no longer had any doubts of success, any fears of failure. By the grace of the god, he was invincible and omnipotent, beyond the touch of any other power on earth.

"My son," he said, joyously embracing Bruno. "Bruno, Bruno, my own true son!"

"Okay," Gussie said, "it's your turn."

"My turn?"

"Yes, your turn. I've told you all about myself, told you on the phone. How Mom and I went out to the Coast. About my career and Buddy Weston and that lizard shit, Philip Steadman. Told you just about everything. But whenever I ask what changed you—and you have changed, Brad—you say something like, 'Oh, I guess I just grew up.' But I know it's more than that. Why won't you tell me, Brad?"

"Well . . . it's not something I can talk about on the phone."

"We're not on the phone. We're Brad and Gussie, alone together in a hotel room, and we can talk. So tell me. . . ."

It seemed to her she could still feel the bruising pressure of Brad's lips on hers. God, what a welcome kiss! When she had turned to Bruno again and extended an olive branch,

"Bruno, it really is good to see you, but . . ." the sheriff had given her a tight smile and a nod and said, "Another time." He had even shaken Brad's hand before leaving. Might he never return!

Brad had ordered dinner from room service, bless him, and now, having eaten and feeling much better, she sat at the head of the bed, her crossed legs bare and attractive (she hoped), while Brad lounged in a chair, his tie pulled loose and his shoes kicked off.

Her Brad.

"Tell me, Brad," she said again, softly.

He nodded. "I've never told anybody. Didn't feel like I could tell it, not so they'd understand. Or maybe I was saving it for you. . . .

"I missed you guys after that last summer, Gussie. I never would have admitted it back then, even to myself, not my style, but I really missed you. I hardly remember my mother, you know, and my dad and I were never close, but all through high school and even before, I had you guys."

"Your own little family."

"That's right. You the mama and me the daddy. And when we formed our secret coven, that made it seem even more real. Even though I knew it was all going to end at the end of the summer."

"You *ended it*, Brad," Gussie reminded him.

Brad nodded. "The more fool I. Thinking I didn't need you, even though I had a little ache in my heart. Thinking I could always start another coven or find another convocation. And after a while I found that at times I *could* sense or recognize other cult members."

"Yes, I know."

"The trouble was, none of them were anything like our little coven or what I imagined the Balthazar Convocation to be. You see, I had constructed a kind of romantic vision of Luciferians as being the secret movers-and-shakers of the world, people who held the *real* reins of power. And that was what I wanted. Power. I wanted *in*. But what did I find? First, some ivory-tower types who did little but adore themselves for not allowing their oh-so-superior intuitive powers to 'corrupt' them. And then, a gang of splatterpunk perverts who were into things like domination and pain."

"People like Bruno Krull," Gussie said.

"Like your friend Bruno," Brad agreed. "I swear to God, some of these people, and more than a few, live on the very edge of insanity—they'll kill you on a whim. And why not? They're superior creatures, after all, godlike, reading minds and foreseeing the future, so what can touch them? Or so they believe."

"Did you ever approach Mr. Balthazar about his convocation again?"

Brad nodded. "When I came back for Christmas vacation. He put me off. And my own father," he added with a touch of bitterness, "when I brought the matter up, he pretended he didn't know what I was talking about. Told me to go back to school and do some growing up.

"So I did that. Went to school year-round for three years and busted my ass trying to make my old man proud of me. But if he was, he never showed it."

"I'll bet he was."

Brad shrugged. "Probably. He really wasn't such a bad old guy, just not much on emotional display. But when he dropped dead of a heart attack, he was no longer there to please and I lost all interest in school. The funny thing was that I had looked forward to studying law. I knew I could really learn a lot from my old man."

There was a note of wistful pride in Brad's voice that told Gussie he loved his father and had forgiven him.

"So, Gussie, I just dropped out and took off. Looking for something, I guess. I had suddenly discovered I was a wealthy young man, very wealthy indeed, and for the next couple of years I just bummed around the world. I ran into Luciferians now and then, but by that time I had a pretty supercilious attitude toward them. Thought I was better than that crap."

"You were better."

"Then, in Rome, almost exactly two years ago, I finally found what I was looking for.

"It was a sultry Saturday evening, I remember, and I'd been in Rome almost a week, by myself, taking in the usual tourist sights and getting the feel of the city. Usually I don't mind traveling alone to new places and exploring on my own, but by then I was beginning to feel the need for some companionship, so I went into a little *ristorante* in the Via Veneto for a bite to eat and a cup of coffee, hoping something might turn up. It did.

"When I finally got seated, alone at a dinky little table, I didn't see or sense anything promising—I might as well have been alone in a midtown Manhattan restaurant—so I stopped paying much attention and read a guidebook while I ate. But as I was finishing, I suddenly had the feeling that I was *not* alone. I don't mean that there were or weren't other patrons in the place—the place was crowded—I mean that *I*, sitting there at my little table, wasn't *alone!*

"Well, that was hardly a unique experience, of course. Soul calls out to soul, so to speak. So I just waited to see what would happen, and almost at once the thought came to my mind: *Demon people!*

"*Demon people*—it was a term or phrase I'd never used. And I wasn't using it then. Someone else was. Someone nearby in that room was thinking that *I* was one of the *demon people*.

"And furthermore—it came to me in a flash—whoever that someone was, he—no, *she*—thought that *I*—my *demon* self—looked something like a goddamned *monkey!*

"*She*, whoever she was, was *laughing at me*.

"So I looked up and around, and there, a couple of tables away, sat this good-looking auburn-haired woman, mid-twenties, gazing directly into my eyes. She was sitting with this big, handsome guy, a few years older—long, blondish-brown hair and darker, curved, flyaway eyebrows, very striking. The woman still seemed to be laughing at me, though not in any mean way, and the guy grinned and held up his wineglass in a friendly little salute. So I smiled and nodded back and saluted with my coffee cup . . . and noticed that the guy looked familiar. Very familiar.

"He said something to the woman and got up and walked over to my table, and just as he stuck out his hand and spoke, I recognized him.

" 'Pardon me,' he said, 'I'm Adam Valliere. We really

didn't mean to be rude, staring at you like that, but haven't I met you somewhere before?'

" 'No, Mr. Valliere,' I said, taking his hand, 'but you've stared at me from the picture on your book jacket often enough.'

"Adam Valliere, author of *Children of the Griffin*. What a coincidence! Or so I thought.

"Adam invited me over to his table and introduced me to the woman, Elspeth Tremaine . . . 'to whom I am but the humble consort.' He smiled when he said that, and Beth, as she's called, laughed, but I could tell he was serious. There was something about Beth that suggested great, quietly contained power.

"Adam and I discussed his first book on the Griffin cult, and he told me about the new one he had coming out, and before long I found myself telling him and Beth all about our coven and Balthazar and Freya. I couldn't stop talking. I was perfectly frank about my power ambitions and my disillusionment. I said if the vows he'd taken were anything like the ones I had, there didn't seem to be any great danger in breaking them. At that, his face went kind of grim and shut down, and he said, 'Don't count on it.'

"Then, when I finally wound down, Beth turned to Adam and said, 'Darling, I have a marvelous idea. Let's take Bradford with us this evening.' 'Well, of course we're going to take Bradford with us, if he'll come,' Adam said. 'Bradford, it's just a small, informal party, our own little rogue coven, so to speak. Some drinks, some conversation. I'm sure you'll find people there who interest you.'

"What else could I do but go?

"When we stepped out of the restaurant, a limousine pulled up as if on signal, Adam swung open the door, and Beth drew me into it, literally, by the hand. Adam followed, slamming the door, and we were instantly off, hurtling through the busy streets.

"A few minutes later the limo all but screeched to a stop in the Via Sestina, not far away. We got out and entered a building and, practically bracing me by the elbows like a prisoner, Adam and Beth led me upstairs to the apartment where the party was being held.

"By the time Adam rang the doorbell, I was beginning to wonder if I wasn't making a mistake. I had the feeling that something was going on that I didn't know about and maybe didn't *want* to know about. It even occurred to me that I could turn and bolt like a fool. But of course I didn't. Adam and Beth kept smiling reassuringly at me, maybe *too* reassuringly, and Adam had put his big, long arm ever-so-casually over my shoulders, so that I had the feeling I couldn't get away even if I wanted to.

"The door opened, and I swear, I felt Beth mentally *pushing* me into the foyer. I almost turned around and said, 'Don't *do* that!'

"After that, I've got to admit, my apprehension began to fade. A dozen or more guests, men and women, most of them older than the three of us, had already arrived, and I certainly didn't sense anything menacing about them. Our hostess was a very old, very beautiful Asian woman who spoke English with a French accent, and she projected some of the same power that Beth did, but she seemed completely benevolent. Adam startled me by introducing me to the party as 'a somewhat disillusioned member of the Order of the Griffin—I think some of us here know how he feels,' and there was some good-natured laughter.

"I was then let loose on the party, or the party was on me, and I had a very good time. The guests were a varied lot—Italian, French, German, American . . . an actress, a philosophy professor, some kind of police commissioner . . . and, without pressing, they all seemed eager to show me a pleasant time. Most of the talk had to do with art and politics, and I soon forgot that some of them, apparently, like Adam, were or had been Children of the Griffin.

"My apprehension gradually, almost unconsciously, began to return, however, as two things became apparent to me.

"I was not just another one of the guests at the party. I was the principal focus of attention, even if the others did politely, or guilefully, try to hide the fact. I was, in fact, being sized up. Evaluated, as it were.

"*And* the others were waiting for something to happen. I could feel the tension building, like barometric pressure or an electric charge, and for the second time that evening, I had an impulse simply to *bolt*. But when I looked into the foyer, Adam and Beth were standing by the door as if guarding it, and I knew I could never get past them.

"I looked around the room. Everyone had fallen silent and was standing perfectly still, smiling at me. But in the soft, shadowing light of the room, they had the faces of smiling gargoyles. The old Asian lady, our hostess, smiled at me as if pleading for understanding, but she looked as dangerous as some beautifully scaled adder.

"As I stood there, surrounded, my fear grew as never before in my life. I tried to hide it, I tried to smile back, but my whole body was trembling, and my bowels, bladder, and legs threatened to give way at any instant. The whole room, the entire apartment, seemed to tremble and vibrate with my fear. *Something* out there was coming for me. To punish me, perhaps. To destroy me for breaking my Luciferian vows.

"And I could only wait for it.

"I waited. And just when I thought I could bear to wait no longer, there came a knock at the door.

"No doubt it was just a gentle knock, a tapping. But to my ears and soul, it was like thunder, a great crashing, reverberating sound. *Bam! Bam! Bam! BAM!* Never had Fate knocked louder at the door.

"Adam opened the door and said, 'Good evening, Professor.'

"A tall, thin man—long, handsome face, hollow cheeks, raven and silver hair—stood there looking directly at me from under fierce brows. He was wearing black clericals and a Roman collar, that little glimpse of white.

"Beth said, 'Good evening, Uncle Nicky,' and lifted her face to kiss his cheek. The priest said something about being sorry he'd been detained, but he never stopped looking at me. And smiling.

"He came toward me, holding out his hand.

" 'Uncle Nicky,' Beth said, 'this is our new friend, Bradford Holland. Bradford, I'd like you to meet my uncle, Monsignor Nicholas Crown.'

"Our hands met. And something happened to me. Something cataclysmic.

"The priest had a nice, firm, loving grip—I can't describe

it in any other way—and the kindest eyes in all the world. As I felt that hand and looked into those eyes, I found my view of the entire world changing, explosively, all my values shifting and changing, everything coming into a new and radically different focus. It was a revelation, and it was beautiful.

"*But of course!*

"How had I ever got it all so wrong?

"At that point, I wasn't frightened, Gussie, I was simply in shock. But I understood clearly that this man hadn't come here to destroy me. On the contrary, he had come here to keep me from destroying myself!

"More than that, he had come here to ask *me* to help *him!*

"I couldn't help myself. As we stood there shaking hands, I began to laugh. Laugh from simple relief and from pure, unrestrained joy. Father Nick, understanding, nodded and began to laugh with me. We stood there, nodding at each other and laughing like a pair of fools, and then Adam and Beth began laughing, and finally the whole damn room was laughing. It was all so goddamn funny! The joke was on me, of course, but that was all right. Something wonderful had happened, and I wasn't sure what it was, but for the first time in my life I found I could really and truly laugh at myself, without embarrassment or private reservations or secret resentment.

"You see what I'm saying?

"Hell, Gussie, I was saved!"

Brad sat quiet, remembering. His face was that of a man now, not a boy, but Gussie thought that never in the old days had she seen such a look of gentleness and peace and beauty on it.

"Sounds like maybe you were 'scared straight,' " she said, smiling.

"Yeah," Brad agreed with a laugh, "or maybe the Stockholm Syndrome—'If you can't beat 'em, join 'em.' But it wasn't that, Gussie, it was a genuine conversion experience, and it lasted. Not that I turned Catholic or anything like that—strictly speaking, I'm not even a Christian. But I learned from Father Nick that the Prince of Power is *not* the true god of this world and never will be. Power, properly used, is a good and necessary thing. But power without compassion, love, *caritas*, whatever you want to call it, is like justice without mercy. It turns everything that is into a vast meaningless soul-grinding machine, a psychotic nightmare, a shriek of despair in the everlasting darkness.

"But that's always been obvious, hasn't it?" Brad said wryly. "Except to a punk like Bradford Holland."

"Bradford Holland, my darling, is not a punk. He never was. He was always searching, seeking, hoping, and he kept it up until he found what in his heart he always wanted.

"But," Gussie added, "it sounds as if he had a little help."

"Yeah, you're right. That meeting in the Via Veneto was no accident. Beth and Adam had been on the same flight with me from New York to Rome, and she had identified me as one of what she calls 'the demon people.' She didn't give me any further thought until I turned up in the same hotel with Adam and her. Then she got interested in me—her pet 'monkey.' She persuaded Father Nick to 'open a file' on me and asked Adam to run a background check. He's rich—he employs the same investigators I do! Within forty-eight hours, they knew all about me.

"Now, Nicholas Crown just happens to be a pretty well-known psychic detective, so-called—"

"I *knew* that name was familiar!"

"He's the guy who finds the missing body or who points toward the clue or the suspect when the police don't have any. He's also a dedicated enemy of the Children of the Griffin, because years ago they murdered his sister. But that's another story."

Brad didn't have to spell it out any further. "He saw possibilities in you," Gussie said. "You said he came to the party to ask you to help him. He recruited you into his little band of . . . demon-busters."

"That's right. He insisted that I go back to school and get my law degree, but I spend all the time I can with him, and he's been training me." Brad grinned. "As a demon-buster. I love that man, Gussie, I really love him. I want you to meet him."

"You finally found the father you always wanted. And the family too, I suppose."

"No, Gussie, *you're* still my family. You and the rest of our little coven. And like it or not, I'm still the daddy."

• • •

Which left unanswered the question, What was the daddy going to do for his family? What *could* he do for his family? He was here to protect it, but a daddy could hardly hover over his children forever.

"Listen, Brad, we'll soon all be going our separate ways, and in the long run we'll all have to look out for ourselves. But knowledge is power. Why don't you get together with the others as soon as possible and tell them everything you've told me. Tell them everything you've learned about the Children of the Griffin. Tell them about these mind-games they play, so that we can all be on guard against them."

"You can help with that, Gussie," Brad agreed. "Tell the others what your friend Steadman did to Buddy Weston, how he killed the poor guy without ever laying a hand on him."

"All right, I will. Maybe Derek will have something to contribute too. If those articles he writes are for real."

"They are, the ones I've read. Enough so to make some people unhappy with him."

Brad got up from his chair and walked about the room, considering the situation. "Tell you what. I saw lights in the St. Claire house when I was cruising around waiting for you, and Derek told me he and Joanne were going to get here earlier than they expected. They should all be here by now. So let's *have* our reunion. Maybe a dinner party, tomorrow night if everybody can make it. What do you think?"

"Sounds good to me."

Brad took a small, battered black notebook from his hip pocket and thumbed its pages while he thought out his plan. "We've got to make some phone calls. I've got the numbers."

"But it's way past eleven!"

"It can't wait. Tell them we're both here. Tell them we got in late—"

"Wait a minute. You want *me* to tell them?"

"That would be best. I don't think Duffy cares for me much anymore, not that I blame him. Except for Derek, I don't think any of you wanted anything to do with me after that summer, you blamed me for a lot of unhappiness and you were right. But you can talk to Nicole and Joanne and Lily.

They'll listen to you, where they might not to me. You can work on the women and set it up."

"Oh, God!" Laughing, Gussie shook her head. "You haven't really changed, have you? The Evil Elf strikes again! All right, whom do I call first?"

Brad sat down on the side of the bed, close to her, and handed her the open notebook. "Call Nicole. Let's break the Duffy barrier."

Gussie looked for the St. Claire listing in the notebook, picked up the handset, and tapped in the number. The *brrrr* of the ringing began.

"God, you've got marvelous legs," Brad muttered thoughtfully.

" 'Bout time you noticed."

"*Splendid* legs!"

"Shh! . . . Nicole?"

Nicole was answering, her voice at first a little hesitant and worried by the lateness of the call, and then filled with delight when she realized who was calling. "Oh, Gussie, Gussie, this is so wonderful!"

Minutes later, it had all been arranged. By great good luck, Joanne and Derek had been at the house for dinner and hadn't yet left, and Gussie spoke to both women. Nicole was tied up part of tomorrow, but they would all visit when and as they could during the day and then get together for dinner in the evening. Arrangements to be finalized tomorrow.

Brad conceded to Gussie that the call to Lily could wait until morning, and Gussie took her hand from the phone.

"It's going to work out," she said.

"Yeah, it's all going to work out."

They sat there on the bed, not quite touching, smiling at each other. It seemed to Gussie that never, even in the old days when they were lovers, had they been this close. Surely if that Beth Tremaine woman could see Brad at this moment, she would see, not a monkey creature, but an angel whose beauty stung her eyes. As it did Gussie's. She reached out to dim the lamp.

Then, without a word, or even a thought, they slid into each other's arms, and for a time, they simply held each other.

CHAPTER
17

Gussie loves Brad, Nicole thought, feeling warm and happy for the two of them. *Gussie loves Brad, and Brad loves Gussie.*

That had been obvious to her from the moment she laid eyes on the two of them together that afternoon. The whole gang had gathered down on the little strip of beach in front of the house, and except for the added presence of Lily, it had been like old times—the Evil Elf holding court, with Gorgeous Gussie clinging to his arm and to his every word.

But it had been disconcerting, remembering Freya's comforting presence the previous afternoon, to listen to Brad's chilling warnings against the Luciferians and Gussie's story of what that awful "lizard man," Philip Steadman, had done to Buddy Weston.

"Luciferian or not, I like Freya Kellgren," she said, bewildered, as they sat on the beach, "and my daddy loved her, and I just can't believe . . ."

"Nicole," Brad replied gently, "I liked Freya too, and I think she kind of liked me. I'm just saying that *sometimes* these people can be extremely deceptive. *Sometimes* their lovely personalities are about as deep as an oil slick on a wet pavement—and just as dangerous. So when you're dealing with them, be very, very careful."

Then, as if to lighten the mood, Brad turned to Nicole and said, "Hey! Do you guys still do that judo stuff? I used to love watching it. How about showing us a little?"

Their old judo-dance routine. They had taken it up again for exercise, working out in Paraclete General's gym. That afternoon they were limited by the fact that they were wearing bathing suits, but at Brad's insistence, they performed a few throws and recoveries with slow-motion grace and wound up with Nicole's most spectacular move, an overhead throw. With Duffy's cooperation, it worked perfectly. Pivoting and ducking under his right arm, she seized his right wrist and wrapped her right arm across his chest and around his neck. Her right side and her back molded itself to his, and pulling with both arms, she bent quickly forward, levering Duffy up into the air until he was upside down. At that point, had he been an unskilled opponent, she could have dropped him on his head or slammed him down on his back. Instead, she guided him as he did a graceful backward somersault through the air and landed lightly on his feet facing her.

Brad led the applause, and Nicole, flushing with pleasure, realized for the first time what a knack he had of making others feel appreciated.

Now he sat at the head of the table in the dining room at the Moonlight Inn. Actually, the table was round, but Brad had insisted that *he* was giving the party, and there was no doubt that *he* was at the head and presiding. Nicole smiled to herself. Same old Brad . . .

Gussie, Nicole, and Duffy sat at his right, and Joanne, Derek, and Lily on his left, around the table. Lily and Duffy thus sat side by side, at times talking softly, laughing, a little party of two.

Well, that was all right. It was now apparent to Nicole that this return to St. Claire, and the reunion, was the best thing that could have happened to Duffy. Her grandmother might have helped heal Duffy's soul, but she hadn't given him back the five friends he had lost through guilt and shame. Now he had them again. He had made his peace with each and every one, even Lily, whom he had most wronged, and Nicole was damned if she was going to feel jealous.

Duffy was chatting with Derek, about some ancient basketball game, apparently, and Nicole wondered if Derek had his little palm-sized tape recorder in his pocket, set to run. She wouldn't have put it past him. There had been an awkward moment the previous evening, when he had flourished the recorder and, over her protests, had attempted to "interview" her, but Duffy had quickly stepped in. "Look, Derek, we love you, but Nicole invited you into her house for dinner, not to be questioned about some old business she'd rather forget."

"Hey, I don't mean any harm. To a lot of kids, back then, she was a kind of heroine. Her claim to fame."

"She doesn't want it. Please, Derek, just drop it."

Derek had pressed no further, and the rest of the evening—capped by Gussie's phone call—had been very pleasant. Nicole had been pleased to observe the return of some of the old affection and rapport between Duffy and Derek. They could still look at each other and burst out laughing at some punch line known only to them.

And now, looking at Brad in the dimly lit, almost deserted dining room of the Moonlight Inn, Nicole could not believe there was anything superficial or deceptive about Brad's love for his friends or for Gussie. There was a sweet simplicity and an openness about it, unforced and asking nothing in return, that could only be genuine. Gussie had moved closer to Brad so that she could lay her head on his shoulder and he could put an arm around her, and it seemed to Nicole that their faces actually glowed with the light of their love. *Gussie loves Brad. And Brad loves Gussie.*

"Going on eleven," Joanne murmured, looking at her watch.

"Yes," Lily said, "and I have to be up early. Missed half a day today. We're computerizing, and I'm in charge."

Duffy looked questioningly at Nicole, and she smiled and nodded. Time to go.

It was a sad and yet somehow lovely moment, the conclusion of their reunion party, and it was still Brad's job to preside. Gussie removed her head from his shoulder and sat up. He tapped his glass for attention, and got it.

"My friends," he said, "about seven years ago all of us here except Nickie took some pretty ridiculous vows. Fortunately, a Higher Power said, 'Hey, forget it!' "

Smiles and soft laughter.

"More importantly, we promised each other that in seven years we would have a reunion. You all know that as the time approached, I had doubts about its wisdom. I was wrong. I only hope this reunion has meant as much to you as it has to me, because"—Brad looked slowly around the circle of friends—"since I got here yesterday evening, you guys have given me the greatest time of my life." He looked intently at Gussie. "Bar none."

Some more soft, comfortable laughter, and applause. Gussie made a small, almost-invisible kiss toward Brad. Her eyes and Brad's seemed to glisten in each other's light.

"It's been great," Brad continued, "but Gussie and I are leaving in the morning, and I don't think it's likely that all seven of us will meet again at the same time. But let's do meet. And not wait seven years."

"Here-here!" Duffy said, and Derek applauded.

"And now, my friends . . ." Bradford took Gussie's left hand in his right and Joanne's right in his left. At almost the same time, as if they shared a single thought, the others joined hands.

"I hereby declare the coven forever dissolved," Brad said, "but may this circle of friends be forever unbroken."

He leaned toward Gussie, and somehow Nicole knew exactly what was going to happen. Brad and Gussie kissed. Then Brad turned to Joanne, and they kissed.

Gussie and Nicole turned toward each other and kissed, and it was no symbolic social kiss. Lips warm and soft and slightly parted, it was a loving kiss, a touching of flesh and souls. As Nicole glanced across the table and saw Joanne and Derek kissing, she could believe that there was hope for them after all.

Derek turned to Lily, and Nicole to Duffy. She tried to put all the love she felt into that kiss.

Duffy and Lily turned to each other and kissed.

"Well, all right, guys!" Brad said cheerfully. "Gussie and I love you all and hope to see you again soon!"

There was more laughter and applause and the scuffing sound of chairs being pushed back. Duffy and Lily were still looking at each other.

Had their kiss lingered a trifle long?

"Old girlfriends are meant to be kissed."

Oh, yeah?

Nicole thought of the dread St. Claire anathema and wondered what it might do to Lily, and hated herself for it.

There were more hugs and handshakes and more kisses and promises to "keep in touch" and to "see you soon." Then, as the other five moved toward the foyer and the door, Brad gently returned Gussie to her chair and sat her down. "Quick trip to the men's room," he said softly in her ear, "I'll be right back. Is there anything . . . ?"

"No, I'm fine."

Oh, was she ever fine. Very fine, and mellow, mellow, mellow, and as happy as she had ever been since that day, oh, how long ago, when she had first fallen in love with Bradford Holland. Wonderful, how in spite of all the shitty things that happened, sometimes things really did work out.

The room gave a slight spin, a momentary lurch. That surprised her, because she didn't think she had drunk all that much—maybe three or four drinks, whatever she'd found before her, spaced out over the evening. She had better be careful, she didn't want to spoil the evening for Brad.

But there was a fresh drink, apparently a liqueur, in front of her, and where had *that* come from?

"From a fan," said Lynn, their waitress, materializing as mysteriously as the drink. "From an admirer who shall be nameless."

Gussie didn't want the drink, but she sipped it as a courtesy, and it was orange-lemon-cinnamon delicious.

"Thank Mister or Miz Nameless, as the case may be," she said, and added, to discourage any further moves, "I shall depart momentarily with my Shig . . . Sig-nificant Other."

"No hurry, Jessie. It's good to see you."

Good to be here. Oh, how good to be here!

Moments later, at Brad's touch, a hand on her back and another under her arm, she seemed to float up out of her chair. She had no sensation of effort, of lifting herself, at all. She reached for her purse, and he slowly wafted her through the darkened, near-deserted room. *I am a mermaid,* she thought, *a mermaid almost asleep and drifting through shadows, but soon he will awaken me and I'll be a real woman. . . .*

Piano music tinkled from the bar, busy even on a week night. It faded as they passed through the brightness of the foyer and out the door to the porte-cochere. Brad's car was already waiting for them.

Forgive me, Brad, for being a little tipsy tonight. I promise you, my darling, that when we get back to the hotel I shall be quite sober enough to make love, and I shall make love to you, I shall make such love . . .

Still adrift, she found herself entering the car and settling into the passenger seat. Hearing the door shut, she automatically reached for the safety belt and fumbled it into place. It hardly seemed worth the effort, but . . .

She laid her head back and closed her eyes, and a moment later, she felt the car moving slowly, smoothly off. It made a turn and gained speed. The windows were open, and the cool night air caressed her face. The car made another turn or two, and then, as it sped yet faster, seemed to be rising. The engine was so quiet that they might almost have been in a sailplane, floating on thermals through the night sky. The seat of the car held her like a great comfortable hand, and she thought of being in Brad's hands, in his arms, while his lips explored her body. Soon . . .

She might have dozed briefly. It seemed to be taking rather long to get back to the hotel, and when she opened her eyes, she saw only a few scattered lights in the darkness, not the lights of St. Claire's streets.

"Where are we?" she asked, disoriented.

"I thought we'd drive around the lake. Get a little air before going back."

"Ah! Good idea."

She took a deep breath of the refreshing night air, and smiled as she caught a glimpse of Brad's profile by the panel lights. She closed her eyes again.

She almost roused up when the car stopped and she sensed Brad getting out. Were they back at the hotel? No. They were moving on again, over a much rougher road. A memory returned, dreamlike, of how high school kids had used the forbidden service roads in the park as lovers' lanes.

The car bounced and jounced.

What in the world . . . ?

She opened her eyes and scooted up in her seat. Where were they? The headlights revealed a narrow, winding dirt road, little more than a path, cutting through dense forest. On either side of the car, she saw only darkness.

Where in the world was Brad taking her?

Suddenly she was totally awake and sober, her mind racing. Something was wrong! She looked at the car's dashboard and didn't recognize it. She had paid little attention to Brad's car, a Porsche, but this certainly wasn't it. Fear impaled her like a barb in her heart.

"Brad—what the goddamn hell . . . ?"

The car slowed to a stop. Brad killed the engine and the lights and released his seat belt. As he opened his door to get out, the dome light came on.

Gussie knew the truth before she even looked at him, and her heart pounded, her nerves screamed. She had been tricked. Her every instinct had told her to keep her guard up, but all she had been able to think of was Brad, Brad, Brad, all that had mattered was Brad and her love for him, and they had taken advantage of that weakness.

As she stared at him, Brad slowly turned toward her, that idealized, impossibly handsome face, that mask, now wearing the ugliest grin in the world . . .

"End of the line, Jessie," he said.

. . . and, in that strange shift in perspective that she had first witnessed seven years ago, the face became that of Philip Steadman.

"*You son of a bitch!*"

The simple epithet was hurled with such unadulterated venom that Steadman's grin vanished as if slapped off of his face, and he reared back to escape Gussie's searing anger.

"End of the line, Jessie," he repeated. "Or should I say

Gussie? Isn't that what your friends call you? Gorgeous Gussie?"

By that time, Gussie had thrown off her seat belt, flung open her door, and was out of the car, purse in hand. She marched past the rear of the car, giving thanks that she was wearing flats. Somehow, even in the dark, she would find her way back along the service road to the main road, and then . . .

"You're not going anywhere, Jessie."

She came to a dead halt as Steadman's words brought a terrifying premonition. It was true: *she wasn't going anywhere.* She felt the barb in her heart again, cutting deeper.

She looked back over her shoulder toward the car, but she could no longer see it. Steadman had closed the doors, and all the lights were off. Not a star shone anywhere, and if the moon had begun its rise, she could not yet see it through the dense forest. And yet she could see Steadman's face, perhaps thirty feet away, as clearly as if he burned with his own infernal light. It seemed to hang in the darkness like a lantern, like a glowing human mask behind which she could clearly see the scaled monster that she had only glimpsed at Malibu. Hatred burned in its eyes like gaseous blue flames.

The mask was coming toward her.

And she wasn't going anywhere.

For a moment she felt utterly paralyzed, and then she realized why. Something else was coming toward her through the darkness from the other direction. She sensed it, though she couldn't yet see it.

Her breath was ragged and gasping, and she tried to hold down panic. She considered plunging through the brush on one side of the road or the other. She didn't think she would get very far. No, in those woods they would soon be on her like hounds.

Then what the hell could she do?

Her bowels were hot liquid and she was close to vomiting. She knew that Steadman wouldn't have brought her here merely to frighten her or to abuse and abandon her. No, his vengeance would go far beyond that. He had made that clear. If he had his way, she would never leave these woods alive.

What could she do?

The answer came resoundingly, as terror transformed to life-saving rage: *Kill the sons of bitches!*

Her feeling was that there were only two. If she could take one out quickly, she would have a chance at the other.

But how to do it?

A personal-defense instructor had once told her: *"You are almost never without a weapon of some kind. A tightly rolled newspaper can stun a nerve or break a bone or burst an eardrum. A stiletto heel can be just that—a stiletto. An ordinary pencil or a ballpoint pen can be as deadly as a switchblade."*

Turning away from Steadman, she reached into her purse and quickly found what she wanted. The plastic teeth of the comb bit into her fingers. She turned back again, half crouching defensively and whimpering to show fright, her purse before her and her weapon hidden behind her.

Steadman stopped directly in front of her. He grinned a lizard grin, flickering blue and green behind the mask, and flexed his fingers.

"You hurt me, Jessie," he said softly. "You hurt me badly. Would you like to try again?"

Gussie looked imploringly at him for only an instant. Then, with a despairing cry, she raised her purse over her head as if to strike at his face. Laughing, Steadman threw his arms high to ward off the harmless blow.

A warrior cry broke from Gussie's throat. She brought the rat-tail comb around from behind her, and with all her strength, drove the long, pointed handle up, up, *up* through the soft underside of Steadman's chin, *up* through his mouth and into its roof.

Had she gone for the heart, the comb might have broken on Steadman's ribs, but the thrust through flesh had been powerful and straight. With a long, choked scream, Steadman scuttled backward, off balance, until he fell to the ground. He yanked out the comb and flung it away, but Gussie knew he was strangling on his tongue and his blood, and she ran forward to stomp him while he was still disabled. Simply leap into the air, knees raised, as she had been taught, and then stomp him with all her falling weight until he was dead, or at least no longer a threat.

Steadman looked up at her with terrified eyes.

Perhaps the flicker of dismay she felt, even in that moment of rage, slowed her for the merest instant. She would never know. As she was about to launch herself feet-first at Steadman, an arm encircled her waist from behind and lifted her back and up. She screamed and clawed at the air, screamed and kicked and clawed, but she was lifted high and still higher, and held there. Then she was not dropped, but thrown, hurled, with incredible force to the hard, bare, rutted ground.

Never before in her life had she been hit as hard as the ground hit her, and she screamed, as ribs broke and splintered and pain blazed through her body.

She might have lost consciousness then, but not for long.

Pain returned, and with it came light. She seemed to feel that light, that hellish light, before she actually saw it.

She heard Bruno Krull's low, throaty chuckle. Steadman was sobbing.

Brad, Brad, help me!

"Don't expect your boyfriend to rescue you this time," Bruno said as if in answer to her plea. "He's still back at the Moonlight Inn, getting his beauty sleep. We've seen to that."

". . . kill the bitch," Steadman moaned. A foot slammed into Gussie's belly, and she felt another volcanic burst of pain.

"Not like that, goddamnit," Bruno said, "we want her conscious."

Brad, please! Mama, Mama!

Someone grasped her hair and raised her head. "Are you with us, Jessie?"

Mama, please help me!

"Yeah, she's with us." The hand released her, and her head fell back to the ground. "Pick her up—*gently.*"

There was no way anyone could have picked her up gently. As hands reached under her armpits, grasping her from behind and lifting her, she was in agony, driven almost mindless with pain. *Mama! Brad!*

"Can you see me, Jessie?"

She seemed to be dangling from Steadman's forearm. He yanked her head up by the hair. At first she could see only that strange light, yellow and red and blue, that seemed to rustle with unseen and half-glimpsed life. It was as if Steadman and Bruno had brought a little part of hell with them. Then she saw Bruno, but only through a haze of pain, and she couldn't be sure she wasn't hallucinating. Her drinks, or at least that last one, had been drugged, she was sure.

Bruno was wearing a hooded black cloak, and as with Steadman, his face seemed to mask a different inner self, something demonic that she had sensed the night before. Her vision blurred and she might have passed out for a time, because when she saw him again he was naked. She could now seen his demonic self clearly—the catlike muzzle with the long sharp teeth, the female breasts, the penis spearing out of the vulva. But she was beyond shock, and somehow that didn't surprise her or even, in itself, horrify or frighten her. What did she care if Bruno Krull and Philip Steadman were human or demonic in form, men or monsters? It made no difference— they were going to kill her.

They were going to take her from those she loved.

From her mother and Brad. From those lost friends she had found again. From all she held dear. And they had no right. What had she ever done to them?

Oh, Mama, Brad!

Demons trod the earth, stalking the innocent and the not so innocent, looking for chances to humble and degrade and kill. Demons, filled with hatred and contempt and envy, because they could not be—perhaps *dared* not be—quite human. Demons without the capacity or the courage for compassion. Demons who considered it a weakness to share the pain and joy and sorrow of others. Demons driven by an insatiable lust for power over the humanity they so despised. Gussie understood that now.

A hell of a lot of good it did her—she was going to die.

Bruno stepped up to her. He grabbed the front of her dress with both hands and tore it open, all but tore it off of her. Claws raked her flesh as he tore off her brassiere and underpants. He stood before her with his right hand hung low, palm toward her, claws spread apart.

"Are you ready for it, Jessie?" he asked, grinning. "Are you ready for it, huh?"

Oh, please, Mama, help—
Gussie screamed as, with one swift, powerful movement, Bruno brought the claws tearing up through her belly.

She knew this was not the end of her terror and her pain. She knew this was only the beginning.

CHAPTER 18

He had dozed off, and it took him two or three seconds to recall where he was. Not in the cottage on Martha's Vineyard, not in his room at the hotel, but sitting on a john in the men's room of the Moonlight Inn.

Still half-asleep, he blinked and shook his head. He'd only had a couple of martinis and some wine over the course of the evening, but the drinks must have hit him. He'd felt fine until he sat down, but then . . . but then . . .

Sleep, Bradford . . .

Jesus, *no!* He had to get a move on, not fall asleep again. Gussie was waiting.

With an effort, he made himself stand up, arrange his clothes, and step out of the shadowy booth into the glare of the men's room. His legs felt almost paralyzed as he staggered over to a washbasin. He washed his hands and, still trying to shake off his daze, threw some cold water on his face. His eyes looked puffy in the mirror.

The dining room was empty when he returned, every table cleared and most of the lights off. That didn't surprise him—theirs had been one of the last parties to leave. He was a little surprised not to see Gussie, but then he realized she must have followed his cue and gone to the women's room. He sat down to wait for her.

Gussie! He still could not comprehend the magnitude of the miracle that had happened, the gift that he had been given. This girl, this young woman, who had once loved him and whom he had treated so shabbily, loved him still, loved him more than ever. And she accepted *his* love, poor thing that it was, accepted it as if it were treasure.

But where the hell was she?

Maybe she hadn't gone to the women's room, maybe she had spotted an old friend and gone into the bar, maybe—

As he glanced at his wristwatch, all thought slammed to a dead halt.

Twelve twenty-three.

But that was impossible.

The party had broken up and he had gone to the men's room at about eleven.

He stared at the watch. The long, narrow, golden hand steadily ticked off the seconds against the ebony face. Twelve twenty-four.

If his watch was right, and he felt an unholy dread that it was, then he had been in the men's room for over an hour.

Where was Gussie? What had happened to her?

He got up and walked unsteadily toward the bar—he felt as if the earth's center of gravity were shifting under him—hoping that this was all just some crazy mix-up, some confusion on his part, that his watch had gone loco on him. He would find Gussie in the bar in earnest conversation with some old friend, and she would look up and smile and wave at him and—

She wasn't there.

Three tables and a couple of booths were occupied, and a few people sat on stools at the bar. The pianist was gone, and the clock on the wall, a little advanced, said twelve thirty-five.

Lynn Briggs, their waitress, was now working behind the bar. She was a good-looking freckled redhead in her forties. She smiled at Brad and said, "Welcome back."

As if he had left. As if he had left and had now returned.

He tried to smile back, tried to sound casual. "Lynn, as a matter of curiosity, did you happen to notice what time it was when we left?"

Lynn cocked her head and thought. "Mm, party broke up about eleven, I guess."

"That was the others. They went first."

Lynn nodded. "I remember. You and Jessie left about five or ten minutes later."

"You saw us leave."

"Not really. I wasn't paying any attention. But it's hard to mistake that head of blond hair, even from a distance. Why do you ask?"

"I was just wondering."

Brad's mind felt like a compass whose needle kept spinning back and forth erratically, without ever settling on a single direction. Why would Gussie have left like that? And with whom?

What the hell was going on?

The fact was, he was completely baffled. And frightened. He recalled his deep misgivings about the reunion. Now, once again, they seemed valid. Why hadn't he done more to discourage the others from returning here? What would happen to them now? What terrible thing might already have happened to Gussie? He felt like a man forced to look into the darkest of shadows, terrified of what he might find there.

Don't panic, he thought. Don't let your goddamn imagination run away with you. The first thing to do is to check the hotel.

There was a pay phone and a directory near the front door. He looked up the number and tapped it in. A male voice answered.

"Give me room five-fifteen, please."

The phone began ringing.

Perhaps because it was so late, the clerk let the phone ring only five times.

"No answer, sir."

"Try again. This is important."

Five more rings.

"Still no answer, sir."

"Look, she's expecting a call from me. Give it a good try."

Ten more rings.

"Sorry, sir."

"Thanks anyway."

Two full minutes of intermittent ringing and no answer. She wasn't in her room. Then, where?

Jesus God, where!

It was crazy to think that she might be in the women's room, but Brad went to check it out anyway. He opened the door and looked in, almost afraid of what he might see.

Nothing. Empty booths, the doors ajar, a mirror over a row of sinks, no one.

Where next? The parking lot.

The parking valets were long gone, and the lot, behind the restaurant, was nearly empty. The mercury vapor lamp tinted it an eerie goblin blue, but at least there was light. Despite a sense of dread, like a whimper rising in his throat, he made himself get a flashlight from his car and look around and under and into every car in the lot. He then looked into the surrounding brush and brambles.

Nothing.

Thank God.

He went back into the bar. Lynn, looking perhaps a trifle perplexed, smiled at him, and he said, "Cup of coffee, please, Lynn."

What should he do now? The crazy thought occurred to him that he could just sit here on a bar stool and wait for Gussie to come back. As he recalled, the Moonlight Inn closed at two. Sometime before then, Gussie would come wandering in. She would tease him about falling asleep in the john, gently bawl him out, and they would leave together to live happily ever after.

Except that he knew in his poor terrified heart that *it wasn't ever gonna goddamn happen!*

Oh, Gussie, God, what have I done to you?

He could go back to the hotel and pound on her door loud enough to wake the dead (oh, Jesus, don't even think that!) though he was certain she wasn't there. Or he could check with Duffy or Derek, find out if Gussie was with them, see if they had a clue.

Even under the circumstances, he was reluctant to phone

at this hour but, hell, he didn't need to. He had his mental radar, still sensitive to his friends, and he might be able to pick up something just by driving past their places. Then he'd bang on a door if necessary. He hurried out of the bar.

As he drove through the quiet streets of the town toward the lake road, he began feeling better. He was *doing* something. He even had the feeling that he might be on Gussie's trail, though he knew that in his emotional state such feelings could be deceptive.

Once on the lake road and past the old Johnson place, he slowed down. There was little traffic at this hour on a week night, and when he came to the St. Claire house, he crawled by. Not a light shone in the house. He wanted so badly to sense Gussie's presence there, to sense it the way he had sensed her arrival at the hotel on Monday evening, that any psychic impressions he might have had were overlaid by wishful thinking: he *had* to find Gussie, she *had* to be all right!

As he rolled past and picked up speed, he had half a notion to go back and ring the bell, pound on the door, make sure Gussie wasn't there. But then he saw light in Derek and Joanne's place. He turned into their drive and coasted down the slope to the cabin.

Joanne had gone to bed, up on the sleeping balcony, but Derek was still awake and dressed. A laptop was open on a table back in the kitchen area, under the balcony, and beside it lay a scattering of legal pads, loose-leaf notebooks, and ballpoints. Derek cleared the laptop's screen before Brad could see what was on it, and in that instant, he knew that his old buddy had been carefully noting down everything Brad had told them that day about the Luciferians. Because he had little respect for Derek as a journalist, he had spoken "off the record," but at the moment, he didn't give a damn what Derek wrote.

While Derek sat comfortably on an old-fashioned cushioned wicker chair, smoking and grinning, Brad paced and told what had happened.

Derek thought it was all very funny. "Oh, man," he said, when Brad was finished, "asleep on the john for over an hour—it's like, Welcome to Hemorrhoid City!"

"Could I use your phone?"

"Go ahead."

Perhaps the clerk recognized Brad's voice, because he let the phone ring a full ten times.

No answer.

"Well, hell," Derek said, "it's not even two yet. If you want company, you can bunk-out on the sofa. Use the phone some more. I'll be up another hour or so."

"No, I'd better get back to the hotel."

But he could not go back to the hotel, simply to lie awake listening for the sound of Gussie's door. He had to do something. After leaving Derek, he headed west again, around the lake. *Goddamnit, Gussie, haven't you punished me enough?* He was beginning to get a little angry, and that was good—not because his anger was justified, but because it helped him suppress his fear.

He was going to find Gussie.

He was a psychic detective, wasn't he? Maybe a goddamn bumbling amateur psychic detective, not nearly in Nicholas Crown's league, but Father Nick said he had talent, he was better than he knew, and one way or another, he was going to find Gussie before this night was over.

As he drove along the dark, nearly deserted road, he worked to calm and clarify his mind. A mantra, a koan, a silent "Our Father," paying close attention to its meaning, would do it. He might not be a Christian, but he had found that an "Our Father" worked nicely.

He had just passed the Balthazar place when he noticed something.

On his way from the restaurant to the cabin, he had had the feeling, perhaps illusory, that he might be on Gussie's trail. As if she had left psychic traces behind her.

He no longer had that feeling.

He had been on her trail but had lost it.

He turned around in the first driveway he came to and started back, driving slowly, as if feeling his way.

Hope, he knew, was like the scent of fresh, clean air. That was what he wanted, what he strained for, but his guts cramped and he could hardly breathe. If Gussie wasn't with Nicole or Joanne, what in God's name was she doing out here at this time of night?

He was back within a few hundred yards of the Andersons' cabin when he sensed Gussie again. Or rather not Gussie but her traces, her psychic spoor, and now there was no mistaking it. It was like her voice, faintly heard, when she sang some sweetly haunting melody of love, low and soft and rich in happiness.

Why should he find that to be so terrifying, as terrifying as any scream in the night?

It was terrifying because it was inexplicable. It was almost as if he were being lured by a siren song, as if he were meant to follow . . . and find what?

But that had to be bullshit; he was thinking crazy. He pulled over to the side of the road and sat for a moment, again trying to calm his nerves. *"Our Father Who art in heaven . . ."*

He looked in his mirror and then back over his shoulder. The road was deserted. He slowly, carefully began to back up. A hundred feet. Two hundred. He stopped.

Gussie hadn't come this far west. He was sure of it. He had never before had this kind of experience so . . . definitively.

He remembered there was a turnoff near here. He rolled slowly forward, his eyes searching the berm, the ditch, the edge of the woods, in his headlights. He had missed it while backing up, but now he found it—an old seldom used service road, its entrance overgrown with weeds. Kids had sometimes used it as a lovers' lane, and perhaps they still did. Some of the weeds had been run over and crushed.

Again, he pulled over and tried to calm himself and gather his wits. Again, he asked himself why in God's name Gussie would leave the Moonlight Inn to come out here? And with whom? He tried to open himself up to the traces of any other presence that might have been with Gussie, but he got nothing . . .

. . . except, perhaps, a faint, veiled sense of evil, a low, muted counterpoint to Gussie's melody . . .

. . . but that might be nothing but a reflection of his own sense of dread.

Stop wasting time; Gussie needs you; let's get going.

He put the car into gear, eased forward, and turned onto

the service road. A slight dip, a rise for a few yards, and then a leveling, and he was into the woods, his lights revealing a path of sorts through the undergrowth. A rusty chain that had once blocked the way lay across the road. It might have been down for an hour or for years.

Brad edged forward slowly at first, getting the feel of the road. It was a single lane, still rutted from past use, with occasional clearings of each side to allow vehicles to pass. Branches long untrimmed scratched softly against the roof and sides of the car. The headlights only emphasized the darkness around and overhead, and Brad had no sense of spaciousness or of open forest. Rather, he felt blanketed, cocooned in darkness, as if he were following a long dark tunnel down into hell.

Gussie had come this way.

She had not come back.

Suddenly Brad could no longer bear this crawling through the woods at a snail's pace. He had to find Gussie and find her fast. He found himself pressing down on the accelerator, and he began pounding on the horn, as if that would somehow clear the way. The Porsche took off like a frightened gazelle, bounding through the night; the horn brayed. Gussie, do you hear me? I'm coming for you, damnit! The car bucked and bounced, swayed from side to side, scraped against a tree on a curve, missed another tree by inches, headed for another—

You damn fool, you're going to kill yourself!

He hit the brakes and slid to a halt.

If he killed himself, there'd be no one out here tonight to look for Gussie.

Trembling, he leaned on the wheel and gasped for breath. Tears came to his eyes.

Gussie, where the hell are you?

He killed the lights. He had no idea why. Perhaps he wanted to see what they couldn't show him. Perhaps he didn't want to see what they could. Something out there . . .

He turned off the engine and, leaning out the open window, listened. The night was oddly silent. After a moment, he heard the click and trill of a few insects, nothing more. There wasn't even a firefly in sight. Gussie was somewhere out there in that darkness, out there still, somehow he knew she had to be . . .

Something whispered in Brad's mind like a faint echo of the evil music he had heard earlier, the counterpoint to Gussie's lovely tune:

"End of the line, Jessie . . ."

Fear crawled up Brad's spine like a giant spider and settled on his shoulders. *Oh, no, no, no, no . . .*

He got out of the car. He brought the flashlight with him but didn't immediately use it. He put it in a pocket and closed the car door. He waited for his eyes to adjust to the night. For the first time, he noticed that the moon had risen, its milky borrowed light filtering down through the trees onto the road.

"End of the line, Jessie . . ."

No, no, it was not, could not be, true. Brad raked a hand down over his face, found he was crying.

Tear-blinded, he walked ahead, beyond the car, slowly at first, afraid of what he would almost certainly find. Then faster, stumbling, desperately trying to deny what was about to happen.

He knew.

It was all there in his mind now, but he refused to see it, could not bear to see it. The whole thing, everything he was about to find, the body broken and torn, was burned into his mind, but rather than see it, he ripped his mind apart. Better to escape into madness than to see what was about to come. He could not, could not bear it. He wanted to turn and flee, anything to escape the next few minutes, the next hours, the rest of his life, but he could not do that. She was Gussie, his Gussie, and he had to go to her. He stumbled forward. *Gussie, I'm coming to you, I'm coming!*

A moment later, a great, long, agonized cry of endless despair and everlasting grief floated out over the vast dark forests of St. Claire, the cry of a soul self-condemned and eternally damned.

.   .   .

The thumping on the back door and the ringing of the door-bell never stopped as they ran down the back stairs. Nicole was still pulling on her robe and Duffy belting his when they reached the kitchen. Duffy turned on the kitchen lights and then the porch lights, and they saw Brad's face pressed against a glass pane in the kitchen door. It was a ghastly clown's face, twisted, distorted, blurred.

Duffy unlocked the door and flung it open. Brad staggered into the room. His clothes were disheveled and soiled, one knee of his trousers torn. He fell sobbing into Duffy's arms as if he no longer had the strength to stay on his feet.

"Brad," Duffy said, "for God's sake!"

His eyes tightly closed, Brad shook his head. His lips moved, but he seemed unable to speak.

Nicole's whole body clenched up with dread. "Brad, what is it? What's happened?"

Brad whispered something. "Gussie . . ."

"What? What about Gussie?"

"Gussie's dead."

For a brief moment, the words hung meaningless in the air. Then Nicole understood but couldn't believe. No. No, that was impossible, Gussie wasn't dead. Brad was talking some horrible nonsense. Gussie had been with them this evening, just a few hours ago.

"What do you mean? What happened? What do you—"

He shouted it now, almost screamed it: "Gussie's dead! They killed her! Gussie's dead!"

That, somehow, made it real for Nicole. Gussie was dead. Their Gussie. Gussie was dead, and nothing was going to bring her back. No wonder, then, that Brad looked like a grief-stricken child. A child with his heart torn out.

Duffy dragged him to a chair and sat him down. "Who killed her, Brad?" he asked. "What are you talking about?"

Brad shook his head. He didn't answer, but his cry of grief seemed to have calmed him somewhat. He took a deep breath and released it in a long shuddering sigh.

"Gotta call the cops," he said after a long moment.

"First tell us what's happened. Maybe we can help."

Brad's eyes said no one could ever help, but after some

urging, he briefly recounted what had happened after the others had left the Moonlight Inn.

"Never mind the psychic stuff, just say I had a hunch. After I left Derek, I remembered that old service road the kids used as a lovers' lane. I drove up it a ways and got out of my car and looked around. And I found her." Brad's voice broke. "All torn up like . . ."

To her horror, Brad slowly lifted his eyes to look into Nicole's, and she knew exactly what he was thinking, what he was seeing: a man's torn body in a dark parking lot, Nicole nearby with blood on her face. She wanted to cry out, *No, Brad, I didn't. I couldn't do that! Not to Gussie. Not to anyone!*

Brad nodded, lowering his eyes, and she sensed that he was sorry for even having the thought.

"I think I sort of went nuts, Nickie," he said, "and maybe I still am. I went back to my car and tried to drive back the way I'd come, but I couldn't. I banged up the car trying to turn around. I got out and started running back, but somehow I wandered off the service road and got lost. I finally spotted this place."

Sitting hunched over on the kitchen chair, Brad looked small and shrunken and gray-faced, all the clown-color now burnt out of him. He made Nicole think of a smoldering ember: if she had turned off the kitchen lights, she would have seen the pain burning beneath the ash.

"It's my fault she's dead," he said after a moment, softly. "It's my fault. I started the coven—"

"This has nothing to do with the coven," Duffy said sharply.

Brad, staring into the distance, didn't seem to hear him. "I started it. Gussie only went along with it to please me. I drew you and the others into it. I'm responsible for everything that happens because of the coven."

"Nothing has happened because of the coven," Duffy insisted, "and anyway, we're all responsible for ourselves."

Brad looked up at him. "Just a few hours ago everything seemed so wonderful. I had all you guys back again. You didn't hate me or—or find me disgusting for what I did seven years ago. You *liked* me."

Nicole covered her eyes with her hand. "We love you, Brad—stop breaking my heart."

"Gussie loved me. After all these years, I had her again, and she loved me. That was the most wonderful thing that ever happened to me—Gussie's love. And my love for Gussie. We were both so happy, so goddamn endlessly happy. And now . . . suddenly she's dead. She's gone. Because of me."

"Brad, no!" Nicole sobbed.

Brad shook his head. With the weariness of a frail old man, he slowly pulled himself to his feet. "I've got to call the police."

A police sedan, running silent but in a great hurry, arrived in a very few minutes. Nicole and Duffy watched from the veranda while Brad met it in the driveway. A deputy got out of the passenger side and came around. Brad showed him identification, said something Nicole couldn't hear, and gestured toward the house. The deputy nodded and said something, and he and Brad got into the car.

"I'm surprised they didn't want to talk to us," Nicole said.

"They'll be back."

They watched as the car turned and drove off.

"Brad thinks I could have done it," Nicole said when the car's red taillights had disappeared in the darkness.

Duffy turned toward her with a look of incredulity. "Honey, Brad thinks nothing of the kind!"

"I didn't say he thinks I did it. I said he thinks I could have done it."

"But Brad likes you!"

"Wrong. Brad loves me. And I loved Gussie, and he knows that. But he still thinks that, given the opportunity, I could have done it."

Duffy enfolded Nicole in his arms and drew her to him. "Well, Brad's wrong. My heart aches for Brad, but on this subject, I don't give a damn what Brad thinks. Now let's go back to bed. There's going to be a lot of traffic along this road pretty soon, and I don't care to see it."

.   .   .

Timothy Balthazar came to his aid. Gave him counsel and support. Guided him through the nightmare. Uncle Timothy. His godfather.

Uncle Timothy was suddenly there when the sheriff was questioning him—with surprising gentleness—under the harsh lights of an interrogation room. Uncle Timothy assured the sheriff of Brad's complete cooperation and obtained his release. Uncle Timothy took care of everything.

Hardly aware through the haze of his misery, Brad found himself in a police car, heading back to his hotel with Timothy at his side.

"I've called a doctor to see you, Brad. You're obviously exhausted and need rest. He'll meet us at the hotel."

The doctor was there when they arrived. Brad knew him slightly—a Dr. Frank Stranger. While Brad put on pajamas, the doctor prepared a hypodermic. "This is just a relaxant, Brad. Not much stronger than a couple of drinks. . . ."

Looking at the glistening tip of the needle, Brad was suddenly apprehensive. Gussie had been killed. Why was he being so trusting? Why . . . ?

Reluctantly, Brad let the doctor swab the inside of his elbow with chilling, pungent alcohol and insert the needle.

He felt himself relaxing almost at once.

"And now," Timothy said, "into bed, young man. Thank you, Frank!"

"I'll meet you downstairs," the doctor said, leaving.

While Brad slid under the sheet, Timothy closed the shades and drew the drapes, darkening the room. Then he pulled a chair to the side of the bed and sat down.

"You're going to need a car, Brad, while the police have yours. I'll arrange for a rental. Just ask for the keys at the desk."

"Thank you."

"How do you feel?"

"Like I'm about to drift off."

"Good." Leaning closer to Brad, Timothy lowered his voice. "Bradford, listen closely. I'm going to let you go to sleep now. Are you relaxed?"

". . . Yes." Brad felt the tension draining from his body as he drifted further toward sleep.

"You are going to sleep. You are going to sleep and you are going to sleep deeply, and while you sleep I want you to remember this. *You* are going to find poor Jessie's killer, Bradford. *You* are going to find him. You are going to use all the skills you have acquired from Monsignor Crown . . . oh, yes, I know all about Monsignor Crown . . . and you are going to use those skills to find Jessie's killer. Only you can do it, Bradford, only you. Sleep now, Bradford, but while you sleep"—Brad's eyelids were heavy, almost closed, but he saw Timothy's big face, with the oddly colorless yet piercing eyes, looming over him—"while you sleep, remember. Jessie's killer is somewhere out there in the dark. Somewhere out there in the dark. And you must find him. The police will never find him without your help. You must find him . . . out there in the darkness . . . tonight. Tonight, Bradford. Now, sleep . . ."

Timothy was still talking as Brad fell asleep.

CHAPTER
19

G ussie was dead.

    That was Nicole's first thought, barely articulated, upon awakening. Gussie was dead.

The impossible, the monstrous, had happened. Beautiful, loving, supremely happy Gussie had been wantonly slaughtered, her body left to rot in the woods like abandoned garbage.

Gussie was gone.

They had discovered something yesterday, she and Gussie and Joanne. They were one. The way Duffy and Brad and Derek, in the old days, had been one. Maybe it had started that terrible evening eight years ago at the mall, she couldn't be sure. But aside from Duffy, they were the two friends Nicole had most hated to leave behind when she and her grandmother moved to New York. And yesterday when she saw them for the first time in years . . .

    . . . yesterday something wonderful had happened. She had been delighted to have, first, Joanne back, and then Gussie. She had greeted each as a dear old friend. But she had sensed that long ago, after she had left St. Claire, something had happened between the other two women. Things to do with the coven, perhaps, which neither really blamed the other for, but which neither could quite forgive. The coven had poisoned their friendship.

But Nicole had reached out for both of them at once, and it was one of those rare times when it seemed to her that she had some of her grandmother's magic. She had brought the two women, and herself, together again in love and forgiveness and understanding. They had become one.

And, Lord, what a wonderful, strengthening thing that had been—talking, reminiscing, confiding! Talking to Gussie and Joanne was better even than talking to Freya. The crazy, happy thought had crossed her mind, What did she need with Freya when she had Gussie and Joanne?

They were three singular ladies who made up more than the sum of their parts.

But now, suddenly, Gussie was dead.

Slaughtered, all life and love and beauty gone. All hope, all dreams, all happiness.

A great yawning void opened up in Nicole.

It was well past noon, and when she went downstairs, she found the house full of people. Police uniforms. The sheriff. Mr. Balthazar—what was he doing here? And Dr. Stranger?

"Mr. Balthazar asked me to check out Bradford this morning after his ordeal and, while I was at it, to look in on you. But Duffy said you were sound asleep, and under the circumstances, that was the best thing. You look fine."

"Thank you, but . . ." Nicole still felt dazed from her long sleep. "I don't understand. Mr. Balthazar . . . ?"

"Everything's under control, Nicole, don't worry. Bradford's father was a good friend, so I'm looking out for his interests. I'll keep an eye on yours too, if you wish—your grandmother would want that."

"Thank you."

The police wanted a "statement" from her, it seemed. So she sat at the kitchen table and answered questions. She told about Gussie's phone call Monday night and the party last night and Brad's pounding on the back door early this morning . . . all the while sipping black coffee and nibbling toast that did nothing to assuage her growing hunger.

If only she could talk to Freya . . . once again she needed Freya. . . .

Finally the police were finished with her. Actually, it hadn't taken very long. People began to leave the kitchen, the house. Mr. Balthazar, Sheriff Krull, Duffy, and Nicole remained at the table, the doctor and a couple of coffee-drinking cops looking over their shoulders.

"Nicole," the sheriff said in a kindly, confidential voice, "about Brad. I can tell you're concerned about him. Now, I really shouldn't discuss the case with you—"

"No, you shouldn't," one of the cops said firmly. He was a tough, weathered-looking man, someone important from the state police. Nicole had been introduced to him—she thought his name was Laughlin.

Neither the sheriff nor Mr. Balthazar showed any signs of having heard him. "But off the record," the sheriff said, "I don't believe for one minute that Brad did it."

Nicole looked at him in surprise. It had never occurred to her that Brad might be a suspect.

The sheriff smiled smugly. "While poor Jessie was being attacked," he said, "Brad Holland was in the men's room at the Moonlight Inn. He had fallen asleep there, and Jessie left with another man."

"You don't know that for sure," Laughlin said angrily. He didn't like being ignored. Or perhaps he didn't approve of the way the case was being handled.

The sheriff smiled back over his shoulder at the man, and returned his attention to Nicole. "For absolute sure, no. But we've already talked to some of the bar regulars, and they tell us there *was* a guy, they're pretty sure it was Brad, asleep in the men's room for over an hour."

"*But*," Laughlin said, "if Holland left with Lindquist at about ten after eleven, as the Briggs woman said—"

"She couldn't say for sure it was Holland."

"He'd have almost an hour and a half—"

"To get to the scene, slash Jessie, and then manage somehow to clean himself up. Change into clean clothes and dispose of the bloody ones and *then* return to the Moonlight Inn. No way."

"I still think he's good for it," Laughlin said. "I'm not saying he *did* it. I'm saying he's *good* for it."

The sheriff shook his head. "I know him, Joe, I know all about him. And his alibi, the way he cooperated, his whole demeanor—"

"Aw, come on," Laughlin said disdainfully. " 'He was such a nice, quiet boy, such polite manners.' You a human polygraph, for Chrissake? Demeanor!"

"Yeah, demeanor. No, I'm convinced. Brad Holland did not kill Jessie Lindquist."

The sheriff smiled complacently. Point proven.

What is wrong with this picture? Nicole thought dazedly.

Why should the sheriff seem almost pleased at losing a suspect, if indeed he had? Of course, she barely knew Bruno Krull, but she would have expected him to react more like Laughlin, keeping all possibilities open till the very last moment.

For that matter, who was actually in charge here?

The answer came to her at once.

Timothy Balthazar was in charge.

Timothy Balthazar said little, listened intently, and kept his face carefully blank except for the occasional smile. But he was the power in the room. If the sheriff did most of the talking, he spoke for Mr. Balthazar. And if Laughlin objected, took exception, seemed irritated, well . . . that was his role. She felt as if the whole scene since she had arrived in the kitchen had been concocted and played out for her benefit.

But why?

She wished all these people would leave right now. She wanted to call Freya, to talk to Freya.

The sheriff granted her wish. "Just a couple more things," he said as he stood up from the table. "Jessie Lindquist was a celebrity, and this is going to turn high profile. Already more people know about Jessie than need to, and in the next day or two the media will probably start hitting on you—"

"We've got nothing to tell them," Duffy said, looking to Nicole for approval, "or at least no more than it takes to get them off our backs."

"Good for you," the sheriff said. "This could turn into a circus. The other thing is, I'd like you to stay around a few days until we have this cleared up, just in case we need you."

"We'll do that, Sheriff," Nicole said.

Timothy Balthazar and Dr. Stranger were the last to leave the house. Nicole and Duffy walked them to the front door.

"This morning before you joined us," Timothy said, holding Nicole's right hand in both of his, "I again tried to tempt Duffy with a future in St. Claire. I truly believe it could be brilliant."

"Duffy has a brilliant future wherever he goes, Mr. Balthazar."

"Perhaps that's the real reason I want him to come back. Perhaps you will persuade him not to close his mind to the possibility."

"We'll see."

If Duffy ever came back to St. Claire, Nicole was reasonably certain it would be without her.

"Call me," Timothy Balthazar said to Duffy, "at any time, about anything."

When he and the doctor had left, Nicole turned to Duffy. "He made you some kind of offer?"

"Not exactly. But he hinted at several stars and a large part of the moon."

And Lily, Nicole thought miserably. That was irrational and unfair, but still she thought it.

Freya. She had to talk to Freya again. She had found such comfort in talking to Freya before, and Freya had said to call her at any time. But before she could get to a telephone, she felt Duffy drawing her into his arms. And that was what she needed right now, to be rocked in Duffy's arms, to feel his breath on her face, to hear his whispers in her ear, to feel herself growing warm and limp in one of those moments when they seemed to meld together, her anxiety absorbed and dispelled by his strength, his love, his steadfastness—

The phone began to ring.

Freya!

Bursting free of Duffy's arms, she picked up the handset before the answering machine kicked in.

"Yes? Hello?"

"Killer!" shrieked a strange voice. "Murderer! We know you killed her! Same as you killed Buster Dugan! Only, *this* time you won't get away with it, *this* time you'll pay!"

Once again Nicole had the sensation of being slammed in the face, a shattering, blinding blow. "Who is this? Who—"

"You crazy woman, you stay away from St. Claire! We know what you are! Werewolf! *Werewolf!*"

Thank God for Freya.

In a way, she had rescued them from Derek and Joanne—well, from Derek, anyway. When they had come up to the house that afternoon, Nicole had welcomed Joanne as a source of strength and understanding. But not Derek, with his tape recorder and his camera, wanting to get "the whole story" and take pictures. She wanted to like Derek, and she had no doubt that he was appalled by Gussie's death, but his grief had struck Nicole as surpassed by his ambition. He had finally gone off to see if he could get pictures of the crime scene. Joanne, looking ashamed for him, had invited them to supper, but by that time, fortunately, Freya had already asked them.

In the early evening, they drove around the lake to Freya's house. Lovely in a white loose-fitting summer dress, she greeted them with a smile and exactly the right degree of gentle cheerfulness. "The grill's set up in the backyard. I'll bet you're both ready for a drink." Already Nicole felt a slackening of tension, a closing of the void within her, a wonderful sense of relief.

They went through the house and out into the backyard, where a bar had been set up on a picnic table. At Freya's request, Duffy mixed drinks. Though they had met only once before, at Julia St. Claire's funeral, Duffy and Freya found themselves chatting as easily as old friends; and once they were settled in lawn chairs with their drinks, Nicole found she could discuss Gussie's death calmly, if sorrowfully.

"And they have no idea who did it?" Freya asked.

The lizard man, Nicole thought, remembering Gussie's story, but that was hardly an answer. She shook her head. "Apparently not, or if they do, they're not saying."

While Duffy lit the charcoal and made a second round of drinks, she told Freya about the vicious phone call she had received that afternoon and then—she had already told Duffy—about her trip to town on Monday and her ugly encounters with the man in the liquor store and the woman at the supermarket checkout. It now all seemed so trivial that she told it lightly, almost as an amusing anecdote, but Freya didn't smile.

"Remember what I've told you. Accept yourself for what you are and regard their insults as inadvertent compliments. And if they really give you a hard time—show 'em your teeth, baby!"

Duffy applauded vigorously.

At eight-thirty, with their meal finished and the sun setting, they moved inside. Duffy asked if he could use the telephone. He returned to the living room a minute later looking concerned.

"It's Brad," he explained to Freya. "He was in pretty terrible shape this morning. I've tried to call him several times, but all I get from the hotel is 'Sorry, Mr. Holland is not accepting calls.'"

"If you're worried, Duffy," Freya said, "couldn't you just go to the hotel and check on him?"

Duffy could do that. Brad had given them his room number, five-seventeen, and Duffy could go bang on his door and then get back here as soon as possible.

"Oh, there's no need to hurry, Duffy," Freya said. "Bradford may need you. If he does, I'll see that Nicole gets home."

"Well . . . if I'm held up," Duffy told Nicole, "I'll give you a call." He expressed his appreciation to Freya and left.

"And now, Nicole," Freya said, smiling, when they were alone. "And now I wonder if you've given any further thought to my . . . to my 'outrageous' suggestion."

Nicole laughed. "That I 'accept' my craziness?" She shook her head. "I don't think I could ever accept something that I know destroyed my grandfather."

"But don't you see, by accepting our nature we can learn to control it. . . ."

Much of what Freya had to say appealed to Nicole, yet she found herself reluctant to yield to it. She sensed an unspoken message—*Be what I will you to be, Nicole*—and she had no intention of going that far. Still . . .

The next hour went by so swiftly that Nicole was surprised to discover it was a quarter to ten. She had a faint sense of alarm. Why hadn't Duffy called as he had promised? Usually he was very thoughtful about keeping her informed. Still, if he had found Brad to be all right and was on his way back, there was no need to call.

Half an hour later her growing worry had begun to turn into mild anger. That was her choice: worry or anger. Duffy had promised to call, and it would be better that he had broken his promise than that something had happened to him.

"Freya, may I use your telephone?"

"Of course."

She called the Hotel St. Claire, asked for room five-seventeen, and was told that that room was not accepting calls. But that didn't mean anything. Duffy and Brad still might be there together. Or they could be anywhere.

The great aching void began to open up again.

By a quarter to eleven, she felt as if she couldn't hide her growing anxiety from Freya any longer. Forcing a smile, she said, "Well, I guess my wandering boy is out on the town, and I'm keeping you up and frankly I'm beat after today, so I'll just call a taxi . . ."

No, no, if Nicole wouldn't stay, Freya would gladly drive her home.

And she did.

Come home, Duffy, and I'll stop being scared and angry the minute I take you into my arms. That's all I want right now—to tell you I'm mad as hell, 'cause it's dark and dangerous out there and I got scared when you didn't call!

She checked the answering machine, but it had been left off. Just as well, she thought; who needed more messages from the friends of Buster Dugan? She and Duffy had left some lights on in the house, and she turned on a few more. If Duffy spotted them, he would come directly home rather than going to Freya's.

Then she went upstairs and took a leisurely shower.

Oh, Duffy, be safe!

She wondered if Gussie's mother had been notified yet. Surely she had been, and at the thought of what that woman must be suffering, all the shock and grief Nicole had felt that morning returned.

Oh, Duffy, come home. Be safe and come home!

She had just slid between the sheets and turned off the light when she heard the faintest of clicks. Duffy was home at last. Safe behind their locked doors. She felt such a tide of relief that she nearly called out to him, *Duffy, oh, Duffy!* all her ire quite vanished. Oh, she would chide him for not calling, of course, but only while she held him close.

He would be on the back stairs by now, likely, and in a moment more in the hall . . .

She frowned.

She smelled something . . .

. . . something strange and unexpected . . .

. . . strange and yet shockingly familiar. . . .

Her body went rigid between the sheets.

The odor grew stronger, a very distinctive perfume that included, perhaps, the scent of a woman's body.

She had smelled it before.

Oh, yes, she had smelled it before. A thought came to mind, a possibility so painful that she immediately denied it. *He wouldn't have, no, no, he wouldn't have!* Tears filled her eyes.

As the door opened, light from the hallway cut through the darkness of the room. She rolled away from it and hid her face in her pillow.

"Nicole?" Duffy said softly, as if fearful of disturbing her.

For a moment, she couldn't speak. She struggled to keep her voice steady. "Why didn't you call?"

"I did. I called Freya's a couple of times. Later I called here. Nobody answered."

That was possible, she supposed. He might have got Freya's number wrong, and she didn't think he would ever lie to her, but . . .

"Did you see Brad?"

"No. Nicole—"

"Go take a shower."

"Nicole, please—"

"I can smell her. Go take a shower. We can talk later."

When Duffy returned from taking his shower, the smell

was gone. But when he slid into bed with her and touched her shoulder, she didn't move but lay still with her back to him. The terrible hungering void within her was widening, but she knew she would not find surcease in his arms tonight. Perhaps she never would again.

Weeping silently, she pretended to sleep.

"Jessie's killer is somewhere out there in the dark. . . ."

Brad sat at the dimly lit hotel bar, staring at his drink, not sure of how he had got there or of how many he had had. Sure only that Gussie was dead and that he was to blame.

If only he had somehow kept her from coming back here . . .

If only he had never heard of the goddamned Children of the Griffin . . .

If only . . .

Too many if onlys. But no matter how much he blamed himself for Gussie's death, the fact remained that he had not killed her. Someone else had.

Gussie's killer is somewhere out there in the dark. . . .

He had started awakening that evening at a little before nine, when someone had knocked on his door. Unable to answer, he had awakened slowly and in a stupor, but with the painful knowledge that Gussie was dead and lost to him forever.

Finally he had gotten up and shaved and showered, hoping that that might revive him. A drag at his Scotch bottle had stimulated his appetite, and he had realized that he had had nothing to eat since the previous evening. Even in grief, it seemed, the body demanded to be fed, and so, since the hotel dining room was closed, he had claimed the rental car Timothy had arranged for and had gone out for something to eat, a hamburger and fries, barely tasted. On his way back to the hotel he had stopped at a tavern for a couple of drinks and then had somehow found himself in the hotel bar. Drinking. And firmly intent on closing the place.

Or maybe not.

He owed Gussie a lot more than grief. And he wasn't a student and disciple of Monsignor Crown—of Father Nick—for nothing.

He remembered following Gussie's psychic traces last night . . . and thinking there might be traces of another presence, an evil presence, as well. If he were to go over the ground again . . .

But he mustn't wait too long, or the traces, the clues, might be obliterated. Even tomorrow might be too late.

Brad put some money on the bar and climbed down off of his stool. He had no idea of how much he had had to drink, but he felt quite clear-minded and steady on his feet. And he had to do this, he had to do it for Gussie.

Bradford Holland went out into the night to look for a killer.

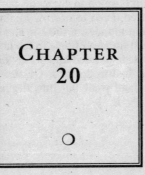

CHAPTER
20

Nicole dreamed.

She was sleeping only lightly, surfacing now and then and sinking back, aware of thoughts and images that immediately vanished. Then, as if some decision had been made, she found herself sinking deeper into sleep, farther into a darkness where she seemed to be looking for Duffy. I'm not angry, she wanted to tell him, I do understand about Lily and I'm not angry, I love you and I'm sorry I turned my back on you. I want to be with you. Hold me close. Share my dream. Share my dream. . . .

She got no answer.

Please, Duffy. . . .

Still no answer, but . . .

. . . she saw something.

Dimly at first, soft, warm flesh colors in the dark, but as she drifted toward them they rapidly came into focus. Duffy. Duffy and Lily, she realized with dismay.

Duffy and Lily as they might have been yesterday evening.

Duffy's long, bare back. Lily, an odalisque, reclining beneath him on something silken, her arms extended in welcome . . .

Only with the greatest effort could Nicole stifle her cry of pain as she retreated back through the dark toward wakefulness.

They sat in the candlelit near-darkness of the tower room, almost invisible to one another in their cloaks. There were no flaring lights this time, no baleful howling, no sense of other presences, but the room seemed vibrant with their shared concentration.

Sleep, Nicole . . .

Dream, Duffy . . .

Freya was ready.

One's powers waxed and waned, of course, even as they increased over the years; but never had Freya felt stronger or surer of herself than she did tonight.

Or perhaps her certainty of strength was a measure of her growing desperation. She needed this kill. When she looked in her mirror, she felt the need as never before. As far as she was concerned, that was what this summoning of the Bradford coven was all about, had been about from the beginning, and to hell with Timothy and his lost Alida. She had instigated the return of the coven, and the reconciliation or punishment of its members, solely for the benefit of Freya Kellgren.

She had, of course, considered punishing some of the coven on her own, particularly Bradford and Jessie, who were unlikely ever to be reconciled with the god of this world. But she had been afraid. Afraid of acting openly against Timothy's wishes. Afraid of the fabled Monsignor Crown, who was Bradford's mentor. Afraid of Philip Steadman, who claimed Jessie for his own. Afraid of Julia St. Claire and, until recently, afraid even of Nicole St. Claire.

But no longer. Not only did she have Timothy behind her, but there was also Philip. Oh, yes, there had been a certain affinity between them ever since they had met years earlier, and now that Jessie was out of the way . . . Philip had appeared at her house in the small hours of the morning, his eyes bruised and his jaw bandaged, hardly able to speak, but, oh, how they had celebrated his vengeance!

*So you see, Timothy, when this business is over with, I won't
need you anymore. Maybe no one will need you anymore.*

She quickly veiled the thought, turning her mind to the
matter at hand and dropping further into that twilight state
that would enable her to travel out-of-body.

Lily broke the silence with a low, soft laugh of childish
pleasure. Freya opened her eyes slightly. Lily and she sat to
Timothy's right, and Bruno and Philip to his left, a circle of
five. The tapestry had been brought up from the chapel and
hung on the wall behind Timothy's back, and in the flickering
candlelight the magnificent griffin seemed to glare down at
them and grin in anticipation.

Lily's eyes were closed. "He's dreaming," she said in the
slurred voice of the half-asleep. "He's dreaming of me again
and he wants me so bad, and—and *she sees!*" She laughed
again, the giggle of a naughty child. "Sleep, Duffy, sleep and
dream and I'll give you such a sweet dream . . ."

Freya closed her eyes again and sank further into her
trance. *I am coming for you, Bradford. . . .*

"By now," Timothy said quietly, "Bradford should be on
his way. So let us prepare ourselves. It is almost time."

"Yes," Freya said. "I am ready. He will find me waiting for
him."

"No," said Timothy Balthazar.

The word was spoken softly and gently, but it startled
Freya. What did Timothy mean, *no*? This was what they were
here for, what *she* was here for, what she needed, what was
owed to her—

"No," Timothy said again. "No, Freya, not you. Nicole."

She stared at him, unbelieving, as his meaning sank in.
"But Nicole isn't ready yet. I've had only two short sessions
with her—"

"She is ready for what I have in mind. I sensed it when I
was with her this afternoon."

"Well, what *do* you have in mind? You know it's almost
impossible to make a person act against her deepest convic-
tions, and Nicole hasn't yet accepted the idea of attacking her
enemies, let alone a friend!" Freya glanced at Philip's hollow-
eyed, bandaged face in hope of getting his support, but he
merely leaned toward her sympathetically.

"Freya," Timothy said softly, patiently, "what you say is true, but often a person can be tricked, be made to believe, for example, that a friend is a deadly enemy—"

"Not Nicole!"

Timothy was silent for a moment. When he spoke, his voice was softer yet, dangerously soft.

"My dear, I shall explain briefly. You have told me how as a child Nicole had certain cherished dreams. You have told me how she sometimes, perhaps a number of times, *lived out* those dreams, leaving the house at night and running through the woods, even as her grandfather did. You have told me how she once killed a rabbit—"

"I don't think she's going to mistake Bradford Holland for a rabbit!"

"*Listen to me*! Tonight with our help Nicole St. Claire will have that cherished dream again. If we are entirely successful, she will live out the dream and attack Bradford. I grant you that that is highly unlikely. But if she even approaches him, his worst fears will have been confirmed. He will feel honor-bound to report that he was menaced by a wolflike madwoman—Nicole St. Claire—and, oh, how the people of St. Claire will love that!"

Freya groped for an objection. "But if she does no such thing—"

"At the very least, Nicole will be driven deeper into madness by the dream, because as with her grandfather, the dream represents what in her heart she wants most. And as with her grandfather, her forbidden desires are tearing her apart."

Freya, silent, still protested inwardly. Lily and Bruno sat unmoving, eyes closed. Philip reached over and for a moment touched her arm.

"We need you with us tonight, Freya," Timothy said. "We need your strength to accomplish our goal, and there is no time for argument. Help us. I promise you that, as in the past, you will be richly rewarded."

"I want Bradford Holland. If he survives this night, I want Bradford."

"If Bradford survives this night, you shall have him. You have my word. And now . . ."

Lily and Bruno stirred and straightened in their chairs.

Bruno chuckled softly. The eyes of the beast-angel on the tapestry seemed to glow and a hot breath to sough from its throat.

". . . let us begin."

Brad pulled the rented Accord over to the left-hand side of the road and killed the engine and lights. Looking through a scattering of trees at a scene painted in shades of gray and silver, he could see the St. Claire house at the head of the long, sloping front lawn. No light showed at any of the windows.

He released the seat belt and consciously relaxed, trying to open himself up to whatever impressions might come to him. What did the house in the moonlight tell him?

Nothing, it was simply a house he had known from boyhood, a house that held a few, mostly pleasant, memories. The house where Mrs. St. Claire and little Nickie had lived.

Nicole, did you kill Gussie?

He hated himself for having that thought. When it had occurred to him that morning and, looking up into Nicole's eyes, he had realized she was reading his mind, he had been appalled. *No, Nickie, I didn't mean it!* But it was too late. The thought could not be undone.

At least she hadn't blamed him. She had shared his bewilderment and grief, and for that he loved her. Yet the thought persisted, like a tumor implanted in his brain by some evil surgeon.

Nicole, did you kill Gussie?

Brad couldn't help himself. He remembered the old stories, stories about the Werewolves of St. Claire and about Nicole's grandfather. Wolves did not ordinarily attack and kill humans, but an afflicted woman might.

The sheriff had said something that morning about the crime scene being roughly three quarters of a mile from the St. Claire house. Four thousand feet, maybe less. Wouldn't it be possible for Nicole to leave the house while Duffy was asleep and . . .

. . . and what, for Chrissake? Go looking for prey? And just *happen* to find and attack a friend?

Yesterday—or rather Tuesday, the day before—as he listened to the women talk, Brad had for the first time become aware of all the crap Nicole had had to put up with throughout her childhood—an agony of insults because of her family background, her lycanthropic symptoms, and even her cute little pixie ears. And here he was, Bradford Holland, who purported to care for her, making up fantasies like some slavering, ghoulish St. Claire yahoo. *Nickie, forgive me!*

He was getting nowhere, just sitting here in the dark on the wrong side of the road. Before long, a cop was going to pull over and ask him to step out, and he didn't need that.

He refastened his seat belt. He would drive back to the service road. Perhaps stop to talk to Derek and Joanne if their lights were on. If the cops hadn't somehow blocked the service road, he would drive up it, see if he could get as far as he had this morning.

Or if for some reason he couldn't drive up it, he would walk. For the moment, at least, the moon was bright—surprisingly so. He ought to be able to find his way back to . . . to where it had happened.

He assumed the police had taped off the crime scene, and he wondered if they had posted a guard for the night. He doubted it—they had probably worked like hell all day to get what they needed from the scene. In any case, he would get as close as he could, guard or no guard, and this time he wouldn't panic. This time he wouldn't go mad with shock and grief. This time he would find something, some psychic clue, that would point to Gussie's killer.

He started the engine, turned on the lights, put the car in gear. As he rolled back onto the road, he wondered what he would find waiting for him in the dark.

Nicole drifted between fleeting dream-state and dim consciousness, where the hunger was now a constant, unremitting, gnawing void.

She didn't think she could take it any longer.

Worse, she didn't think she *wanted* to take it any longer. She wanted to end it . . . had to end it . . . somehow.

There was a way.

She slid out of bed very slowly, careful not to awaken Duffy. He couldn't help her now, and she mustn't let him stop her. Dreamlike, she made her way silently through the darkness of the bedroom.

In the bathroom, she eased the door shut, with no squeak of a hinge or click of the latch, and even then she didn't turn on the light. Enough light came through the one small window.

She opened the medicine cabinet over the sink, took out the plastic vial of capsules, closed the cabinet again.

She stared at the vial in her hand, dimly seen, a fistful of oblivion. Because of her extreme reaction to tranquilizers, she had been tempted to throw them out. But she didn't dare. They were her last resort.

She wondered what would happen if she took, not one, but two or three of them. Four or five of them, with whiskey. All of them, the whole vial.

That thought started her crying. Because she couldn't do that to Duffy. The thought of him finding her like that, perhaps still breathing, and trying to save her . . .

"But, Grandma," she whispered, "I've been good for a long time."

"You have always been good. You are a good person."

"No, I'm not. I'm bad . . . sick. I hate what I am."

"Nicole, self-hatred solves nothing. And neither does self-pity. Snap out of it, young lady!"

Sometimes remembering conversations with her grandmother, or making up new ones, did help. All right, she wouldn't take a tranquilizer tonight. Not even one, let alone a handful. Her crying quickly eased, and she put the vial back into the medicine cabinet.

"Just the same, why can't I be like other kids, Grandma?"

"It's more important to be yourself. Your best self if possible, but yourself."

"Sometimes I just want to die."

"Well, then, we'll have to do something about that, won't we? . . . have an adventure."

"What kind of adventure?"

Unfortunately, there was no answer to that question, but neither was she ready to slip quietly back into bed with Duffy. Duffy, with his secret dreams of bliss with Lily.

Now, be fair, she thought. You don't know that Duffy was

dreaming of Lily. The chances are that that dream was entirely your own, caused by your jealousy and hurt.

Her yellow terry-cloth robe was hanging from a hook on the bathroom door. She took it down, slipped into it, and tied the belt. Again with great care to make no sound, she opened the hall door and, without conscious plan, slipped silently along the dark hallway to the back stairs. She descended the stairs so slowly and carefully that she seemed almost to float.

In the kitchen, a little light filtered in through the windows. She turned off the security system and opened the kitchen door. She hesitated only a moment, then went outside, closing the door behind her.

She stepped down off the porch, enjoying the feel of damp grass under her bare feet. Raising her head, she gazed at the treetops, black against the night sky, and the clouds scudding across the moon. She drew a deep breath, savoring every nuanced odor of growth and decay on the night air.

She felt better now. The void, the hunger, was still with her, but somehow she found it easier to bear. She remembered something Freya had told her. *"When you fully accept the wolf in yourself . . . then you will find yourself fully in control. . . ."*

Perhaps.

She loosened the belt of her robe and, with a shrug of her shoulders, let it fall to the ground. She stood naked in the night. The moonlight was milk on her body, and the breeze licked at it like a lover.

She had loved this as a child, this luxury of being naked in the open air. Later, it had become one of her secret pleasures, to be indulged in only rarely and at night. A little girl rolling in the grass. Sometimes it was difficult to distinguish those memories from her wolf-dreams.

She raised her arms above her head and stretched luxuriously, tightening and limbering the muscles of her back, buttocks, and legs. The hunger now, oddly, felt good.

There was a way to satisfy it.

"An adventure, Grandma."

"Nicole, don't!" her grandmother said.

Nicole heard, faintly, but for once she paid no heed.

She lowered her arms. As in a dream, she walked across the backyard and into the woods.

After turning onto the service road, Brad stopped for a few minutes. What had happened here? His impression of Gussie's passing this way had faded, but that was hardly surprising. There had been a lot of traffic, police traffic, along this road in the last day, which meant a lot of loss and overlay of different psychic energies.

In any case, he sensed nothing new that might be useful to him.

He continued along the road. He was no woodsman or forest ranger, but at one time this area of the park had been familiar to him, and it now seemed as if every foot of the road, every twist and turn and overhanging branch his headlights struck, was emblazoned in his memory. He recognized the exact point at which, in a kind of panic, he had jammed down the accelerator and begun pounding on the horn. This time he slowed down, but he still recognized the pattern of bouncing and swaying he had put the Porsche through, and he saw the tree he had scraped against. There ahead, after another curve and a couple of trees narrowly missed, was the place where he had hit the brakes. The Porsche was gone now, but he saw several raw scars on trees he had banged into, trying to get the car turned around.

He stopped the Accord in approximately the same place he had stopped the Porsche. This time he was calm and should have no trouble in getting turned around. He killed the engine and the lights and got out of the car. He closed the car door softly, as if not to disturb the scene. He relaxed, closed his eyes, let himself sink into a state of passivity. Waited.

Nothing came to him.

When he opened his eyes, the night seemed brighter, but only for a moment. Passing clouds bloomed white, turned to gauze as they passed over the moon, and then darkened as they obscured it. The road ahead vanished in darkness.

He couldn't have said now if he had found Gussie a hundred feet down the road or a hundred yards. More like a hundred yards, he guessed, or even farther. He would go the rest of the way on foot, as he had last night.

He moved down the road, taking his time, making his mind as nearly a tabula rasa as possible. After about fifty feet the road curved slowly off to the right. He didn't remember that, but he kept on going, expecting to encounter a crime-scene tape and possibly a police guard at any time.

He went another two hundred yards and encountered nothing of the kind. Something was wrong. He didn't recognize the terrain at all. By now he was headed west, toward the Balthazar place, and the road was climbing. He was certain he hadn't come this way last night—his road had descended slightly. He must have somehow made a wrong turn.

He hurried back the way he had come, slipping and sliding in the dark.

He was almost back at that first curve when the moon came out and revealed what he had missed: a split in the road. His mistake had been in following the wide, obvious curve—its ruts had guided his feet in the dark—instead of continuing straight on. This time he took the other, narrower branch, heading south.

This had to have been the way he'd gone the previous night. The road looked familiar, and it had the gentle downward slope that he remembered. But once again, after two hundred yards or more, he saw nothing that reminded him of a scene that had been burned into his brain forever. He could not believe that the police in going about their work had completely obliterated it, had changed the very landscape.

He stopped, closed his eyes again, tried to relax and clear his mind. What did this road, these woods, have to tell him?

Nothing. He felt no remnant of Gussie's presence or of that evil that had accompanied her.

Never mind, he wasn't about to give up. He would go back to the car and drive the road, drive until he found what he was looking for. He turned and walked rapidly back the way he had come, a hundred yards through the darkness, two hundred, three . . .

The car wasn't there.

Ahead of him he saw only a narrow, empty service road, and now he wasn't even sure it was the same one he had come in on.

He walked a few yards farther, and *this* road curved off to the *east*!

Where the hell was he?

How the hell had he gotten here?

Suddenly he found himself undergoing a strange, startling shift of consciousness. He had the sensation of awakening from some obscure, frightening dream and finding that it had come true. He wasn't supposed to be here! He was supposed to be back at the Hotel St. Claire! *What the goddamn hell?*

What had *happened* to him?

He remembered having awakened around nine. He had shaved and showered and gone out for something to eat. He had had a couple of drinks at a tavern and returned to the hotel, and then . . .

He remembered sitting half-drunk in the hotel bar, remembered grieving for Gussie, remembered thinking he had to do something to help find her killer. He had gotten up to leave. After that, he dimly remembered sitting in his car near the St. Claire house, but . . .

. . . *what the hell was he doing out here, wandering around alone in the middle of the night? Trying to find a killer? He was too damn drunk even to find his way! Was he crazy?*

His heart beat faster. He could hear it in his ears.

Never mind. He was sober now, or almost so, and he could take care of himself. The lake was directly to the north, and his sense of direction was good. All he had to do was head north, more or less, make his way through the woods, and before long he was bound to come to the lake road. In the morning he would come back to retrieve the car and find out what he could learn.

He left the service road and struck off through the woods. For the moment, at least, the moon was unobscured by clouds, and he could see his way easily, as he ducked the occasional tree limb and pushed through foliage. There was nothing to be afraid of, nothing at all. If he bore a little east, he should see the big St. Claire house looming up out of the darkness before he even reached the lake road. That was what had happened last night. As long as he kept his wits and didn't panic—

Somewhere in the distance a dog howled, a long, mournful howl, floating for miles over the woods, the fields, the town of St. Claire.

Brad's body was sticky with sweat, but the trickle of fear down his back was like ice water.

A breeze swept through the woods, like a breath blowing out candles. Slowly the woods darkened, darkened utterly, and Brad felt as if he were going blind.

Like an insect boring into the very center of his brain, a voice seemed to whisper to him.

"End of the line, Bradford . . ."

In the darkness, Bradford Holland began to run.

He was running through brilliant patches of moonlight, every tree and shrub of the forest clearly etched. His thundering heart filled his chest until he could hardly breathe, and his legs, as he stumbled and fell and rose to stagger on, felt like broken sticks. At one point, when the moon was still hidden, he had run directly into a deadfall, and a tree limb had speared into his left side, cracking a rib and tearing a flap of skin away. Another limb had narrowly missed his right eye, and he tasted blood as it ran down his face and into his mouth.

Something was after him.

The howling had stopped, but he would have sworn he heard something running through the woods alongside of him, at one moment on his right, the next on his left, and when he paused, gasping for breath, he thought he heard something huffing and panting nearby in the dark. At times, it sounded like muffled laughter.

Nickie, he thought, *help* me; don't *do* this to me!

But that was crazy, he was trying to get *to* Nickie, for God's sake, *to* Nickie and Duffy. If there was really any danger, they were his hope. Nickie would never harm him, not him nor anyone else.

He began running again. *Nickie, help me! Guide me to your house. Let me home in on you. Am I getting through to you? Nickie?*

He was running from Nickie.

He was running *to* Nickie.

To Nickie and Duffy. He would be safe when he was behind their locked doors. But where was the lake road, where was the house? Surely he should be near it by now.

The panting, slavering sound followed him.

Then he was out of the woods and running across a grassy open space. His feet hit a down slope, he slid, hit bottom, and his momentum flung him forward, hard, against the other side of a ditch. His left side exploded in pain like a grenade going off.

For a moment he could only lie still, gasping, his face pressed into gravel. Slowly he raised his head. Before him lay a smooth, dark, open surface, and beyond that a few more trees on a decline.

He realized he had reached the lake road. He was lying in the roadside ditch and on the shoulder. But exactly where? Looking about, he thought he saw the roof of the St. Claire house rising above the trees to the west. He had borne east more than he had realized, and now he was somewhere near where he had parked earlier. If only he could reach the house, as he had last night, if only he could get to Duffy and Nickie . . .

Something stirred in the woods behind him. Perhaps only some small animal, or perhaps . . .

He heard a sound like smothered laughter, and . . .

. . . he saw a hysterical child sitting on the pavement in a dark parking lot, blood on her face, and nearby the savagely mangled corpse of the man who had attacked her.

. . . he saw Gussie lying in these woods only hours ago, her lovely body even more ripped and torn, more desecrated, than Buster Dugan's.

. . . in horror, he saw himself lying on the edge of Lake St. Claire, the surrounding water tinted crimson. . . . *You sons of bitches! Bitch and son of a bitch!*

Not for nothing was he Father Nick's student and disciple, and now he understood. It was an understanding he should have arrived at much earlier, but the shock of his grief had prevented it.

"Nickie," he cried out aloud, "they're trying to *use* you. They're trying to *make* you do it. They're doing their god-damnedest to *push you into it!* Freya, you treacherous bitch, you think she's yours, but she isn't! She'll never be!" His voice was fire in his throat. *"Nickie, Nickie, they can't make you do it! Fight them, Nickie, fight them, they can't make you do it!"* The only answer was more choked laughter somewhere in the darkness.

Maybe they could make her do it.

He looked toward Derek and Joanne's place. Too far. He couldn't see a light from here even if there was one.

Like Gussie, he was going to die.

He had allowed himself to be drawn back to St. Claire and into its dark woods, and now *he was going to die.*

But not by God without putting up a fight. Brad Holland might not be a big guy, but he could by God be dangerous.

"I'll kill you, you cocksuckers," he raged. *"Come and get it!"*

The only answer was silence.

Then he heard something that gave him hope.

Traffic.

Actually, he seemed to feel it more than hear it. It was a faint vibration in his body, pressed against the ground, a humming in his head. And when he looked to the east, toward town, he saw headlights in the distance.

The lights were coming slowly, but he hurried to his feet, for all the pain it cost him. There was little traffic along the road at this hour during the week, and this was probably a cabin-dweller returning home from God only knew where. If he could only stop him and explain that he had to get help, a cab, the police, anybody . . .

The police! Brad's hopes raised still further. The car was only a few hundred yards away now, its beams directed straight at him, and coming so slowly as to suggest a cop on patrol.

The car slowed almost to a stop, crawled forward. Brad grinned and waved his arms. He walked into the blinding high beams. It occurred to him that he must look like hell.

The driver hit the horn and held it down.

Brad halted. Like a confused animal, he stood transfixed in the headlights. What the hell . . . ?

The driver gunned the engine twice, two savage roars. The

tires squealed as he burned rubber, and the car shot forward. It pulled over to the left as if to pass Brad—

—and then, to Brad's shock, turned back toward the right lane and headed directly at him.

As he tried to fling himself off the road, Brad felt the car bang against his right thigh like the shoulder of a charging bull. The blow, sharp and painful, sent him spinning through the air. He fell hard, his left side exploding again, the pain beyond anything he had ever before experienced, and rolled down the dark slope among the trees. The sound of the car faded into silence.

. . . He thought he had passed out for a moment or two, perhaps longer. He wanted only to lie where he was until someone came and found him. But that wasn't an option. Gathering his strength, he began the long, hard struggle to get back on his feet . . . gasping, sobbing, clutching at his throbbing left side. He suspected his right femur was cracked and the leg wouldn't hold him, but it did. By an act of will, gritting his teeth against the pain, he *made* it hold him.

He was alone again, all alone in the dark.

Not quite.

The thick, clotted laughter was closer now.

As he turned toward it, it turned into a growl, a snarl, a roar.

Brad screamed his defiance.

That was when for the first and last time he saw the beast in all its hot-eyed, saber-fanged, demonic beauty—when it came at him.

CHAPTER
21

Duffy awakened slowly. At first he thought that the steady whispering sound was rain, and he took comfort in it; he had always liked sleeping to the sound of rain. But something about the quality of the sound was wrong, and a growing unease made him open his eyes.

Even before he was fully awake, he knew what was happening. Nevertheless, he lay still for a moment, listening in the dark, as if to check the evidence. When he reached behind him, Nicole wasn't there, nor could he see her in the other bed, and the susurrus he heard was coming from the bathroom.

"Aw, Nickie," he said softly as he sat up and swung his legs out of bed, "Nickie, I am so sorry!"

Nicole had come back to St. Claire desperately seeking help, and instead she had been made to feel threatened and insecure—the very worst thing for her—almost from the hour of her arrival.

And he, Duffy Johnson, the Great Diagnostician who should have foreseen this, sure as hell hadn't been much help.

Last night he had known she was upset, and he had known why. Why hadn't he done something about it? Why hadn't he explained? All right, Nicole had been in no mood to listen, or to talk, had been asleep or pretending to be by the time he came to bed, but he could have tried. He could have said, Please, Nickie, listen to me! But he had been tired, and he had thought, What the hell, let it wait till tomorrow. He hadn't even whispered, I love you. Please, Nickie, darling, don't ever doubt it.

But God give me strength . . .

Nicole was having an attack; he knew that. But what was she doing in the shower? He had suggested showers and warm tubs, but she had never found them to be much help. Well, whatever was going on, he could handle it. He *had* to handle it.

He turned on his bedside lamp and went to the bathroom door. It was closed. He turned the knob and eased the door open an inch, expecting to see light, but there was none. That wasn't good. Why would Nicole be showering in the dark? He tapped on the door, called out "Nickie," and stepped into the bathroom. He turned on the lights.

The sliding door of the shower stall was half-open. Nicole was huddled on the floor of the stall, sobbing, as the water poured down on her. Softly calling her name, Nickie, Nickie, Nickie, Duffy turned off the shower and knelt over her. He drew her into his arms. "Nickie, come on, come on, Nickie, darling . . ."

She made a sound: ". . . bluh . . ."

"What? What is it?"

". . . blood . . ."

For an instant he saw Nickie's body covered with blood, drenched in blood, and he realized that she had been trying to wash the blood away. Wash it away in a dark bathroom where she wouldn't have to see it.

"No, Nickie," he said gently, "there is no blood."

She looked at him with eyes that had seen the worst that hell had to offer. "I killed him," she said.

"No," he said, rocking her, "you haven't killed anybody. It was just a dream, like a couple of weeks ago when you dreamed about Chucky. Remember?"

"But the blood . . ."

"There *is* no blood," he repeated. "Look at the bathroom floor. Look out in the hall. There is no blood. It was a bad, bad dream, but it's over. Now, come on . . ."

She put herself into his hands like a weary but trusting child. She allowed him to help her to her feet and out of the shower stall, and stood perfectly still while he patted her dry from head to foot. She made a pass at drying her own hair and wrapped a towel around it. He took her back into the bedroom, helped her into fresh pajamas, and pulled on a pair himself. All the while, he continued to speak reassuringly to her, tried to send out the most comforting thoughts. But he had a feeling that he wasn't getting through to her, that her thoughts were far away, that he was failing her again.

He was goddamned if he was going to let that happen.

"Now," he said, when they were ready. "Do you want to tell me about it?"

They were sitting on the edge of the bed, she within the circle of his arms. She looked up at him as if he had distracted her from her thoughts.

"Look, if you'd rather not . . ."

"No, it's all right. I dreamed . . ." Some of the fear came back into her eyes, and she spoke in a whisper. "I dreamed I killed Brad."

"Very upsetting," he said after a moment. "I know that kind of dream . . . you kill a family member or a friend, and it's awful. But why . . . ?"

"Because I was angry with him. Angry because he was afraid of me. Angry because he thought I was capable of killing Gussie. Someone I loved."

So you killed Brad, Duffy thought, whom you also loved. Dream logic. Nightmare logic.

"The dream wasn't so bad at first," Nicole continued after a moment. "I mean, it was bad when I was half-asleep and felt a spell coming on, but then I dreamed that I went out back of the house and looked at the moon and I felt better. That's the part I remember most clearly. It still seems real to me. I was wearing only my robe, and I took it off and started walking naked through the woods. Running through the woods. It was like the dreams I had as a kid. I was happy. So happy I even looked up at the moon and cried out to it. The moon was like the face of God. But then . . ."

Nicole seemed to be looking at something beyond the light of the bedside lamp, and her nostrils flared slightly.

"But then?"

". . . I picked up Brad's scent and started following him. At first it was all in fun. I didn't mean any harm! I chased him, staying in the shadows. I laughed at him. Then I realized he was scared, and that's when I started getting angry.

"After that it gets more and more . . . vague . . . confused . . . and I can hardly remember. All I know is, I was after Brad. I was *so* angry, *fiercely* angry! I wasn't at all scared, not the way I was that time . . . that time in the parking lot."

He was shocked that she should even refer to that distant episode. It was something never to be mentioned, and it hadn't been, not once, since they had been together.

"Not the same thing, Nickie, *this was a dream!*"

A dream, yes, but she was back in it: "This time, *I* was the aggressor, and I was after him—"

"Only in a dream!"

Nicole shook her head. She covered her eyes as if to protect herself from some terrible sight. "All I know is, I saw Brad's face glowing in the dark, glowing with fear and hatred, as if *he* was going to attack *me*. And then I think I charged at him, and . . ."

She collapsed against his chest. "I don't remember! But I still have this terrible feeling of guilt . . ."

"Hush."

". . . as if I really did kill him!"

Rocking her, Duffy tried to send her healing thoughts. Perhaps he succeeded: he could feel her gradually relaxing, as she entered the quiet cove of her own thoughts, that very private place to which she sometimes retreated. He waited for her to invite him in.

Finally, she turned in his embrace and reached up to interlace her fingers behind his neck. She looked up at him, gratitude shining in her eyes, and smiled a bittersweet smile.

"You poor guy," she said.

"Why poor?"

The smile twisted a little and the eyes saddened. "Because you have me on your hands and I am so screwed up."

"Nonsense. We've got a problem, we know that, and we'll work it out yet."

She laughed softly. "You sound like my father."

That reminded him: "How do you feel about Freya now? Do you think she'll be able to help you?"

Nicole's smile vanished and she looked away from him. "I don't know. I like Freya. Some of the things she says about self-acceptance might be my grandmother talking. But she pushes them to such an extreme. For instance, she'd probably say I should *enjoy* my dream, I should *enjoy* the thought of destroying my enemies."

"But Brad isn't your enemy—"

"She even says I may think I'm getting worse before I get better, but I should just go with it. Not even try to get better."

At those words, Duffy lost any hope he might have had of Nicole's getting help from Freya Kellgren. He didn't care if Nicole's father had loved Freya; he had a frightening vision of the woman deliberately leading Nicole down a path of evil and madness.

But he couldn't say that to Nicole. He said, "Then to hell with her."

Nicole's smile returned briefly, and she shook her head. "I'm not ready to write Freya off just yet—but . . ."

Nicole looked, unsmiling, into his eyes for a long moment. He had no idea of what she saw there or what she was thinking. His heart seemed to pause. Then her fingers slipped away from his neck, and she left the comfort of his arms. She moved on her knees to the center of the bed and sat again, her legs folded under her, facing him.

"Duffy," she said, "we have to talk about something. Something very important."

The breath slowly went out of him and didn't want to come back. "Won't it wait till morning?" he managed to say.

"No. Too often we've both let it 'wait till morning,' and when morning came it didn't get said. I've been thinking about this for some time, and we'd better talk about it now. Tonight."

He didn't want to talk about *this*, whatever *this* might be, not tonight or at any other time. But he saw that Nicole was offering him no choice.

"All right," he said, "what is it?"

Darkness . . .

Freya, her eyes closed, seemed to be returning through darkness from a very great distance. Perhaps, exhausted from her efforts, she had actually fallen into a dreamless sleep for a time, but as she regained normal consciousness, she felt certain she had succeeded in her task. It was as if she herself had had the dream she had urged on Nicole, or at least some part of it. Nicole had left the house, Freya remembered that. She had stood naked in the night, had gazed at the moon, had sniffed the night air. She had started running through the woods, a gentle pace at first, and then faster, faster . . .

She remembered little after that. She and Nicole were not yet so attuned as to easily share dreams. But she remembered enough.

Her eyes remained closed, but she heard the others stirring, a sigh of satisfaction, a laugh, the rustling sound of a cloak being thrown aside.

"I did it!" Lily whispered. She sounded as if she, too, were returning to normal consciousness. "I did it!"

I did it, you little fool, Freya thought, *I* did it, and with damned little help from the rest of you!

"I did it!" Lily repeated, full of little-girl joy. "I really think I did it!"

"Yes," Timothy rumbled, laughing with her, "I really think you did."

"Oh, she did it, all right," Bruno agreed, with his low, thick-voiced laugh, and Philip laughed too. She heard Philip stand up, drop his cloak, and move away from her.

What was going on here? Something Freya didn't understand.

"I killed him," Lily said. "I'm almost sure I killed him."

Freya's eyes were instantly wide open.

Lily was smiling broadly even while tears, golden in the candlelight, ran down her cheeks. Her body, though abraded and blood-smeared, had never looked more youthfully beautiful.

This was not right, this was not what was supposed to happen!

What was going on?

Timothy had moved closer to Lily and had an arm around her shoulders. "Do you remember . . . ?" he asked.

"Not much," Lily said, sniffling and wiping her nose on her hand. "Not much, but I saw his face just before I did it, and"—Lily's own face went crimson with childish rage—"and he hurt me! He hurt me! Look at me, I'm bleeding. He hurt me!"

"Now, now," Timothy said comfortingly, "you'll heal quickly, I'm sure. And before long you'll learn how to restore your materialized body as fast as anyone can damage it. You'll be invincible!"

"I don't care," Lily wailed, "he hurt me! I hate him!"

"But he's dead, my dear, and you're here."

As if to make the point, Timothy drew her closer, cupped a breast in one hand, and kissed her. Philip had come to her other side, and when she looked up, he leaned down and kissed her in turn. And Bruno, not to be outdone, dropped to his knees between her spread thighs and buried his face in her belly. Then all four of them were laughing. Laughing uproariously, laughing hilariously, laughing, laughing, laughing . . .

. . . laughing at Freya.

Or so it seemed to her.

She had been tricked, deceived, deliberately cheated. While at Timothy's insistence she had been doing everything in her power to give Nicole the dream, Lily had traveled out-of-body to make the kill. The kill that should have been Freya's, that she needed, that she had been promised. *"If Bradford survives this night, you shall have him. You have my word."* Oh, yes, Timothy. How clever of you!

They had all been in on it. She saw that now. She saw it in Lily's insolent eyes as she looked at Freya over Bruno's head. She saw it in Bruno's grin as he looked at her over his shoulder. She saw it in Timothy's sardonic smile and the indifferent shrug of his shoulder. As for Philip, in whom she had placed her hopes . . .

. . . clearly Philip was interested only in beautiful young Lily. Like Timothy. Like Bruno. Philip saw in Lily a possible replacement for Jessie Lindquist. Timothy saw in her a powerful ally more easily manipulable than Freya. And Bruno, always close to Timothy, had resented Freya for years.

Now the four of them were freezing her out. After all these years, *Timothy* was freezing her out, and the others would do his bidding.

Oh, yes?

To hell with them! If they thought Freya Kellgren could be dismissed so easily, they were wrong. She had made Timothy Balthazar what he was, he would never have had his convocation without her, never the power and the glory, and what she had made, she could destroy.

And would.

It's over, Timothy.

You don't know it yet, but it's over!

Look at them—men of three generations, slavering over Lily's fair young body, licking the blood away like vampires. The four of them writhing together like maggots on Bradford Holland's rotting corpse.

They had to die, all of them. Somehow she would destroy them. She no longer feared Timothy, her anger had wiped out any residual fear, and what did she have to lose? She had to play along for now, but sooner or later . . .

Freya was sick to the point of nausea on the chemistry of her rage, but of course she couldn't let that show. Not now. She must veil her thoughts and emotions, but over the years she had learned to do that so well. . . .

She smiled. "Clever Timothy. You did what you thought best, of course."

"Of course."

"Lily's turn tonight. But my turn will come."

Timothy nodded. "There are still three unreconciled members of the coven."

"None of them worth a damn compared to Bradford, though." Freya's voice had a steely edge. Best not to appear too easily appeased.

"I didn't lie when I said that *if* Bradford survived you would have him," Timothy said. "In any case, you *will* be well rewarded."

You can count on it, Timothy.

Freya smiled again, briefly. "Be that as it may. We still have work to do. When do we finish it, Timothy?"

"Very soon. In a single stroke, I think." To Lily he said, "My dear, I don't want to risk anything happening to you. With your newly developed skills, you can travel out-of-body, so perhaps you should remain behind and—"

"Oh, no!" Lily said quickly. "I want to be there! I want to be conscious and in control at every moment. I want to look into dear Duffy's eyes when he's dying and afterward remember every delicious detail. I want—I want—"

"You want the Rapture," Timothy said.

"Yes. I want the Rapture." Lily smiled at Freya. "Of course, if Freya is afraid of the risk—"

"Freya is afraid of nothing," Freya said. "Freya will be there."

"Duffy, I think it's become pretty obvious that we can't go on living this way."

Nicole was sitting in the penumbra beyond the bedside lamp. He wanted to draw her back into the light, back into his arms, but when he moved toward her, she held up her palms as if to press him back and shook her head.

"No. Let me finish. You've had a very difficult year, thanks to me—"

"One of the best years of my life, thanks to you."

The words were glib, mouthed automatically, but he recognized at once that they were true. Whatever the strains of the past year—and they had been great—Nicole had been a blessing to him. Her love, her faith in him, had been a recurrent source of strength. That was something to keep in mind when the going got tough.

"It's sweet of you to say so. But, Duffy, the fact remains that you are about to begin the long hard grind of your internship and residency. And if there is anything you *don't* need for the next three or five or six years, it's a crazy live-in girlfriend, driving you nuts with her fits and spells."

"So what do you propose?"

Nicole laced her fingers, rested her face on the double fist, and closed her eyes. She spoke slowly, as if thinking the whole matter through again.

"When we get back to the city, Duffy, I'm going to sign myself in to some place where they can look after people like me. You won't have to worry about me anymore. I'll go on seeing Freya if they'll let me—don't worry, I'm not giving up on myself—"

"Oh, fine. Great solution! But it overlooks one thing, I happen to love you. What happens to that?"

Nicole managed a small, rueful smile, and he saw that she had no intention of offering false hope. "I don't know. Probably sooner or later you'll find someone else. If you're lucky, you'll find someone who's strong and healthy, someone who adores you and can give you the kind of support you're going to need. Maybe someone like . . . like Lily."

"Like Lily." He could not believe she was saying this.

"Oh, honey . . ." Nicole suddenly came forward on her knees, moving into the light, and laid her hand on Duffy's. "Baby, don't think I've stopped loving you. I'm jealous as hell of Lily. I think I've loved you all my life, in different ways—little-girl ways, growing-up ways; love for my cousin, for a friend, for the big boy next door. And last year when we met again I realized that all the Duffys I had ever loved, and maybe a few I had yet to meet, had somehow been rolled up into one wonderful new Duffy. And, oh, how I fell in love with him!

"So believe me, that hasn't changed. I do love you, Duffy, and one way or another, I think I always will. But in this world, love does not always conquer all. And I'll be damned if I'm going to let my problems blight a future and a career that you and I and your family and even my grandmother have dreamed of. I simply cannot let that happen. I couldn't live with it."

"And that's it?"

"That's it."

"You're going to put yourself into some goddamn nursing home . . ."

"Where I'm not the only one who howls at night."

Nicole sat back again, smiling, though Duffy could see the tears in her eyes. "Oh, don't look so grim, Duffy. I'm not going to just disappear, you know. Who knows, medicine does make progress . . . maybe things will work out for us yet."

"But you don't really believe that's going to happen, do you."

"I want what's best. For both of us."

Duffy put a hand over his eyes.

Now, let's get this straight, Duffy. This girl loves you. You'd be a fool ever to doubt it. You know she's not just looking for an excuse to break up a relationship she's tired of, and she's not fishing for reassurances. You know her, and you know she means what she's saying. She's ending it, Duffy; she's telling you it's over. She's offering you a way out.

This girl—no, this woman—this woman loves you so much that she's willing to give you up for the sake of your career and your future happiness.

His hand dropped from his eyes, and he looked at Nicole in absolute awe.

You stupid son of a bitch, why did you ever think that you deserved her?

A wonderful warmth spread through him, and he laughed quietly. He had feared that their little world would be changed, and that was happening, though in a way he hadn't anticipated. He now knew exactly what he had to do next.

"Got it all figured out, haven't you, Nickie?"

His laughter, his smile, had surprised her. "I think it's for the best."

"Even got a girl in mind for me."

"I think she still feels something for you, Duffy."

"And I feel something for her?"

Nicole nodded slowly. "I think so."

"All right, let's dispose of Lily once and for all. You know I saw her last night."

Nicole shrugged.

"When I couldn't get hold of Brad at the hotel, I went looking for Lily. You're right, I did feel something for her. Call it unfinished business, maybe better left unfinished. But now it is finished, and I hope you'll believe that."

"I'll believe anything you tell me. But you don't have to tell me anything."

"I caught her at the library just as it was closing. She wanted to go to her place, but I made an excuse, I said I wanted to go to Finnegan's Bar.

"So we spent nearly two hours in a booth at Finnegan's, while Lily tried to sell me on the glories of St. Claire and all the fame and fortune that would accrue to me if I were to return as Timothy Balthazar's protégé. And furthermore . . ."

Duffy didn't know how to say the next part. It sounded so goddamned ungallant to talk about Lily this way—she deserved better. But Nicole deserved the truth.

"Furthermore, I got the distinct impression that if I wanted her, Lily was part of the package. She and I could seal the deal that very evening. All I had to do was take her home and screw her, and the package was mine."

"How nice for you," Nicole said faintly.

"Nice, hell. It was sad. I know this sounds egotistical, but it was as if in seven years she hadn't changed toward me a bit. *Just love me, and I'll do anything you please . . .* be *anything you please.* And God knows she's a beautiful woman. But, Nickie, when I looked into her eyes, over and over again I got this crazy feeling that, really, *there was nobody home.* There was no stable, fixed *some*body in her that I could get to know and rely on. It was like looking into a dark, empty pit. *I'll be anything you please.*

"You're the psychologist, you tell me. Does this make any sense?"

"I think so. Some people need others to validate their existence." Nicole smiled. "And, of course, she was trying to seduce you."

Duffy didn't return her smile. He shook his head. "If she hasn't changed, I sure as hell have. I'm not a screwed-up adolescent kid anymore. And if I learned anything last night, it's that I don't want an adoring, *without-you-I'm-nothing* cipher as a partner in this life. My God, we'd have nothing in common but sex, and we'd end up hating each other. I want a woman, Nickie, a real woman, with a mind and a heart and a soul of her own.

"I finally took her home. For what it's worth, I told her—as gently as I could—that I thought your coming back to St. Claire was a mistake. And since I couldn't see a future without you, I doubted that either of us would be coming back here again. Was I wrong?"

"No, Duffy, I'm sure you were right."

"If I'd known last night what I know now, I could have told her something else." Gently, Duffy placed his hands on Nicole's shoulders and turned her so that he could look into her eyes. "Nickie, will you marry me?"

Nicole's eyes widened. Her mouth moved until words finally came. "But . . . we've always said, this is such a strenuous period for both of us . . ."

"Yes, I know, we've found all kinds of reasons for not talking about marriage. Our studies; your money and my ego. Well, to hell with that. I love you and I want to marry you. And I'm going to do it, Nickie, if I have to get down on my knees and beg. *Nickie, will you marry me?*"

For a moment Nicole was perfectly still. Then, with a joyous little cry, she was in his arms.

"But it's crazy," she said moments later as they lay entangled, her head on his shoulder. "I can't possibly marry you now."

"Why not?"

"I've told you why not. And why would you want to marry me?"

"Because I'm selfish as hell and my Nickie is a prize beyond compare. And if you think I'm going to let you get away from me by going into some kind of nuthouse or nursing home, you really are crazy. Go ahead, sign yourself in, if you think that's best for you. But I'll be there with you every hour, every minute that I can get away from the hospital. I'll feed you when you're in your straitjacket and sleep with you in your rubber room. We'll be known as the happiest, lovin'est couple in Bedlam."

Nicole rose up onto an elbow so she could look into his eyes. "But your career . . ."

"My career will go just fine. I want to hear less about my career and more about yours. I don't tell you often enough how proud of you I am. Really, we've only got *one* career, Nickie, and that career is *us*."

She was crying, just a little, and when she lowered her face to kiss him, he could taste her happiness in her tears. It filled his heart. Between them, two hearts, one happiness.

That was when he realized she was healing.

Right at that moment, in the certainty of his love, she was healing.

He could feel it, a strengthening within her, the filling of a void, an easing of her soul. A new completeness.

Why hadn't he understood? The death of Nicole's grandmother had left her virtually alone in the world and terribly insecure—the probable cause of her attacks. Fortunately, when the attacks came on, she had always found relief in Duffy's arms. But she had also sensed his weariness with their situation, his occasional wish to escape, and that had only aggravated her condition. A vicious circle.

Tonight, when she had found the strength to give him up and he had refused to let her go, they had broken that circle.

Perhaps forever.

"You're going to be all right," he whispered.

"I know."

"We're both going to be all right. Nicole, I'm asking again. Will you marry me?"

"Yes," she said. "Yes, Duffy, I will marry you."

"Let's do it right, the way Aunt Julia would have wanted. In a church—"

"Hush, my darling," she said as she began unbuttoning his jacket, "time enough for that. It's late and we're going to sleep till noon, but first . . ."

"First?" he asked. "What have you got in mind?"

"I think you know. I love you."

Duffy dreamed.

He dreamed that Nicole had awakened early, long before noon, and was slipping out from under the sheet. He felt her bending over him, felt her breath on his cheek, and then her lips as she kissed him. He smiled in his sleep. . . .

Now, as if he were a ghost in the room, he saw her, saw both of them, Nicole kneeling naked over him on the bed. Her smile was like a reflection of his own, and he felt her radiant happiness. He shared it. It made all the more poignant their grief for Gussie, and Duffy felt something like survivor's guilt. But the happiness wouldn't go away.

Thunder rumbled distantly and Nicole's smile vanished.

Carefully, she moved off of the bed and went to a window. The sky was mottled gray and a breeze waved the treetops.

She went into the bathroom. When she came out, she was wearing a green bikini and her yellow terry-cloth robe. She bent over Duffy and kissed him again, and left the room.

Still dreaming, Duffy followed, an invisible voyeur.

Nicole went down the stairs and out the front door.

On the veranda she paused and stretched and inhaled deeply of the fresh air, still cool in the early morning. Duffy could almost feel it filling her lungs, bringing with it a wonderful sense of well-being.

Thunder sounded a little closer, a little louder, and Duffy felt a touch of apprehension. Nicole, he thought, maybe you'd better not . . .

But she hurried down the veranda steps, down the long front lawn, the grass still dewy under her bare feet. Duffy followed.

At the road, Nicole paused to let a car go by—

Nickie, maybe this isn't such a good idea!

—and then crossed. She continued down the slope, through a scattering of trees, toward the beach.

She was near the verge of the grass and about to step down onto the beach, when out of the moils of Duffy's unconscious mind his fears exploded. The very *tone* of his dream changed, like violins and cellos suddenly bursting out in cacophonous banshee wails.

This was wrong, all wrong, Duffy realized in nightmare horror.

Nickie shouldn't be out here in the early morning all by herself.

She shouldn't be out here at all!

Something was about to happen, something so awful—

Nickie, come back!

Nicole hopped down onto the beach. She curled her toes in the gravelly sand and began taking off her robe.

Duffy tried to make himself known to her. *Nickie, please, please, listen to me! Nickie, come back to the house. Come back to the house right now! Don't do another thing, just run, run, run, Nickie, run back to the house!*

So often they were attuned, sharing thoughts and dreams,

but now it was as if he were shouting into a void. Nothing carried, nothing sounded in Nicole's mind. Smiling, she threw her robe onto the grass and looked around.

Nicole, don't!

She was alone. There were few boats out on the water on this gray morning and none nearby. The only thing unusual she saw . . .

There was something in the water, a dark, low-lying mass, half-submerged near the edge of the beach, perhaps a hundred, two hundred feet away.

She started toward it.

No, Nickie, don't look. Come back! Duffy followed closer, trying to force his way into Nicole's mind. *Nickie, come back!*

Now Nicole began to share Duffy's apprehension, but that only caused her to hurry. Whatever the object was, it wasn't supposed to be there. It hadn't been there yesterday.

Duffy was in her mind now, seeing what she saw, feeling what she felt. Her worst fear—his—was coming true. There was a heap of clothing lying in the water, perhaps a body. He felt her sense of dread, her quiver of revulsion. Her heart began to slam.

Nicole, please! he told her, even as she told herself, *Don't go any closer. Go get help. Go back and get Duffy.*

She couldn't do that. If there was any chance at all that the man—it seemed to be a man—was still alive . . . she continued forward.

Nickie, no!

The heap of clothing was red and ragged.

She knew then, somehow she knew, and she wanted to turn and run, but she forced herself to go on, closer, closer still . . .

. . . until she saw who it was, lying facedown in the still, crimson water, the torn and bloody face turned to one side, a dead eye open and staring.

As Duffy slammed back through darkness into his own body in the bedroom, he heard Nicole's long, anguished scream in the distance, echoing his own.

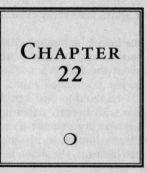

CHAPTER 22

Though Nicole's cry barely reached Duffy's ear through the open window, it pierced his mind like a white-hot needle that etched a single thought: *DUFFY, DUFFY, DUFFY, HELP ME, HELP ME, I NEED YOU!*

As if hit by an electric charge, a thousand-volt surge that fired every nerve and muscle, Duffy found himself flung from the bed. He grabbed the first piece of clothing he saw, a pair of jeans draped over a chair. Pulling the jeans on, he shoved his feet into a pair of moccasins and ran from the room. He went down the front stairs in four long, pounding strides. His only thought now was like a repeated shout in his head: *GET TO NICKIE, GET TO NICKIE—NICKIE, I'M COMING!*

He ran through the front door, leaped from the veranda, and sped down the lawn. At the road, he barely paused. He glanced both ways at the traffic, judged that he could make it across, and kept running.

Only then did it occur to him that he might be reacting, not to Nicole's scream (had that faint sound even been a scream?), but to a nightmare, a mere dream, that the stresses of the last day might have upset his emotional balance and impaired his judgment, and that Nicole might be back in the house and perfectly safe in the kitchen, and O God, O God, how he wanted that to be true!

But he knew it wasn't.

There, on the grass near the beach, lay Nicole's yellow robe.

He saw her just before he jumped down onto the beach. She was about a hundred feet away, stretched out on the sand and facing him, as if she had fallen. She was kicking and pawing at the sand like a wounded animal struggling futilely to get to its feet. As he raced toward her, she reached out to him. Her eyes, wide with horror, rolled up in their sockets, and another long, hoarse cry rent her throat.

But when he threw himself to his knees before her and tried to take her into his arms, she shook her head fiercely and waved him away. Her long cry ended, her horrified eyes closed, and she began to cry, painful, wrenching sobs. Lowering her head almost to the sand, she pointed back over her shoulder. He struggled to understand what she was saying.

". . . Brad . . . please . . . Brad . . ."

"What about Brad?"

"My dream . . . it wasn't a dream. I killed him."

He remembered now. Brad had been in his dream or vision or whatever it had been. Brad had been in the last and most terrible part.

Slowly he stood up. He looked in the direction Nicole had pointed, along the water's edge, and saw what they had both seen only moments earlier, something that might have been a sodden pile of clothing lying half out of the water.

That couldn't be Brad. Brad couldn't be dead. This all had to be some kind of mistake, an illusion, a horrible misunderstanding. If that was Brad, he might have been in the water only a few minutes, and that meant there was a chance, however remote, that he was still alive. Duffy had to save him. *NOW!*

Again, Duffy felt himself hit by an electric charge. He sprinted—

Aw, jeez, Brad, you fuckin' dork, what've you got yourself into?

—ran with all his remaining strength. Threw himself down on his knees in a spray of water and wet sand near Brad's head, and, unable to stop himself, howled.

Aw, jeez, Brad . . . ?

Brad lay with his torn face half underwater, an eye open, his nose pushed into the sand. The water around him was stained red. Already certain that Brad was dead, Duffy nevertheless grabbed his hair, pulled his head out of the water, and felt his neck for a pulse. In that same instant, he saw that Brad's other eye was missing and that his neck had been deeply slashed.

Aw, Jesus, Brad!

Whatever had killed Gussie had gotten Brad as well. What else—who else—could it have been? It had killed with the same unbridled savagery.

Duffy laid Brad's head down carefully on his knee. He found tears running down his face, and the pain in his throat and his chest threatened to tear him apart.

Fuckin' little dork . . .

Something, some sound perhaps, caused Duffy to look up. The few boats on the water were at some distance, but it seemed to Duffy that people were looking his way. Undoubtedly others had heard Nicole's screams, they would have carried far over the water, and someone would soon come to investigate. Maybe someone had phoned the cops already.

He had to get Nicole back to the house and take care of her. That came first, absolutely first, *he had to take care of Nicole!*

But what could he do for Brad?

He couldn't just leave him, lying here in the water, could he?

That was exactly what the cops would say he should do—don't touch the body. Just leave it where it is.

He was sorry, but he couldn't do that. Not to Brad. He couldn't just leave him in the water.

Standing up, he grasped Brad under the arms, lifted his upper body, and pulled him up onto the beach.

He screamed when he saw Brad's gray entrails dragging behind in the sand.

Screamed a low, strangled cry of horror and grief and

rage. He wanted to cry to high heaven for vengeance, vengeance for Brad and Gussie.

But this was no time to lose control. He had to hang on. Had to! Right now Nickie needed him, and Nickie came first. Gently he lowered Brad onto the sand and hurried back to Nickie.

Trying to soothe and reassure Nicole as he had so often in the past, Duffy got her back into the house and up to their bedroom. Huddled in her robe, his arms around her, she was weeping almost soundlessly. He tried to fathom the depths of her pain and despair and found he could not. All he could do was try to communicate his unremitting love and protective strength.

He helped her out of her robe and bikini. When he started putting her pajamas on her, she shook her head *no* and headed for the bathroom and the shower. She felt polluted, he knew, once again polluted by Brad's blood—by a death of which he was certain she was blameless. As she turned on the water, he cobbled up a prayer from phrases learned in childhood. *"Bless, O Lord, this water to Thy use and cleanse my darling of the sins of others. You can forgive them, O Lord, if you want to, but first give me a chance at the bastards. . . ."*

To hell with St. Claire!

To hell with St. Claire and Freya Kellgren and Lily Bains and the whole goddamn lot. To hell with 'em all!

We are outta here!

Early this morning it had seemed that Nicole had reached a turning point, that she was on the mend at last. They had both been filled with such hope, such joy, such confidence in the future. But that evil trickster, the god of this world, had mocked them. That brief, sweet hour had turned out to be just a prelude to one more horror.

Duffy couldn't quite steady his voice. "I'm going downstairs for a minute. Call the cops and get you something to drink. Okay?"

Nicole nodded, seemed to say yes.

He called 911 from the kitchen phone. He described as clearly as possible where the body was and assured the voice on the telephone that he would await the police. The voice tried to keep him talking, but he hung up. There was nothing more he could do for Brad, and Nicole needed him.

When he returned to the bedroom, carrying a large tumbler of ice cubes and a bottle of Scotch, she was already out of the shower and toweling herself and she seemed calmer. Feeling the need to touch her, to convey his love with his hands, he helped her into her pajamas, then picked her up gently and sat her on the bed.

He poured some Scotch over the ice and handed her the glass. She took a big sip, closed her eyes, and swallowed.

"Anything more I can get you?"

She shook her head.

"Maybe this once you should take a tranquilizer."

She shook her head harder, her hair falling about her face, and whispered no.

"Be back in a minute."

He went into the bathroom to inspect the medicine cabinet. He hoped Nicole had brought along something mild that might help her relax and doze off, but there wasn't even an ibuprofen. Reluctantly, he took one of her orange and white capsules from its vial and returned to the bedroom.

When Nicole saw the capsule between his fingers, she put a hand to her face and began to cry again.

"Hey, no!" Quickly Duffy put the capsule down beside the whiskey bottle and drew her back into his arms. "You don't have to take the goddamn thing, you don't have to take a thing you don't want, not even an aspirin!"

When her tears had subsided, he explained.

"It's just that you've undergone a terrible shock, we both have, and we've got a hell of a day ahead of us. The police should be here any moment."

"Oh, God!"

"When they question you, just tell them what happened. You went out for an early swim and found Brad. You screamed and I came running and found you. That's all."

"But if I killed Brad—"

"You didn't kill him," Duffy said firmly. "We talked about this. You had a bad dream last night, and remembering other bad things in the past, you feel like you *might* have killed him—"

"And Gussie too."

"Oh, come on, Nickie. *Twice* you left the house in the middle of the night without my knowing? Half the time, you can't go to the bathroom without waking me up. You nearly woke me up this morning, kissing me."

"But why would I dream . . . ?"

"I don't know. I don't have all the answers, not yet. But I can tell you this . . ." Duffy groped for something persuasive, something that might reassure Nicole. "This morning, after you kissed me and left, *I* had a dream. I don't remember most of it, but it was about you. And at the end of it, I *was* you. I *was* you, *discovering Brad's body.*

"That was what woke me up and sent me out to find you, Nickie. I shared your experience the same way we sometimes share dreams. Now, I may be wrong, we may find a better explanation, but it's possible, just possible, that in your dream you clairvoyantly shared the killer's experience."

Nicole was very still, frowning slightly, gazing into the distance as she examined the possibility. Her frown deepened and she shook her head. No, no, she was thinking, there was more to it than that.

However . . .

Her frown eased and for a moment her eyes closed. She leaned back against the head of the bed and let out a long sigh. A single tear rolled down her cheek.

"Poor Brad," she said with quiet grief. "Poor Brad and poor Gussie. What kind of . . . monster would do such a thing?"

With a feeling of immense relief and gratitude, Duffy embraced Nicole again. She had taken a terrible beating in the last few days, but she wasn't defeated.

"Listen," he said, releasing her, "you need some rest. Get back into bed. Maybe I can keep the cops off of you for a while."

"I hope so."

"And then we're getting the hell out of here. If the sheriff doesn't like it, fuck'm. Tomorrow or the next day latest, if he doesn't lock us up, we are gone."

Nicole smiled and nodded. "The sooner the better. Would you close the blinds, please?"

Duffy kissed her forehead and went downstairs to await the police.

People were kind.

The first to arrive was a tall, comely female deputy, Patty Cantrell, whom Duffy remembered from high school. The rain was just starting, as she trotted briskly from her car to the veranda where he waited. Her eyes filled with pain, as he briefly recounted what had happened that morning.

"Oh, no. Not little Brad!"

Duffy nodded.

"How's Nicole taking it?"

"I sent her back to bed."

"That poor kid. I never actually knew her, but . . ." Patty looked embarrassed.

"But you knew about her. It's okay, Patty."

"I still think of her as a kid. . . . Duffy, I hate to ask, but would you please show me where . . ."

There was no need. As she spoke, police cars and vans began skidding to a halt on the road below. They came without sirens, no doubt unwilling to draw a crowd any sooner than could be helped. Doors slammed and uniforms started down the slope toward the lake.

Duffy said, "They're going to find him before I can show you, Patty."

Patty nodded. "We're going to have to work fast, with this rain. It could destroy evidence. I'd better get down there." She took Duffy's hand. "Duffy, the sheriff will want to talk to you. You aren't going anywhere, are you?"

"Of course not."

"I'll do anything I can for you and Nicole, anything at all."

"You're a friend, Patty. I thank you."

Patty gave his hand another quick squeeze and hurried back to her car.

She was hardly out of the driveway when a black Lincoln turned in. Timothy Balthazar, uncharacteristically tieless and in shirtsleeves, got out from behind the wheel. He walked toward the veranda like a burdened man. His eyes looked moist and weak, and he breathed as if he had been running.

"Duffy, what can I say?"

Duffy shook his head.

"Bruno . . . the sheriff called me. He knew I'd want to be informed. I hope I'm not intruding, Duffy."

"Not at all. Mr. Balthazar, please come up out of the rain."

Balthazar climbed heavily up the stairs. "First that lovely young woman and now Bradford. At least his father isn't here to grieve. When I think of what Connie Lindquist must be going through . . ."

As he spoke, another car, expensive-looking, pulled into the driveway. Balthazar glanced at it, then looked back at Duffy. "Dr. Stranger. Duffy, I'm afraid I'm being terribly officious, you're a doctor, after all—"

"Not even an intern yet."

"—but I thought you might want to see someone, and Frank's my doctor, so I called him."

"I'm glad you did."

Dr. Stranger came toward the veranda, black bag in hand. He held up his other hand before Duffy could speak.

"Duffy, I'm here as a friend, I'm sure you don't need me, but Timothy felt—"

"He was right. A doctor shouldn't treat his own family, and Nickie and I . . . I wish you'd take a look at her. Finding Brad like that was pretty rough on her."

Dr. Stranger followed Duffy into the house and up the stairs. Nicole lay facedown in bed. She had finished the whiskey in the tumbler, and the capsule was gone. The doctor did a quick, efficient examination, while disturbing her as little as possible.

"Color's good, pulse, respiration . . ."

"I gave her a tranq and a shot of booze," Duffy said, showing Stranger the medicine vial. "They tend to hit her hard."

Stranger read the label and nodded. "Can't hurt her. Rest is the best thing for her. She'll probably sleep most of the day." He took another vial from his bag and tapped a few pills into a small envelope. "She'll need a couple of these to help her sleep tonight. Take a couple yourself if you want."

Even Bruno Krull, when he finally appeared, was kind, or

tried to be. He explained that it was impossible to completely seal off a park so large that it occupied much of the western end of the county. However—

"The park is closed to newcomers, and state police are at all the exits, canvassing everyone who leaves. We'll probably have a mass exodus of campers by this afternoon, but they'll all be checked. If the killer's nutty enough to stay around, we'll find him."

He held down his exasperation at not being able to question Nicole immediately.

"Dr. Stranger said she'd probably sleep all day, if not longer," Balthazar explained, "and that she should have at least twenty-four hours of rest. But I'm sure that Duffy can tell you all you need to know."

They were again at the kitchen table, with uniformed and plainclothes police officers coming and going. Duffy told his story as accurately as he could, without, of course, any reference to his dream.

"*You pulled the body up out of the water?*" the sheriff said unbelievingly.

"I know I shouldn't have—"

"You know you shouldn't—if you knew—"

"I couldn't just leave him there. It was *Brad,* for God's sake."

"You deliberately disturbed a crime scene—"

"I'm sorry. I couldn't help myself. I guess I went a little crazy."

The sheriff shook his head at the wonder of it all. "You moved the body. I should pull you in. I could, you know."

And yet, oddly, the sheriff didn't seem as angered or upset as Duffy might have expected. In fact, he seemed almost amused.

"We found the car you rented for him, Mr. B., in about the same place where he left his own. After leaving the car, he probably came through the woods more or less the same way he did before, but this time he bypassed this house. He crossed the road, and apparently that was where he was attacked. He was carried, dragged, or pursued down into the water. What with the rain and Duffy's having moved the body, it's hard to tell. Duffy, do you have any idea of what he might have been doing out there last night?"

"Only one. He might have been looking for clues."

"*Clues?*"

"Psychic clues. Brad was a disciple of Monsignor Nicholas Crown. Monsignor Crown is some kind of psychic detective. Brad said he'd been working with him for a couple of years."

The sheriff shook his head again. "Great. A woman is killed, obviously by a maniac. So Brad, playing psychic detective, goes back to the same place in the middle of the night and gets himself killed by the same loony."

The *same* . . . ?

At those words, an odd question began to tease at Duffy's mind, he didn't know why. The answer, surely, was obvious. But his diagnostic sense sometimes suggested to him that something important had been overlooked or that the data had been misinterpreted, and he had that feeling now.

He waited until the others had left and he was alone at the table with Balthazar and the sheriff. "Sheriff, one question. There's one thing that everybody seems to be taking for granted. Are you sure, really sure, that Gussie . . . that Jessie and Brad met the same killer?"

The sheriff looked at him sharply. "What? You think maybe we've got two or three maniacs running loose? A whole gang of them?"

"I'm just wondering—"

The sheriff leaned over the table toward Duffy, and any suggestion of kindliness in his manner vanished. "Duffy, the two victims were killed in exactly the same way. They were ripped, torn, slashed from sternum to groin. They were chewed up and spat out and maybe partly eaten. Their throats were mangled, and their genitals. And, Duffy, I will guarantee you this." The sheriff leaned still closer to Duffy, as if to spit in his face. "Anybody, Duffy, who kills in that kind of rage, in that kind of limitless, butchering blood-frenzy, has got to be stark staring, raving mad. No matter how rational he may appear to be on the surface, he has got to be totally insane."

The sheriff sat back and grinned. "Now, do you really think there could be a whole gang of such loonies roaming the St. Claire woods? I'm telling you there's only one."

* * *

Nicole was sick.

Sitting in her pajamas and robe on the shadowy back stairs, listening, she fought the nausea that rose in her belly like dirty, oily water, fought the series of heaves that forced acid up into her throat and wrung tears from her eyes, fought to remain silent and undetected.

Only one, the sheriff had said.

And we all know who she is, don't we, Sheriff.

All of St. Claire knows.

Heretofore Bruno Krull had masked any hostility he might have felt toward her. But no longer. He had a killer to bring in, and as far as he was concerned, she was upstairs in this house.

Could he be right?

No . . .

Nicole closed her eyes and breathed deeply and regularly to subdue the nausea. *I will not be sick! I will not be sick! I won't let you do this to me, Bruno Krull.*

Duffy said she hadn't killed Gussie or Brad, and despite her nightmare and her guilt feelings, she believed him. She had to! No doctor had ever thought her dangerous, and if she had been, surely Duffy, of all people, would have known. When she calmed herself and used common sense, she knew that to be true. She was not the killer.

Then who could it be?

Probably someone unknown to any of them.

Or perhaps someone known only to Gussie and Brad.

Or perhaps . . .

She recalled something Duffy had said about Bruno on their first night back in St. Claire. *"Diagnosis: psychopath. Prognosis: homicide. Sooner or later that son of a bitch is going to kill somebody. If he hasn't already."*

Oh, sweet Jesus! Was it possible . . . ?

She didn't want to believe it. If the sheriff was the killer, who could they turn to for help? The state police? Excuse me, Officer, but we suspect the sheriff of being a psychopath and perhaps a murderer as well.

Lock the little lady up. Everybody knows she's sick and a killer herself.

Mr. Balthazar? He had been her grandmother's lifelong friend, if in a qualified way (Nicole felt), and goodness knows he looked favorably on Duffy. Or had seemed to. But the sheriff was clearly his man, and yesterday hadn't she had the feeling that, for better or worse, Mr. Balthazar was orchestrating the whole scene?

And wasn't he now?

Timothy Balthazar, leader of the oh-so-respectable convocation . . .

. . . of which Brad's little coven had been a part. Something Brad had said came back to her: ". . . *these people can be extremely deceptive. Sometimes their lovely personalities can be about as deep as an oil slick on a wet pavement—and just as dangerous. So when you're dealing with them . . .*"

Her thoughts were broken off by the sound of Duffy's voice. ". . . been thinking about moving into town . . . hotel or maybe a motel, but I don't think Nickie'd go for the idea . . . people staring at her . . . and, my God, we'd feel like prisoners, locked up in a motel room."

"You're right, Duffy," the sheriff said, "and you're probably as safe here as anyplace, as long as you don't go out after dark. At least not alone."

"Duffy," Balthazar said, "I have a suggestion. I have plenty of empty space up at my house . . ."

NO, DUFFY! Nicole screamed in silent alarm. *No, Duffy, no, no, no!* However unlikely the ugly suspicion that had arisen in Nicole's mind, Balthazar's offer seemed to confirm it, and she sent out her message furiously. *No, Duffy, don't accept! You mustn't. No, no, no, no . . . !*

"That's awfully kind of you, Mr. Balthazar, but I don't think so. I'll ask Nickie, of course, but I'm sure she'll prefer to stay in her own house."

Oh, thank God!

"They'll be safe, Mr. B.," the sheriff said. "We'll keep an eye on 'em. Duffy, if you see a car parked out front tonight, don't worry about it. It'll be one of ours."

"Well," Balthazar said, "if you change your mind . . ."

When she heard Balthazar and the sheriff taking their leave, Nicole went silently back up the stairs. She was suddenly weary beyond belief. She needed rest, she needed strength, to get through the hours ahead.

Simply *leaving* St. Claire was no longer possible. Of that, she was certain.

They would have to escape.

When she awakened, she was surprised to find that it was after six. She had fallen asleep almost the instant she had lain down, and her sleep had been deep and, as far as she could remember, dreamless. For a few minutes she felt dazed and disoriented, but as she performed her ablutions, she quickly gathered her wits. Brad and Gussie . . . the sheriff and Mr. Balthazar . . . *escape.* . . .

The day was overcast, promising more rain, but that hadn't discouraged the curious. Peering cautiously out of a front window, Nicole saw that the "circus" the sheriff had predicted was in full force. Gawkers were everywhere, some of them even coming up onto the lawn, where a female deputy seemed to be warning them away, others staring at the large areas on both sides of the road that the police had taped off. A number of police vehicles were parked along the road, and car after car went by in both directions, all of them slowing to a crawl as they passed the house.

This was the house where the Wolf Girl lived. The last of the infamous St. Claire's.

St. Claire had once honored and loved her family, Nicole recalled. No longer. . . .

She was pleased to note that the only feeling in her stomach was hunger, not fear. During the hours of rest, fear had been replaced by a steely determination to survive. She and Duffy were getting out.

She dressed for comfortable travel: jeans, a lightweight sweatshirt, slip-on deck shoes. She was halfway down the back stairs when she paused, hearing Joanne's voice. She trusted Joanne and wanted to help her if possible, but Derek . . . she would have to be careful. Circumspect, her grandmother would have said.

They were alone, Duffy and Joanne, at that favorite gathering place, the kitchen table. Duffy looked ragged with fatigue, and Joanne was white-faced, but they both managed a smile as she entered the room.

"Hey," she said as she hugged Joanne, "that's some mob scene out there. Been going on all day?"

"Most of the day," Duffy said, looking at her curiously. "TV people, the works. You feeling all right?"

"I'm feeling fine, considering. But awfully hungry." She went to the refrigerator for orange juice.

"Tranquilizer wear off?"

"I never took it. You know how I hate those things." She saw the question on Duffy's face. "I didn't want to talk to that maniac sheriff, but I didn't want you to have to lie to him, either. So I put the capsule back and pretended I was asleep. Actually, I did go to sleep"—Nicole looked at the stairs and then back at Duffy—"but that was later. Quite a bit later."

She saw understanding on Duffy's face.

Joanne smiled wanly. "You two passing messages over my head?"

"I'm sorry, Joanne. I was telling Duffy that while he was down here talking to the sheriff and the police and the ever-helpful Mr. Balthazar, I was on the back stairs listening. Where's Derek?"

"Somewhere with the sheriff. Tape recorder in hand."

"All right, now listen to me." Nicole sat down at the table across from Duffy and faced Joanne. "Duffy and I have decided to leave here just as soon as the sheriff will let us . . . or even a little sooner. We strongly suggest that you and Derek do the same. Don't tell anybody, not even Mr. Balthazar, just *go.*"

Joanne looked as if Nicole were confirming her worst fear. She shook her head hopelessly. "Derek will never leave now. He's obsessed with his book. He hinted to the sheriff that in return for his cooperation he might make him the hero. And"—Joanne's face crumpled and she covered it with her hands—"Jesus . . . Jesus . . . Jesus!"

"Joanne!"

"I am so scared." Joanne's voice became a small, pinched shriek. "*I am so scared!*"

"Joanne?"

Nicole jumped up and threw her arms around Joanne.

"I am so scared. We all came back, all of us, such good friends, and now two of us are dead, and I am scared—"

"Sh! Sh! Sh! You're going to be all right."

"And Derek's gone crazy, all he can think about is his goddamn book, and I—I—"

"Sh! Sh! I'm here for you. I'm here for you and so is Duffy, we're both here for you. . . ."

Nicole held and soothed Joanne as Duffy had so often held and soothed Nicole, and it worked. Joanne soon calmed.

"I'm sorry."

"Don't be. We're all frightened. But we're going to be all right."

Nicole held Joanne a moment longer, thinking furiously. Common sense told her not to say another word about their plans. Common sense told her that she had warned Joanne and now she should let Joanne fend for herself. But she couldn't do that, couldn't just abandon her.

She looked at Duffy and saw his resignation. He felt the same way.

"Joanne, how long would it take you to pack and be out of the cabin?"

Joanne laughed mirthlessly. "No time at all. I can be out of there in three minutes. Less."

"Good. We don't know when we're leaving and we may not know until the very last moment. But if there's any way at all that we can take you with us . . ."

Joanne shook her head. "That really would be the end of my marriage."

"So? His lousy book means more to him than you do. You may be married to him, but that doesn't mean you have to risk your life for the bastard—"

To Nicole's surprise, Joanne sprang to her feet, and her hand lashed out rattlesnake-fast across Nicole's face, a stinging blow. Instantly her hands went to her own face, and her eyes widened with shock and dismay.

"Oh, God, Nicole, I'm sorry!"

Nicole pulled Joanne into her arms, tried to soothe her. "No. I'm sorry. God, what an awful thing for me to say!"

"You try to help me, and I slap you!"

"It's all right."

"It's just that . . . maybe this rotten marriage isn't all his fault. I haven't been the greatest wife in the world, believe me. Derek's trying to prove something to me and I've got to help him do it. Maybe I'm more loyal than I thought." Joanne wiped her eyes and cracked a crooked smile. "Hey. Tammy Wynette, that's me."

"You're a good woman, Joanne," Duffy said.

"Thanks, Duffy. Look, I'd better get back."

Nicole walked Joanne to the door. "Joanne, if you change your mind . . . call me. But do it soon."

Looking into Nicole's eyes, Joanne seemed to take her meaning. "Good luck," she said, and she kissed Nicole's cheek. "You two ought to get married."

"We're thinking about it."

"Then I'll see you at the wedding."

Nicole told Duffy her suspicions.

"I could be totally wrong. The sheriff may have nothing at all to do with Gussie and Brad dying, and Mr. Balthazar may be using his influence to keep him off of us. But we really don't know who we can trust. We've got to get out of here, Duffy, and I don't mean tomorrow or the next day. I mean tonight."

Duffy agreed. "Sometime after midnight. In the small hours, maybe, before dawn. That's when people are least alert. I just hope that the patrol car the sheriff promised isn't a problem."

"If it is, we'll cope. Honey, I've slept all day and you look beat. Why don't you rest this evening while I pack and close up the house? We'll load the car at the very last minute and take off."

"Operation Cut-and-Run."

"That's right. But, God, I worry about Joanne. I feel almost guilty, leaving her behind."

"Nickie, you've done all you could for her. Joanne's no fool—she probably suspects we're leaving tonight."

"Then I hope she's the only one who suspects."

The dinner hour thinned the crowd of spectators, as most of them realized that there was really nothing to see. Even the police had apparently completed their work and departed. The telephone rang several times, but the callers left no messages on the machine.

Duffy had, of course, screened all calls, and he hadn't answered or returned any from the media. He reluctantly admitted to Nicole that, earlier, there had been several threatening messages left on the machine. Freya had called and inquired about Nicole and asked that she call back when she felt up to it.

Most of the packing was done and Duffy was getting ready for bed when the telephone rang. Nicole was in the kitchen, and she waited while the machine clicked and the answering message played out.

"Duffy, dear," came Freya's voice from the speaker, "I'm sorry to bother you again, but I haven't heard from Nicole and I've been so worried—"

Nicole picked up. "Freya?" She hated to think of Freya as anything but a friend, but she couldn't afford to let her calls go unanswered or unreturned for fear of arousing suspicion. "Freya, Duffy said you'd called, but I'm afraid I'm still half-asleep . . ."

Oh, yes, Nicole said, she was all right, though it *had* been an awful experience.

"I suppose after all this you'll want to leave St. Claire just as soon as you can."

"Yes, but I don't know when that'll be. I understand that the police want some kind of statement from me. Maybe we can leave after that tomorrow. But Duffy says more likely Saturday. I just don't know."

"I've been hoping I could see you, dear, and perhaps help you."

"Oh, I'd like that, but . . . I don't know when it'll be possible, Freya. . . ."

Nicole hated dissimulation, especially to a friend. She looked for something honest to say, and when it came, the words seemed to burst out of her of their own joyous accord. "Oh, and, Freya?"

"Yes, dear."

"I hope we'll see you in the city soon. Duffy and I are thinking of getting married and we'd like you to come."

Nicole had the sensation of something crashing silently

but violently at the other end of the line, as if she had said exactly the wrong magic words.

"Why, darling," Freya said after a moment, "that's wonderful. You and Duffy couldn't be more right for each other."

A few more words, then, and an agreement to meet in the city very soon, and they hung up. But Nicole felt as if she had caught a frightening glimpse of someone she hadn't seen in a very long time.

The Lady in White.

We've got to get out of here!

Freya sat with one hand still on the phone, her eyes narrowed, her jaw clenched. Though the evening was warm and sultry, she felt herself trembling.

The faithless little bitch.

As if she thought she could fool Freya Kellgren. Freya, to whom she had already revealed so much of her heart. Freya, who had tried to advise and help her. Freya, who had been prepared to take her under her wing and teach her, train her, show her a world of power and pleasure she would otherwise never know.

Had she really thought that Freya wouldn't recognize the guarded tone, the false notes, the veiling of the mind? *That's a game I play far better than you, my girl!* Nicole hadn't spoken a single spontaneous, uncalculated word until she said, *"Oh, and, Freya? . . . Duffy and I are thinking of getting married . . ."*

The simple, mindless happiness in those words, the pure joy! *". . . thinking of getting married . . ."* It was as if Nicole had flung them in her face, a taunt, reminding her of all she had lost or given up.

She picked up the phone again and tapped in Timothy's number, the unlisted phone in his study. He answered at once.

"I've just been talking to Nicole, Timothy. She tried to make me believe that she and Duffy wouldn't be leaving St. Claire for at least a day or two. I wouldn't be at all surprised if they tried to leave tonight."

"Of course," Timothy replied calmly.

"Are you trying to tell me—"

"Freya, I am glad to have your confirmation of what I

have already foreseen. In any case, it doesn't matter. Are you ready?"

"I can't wait."

"Good. Lily and our friend Philip Steadman will be your guests this evening. Bruno will pick you up around midnight—"

"I'd rather come alone—"

"No, a single car will do. Discretion. Use the chapel's outside entrance. We will begin with holy services, of course. Prayers, rededication, a eucharist. We must be spiritually prepared. The better the preparation, the greater the Rapture."

The Rapture. Oh, Timothy, if you only knew . . .

No. Now, of all times, she must guard her thoughts.

She assured Timothy that she would be ready at midnight and hung up.

As for Nicole, she had had her chance. She could join her father in hell.

Tonight was the night, and never had Timothy felt himself to be more of an implacable force, obdurate, inexorable. He was the hand of fate, of the god of this world, for the simple reason that he had to be. Nothing must go wrong. Everything that Timothy dreamed of, everything that he most longed for, depended upon this night.

All was in readiness. Bruno was having the St. Claire house closely watched. At the appropriate time he would tell the deputy on duty that he might as well leave the house and continue his rounds as usual.

Timothy supped late and light, a simple repast prepared by Heinrich, who then retired for the night to the garage apartment he shared with Minna. Heinrich knew when his master wished to be left strictly alone.

Timothy spent the remainder of the evening in his study, meditating and praying.

At eleven-thirty he went to Alida's bedside. She had become a ghostly presence, and if it weren't for the monitors one might not believe she was living. The pale cheeks were thinner than ever, the high cheekbones more prominent, the eyes more sunken. And yet, oddly, this wasting away only emphasized her essential beauty. "You will be restored to me, my darling," Timothy whispered. "It's only a matter of hours now—a few hours and you'll be back. I promise you."

He descended to the chapel like a pilgrim to the underworld. There he lit two candles on the altar, donned a hooded cape, and knelt at the communion rail. He gazed at the beast-angel griffin on the tapestry.

The griffin gazed back.

He would have loved to perform an offering of human flesh on this altar in solemn ceremony before a full congregation, but to attempt such a thing in this day and age would, of course, be most unwise. Steadman was right: all due caution must be observed. But there was a glade deep in the forest that had become sacred over the years, a small, sheltered glen where the soil was rich with blood, though no body had ever been found. Timothy's father had long ago revealed it to him.

It was to that glen and glade, that sacred hellgate, that they would take their human offerings tonight. It was there that they would invoke Lord Lucifer, the Prince of Power, and invite him to join in their revels. And then . . .

Timothy heard someone at the door. The others were arriving.

And then . . .

Timothy felt a wave of sweet pre-orgasmic anticipation ripple through his body.

And then . . .

. . . *let the Rapture begin!*

CHAPTER 23

Sleep, Nicole . . .
    Sleep, Duffy . . .
    Rest . . .
    It's not time to leave yet . . . no, not yet . . . you have plenty of time . . . plenty of time . . . and you are going to need your strength . . . all your strength . . . so . . .
    Sleep . . .
    Rest . . .

The wind moaned through the high sails, white against the stormy sky, and the thunder rumbled like empty barrels rolling loose in the ship's hold. The bow rose and fell, cleaving the dark waves and spewing foam, and as Nicole opened her eyes, she saw distant lightning. . . .

She found herself lying on a bare mattress in the dark bedroom, not quite remembering how she had gotten there, and the dream faded. She had been tired, suddenly so very tired, and she must have kicked off her shoes and lain down for just a few minutes. Now she wanted badly to sleep, oh-so-badly, she wanted to sink back down into that comfortable darkness, but she knew she must not. She must fight her way back to full consciousness. Sleep now was the enemy.

She forced herself to sit up. Duffy lay unmoving in the other bed. The clock-radio on the table between the beds said 2:40. Duffy had set the clock for 4:00, just to be sure they were up, but some instinct told her: *Don't trust the alarm! Wake up now! Stay awake!* They *are out there!*

She slipped her shoes back on, went into the bathroom, and washed her face without turning on the light. There, that was better. There was little left to do. Get Duffy up and dressed. Drink some coffee, pour the rest into a Thermos, rinse the pot. Strip the bed and put the used linens in the laundry bag. Little things, to be done in the dark. Take luggage and laundry out to the car, lock up the house, and take off unnoticed.

They hoped.

Nicole remembered the patrol car parked out front. True to the sheriff's promise, a car had shown up early in the evening, parked a few minutes, and then moved on. Later, it, or another car, had done the same thing. But the car that had appeared at midnight had still been there an hour later when she had fallen asleep. It was like being under house arrest, Nicole thought. If they were seen leaving the house at four or five in the morning, the deputy would surely inform the sheriff, and he would try to stop them.

Suddenly wide awake, Nicole left the bathroom and hurried to a front window. There was no light from the Andersons' cabin or the houses across the lake, scarcely surprising at that hour, and the sky was dark with racing clouds. She could barely see to the end of the lawn. But after a moment, she was certain. The car was gone.

She could have no idea of how long it had been gone. It might reappear at any moment or be gone for the night. This could be their only opportunity to get away.

The urgency of their situation charged her with fresh energy. From now on they had to make every minute count. She hurried back to Duffy and began shaking him.

"Duffy! *Duffy!*"

·   ·   ·

Bad dreams. Joanne had had so many of them this past spring. Not just unpleasant end-of-the-night dreams when she was barely asleep, but bad, bad middle-of-the-night dreams from which she awakened with the same painfully throbbing heart and sick, lingering terror that she felt now. It was as if something were coming for her, as she lay there in the dark, and she was just so damned scared . . .

After a moment, she reached out for Derek, hoping for the hard-bodied reassurance of another human being, evidence that the nightmare, whatever it had been, was really over. But he wasn't there. That didn't surprise her.

She wondered if Nicole and Duffy had left yet. Probably. That had seemed to be the message Nicole had been trying to convey—that they intended to leave at the earliest moment, without anybody knowing.

God, she wished she were going with them!

Maybe she still could. Maybe they were still here. She could wait until Derek was asleep, then go downstairs and quietly phone them and find out their plans. If they were about to leave, she could sneak out to the road and meet them. . . .

Who was she kidding? Either Nickie and Duffy had left already or they weren't going to leave tonight, and in any case she could never do that to Derek. She owed him better than that. Tomorrow, if she still felt the same, she would simply tell him, "Honey, I'm sorry, but I am scared shitless, and you can stay here if you want—I think you're very brave—but I am getting out of here until these killings are cleared up. I love you."

Because part of her did still love him. Or wanted to. And wanted him to love her as he once had.

Her heart had calmed and her terror had abated somewhat, but now she felt far from sleep and she still wanted reassurance. Derek would be downstairs. She would join him for a little while, maybe even lure him back to bed. There were still some sweet moments between them.

The privacy curtain had been drawn and the balcony was in utter darkness. Sitting up, she reached for the bedside lamp, found it, and twisted the switch.

Nothing happened. She was still alone in the dark with her waning terror.

"Derek!"

"It's all right," Derek's voice came from below. "I'm here."

She got out of bed and felt her way toward the balcony railing. Drawing aside the curtain, she could see some faint ambient light from the windows down below, and she could just make out Derek in his pajamas.

"Derek, what has happened?"

"Power out, obviously."

She could now hear wind gusting about the cabin and a tree limb banging on the roof. Perhaps that was what had awakened her from her dream. More bad weather moving in.

"Has it been out long?"

"Only a couple of minutes."

Joanne had always enjoyed the relative isolation of the cabin, but now . . .

"Derek, why don't you give the power company a call? At this hour, maybe nobody's even reported the outage."

"I will, just as soon as I've checked the circuit breakers—"

"No!" Dread gathered again, like a fist clenched in her chest. She had the terrible, inexplicable feeling that she had been through all this before. "Never mind the power company, Derek, phone the police. Nine-one-one. Tell them we think there's a prowler."

"Joanne, I can't tell them that, just because the power is out. We'll have cops all over the place—"

"Just call them, Derek, call them!"

"All right!"

Derek disappeared under the balcony. In the complete silence, Joanne thought she heard the faintest click as he picked up the telephone . . . and then a clatter as he put the handset back.

"Derek, what is it!"

"Goddamn phone is out. First the power and then the phone."

The fist tightened in her chest, squeezing her heart. "But why . . . ?"

"How the hell should I know?"

As he spoke, a hand rapped at the front door and a voice, slightly muffled, asked, "Anybody awake?"

"Good," Derek said, hurrying to the door. "It's probably Duffy. Now maybe—"

"*No!*" Joanne heard herself cry out again. In that instant, it was as if some part of her knew what was going to happen— as if she had been through this before, a recurrent nightmare, always forgotten but inescapable, each time worse than the last, a heart-bursting, mind-shattering premonition of a horrible fate.

She heard herself screaming: "*Don't open the door!*"

But it was too late. Derek was already flinging the door open wide.

The tall, dark, hooded-and-cloaked figure standing in the doorway laughed softly and rushed forward, swinging a fist low and hard. With a horrible gagging sound, Derek crumpled to the floor. A purple fog seemed to fill Joanne's mind, and she thought, astonished, *Why, I'm fainting. . . .*

Then she found herself lying facedown on the floor of the balcony with no idea of how long she had been there. Light pressed against her eyelids like a thin film of blood.

Slowly she raised her head and peered between the pales of the railing. She looked down. The cabin remained in darkness, but within that darkness, now clearly visible, as if illuminated by his own inner light, stood a man. His hood was back and his cloak open, and his naked body seemed to radiate all the gaudy hues of hellfire: flaming reds and blues, sulfurous oranges and yellows.

From the heart of his blazing aura, he grinned up at her. He winked lewdly and said, "We got a date, Joanne."

Bruno Krull. She had encountered him occasionally on visits to St. Claire, and his insolent denuding stare had always caused her to shudder. He strode to the foot of the balcony stairs and started up.

She thought: *I am going mad.*

He seemed to be coming toward her in slow-motion, and so strong was his inner light—or so sensitive her perception— that he was like a transparent anatomical figure; but instead of heart and lungs and guts, she saw something else within him, something emerging so clearly as to all but conceal the human.

On the glowing face, she saw the slanted oval-pupiled eyes and, as his grin widened, the long, sharp fangs. Another stride up the stairs, and she saw the female breasts on the big hirsute cage of the chest.

Yet another, and she saw the strange genitalia, the pizzle, stiff with excitement, emerging from the vulva.

In one part of her mind, she knew she was seeing an illusion, but the illusion represented the true nature of Bruno Krull, the demon he really was.

Rising to her feet, she backed away from him, knowing there was no escape, nowhere to flee or hide. He was on her in one swift bound, lashing out at her with a clawed hand that ripped open her gown and furrowed her skin from breast to belly. As she cried out, more in terror than in pain, he easily picked her up and tossed her onto the bed.

"Please . . . please . . ." She struggled to see the human behind the glow of the demonic mask, as if she could somehow appeal to it. "Please . . ."

Drawing a flask from the folds of his cloak and uncapping it, Bruno shoved an arm roughly under Joanne's shoulders and lifted her. "Take a drink. You'll love it. It'll open you up and, oh, the things you'll see and do!"

As he pressed the flask painfully to her lips, she turned her head away and fought to escape his arms, but she could not. "Drink, bitch," he ordered grimly; "open your goddamn mouth and drink, or I'll break your goddamn teeth."

Her lips already cut, she tasted her own blood as she opened her mouth and, coughing, strangling, let the liquor flow into it.

"Drink!" Bruno Krull commanded again, and she drank until her stomach rebelled and she heaved some of the potion back up, spilling it over her breasts. Bruno Krull laughed, and tilted the flask over his own mouth before throwing it aside.

The liquor blazed its way to her stomach and set her mind whirling almost at once. No, not just her mind. Bruno had lifted her from the bed and now she was whirling vertiginously in his arms in the darkness, as if he were dancing to some mad Luciferian waltz. The only thing she could see was his glowing, grinning, demonic face. The potion she had drunk filled her with a languor that was like despair, and she knew she had to fight it. She sobbed, and tried to rouse herself. She was damned if she was going to suffer meekly any fate that Bruno Krull visited upon her.

She went for his face with her hand and his throat with her teeth. Bundled tightly in his arms, her head on his shoulder, she could scarcely move, but her thumb somehow found a soft hollow in the skull and her teeth bit deeply into salty flesh. Bruno screamed and threw her from him as if he had suddenly found a raging wildcat in his arms.

Joanne hit the floor hard but scarcely felt it. As she rolled, her momentum brought her to her feet and she ran for the stairs.

She was almost there when she felt Bruno's fingers grasp the hair on the top of her head. Her head snapped back and her feet shot out from under her. Again her body slammed to the floor, more painfully this time. Cursing, Bruno wrapped an arm around her waist, lifted her, and flung her back onto the bed.

She knew what he was going to do to her.

As he knelt between her thighs, tearing the remains of her gown away, he seemed afire with his own light. His right eye was already swollen almost shut, and his face and chest were streaked with blood.

A hand came down across her face, a blow that seemed to tear the flesh away, and another hand gripped her right breast and twisted it, a blow, a twist, a blow, a twist, until fire seemed to spread through her body and she was blind with pain. In a high, shrill voice, Bruno was shrieking at her, shrieking something about how he was "going to have you, you bitch, going to have you!" Then his hand released her breast and clutched at her throat, and she felt him trying to penetrate her. She was fighting him, beating at him with her fists and twisting her body, trying desperately to escape, but he was crushing her throat, and she couldn't breathe, couldn't breathe. . . .

Now her lungs were on fire, even as her mind darkened. . . .

This wasn't happening! It wasn't, it was all an evil dream, and she had to escape it, had to wake up, or she would die, she would die in her sleep, die horribly . . .

Please, God, don't let this be happening!

But she knew it was happening.

Oh, please . . . please . . .

Sipping a last mug of coffee in the dark kitchen, Duffy at last felt fully awake. Nicole had returned from making coffee to find him asleep again and had been frantic to get him up and dressed. Apparently the stresses of the last several days had caught up with him, for he had felt utterly exhausted, ready to sink back into sleep and let happen what would.

They had to get out, he had kept reminding himself. That was the object of the exercise. To remove Nicole and himself from the scene. The night and the bad weather were their friends, keeping people away for now; but he had little doubt that the story of the reunion and the Wolf Girl was no longer exclusively Derek's, and in the morning the media would descend upon St. Claire in even greater force than it had yesterday. Of course, the media would follow them wherever they went, and the law, if it wanted them, would too. But let them. At least they would no longer be alone in a big semi-isolated old house on the edge of a forest roamed by a homicidal maniac. Who just might be the sheriff.

Duffy rinsed his mug and put it into the dish rack. It could remain there forever for all he cared. The Thermos was already filled and the coffee machine cleaned up. The luggage was in the kitchen, and Nicole was upstairs taking a last look around in the dark. Duffy smiled. Nicole had insisted that they turn on no lights, not even in the bathroom, for fear of drawing attention. Little ol' Nickie might be a creature of terrible vulnerabilities, but when the situation required it, she could be one heck of a take-charge guy.

He went to the back stairs and called to her.

"Ready to load and leave, Nickie."

"Be down in a minute."

The plan was to carry their luggage from the kitchen door to the side door of the garage. (And this was where Duffy wished he had a gun—in case that . . . *thing* was out there.) Lock themselves in and load the car in the dark. Open the overhead door, back out, and leave, all as swiftly and quietly as possible. And with a little bit of luck . . .

He went to the front of the house, checked the locks on the door one last time, and looked out a living-room window. In the shifting, cloud-diffused moonlight, he could see little other than the ghostlike suggestion of lawn and trees and the road. No car had returned to park out front and keep watch, but the puddles of darkness beyond the trees could have concealed anything.

He felt his way back through the dark hall to the kitchen. He heard Nicole's footsteps overhead and figured she'd be down in a minute. Lacking a gun, he took a butcher knife from its wooden holder, thumbed its reassuringly sharp edge, and slid it under his belt. He looked out the window over the sink and again saw little other than silvery darkness. Certainly no sign of danger. But he realized his heart was beating faster.

"Okay, Duffy," Nicole called softly as she started down the stairs, "let's go!"

Inhaling deeply, Duffy took the plunge. He unlocked the door and pulled it open. Wind whipped at his shirt as he stepped outside and fastened the screen door open.

"Good evening, Duffy," said Sheriff Bruno Francis Krull from out of the darkness, and Duffy's heart crashed.

After a frozen moment, he managed to look around. At first he saw nothing, but then the sheriff laughed, a low, snickering sound, and a dim, shapeless form, its face hidden, seemed to emerge from the night.

"Up a little late, aren't we?"

Duffy stared. As the big man came up the porch steps, his grinning face became faintly visible, and Duffy saw that he was wearing a hooded cloak. Perhaps it was just protection against the bad weather, but Duffy didn't think so. Seven years ago he had worn a cloak like that himself.

The sheriff looked him up and down. He couldn't have missed seeing the knife, even in the dark, but his grin only broadened.

Duffy forced the words: "Anything I can do for you, Sheriff?"

"Call me Bruno. How's Nicole doing?"

"Sound asleep." Duffy raised his voice, praying that Nicole would hear him. "She took a sedative the doctor gave her. I was just . . ."

"Oh, that's good, that's very good," the sheriff said, snickering again, "makes things much easier. Why don't you turn on the light, Duffy?"

Duffy's impulse was to step back inside, slam the door shut, and bolt it. But you didn't do that to the sheriff, did you? Not to Sheriff Bruno Francis Krull, you didn't. Best to play along for the moment. Taking a step backward, Duffy reached inside the open door and flipped the switch for the porch light . . .

. . . and the world went crazy.

At the very instant that the light went on, flooding the porch, the sheriff danced delicately away from Duffy, threw off his cloak with the air of a stage magician performing a brilliant trick—*Ta-daaa!*—and posed, grinning, with Gene Kelly grace.

Duffy stared.

Blood like crimson tears flowed down the sheriff's face from his right eye, which was swollen almost shut, and more flowed from purple wounds on his neck; blood matted the hair on his chest. As if he had dressed hurriedly for this occasion, his shirt was held closed by a single misplaced button, and his fly was unfastened and agape. His hands, his khaki clothes, even his sandaled feet, were stained with blood. With his badge askew on his shirt, he looked like a blood-painted clown-sheriff in some grizzly Grand Guignol comedy.

Duffy laughed.

It was a single, short, hysterical bark of a laugh, but it was a laugh.

That set the sheriff off. Laughing and snorting, choking and braying, he bobbed his head and pointed at Duffy. *Oh, Duffy, if you could only see your face!*

The sheriff was crazy. The sheriff was crazy and he had come here to do something terrible, terrible to Nickie and him, and what the hell could he, Duffy, do about it?

Swinging away from Duffy, the sheriff sought to calm himself. Falling into a limp, slumping posture, the sheriff continued to laugh for a moment, soft, gasping laughter, his pelvis thrusting forward with each little spasm.

"Oh, Duffy, Duffy," he said, wiping tears from one eye and blood from the other, "ain't we got fun? Let's face it. We got more fun than people."

Duffy hardly dared to answer. As neutrally as possible, he said, "Yes, I guess we do."

"Yeah." Cocking a knee, the sheriff scratched his crotch. Not satisfied with that, he reached into his open fly and—*ooh! aah!*—scratched his balls with obvious pleasure.

When he drew his hand back out, his large, half-tumescent cock came with it. Duffy's stomach wrenched when he saw that the sheriff's penis, too, was bloodstained.

"Would you look at that?" the sheriff said proudly. "I fucked Joanne just a little while ago, and already I'm getting it back. Dad didn't like that, me fucking Joanne, it wasn't on the program, but what the hell, the bitch asked for it." Caressing himself, he grinned at Duffy. "What about it, Duffy, you got something here for me to fuck?"

Those words seemed to release something in Duffy. Why was he standing here quailing as if he and Nicole were natural-born victims? They were not. At this moment, *he had the sheriff*—not the other way around! The sheriff might be a killer, but he was also a sick pile of shit. And Duffy Johnson was the doctor.

I want to know you, Bruno!

As he had often done while examining patients, Duffy reached out and touched the sheriff's temple. Bruno yelped and leaped back as if he had been stung by a hornet, but in that instant Duffy glimpsed the demon within, and he knew.

Bruno Francis Krull was not, as Duffy had thought, a madman.

By ordinary standards, he might be a raging sociopath, but he was not delusional. He was no tortured soul, no "cry for help" victim, driven to crimes that in his heart he abhorred. He suffered from no obscure chemical imbalance that skewed his perception of the world and rendered him incapable of empathy. No tumor was devouring his brain and his humanity. No, this was a creature who inflicted pain and death for the sheer pleasure of it—the pleasure of exercising godlike power over others. He did it because he could do it—*and it felt good.*

All right, motherfucker, Duffy thought, *your rules!*

He knew then that he was going to kill Bruno Krull. He, Dr. Duffy Johnson, guardian of life, sworn to the Hippocratic oath, was, with the greatest pleasure, going to tear Bruno Francis Krull's guts out, just as Bruno had almost certainly gutted Jessie and Brad and now Joanne. And not just because the sheriff was a threat to Nicole and himself. He was going to kill Bruno because Bruno, sane or not, was what Duffy most hated in this world, a disease. A disease that preyed on the weak and innocent, a disease as deadly as any Duffy had ever known and infinitely more evil.

Duffy reached for his knife.

He never saw Bruno move. All he knew was that suddenly he was on his knees and clutching at his belly in horrible agony, while coffee rushed up his throat and out his nostrils and mouth. He realized that Bruno must have rammed stiffened fingers deep into his belly, a spearlike blow that, properly placed and hard enough, could kill. He might, at this very moment, be bleeding to death.

He had failed. Failed to protect Nicole.

"Oh," crooned Bruno Krull, "I do that so well!"

Duffy was almost blind with pain, but he caught a glimpse of Bruno's grinning face as the latter pulled his head up and jammed the mouth of a bottle between his teeth.

"Drink, Duffy," Bruno said. "It'll do you good. Make you easier to handle and maybe open those good old 'doors of perception' a little wider. A psychic like you, that ought to be pretty wide."

Duffy gagged and strangled as the liquor burned its way down his throat.

Someone else, a shadowy figure, was on the porch with them. "Get the girl," Bruno said. "Put her under if you have to, but don't let her get away."

Duffy tried to scream his rage, tried to fight, but he could hardly make a sound, could barely move.

He felt himself being thrown over a shoulder and lifted.

And then, for a time, he passed out.

· · ·

She had to get away!

Bruno Krull wasn't alone, and there was no way in the world that she could help Duffy if she didn't get away.

Ever since Nicole had awakened, and perhaps even before, she had had the feeling that someone *might* be waiting outside for them, that *they* were out there somewhere in the darkness, and that was why she had refused to turn on any lights. Their only hope had been to slip away unnoticed.

But that had proved to be a futile, desperate wish. When she had heard Duffy draw the bolt, she had almost cried out *Don't!* in alarm, and then, halfway down the dark stairs, the terrible stomach-churning sense of dread had hit her, and she had known that Bruno Krull was outside. Bruno Krull, reveling in his own unveiled malevolence.

Now the sickness in her belly was turning into something else. Fury. She wanted to leap down the remaining stairs, throw herself at Bruno, and tear him apart. But she knew she couldn't do that. Bruno wasn't alone, and if she was to have any chance of saving Duffy, *she had to get away!*

She couldn't leave by way of the kitchen. She would almost certainly be seen and seized before she got out of the house. Instead, she turned and raced back up the stairs, praying to God that her would-be captor wouldn't hear her and have the wit to run through the house to the front stairs. If he did that, she'd be trapped.

Silently she ran along the upstairs hall to the front stairs. There she paused for just an instant. She saw no one in the murky gloom of the hallway below, but neither did she hear footsteps coming up the stairs behind her. She would just have to take her chances.

She ran, almost fell, down the front stairs.

Then she was at the front door, working the bolts. She pulled the door open, and silent as a shadow, she was out across the veranda and onto the lawn, running as swiftly as she ever had in her life. The nearest forest, the heaviest cover, was a good hundred feet to the west of the house, so she veered that way. Once well within it, she dropped, gasping, behind a thicket and looked back.

For a moment, all was still but for the treetops whipped by the wind. Then, brushed by a feather of moonlight, a movement near the rear of the house caught her eye. She had only a glimpse—a large dark figure carrying something, some-one, over his shoulder. Bruno Krull carrying Duffy, she knew it. As he disappeared into the woods, Nicole rose to follow.

But then another movement caught her attention. On the veranda a second dark figure had appeared. Legs flashed dimly as it ran down the steps, and she realized its phantomlike appearance was caused by a long, hooded cloak. It paused for a moment and seemed to be looking about in all directions. Looking for her.

Though she was certain she was invisible within the woods, the gaze of those unseen eyes under the hood seemed to settle on her. She held herself utterly still, not breathing, trying to silence the din of her heart.

She's not here, she's gone, you'll never find her, she is not here. . . .

Nicole thought she felt a burst of panic from the dark figure. Suddenly it darted around the side of the house toward the rear. But then it turned toward her again, and she realized with dismay that it had put itself between Duffy and her. As it looked about, she felt as if invisible tentacles were reaching out to find her.

The panic she had sensed a moment earlier now hardened into determination. This creature, whoever or whatever it might be, was certain she was nearby, and it was not going to let her escape. It began moving toward her, snakelike—slowly, tentatively, feeling its way. It seemed to Nicole that ever so faintly she could smell it—a rank, sour odor like something out of a thick, rotting swamp.

Then she saw something, an ugly gaseous blue and green flame, flickering within the hood. She thought of Gussie, of Buddy Weston, of their fate, and she knew who this creature that pursued her was.

Philip Steadman, Gussie had called him.

The lizard man.

Duffy seemed to hear a hound baying distantly, two hounds, three in chorus, the sounds intertwining and mingling, echo-ing and reechoing, between high mountains and across dark valleys somewhere deep within his skull.

He saw the light, burnt orange and gold, flame red and electric blue, dazzlingly bright, before he even raised his head from his arms and opened his eyes. Within the light, like pillars of basalt, stood several cloaked figures, their faces obscured by hoods. Three or four? More? Blinded by light, he could hardly tell. He heard Bruno's soft snicker, and the unseen hounds bayed again.

He knew where he was, or supposed himself to be. He was in the very maw of hell. The depths of hell might be dark and silent, but here brilliant light seemed to burst from the earth with a roar, and from it dimly seen wraiths, human and inhuman, the restless dead and demons not yet born, struggled to enter the world to do their master's will. Duffy seemed to feel them as they materialized briefly and plucked at his clothing with skeletal fingers.

It's not real, he told himself, even as he shook with revulsion and terror, *it's nothing but a goddamn drug-dream!* He had to fight the evil brew that deranged his brain, fight to regain normal consciousness, fight to regain his strength. He still felt paralyzed by Bruno's gut-puncturing blow, but he wasn't dead yet, and he had to fight!

For a moment, in spite of his resolve, he sank back into unconsciousness. But then he felt hands on his face and his head being lifted.

". . . wake up, Duffy . . . wake up, dear heart . . . not sleepy time yet, my dear . . ."

Someone was speaking to him in a gently coaxing, chiding voice that, with guilt and dismay, he recognized at once. *No, no, no, Lily,* he wanted to say, *not you, you aren't part of this. You were sweet, you were innocent before you met me . . .* But when he opened his eyes, it was indeed Lily.

Wearing only her cloak, its hood thrown back, she was sitting on the ground immediately in front of Duffy, and she was beautiful. Beautiful and terrible. In the hell-light, her green-flecked eyes were bright with childish glee and her wide smile glistened. But it seemed to Duffy that she reversed the very meaning of beauty, from Good to Evil, and for a drug-maddened moment, he thought he saw scales, green and brown and yellow, shining on her body.

". . . and did you really think you could turn your back

on me a second time? I've waited seven years for this . . .
seven years of loathing you for what you did to me . . . do
you hear me, Duffy? Seven years . . ."

"Lily," he managed to say, "I'm sorry. I tried to tell you
. . . I'm sorry."

"Sorry? Why should you be sorry? I told *you*—I regret
nothing! You taught me the joy of hatred and the sweet bliss of
revenge. Half the town thinks your maniac lover killed Gussie
and Brad, and in a few hours they're going to think she turned
on you—on you and Derek and Joanne. Be sorry for that!"

Out of his half-conscious, muddled brain, a terrible
thought came to Duffy. "Gussie and Brad . . . did you kill
them, Lily?"

"Brad. I killed Brad. I killed the miserable little bastard,
and you should have heard him scream when I went for him.
The way you're going to scream, Duffy, the way you're going
to scream when I go for you."

"God help you, Lily."

"A god does help me, Duffy, the very same god you led
me to seven years ago. And we're going to give you to him,
Duffy. But not yet. First we have something special for you,
something for you to watch. Another offering to our god, and
can you guess who it's going to be, Duffy? Can you guess?"

Lily looked slowly to one side, and Duffy followed her
gaze. Nearby, Joanne lay naked, bloody, and unmoving on the
ground, and beside her, in his pajamas, Derek.

"It's going to be Joanne, Duffy, our dear Joanne."

Joanne was still alive, then, after all. But they were going
to kill her. Right here and now, before his eyes, they were
going to kill her.

"And can you guess who's going to do the deed, Duffy?
Can you guess who's going to offer up our dear, sweet Joanne
if he doesn't want to die?"

Duffy stared into Lily's eyes. He had said that looking into
her eyes was like looking into a dark, empty pit. But he saw
now that he had been wrong—the pit wasn't empty. He was
looking at the demon that dwelt at its bottom.

It was a deadly game of hide-and-seek played in the dark.

Philip Steadman had killed Gussie, she was sure of it.

Steadman and Bruno Krull, they were the killers, and now they had Duffy and they were after her.

From time to time she glimpsed Steadman's demon face, and she saw it now, a lurid green flame suspended in the dark not a dozen yards away, a ghastly flame that illumined nothing. Since she had grown out of childhood and left St. Claire, she had forgotten how terrible some people looked beneath their masks of flesh and bone; but tonight, under the pressure of danger and fear, some part of that gift had been returned to her. She could see with a child's eyes.

From her cover of darkness close to the ground, she could see Steadman looking, listening, *feeling* for her. Each time he turned her way, sheer freezing terror threatened to overwhelm her, but she couldn't let that happen. Terror was a luxury she couldn't afford. Terror was for small children with grandmothers to comfort them.

Grandma, what should I do?

Get help!

But by then it may be too late—

Don't be a fool, child, *GET HELP!*

She could do that. Get to a phone and call 911—the sheriff wasn't the only law in the county. Or she could call the state police, direct. They knew who she was, they'd be here in minutes. And she didn't have to wait for them—she could *still* try to get past Steadman, *try* to pick up Bruno's trail, *try* to somehow save Duffy!

If he wasn't dead already.

No, he *wasn't* dead! She wouldn't let him be dead! They wanted Duffy and her both, they would keep him alive till they got her, and then . . .

She couldn't get back to the house to use the phone there. Whenever she moved in that direction, Steadman moved too, keeping between her and the house. But there was a phone in Joanne and Derek's cabin. And perhaps Derek would have a weapon as well.

That was the key, her one chance. Get to the cabin. She began to back away from that green demon face, slithering swiftly, silently, down through the woods toward the road and the lake.

When she reached the road, she was directly across from

the cabin. For a very long moment, the treacherous moon lit up the road, so luminous that she felt caught by sharp, clinging brambles of light and shadow, and she waited for it to darken. Every lost second made her long to scream. Then the cloud cover returned, and after a last look into the darkness behind her, she raced across the road and down the driveway to the cabin's attached garage.

Something was wrong.

The garage's overhead door was closed, but the side door was wide open.

Joanne, poor frightened Joanne, would never have left a door unlocked and open, would she? Not even by accident. And surely Derek wouldn't have either.

Her first impulse was to run away, simply to run screaming to the nearest door she could find to knock on, but running hadn't saved Gussie or Brad, and she didn't think it was going to save her. Steadman was nearby and he would be on her in a minute.

And there was a telephone inside.

She slid her hand over the wall inside the door and found a light switch. She pushed it up and nothing happened. She flicked it several times. The garage interior remained dark.

She could just make out the back end of the car. She had been in the cabin only once before, briefly on Tuesday, but she remembered that the inside door was directly across the garage from where she stood. She started to close the door behind her, then hesitated and left it partly ajar. Best to leave a path of fast retreat in case it was needed.

Carefully, she felt her way around the car. The inside door would probably be locked, of course, even if the other hadn't been. . . .

Her hand found the knob and slowly turned it.

With a feeling of disbelief, she found the door silently opening. She stepped through.

She was in the kitchen area, directly under the sleeping balcony, and here the darkness was even deeper. She felt for a wall switch and found it, and was not surprised when it produced no light.

What should she do now? Call out softly to Joanne and

Derek? Go up on the balcony and awaken them? No, first she would find the telephone and use it.

She couldn't remember where the telephone was—on the wall or on a counter? She felt blindly over both. She found it on a length of open counter between the kitchen and the living room.

She picked up the handset, ran her fingertips over the almost invisible numeric pad, and hesitated. 911? Or the state police? Both; 911 first. She entered the number and put the phone to her ear.

The phone was silent as the moon.

She tapped the hang-up switch several times, and as she entered the number again, she realized there were no touch tones. And still no line sound. Panic hanging over her like the blade of a guillotine, she hit the hang-up and tried a third time. Nothing. She hit redial, redial, redial, the *, the #, the 0.

The phone was dead.

Keep calm, she told herself, check the cord. Maybe Joanne pulled the plug to avoid calls. Check the cord—

Once again, that fetid smell, that rank, stomach-turning swamp perfume assailed her nostrils.

Swinging around, she looked back through the kitchen doorway into the garage. The outside door that she had left open, her path of retreat, was now closed.

With a little cry she couldn't suppress, she threw herself at the kitchen door and slammed it shut. Her fingers found the lock button and turned it. She slid to her knees against the door, expecting Steadman to start pounding on it at any instant.

What should she do now?

She was huddling in the dark, her fingers still on the lock button. She didn't really know where the lizard man was, though she smelled his presence and felt it. *What should she do?*

She found herself screaming: "*Joanne. Derek. Help! Help, Derek, Joanne, he's here! He's here! Derek! Joanne!*"

In answer, the cabin was as silent as the telephone had been, a dead line.

"Derek," she whimpered, "Joanne . . ."

She rose to her feet and carefully felt her way along the

counter. She realized she had been so intent on finding and using the telephone that she hadn't really looked into the living room. She did so now, across the open section of counter.

The moon had brightened, and she saw a couple of sofas, some chairs, a fireplace, a stereo. Throw rugs on the hardwood floor. An open, unlittered room with a high ceiling.

The front door was partly open, a slit of pale light.

The sickening swamp odor was growing stronger, and she ducked back down behind the counter. Should she run for the front door? Or try the back way out? She had no idea. She took one last look around the end of the counter.

The pale light of the front door widened. Then a large dark shadow with a face of green fire filled it. With a laugh of hungry anticipation, the lizard man entered the room.

"You don't want to die, Derek," Lily whispered, "not like Gussie and Bradford. You don't want to die, and there's no need. You're not like Duffy, he's beyond hope. But you're like us, Derek, like us. Oh, you've broken the vow of secrecy and written about us, but you never turned against us the way Brad did. You never meant us any harm, did you?"

"No."

The words barely reached Duffy's ears. When he opened his eyes for a moment, he saw that Derek was lying supine across Lily's lap. Her left arm supported his shoulders and head. His pajamas had been torn open, and Lily's right hand moved gently up and down his body, stroking the bare flesh. The two of them looked like an obscene parody of Michelangelo's "Pietà."

"No, you never meant us any harm. But we can't let you go on and on, now, can we? There are people who recognize the truth in your 'harmless' little stories and use it against us. People like Brad and his friends."

"I won't write anymore," Derek mumbled drunkenly. He sounded as if he were weeping. "I swear to God I won't write anymore."

"Swear to what god, Derek? We know you won't write anymore, not after tonight, but what god do you swear to?"

"To your god . . . our god . . ."

"Ahh!" Lily sounded deeply pleased, and her fingers

stroked Derek's nipple. "Then you're willing to renew your vows and be reconciled with our god?"

"Yes!"

"And you are willing to make a sacrifice to him, Derek . . . a blood sacrifice?"

"Yes!"

Lily's gaze moved to Joanne, who still lay unconscious on the ground nearby.

"You realize what you are saying?"

"Yes! Yes!"

Lily bent down over Derek and kissed him on the mouth.

"You will be rewarded, Derek," she said after a moment. "I promise you, you will be rewarded. You will survive to tell the story of this night. But not the story of the coven or the convocation—you must forget that. It will be the story of the Wolf Girl of St. Claire, of her history and how it ended on this terrible night. A night which only you survived. Can you do that?"

"Yes!"

"Of course you can. The book will make you famous, Derek. And very wealthy. And if that's not reward enough"— Lily brought Derek's hand to her breast as she kissed him again—"you'll have me, if you wish. I'll be anything you want, everything you could desire. And that will only be the beginning, my darling. Only the beginning."

Duffy lay perfectly still, feigning a relapse into unconsciousness, fighting to clear his mind, trying to reach into the deepest center of his being for some reservoir of strength. *Physician, heal thyself!*

Nickie, where was Nickie? *"Get the girl,"* Bruno had said. But she wasn't here. Surely he would know if she were here. Lily would tell him. Bruno would tell him. Maybe she had gotten away, had found help.

Nickie, run, run, run, and keep on running! And, please, God, keep her safe!

She felt rather than heard the thin, rising wail that tore from her throat.

Steadman laughed again, sure of himself now, and the green face, human and less than human, grinned at her. As he moved toward her, he seemed to grow taller, darker, more massive.

She was trapped. There was nowhere to go, nowhere to hide. She would never make it out through the garage—she knew that without thinking. For the moment she wasn't thinking at all, she was in the grip of terror and operating entirely on instinct and reflex.

She came around the end of the counter, half crouched, her cry reduced to a bleating whimper. Steadman giggled like a sadistic child with a new pet to torment. For a moment they faced each other in stasis, and her cry faded to silence.

They advanced toward each other, weaving slightly. Nicole had no plan. She didn't know what she was going to do from one second to the next. But when they were ten feet apart, she heard herself speak in the low, harsh voice of a stranger:

"You touch me, you slimy bastard, and I swear to God I'll fuckin' kill you!"

Steadman then did exactly what he was supposed to do. The lamb does not threaten the tiger. With a roar of anger, he went for Nicole.

And Nicole waited for him.

Even then, she didn't know what she was going to do—it depended on Steadman. But when in his fast forward rush he reached far out with his long, powerful right arm, instinct and reflex were ready. Her left hand found his right wrist in the dark as if by magic, and the rest was a single, smooth motion she had practiced a thousand times. Steadman howled in outrage and dismay as he found himself lifted from his feet, his legs flailing in the darkness above his head.

Bent forward from the hips, Nicole pivoted and pulled, pulled with all her strength.

Spread-eagled, face up, Steadman flew.

The floor was hardwood on a concrete slab.

Steadman hit it, flat on his back, like thunder.

The reverberation seemed to go on and on, and in that moment, Nicole thought she had killed Steadman. The green fire was out. This was just a big, muscular naked man in a cloak and sandals with his eyeballs rolled up to the whites.

Blood, like black ink, flowed from some kind of bandage under his chin and from the back of his head.

But then, with an animal snarl, Steadman rolled over and reached for her.

Nicole ran.

Turned and ran through the open front door, ran from the cabin, ran for the road. Crossed the road and ran for the woods. Ran toward her grandmother's house. Only when she was sure she was perfectly concealed did she pause and look back, ready to run again at any instant.

Something told her she should try to find out how badly Steadman was hurt.

From where she knelt, she had a good view of the cabin, even in the dark. After a moment a shadowy figure appeared by a corner, but then it merged with other shadows. Another moment and it reappeared, painfully climbing the grade toward the road.

Steadman. Stumbling. Almost crawling. Huddled within his cloak. She could sense his pain as he crossed the road. He was no longer looking for her, he was a wounded animal trying to get back to his own kind, but like any wounded animal, he was still dangerous. She hardly breathed as he passed by only a few yards away.

What should she do? If Bruno and Steadman had cut the telephone line at the cabin, the chances were they had done the same at the house. She could go on to Duffy's old house, try to awaken someone, try to explain, beg to use the phone, but all of that would take time. Time in which Bruno and Steadman could do their worst and disappear.

Grandma, what should I do?

She didn't have to ask. She knew what she *had* to do.

Silently she rose and followed Steadman.

"And should I ever again break these vows, may everlasting torment be my lot."

". . . may everlasting torment be my lot."

"In the name of the Prince of Power, god of this world. Amen."

"In the name of the Prince of Power, god of this world. Amen."

Freya bent down over Derek, where he knelt, lifted his head with one hand, and kissed him on the mouth.

"You're one of us again, Derek," she whispered. "You're a Child of the Griffin, and you've come home to your family. But there is one thing more that you must do to prove your sincerity and commitment. You know that, don't you?"

Derek nodded. He had been stripped of his pajamas and was wearing a black cloak. His back was straight, as he knelt, but his head was down, and Duffy had the impression that he was silently weeping.

Duffy closed his eyes, again feigning unconsciousness. Bruno had pulled him into a sitting position, slumped back against Lily. Now Lily, seeing what he was doing, scratched at his eyes. "You watch, Duffy, or I promise you you'll die blind. You'll never see your little Nickie again."

Duffy watched.

Freya faded back into that dazzling, demon-haunted light as if into shadows, and Bruno took her place. He was naked now, except for his cloak and sandals, and hunching over Derek, his legs apart and his knees bent, he looked like a big blood-spattered troll about to spring.

"Here, Derek," he said, taking Derek's right hand, "you can use this." And on Derek's hand he fitted what appeared to be a set of metal knuckles. But unlike any other such weapon Duffy had seen, the knuckles had two sharp points like claws, or perhaps fangs, attached.

"They're sharp, Derek," Bruno said, fingering the little blades, "very sharp. With these you can rip her up, tear her apart—"

"Gently, Bruno," Timothy Balthazar said from somewhere in that light, "gently . . ." It was the first time Duffy had heard him speak.

Bruno didn't seem to hear him. His one good eye was wide and glistening, and he was grinning like an eager attack dog. "You understand, Derek, somebody's got to die, and it's either her or you and her both. It's your only chance—"

"Bruno, Bruno . . ."

"He's got to understand, Dad."

"Of course he understands. Get the girl."

Derek was now sobbing audibly. Another cloaked figure

seemed to materialize out of the light behind him; it put a comforting hand on his shoulder.

"It will be all right, Derek," Balthazar said, "it will be all right, I promise you. Afterward you needn't even think of it, ever again, and nobody will ever know it was you.

"And the rewards, Derek, the rewards. For one thing, you'll be free of her. You know that she has been unfaithful to you. Oh, not often, but from time to time—that should make it easier for you to rid yourself of her. She doesn't deserve a man like you, Derek. Derek, boy, she doesn't deserve to live.

"But you do. You do deserve to live, Derek. You have such a bright future ahead of you, wealth, fame, all that and more, much, much more."

Bruno had seized Joanne from behind and dragged her up before Derek. She hung unconscious from his arms in a kneeling position, only inches away. Her arms were outspread and her head rolled from side to side as if her neck were broken. Her eyes were closed.

"Do it, Derek," Bruno commanded harshly, "do it now. *Now!*"

Sobbing, Derek raised the knuckles, and Duffy thought, *My God, he's going to do it!*

But then Derek lowered his hand. He looked as if he were about to collapse.

Balthazar leaned down closer to him. "Derek, boy, it'll all be over in a moment and she'll never know. You'll be free of her, and I swear to you that I'll be grateful to you for as long as I live. You'll be like a son to me, and nothing in this world is too good for a child of mine. I promise you. Name your own reward, Derek, and you shall have it!"

Derek started to lift his right hand, but it was as if the weapon were too heavy for him. The hand sank down again.

"I told you, Derek," Bruno said, sounding pleased, "it's either her or both of you."

Balthazar shook his head and held up a hand to silence Bruno. He took Derek's right hand in his and lifted it to shoulder level.

"Derek, I understand how hard this is for you. If it weren't hard, it wouldn't be much of a sacrifice, would it? Close your eyes if you wish. You're kneeling directly in front of

. . . of her." He slowly released Derek's hand as if afraid it might drop. "Now, all you have to do is administer a single blow. Just one blow, Derek, and then you can drop the knuckles, turn away, do as you please, no one will stop you. Bruno will finish it for you. You don't even have to watch. And you'll be spared."

"Do it," Bruno commanded again. "Just do it!"

Derek raised the glittering weapon still higher as if to strike.

Afterward Duffy never knew if he had cried out, *Derek, no!* or not. He did remember that Joanne had lifted her head and opened her eyes and uttered a cry of despair.

And in that same moment, Derek was flinging down the weapon and tearing off the black cloak and screaming his refusal.

With a cry of elation, Bruno threw Joanne aside. Instinctively, Duffy tried to rise, anything to help Derek, but Lily's arms tightened around him.

He heard Balthazar roar: *"No, Bruno, don't!"*

But nothing could have stopped Bruno Krull then. He was suddenly a fanged thing out of a nightmare, more beast than human. Duffy couldn't have said if Bruno picked up the bladed knuckles or used his own suddenly clawed hand, but his right hand came ripping up through Derek's belly, and then across it, two blows of incredible strength, tearing out gray-pink intestines and violet colon. Then he danced aside, laughing, while Derek, screaming, scrambled about on his knees, trying futilely to gather up his own guts and put them back.

Almost at once he stopped. Weeping, his wrecked intestines draped from his fingers, he looked at Joanne lying unconscious nearby and slowly shook his head. It seemed to Duffy that he was asking her forgiveness for having brought them both to this.

Derek fell to one side and rolled over, and Duffy knew he was dead.

Panting, grinning, his right hand dripping gore, Bruno turned to Duffy. "Some people," he said, "just don't know who their friends are."

•   •   •

The scream, though distant, was high and piercing, and she thought: *Oh, God, please, no, don't let it be Duffy, don't let it be Duffy!*

Fighting her way through the underbrush, she ran to catch up with Steadman. Sometimes she caught a glimpse of him in a flash of lightning, but most of the time she followed him by his scent. She had become incredibly sensitized to that particular stomach-wrenching fetor, and not even the winds that were blowing through the forest could keep it from her nostrils.

She seemed to hear, to feel, Duffy urging her to run, to get away, and that gave her heart: he was still alive and she was getting closer.

Then, suddenly, shockingly, she was in the light.

She had been descending a mild slope, literally following her nose in the dark, when she stepped through something like an invisible wall, an opaque membrane unseen and unfelt. One moment she had been in darkness, and the next she had stepped into the farthest reaches of a burning, pulsating radiance. She felt stunned, paralyzed, and exposed, by that light, a creature unexpectedly trapped in amber.

No more than fifty feet ahead of her, Steadman was stumbling toward the heart of the light, a clearing in a small, deep-nestled glen. Nicole remembered it from childhood—she had always thought of it as a strangely evil place and, oh, God, how right she had been! She was looking into the very mouth of hell, a place of demons. Her child's eye could see them, by the hundreds it seemed, flickering, swarming, vanishing and returning, as they tried to enter this world.

And then in that circle, that blinding cauldron, she saw the caped-and-cowled figures—not just Steadman and Bruno, but others as well. Lying on the ground in the arms of one of them was Duffy. And lying nearby were two naked and bloodied bodies that could only be Joanne and Derek.

Her eyes saw, but her mind rejected in horror, what had happened to Derek . . .

. . . and would happen to Duffy and Joanne, and perhaps to her too, for there was no way in the world that she could save them. There were at least five robed figures in the clearing, five to her one. None had seen her yet, but one of them, the nearest, was turning slowly toward her. It was as if that one had felt the intensity of her gaze, had felt the fear and grief in her heart.

That one was Freya Kellgren.

Even at this distance Nicole saw her with such preternatural clarity that they might have been able to reach out and touch each other. This was indeed Freya but not the Freya she had thought to be her friend, and surely not the Freya her father had loved. Under the hot gaze of her child's eye, the exquisitely molded face melted away like a mask of ice and snow, and once again she saw the dark beady eyes, the crooked yellow teeth, the furred muzzle, the animal snout. This was the same Freya she had seen years earlier, in a dream, in a vision, standing over her father's body. This was the true Freya, the demon Freya, the Freya she had feared from childhood. This was the soul of the Lady in White in all its monster vileness.

You killed him, Nicole thought with a kind of astonishment. *You! You killed my father. I don't know how or why—but you killed him!*

Surely she should have known, she felt that she had been on the verge of perception all along, but in her own need, in her desperation to find a cure for her affliction, she had willfully blinded herself. *Daddy, forgive me.*

Duffy, forgive me.

Freya smiled. She was trying to conceal her true self within her beauty, Nicole saw that, but now her beauty fit her like a Halloween mask, grotesque in its falseness. She smiled, and smiled, and held out her arms in welcome and seemed to say: *Come to me. You'll be safe with me. I can save you, you and your lover as well. Come to me.*

Nicole stared, literally struck dumb. In the face of that ugliness, she could not have played false to save Duffy and herself even if she had wanted to. She felt at that moment as if she were slipping into the foulest, the rankest, the most poisonous of cesspools. Not one redeeming spark of beauty shone in the darkness of this evil, and her sense of revulsion was overwhelming and complete as never before. Her stomach cramped, a sulfurous stench brought blinding tears to her eyes, and she could only think, in horror and loathing: *My*

*God, Freya, you are so . . . ugly! I never realized before . . .
you are so horribly . . . terribly . . . UGLY!*

And knew she had committed the unpardonable. She had
spoken only to herself, but she might as well have shouted the
words aloud. She had confronted Freya with a truth she dared
not face, not in a thousand years, a truth that for Freya was
the ultimate insult. That for those with the eyes to see, *she was
UGLY!* And for that Nicole could not be forgiven.

She heard the tortured shriek of Freya's soul.

*If you want your Duffy, come and get him. If you don't, he'll
die, and you after him!*

She didn't know if the thought was Freya's or her own.

She heard a heightened rustling sound, and at first she
thought it was the wind in the trees. But then she heard the
chittering sounds, too high for ears less sensitive than hers,
and in the next moment she felt their wings brushing her face
and arms as they tried to cling to her. Bats. Freya's bats.

Nicole turned and fled in terror.

The god of this world was angry, and so was Timothy Balthazar.

How could everything have gone so wrong, so terribly,
unthinkably wrong? First Bruno had raped the girl, leaving his
semen in her, unmistakable evidence of the crime. Then he
had killed Derek when the boy was in a virtual state of grace,
ready to die rather than harm the girl. If only Bruno had
waited a little longer, until Derek had hurt the girl, however
slightly . . . but, no, Bruno had gone out of control, like a
killer dog that had slipped its collar.

And now Steadman. Steadman, half-dead, pupils wildly
dilated, bleeding from his chin and the flattened back of his
head. Steadman, barely able to speak, telling him that Nicole
had gotten away. She could be anywhere by now. With people
who would swear she had been with them, and not a drop of
blood on her. Identifying Bruno and Steadman as killers. In a
very short time, this part of the forest might be swarming with
the law.

Bruno, Steadman. They were costing him Alida. Unless he
did something about it. At once. He had made a pact with the
god of this world, and he meant to keep it.

He shoved Steadman aside. "Duffy," he said to Bruno. "Put him on his knees."

Bruno grinned at him, and then at Duffy, who lay, apparently unconscious again, in Lily's arms. Lily smiled uncertainly.

"Timothy, no," Freya said, "not yet. Nicole is nearby, and as long as Duffy is alive, she'll come for him—"

"You don't know that."

"Timothy, I have seen her! Just now. She must have followed Philip—"

"Bruno! On his knees."

"Timothy—"

"*Unless, Freya*—"

In an instant, before she could move, Timothy's right hand closed on Freya's throat. He would kill her. He swore by the Griffin, if Freya interfered further he would kill her immediately. His fingers ached for her.

"Unless, Freya," he managed to say, "you would care to take his place."

She knew that she was within a millimeter of death. She was absolutely still for a moment, not daring to move or speak.

"Very well, Timothy," she said at last, "once again, you shall do exactly as you wish, and we shall help you."

Timothy listened for mockery in her voice, but heard none. He allowed Freya to step back, slipping from his fingers. She looked down at Lily, who was watching wide-eyed, her arms still around Duffy. Freya smiled slightly and nodded to Timothy. She was ready.

"Bruno!"

Bruno dragged Duffy away from Lily. As with Joanne, he lifted him by the armpits until he was on his knees, his head hanging forward over his chest. Timothy stepped forward and slapped Duffy hard across the face.

"Come out of it, Duffy! You're just a little drunk, a little drugged—come out of it!"

He slapped Duffy again, and Duffy's eyes opened slightly. "Do you repent, Duffy? Will you be reconciled?" There was no more time for ritual and ceremony, no more time for formal questions, and Timothy no longer cared.

Duffy didn't answer. His head fell forward again.

"Very well," Timothy said, "play that game. I know you're with us, and you know what's going to happen. Freya, give me Bruno's little toy."

Freya had anticipated the command, and she slipped the weapon onto Timothy's fingers as he spoke.

He was almost ready.

He let his anger build, tasting it, savoring it, like fine bitter tea. It had been a long time since he had last killed, and that a kill of no great importance, but this was Duffy Johnson, brilliant young physician and companion to Nicole St. Claire. This was Duffy Johnson, the apostate Luciferian, who had refused all that Timothy could have given him.

He was now going to kill Duffy Johnson. For Alida. His anger throbbed in his head like a drumbeat.

"Lift him higher. Lift him to his feet."

With a laugh, Bruno lifted Duffy, easily. Timothy reached out with his left hand and ripped Duffy's shirt open. Duffy's eyes opened for a second—good, that was what Timothy wanted. Timothy lowered his head, drew back the fanged weapon, gathered up all his strength in his bunched right shoulder for the first blow—

"No, don't. Not yet!"

Timothy gazed at Lily with incomprehension. *No, don't?* Suddenly she was standing in front of Duffy, embracing him. Shielding him with her body. *No? Don't?*

How dared she!

"Get out of my way, Lily."

"But you haven't given him his chance yet, not really! I don't want him to die—"

"Get out of my way!"

The panic on Lily's face turned to little-girl rage. "You can't! He's mine, and he's no good to me dead. I won't let you!"

"Get out—"

Kill her!

The voice pounded in Timothy's head. *Kill her! Kill her!*

Yes, kill her. It didn't matter that the voice was Freya's, urging him on, nothing mattered except that Lily was defying him, Lily was in his way, Lily was suddenly the enemy, and *he was going to kill her!*

And she knew it.

He rejoiced in the look of incredulity that came over her face as he pulled her away from Duffy. This couldn't be happening to her. She was Lily Bains, the favored one, Timothy's lover and Freya's successor. This was supposed to happen to Freya, not to her!

He delighted in her frightened protests, *"Oh, no, no, Timothy, don't!"* as he raised the weapon again.

He exulted in the music of her scream as the metal blades raked bloody furrows across her belly.

And, oh, the shock in her beautiful green-flecked eyes!

But that wasn't enough. Oh, no! There was a better way of finishing the job, one that Timothy much preferred.

Throwing down the metal fangs, he wrapped one arm around Lily and drew her to him, a shoulder to his chest. The other arm he wrapped around her head, and he forced her to look back over her other shoulder . . .

. . . forced her to look up in horror into his grinning face, she knowing exactly what he was doing to her, a thin scream coming from her tortured throat, while he slowly, slowly continued to turn her head . . .

. . . oh, God, this was ecstasy, this was truly the Rapture, not since that long-ago night in Santa Monica had he experienced such consummate bliss . . .

. . . turned her head until . . .

Farewell, sweet Lily!

. . . he heard her neck snap . . . saw her terror-filled eyes go unutterably blank . . . and with a great sigh of satisfaction, dropped her lifeless body to the stony ground.

"And now," he said, "give me Duffy."

Oh, God, Duffy, forgive me!

How far she had run in her panic, a hundred feet or a hundred yards, Nicole didn't know. All she had known as she plunged back into the darkness was that a shrieking horror out of her worst childhood nightmare had seemed to be pursuing her. She had run blindly, tripping, stumbling, while the bats clung to her like Freya's grasping hands. At last they had been left behind, torn from her by the slashing undergrowth, and she had fallen to the ground gasping for breath.

Oh, God, Duffy, I ran out on you. They've got you, and I ran out on you!

She forced herself up onto her knees, forced herself, still gasping, her lungs aching, to stand. What should she do? Get help? There was no time to get help. *What should she do?*

Go back.

I can't go back!

Go back.

I can't, I can't, how can I?

She was powerless against Freya and the others, she knew that. If she went back, they would tear her apart as they had Gussie and Brad and now Derek. They would kill her as they might be killing Duffy and Joanne at this very moment. She had hurt Steadman, but the combat skills Duffy had taught her, mostly in fun, were not nearly enough. She needed something more. Oh, if only . . .

God, please, give me something to fight with!

This was his last chance, his one chance, his only chance. Lily was dead. Duffy had caught a glimpse of her in Balthazar's arms, had heard the terrible popping sound, had felt her soul spinning off into darkness. He had a sense that Steadman was also close to dying and rapidly losing strength. As far as he knew, that left only Balthazar and Bruno and Freya. If he could somehow take care of the two men . . .

He couldn't think further than that. He had to fight for his life, and he had to do it now.

At Balthazar's direction, Bruno was holding him by the waist, facedown: he hung over Bruno's left forearm, his feet dragging on the ground. Bruno held him as easily, it seemed, as if he were a big rag doll. Covertly opening his eyes, Duffy saw Balthazar approaching. The old man was flexing big hard-muscled arms and cracking his knuckles. Far from having spent himself on Lily, he seemed to have gained strength from her death.

"Oh, Duffy, Duffy," he murmured, "you don't know what a pleasure this is. I invite the god of this world to share in it."

Laughing softly, Bruno reached over Duffy's back, grasped a handful of his hair, and lifted his head. "Do it, Dad," he said. "Wring this chicken's neck!"

Like a man straining with all his will to awaken instantly and completely, Duffy put all of his concentration into the moment. Taking a deep, lung-bursting breath, he lifted his left knee as high as he could against his chest. Glancing at Balthazar, his drugged eyes saw as in a haze something, a soul perhaps, so monstrously ugly—multifaceted eyes, a long sucking proboscis—that he might have been looking at the Lord of the Flies himself. But not even that could distract him. He felt a crazy grin crack his face.

He was wearing hiking boots. The edge of his boot-shod left foot found Bruno's right shin.

With all his strength and a great killer cry, he brought his boot down solidly on Bruno's right foot, smashing the bones like twigs.

Bruno screamed and threw his arms wide. Instantly Duffy was out from under Bruno's right arm, and his hands found Bruno's right wrist and elbow.

Duffy hadn't rehearsed the move in months, but it had been programmed into his system from boyhood: a sharp, hard, wrenching, cranking twist of Bruno's arm, accompanied by another killer cry and a twisting pull, and Bruno, reeling forward, screamed again as his elbow shattered, ligaments ripped loose, and his arm tore out of its shoulder socket.

Bruno slammed, almost cartwheeling, into the ground and rolled over, facing Duffy. Duffy might easily have finished him with a kick then, but he did not. Instead, he let himself be carried forward by his momentum and by his absolute loathing of Bruno Francis Krull. He landed with his right knee low in Bruno's belly, crushing his guts and pinning him in place, and in that same moment the heel of his right hand was traveling toward Bruno's face with all the speed and force of an unstoppable battering ram.

Bruno knew what was about to happen to him. He knew exactly. Duffy saw that in his incredulous eyes. In a few seconds, everything had been reversed and now every hope and expectation Bruno Krull had ever had was being taken from him. He, the mighty Bruno Krull, immortal taker of lives, was suddenly and most unexpectedly about to die. At this very moment. And he knew it.

Duffy felt his anguished cry of protest, a cry that would echo throughout eternity: *No, goddamnit, noooooo!*

Yes, Bruno, yes!

The heel of Duffy's hand landed squarely and solidly on Bruno's nose, driving the bone deep into his brain, and Bruno fell back.

Again, Duffy had the sensation of a soul spinning off into darkness.

Good-bye, Bruno.

Then Duffy made a mistake. For an instant, his concentration broken, he hesitated over the body of this man he so despised. When he looked up, he saw Freya a dozen feet away, laughing, her eyes bright with excitement. Balthazar, no longer a figure of terror but only a frightened old man, looked at her angrily; his black cloak flared as he turned sharply away and ran.

Freya paid no attention to him. She nodded at someone behind Duffy. Looking over his shoulder, Duffy caught a glimpse of Steadman standing over him, his hands held high. With what must have been his last remaining strength, Steadman brought his fists crashing down on the back of Duffy's head. Duffy's brain exploded in a great burst of light, and as that light faded, he knew—*Nickie, forgive me!*—that once again he had failed.

God, help me, please! Tell me what to do. Give me strength, the strength of a wolf or a madwoman, I don't care, but give me something . . .

. . . because she was going back.

No matter what the risk, no matter what the cost, she was going back. That was the only way she could possibly save Duffy. The very thought of Freya, monstrous, deadly Freya awaiting her, brought a scream to her throat, but she had to go back.

If only . . .

She recalled the tales of the shape-changing St. Claires who had come to America more than two centuries ago . . . of her great-great-grandfather Stephen Morgan St. Claire, said to lead wolves and perhaps to be one himself . . . tales of the Werewolves of St. Claire.

Oh, if only they could be true!

If only she could be one of them, as she had once dreamed. If only she could be a great dire wolf, then perhaps . . .

That was their only chance, Duffy's and hers and Joanne's—a myth, a legend, a childhood dream. But at least once in her life, when she was twelve, that dream had seemed to come true.

And once, in a dark parking lot . . .

Oh, God, let it be true! Let me be a wolf again, one more time. Make me big and strong and dire. Make me a dire wolf, just for tonight, please, Lord, I beg You!

Quickly, before she could let herself think of the madness of it, she pulled her sweatshirt over her head and kicked off her shoes. She shoved her jeans and panties down and stepped out of them. She looked up through the wind-whipped trees at the darkly savage sky and held up imploring hands. Lightning flickered and thunder rumbled, closer now, and a few windblown drops of rain, cold as sleet, whipped her body.

Please, God, please, for Duffy's and Joanne's sakes, please let me save them, let me at least try!

The storm-darkened sky growled again, as if in reproof.

Oh, please, God, let me be what in my heart I know I truly am, what I once dreamed of being, and I promise . . .

No—no, that was wrong. Some instinct, something she had been taught, told her it was wrong. In near-despair, she tried again, speaking aloud.

"Lord, just let me be whatever You want me to be, wolf or madwoman, and I promise, I swear to You, that I'll never fight it or deny it again. I'll never again curse myself for being what You made me. I'm Your child, and I'll try to be the best, the very best, of whatever I am, but, Lord, please, please . . ."

She couldn't keep this up. Tears streamed down Nicole's face, and she bent forward, trying to cover her nakedness with her hands and arms. She felt so young and defenseless, so completely vulnerable, as if she were twelve again. "Please make me brave, because I am so scared and, wolf or woman, I have to go back now and try to save Duffy, and I think . . . I think we're both going to die, Lord, but I've got to do it!"

Nicole waited.

God was silent.

Then, suddenly, she knew that something was about to happen, it was happening *now,* the earth seemed to fall from under her and instinctively she ducked and crouched, closing her eyes. In the next instant lightning struck, closer, louder, brighter than she had ever before experienced it. The sharp, explosive *BAMMM!!!* like a bomb going off deafened her, and the light burned through her eyelids. Her body tingled electrically and for a moment she was certain she had been hit.

But when she finally opened her eyes and looked up, a wonderful thing happened. In the face of the oncoming storm, miraculously, the clouds began to part one more time and a silvery light shone through them. In another moment, as if a dark velvet curtain had been drawn aside, the moon was revealed in all its dazzling glory, and to the eyes that God had given Nicole, eyes that saw wonderful and terrible things often concealed from others, it seemed to grow larger even as she watched it, seemed to grow until it filled the entire sky.

It was her moon, beloved from childhood, her companion in the night, and as she gazed at it in awe and delight, she felt herself being transformed. Drawing substance from the very light of the moon, she grew larger, stronger, every muscle aquiver, every sense heightened until she smelled a hundred wonderful perfumes—she could *taste* them in the air. Once again, she was a creature of the forest.

But more than that, she was a creature who had rediscovered her true self. And with that realization, her fear vanished—her fear of Freya and her fear of the world. It no longer mattered what the world called her, madwoman or werewolf, or how it judged her. She was who and what she was. She would live and love, she would suffer and die, but in the end she would triumph. Because she was in God's hands. The only true God of this world, the God of wolves and of all creation.

Once again, as in childhood, Nicole raised her face to the moon as to the face of God and howled her joy.

. . .

Come to me, Nicole! If you want your lover, come and take him! Because I have him, and I'm going to have you too! I'm going to have you, little Wolf Girl, I swear by the god of this world I'm going to have you, I'll have you as pet or as prey, but you'll be mine, you and your lover, so come to me!

Freya paused briefly in her summoning of Nicole to save Duffy's life.

She had thrust Philip Steadman aside after he had struck Duffy down, and he, too, had fallen to the ground. Now, however, in a final resurgence of strength he had risen to his hands and knees and was slowly crawling like a great crippled beetle toward Duffy. He was drooling blood and muttering something almost incomprehensible that Freya understood to be a prayer: *Give me life . . . give me life . . .* She understood that he wished to save, or at least prolong, his own life through taking Duffy's. But she could not allow that to happen, even if it were possible. If Nicole sensed Duffy's death she might not come.

Give me life, Philip Steadman prayed, crawling nearer.

"No, Philip," Freya said, kneeling before him. Tingling with anticipation, she cupped his chin in her left hand and lifted his head. She lightly touched his eyelids with two fingertips of her right hand, brushing them back and forth. Steadman whimpered and tried to draw back, but she released his chin and quickly threw her arm around the back of his neck.

"No, Philip," she said again, and Steadman's whimper became a squeal as her lengthening nails, stiletto-sharp, dug under his eyelids. "No, Philip," she said, drunk on the pleasure of his terror as she played with his eyes, "you will give me *your* life. But first . . ." Tightening her grip on his neck, she slowly drove her nails deep under his eyelids, and his squeal rose to a scream as his punctured eyes, like ripe fruit, gave up their purple and crimson juices.

Steadman struggled to escape her grip, but she held him firmly. "How do you like being alone in the dark," she asked over his screams, "how do you like it? Maybe you'd prefer to be with your friends!" With a final thrust, she drove her nails through the backs of Steadman's eye sockets and into his brain. The pleasure of the moment was so intense, wave after wave throbbing through her body, that she, too, went blind, almost lost consciousness, and she never felt Steadman's body slip from her arms.

Gradually her sight returned. Oh, God, this was the most glorious night of her life! Climbing to her feet, Freya wiped her bloody fingers on her body hair and surveyed the carnage by the light of hell. Lily, Bruno, Steadman, they were all dead! All of her nearest and dearest enemies except Timothy and Nicole, and Timothy hardly counted anymore. After tonight, Timothy was nothing. She had proven stronger than Timothy, stronger at last, bending him to her will, and she would deal with him later. For now, there was only Nicole.

She was out there somewhere, howling like a woman demented.

Come to me, little Nickie!

Ugly, was she? Never! She might appear ugly to her enemies and to the enemies of her god, but already she could sense her reward for this night—the renewal of youth and strength and beauty, beauty beyond any she had ever before known, beauty that would unite convocations around the world with Freya Kellgren as their leader and bring about the day when she and her god would rule all.

So come to me, little Wolf Girl! Come to me and grovel at my feet and perhaps, just perhaps, I'll spare you and your lover. I'm your only chance, your only hope. Come to me!

Somewhere nearby, the three-headed hound of hell again raised its bravura carol. The god was approaching.

Come to me, Nicole! Come to meet our god. Come to me . . .

. . . come to me . . .

The whisper in her mind was barely heard, almost unnoticed. She was too filled with happiness, as she danced in the light of the moon, sending her wordless songs of praise and thanksgiving floating on the mountain winds. And when the smiling moon, with a wink and a nod, slid back behind a cloud and the night was dark again, her stomach awakened with an agreeable pang and she thought with delight of the hunt. It was time once again for the hunt. It was time . . .

. . . come to me . . .

But what was that calling?

. . . come to me . . .

And what was that smell, that one special smell, among a hundred others . . . ?

She knew it now . . . the smell of carrion . . . of a fresh kill . . . of blood . . . human blood . . .

Duffy!

Suddenly, like a scream, the human edge of her mind asserted itself, and the sight that only a short time ago she had beheld returned in all its horror. That hellfire-lit, demon-haunted glen . . . the dark caped-and-cowled figures . . . Derek lying slaughtered on the ground and Joanne nearby . . . Freya turning to look at her, and . . .

Duffy!

Freya and Bruno and the others—they had Duffy! They had Duffy and Joanne, and she had to go back and save them!

. . . come to me . . .

Oh, I'm coming, Freya. I am coming. I'm ready to die and you'd better be ready too! *I am coming!*

Welcome, Lord Lucifer, take me, use me!

What better proof that she was the god's favorite could she ask than this?—that he was invading her, using her as his gateway into this world, seeing through her eyes and making use of her strength. She could feel her strength growing, as she was transformed into something far more powerful and dangerous than she had ever been before, something that grew and grew and towered in beauty and burned in the night, something to be worshiped by the strong and feared by the weak.

Take me, O Lucifer, make me one with you! Make me your instrument of life and death! Use me to take your vengeance against those who have offended you! Be with me, O Lord Lucifer. . . .

He was with her, and from her own throat she heard the triumphant roar of the Griffin.

All her years of devotion to the god of this world, all the sacrifices she had made for him, were about to be rewarded. Looking down, she saw that she loomed over the glen and the bodies at her feet like a great beast-angel.

And now one more task for her lord and master, one last task on this glorious night.

Come to me, little Wolf Girl, come . . .

Save for the thinnest edge of human consciousness, all was instinct now.

Oh, the joy of it! Guided as much by scent as by vision, led on by that fierce Griffin cry that tore the night like jagged lightning, she raced back through the darkness. She was meant for this, the hunt, the chase, the battle. Not for her the weakest of the herd, but the strongest of her enemies. Overhead, the bats circled and dipped again, but now, like the other creatures of the forest, they kept their distance, silent witnesses to the battle to come.

I'm coming for you, Freya!

I'm coming, Duffy!

Suddenly she burst from the darkness into the light . . .

Come to me, little Wolf Girl!

. . . and in the heart of the cauldron stood Freya, Freya alone now, Freya grown large, towering dark and immense over Duffy's unmoving body. A Freya who was at once satanic beauty, mighty beast-angel, and the demon who had killed her father. Freya, unholy three-in-one, beckoning and threatening.

Come to me, little Wolf Girl, be my pet or be my prey!

As she raced forward, she felt a single brief thrill of heart-freezing terror. This, she knew, was the moment of victory or of death. But she did not hesitate. All the generations of St. Claires who had come before were with her now, the God of wolves and all creation was with her, and she would not fail them.

Come, little Wolf Girl, come—

In her last strides, she gathered up all the strength in her mighty haunches and all the determination in her heart. Let death take her if it would. This was the enemy, the evil the St. Claires had fought down through the ages and would fight forever. With a great cry of rage and defiance and joy, the Werewolf of St. Claire sprang for the kill.

CHAPTER
24

"Duffy! Oh, Duffy, please!"

Nicole was shaking him. Somewhere a woman was sobbing. Cold rain fell on his face, and for a moment he thought it was blowing in through an open window.

"Oh, Duffy, Duffy . . ."

Then he realized that he was not lying in his bed, he was lying facedown somewhere out in the open in wild grass and weeds. He had no idea of how he had gotten there, but he felt no shock or surprise, only bewilderment. He was a man awakening from a frightening dream, with a few hazy nightmare images still haunting his benumbed mind . . . Derek clutching at his guts . . . Lily screaming something defiant . . . crazy, one-eyed Bruno suddenly dead . . . and then something fanged and dire . . .

Groaning, he lifted his aching head.

"Oh, Duffy, thank God!"

With Nicole's help, he managed, very slowly, to sit up. Clinging to her, he realized she was naked, and somehow that didn't make sense. Why should she be naked? He tried to gather up his wits. They had planned to leave St. Claire, had been ready to leave the house, when Bruno Krull had appeared, and . . .

Nicole kissed him, touching his rain-wet face as if it were fragile. "Duffy, baby, are you all right? How bad did they hurt you?"

"I don't know." His head was throbbing and his abdomen was tender. His whole body ached dully as if he had put it through some terrible exertion, and he remembered, again as in a dream, his desperate attack on Bruno Krull. But aside from that . . .

"I think I'm all right," he said. "A slight concussion, maybe."

The woman was still sobbing.

"I've got to get you away from here," Nicole said. "You and Joanne. Do you think you can help me with her?"

He didn't know if he could. He only knew he had to try. His head seemed nearly to burst as Nicole helped him to his feet.

He looked around, saw Joanne. She lay curled up on the ground, weeping, a naked gray form barely discernible in the wet darkness. Nicole went to her and knelt, trying to get her to sit up.

"If we can just get her to her feet, Duffy, one of us on each side . . ."

As she spoke, lightning struck, a bright, flickering strobe light, and Duffy saw the others.

For an instant he was paralyzed. Then the thunder released him, and he wanted to scream, scream in horror and anguish. *It had happened! It had really happened!* The dead bodies, the torn and bloody bodies, confirmed the nightmare. *It had happened!*

He heard Nicole cry out: "Duffy, don't look. Just come and help me. Don't look!"

But he had to look. Bruno lay on his back almost at Duffy's feet, his face smashed and his remaining eye glistening with rain. The heel of Duffy's right hand ached. *Oh, God, I killed him,* he thought in amazement and grief. *It wasn't a dream. I killed a man!*

"Duffy," Nicole cried out in answer, "you were defending your life!"

That answered his head but not his heart. These people were dead, they had died terrible, violent deaths, and he had played a part in their destruction. He could see their scattered bodies now, even in the dark and the rain. Ignoring Nicole's protests, he walked toward them.

Only a few steps away lay the body of a man half-hidden by a black cloak. His head, turned at an odd angle, was covered with blood, his mouth was open in a silent scream, and his eyes, bloody ragged holes, appeared to have been gouged out.

And there, farther off, lay Derek's naked body, torn open and guts strewn as Brad's had been strewn. Oh, Jesus. Gussie, Brad, Derek, each of them slaughtered, torn apart like so much wasted meat, and abandoned . . .

"Duffy, come back!"

He couldn't. There lay Lily under her cloak, and so oddly twisted. She seemed to be sprawled belly-down on the earth, her head turned, like that of a grotesquely broken doll, so that she gazed up at him. But now her eyes neither accused nor forgave. They were empty. The demon at the bottom of the pit was gone.

Duffy looked around. Where was Balthazar? Had he somehow survived this hideous night? Duffy remembered the fear on the old man's face after Bruno's death, as if he were about to run. And the only remaining cloak on the ground covered a torn body much too small to be Balthazar's.

"Duffy, please!"

Duffy had to lean down close, and even then he didn't know how he recognized her. Perhaps it was the onyx cameo ring and the matching earrings—perhaps he had seen them before without really noting them. Or perhaps it was some slight resemblance of the face. But this face was old and deeply lined and sprinkled with long gray hairs. It was an oddly rodentlike face.

Freya's face and shrunken body looked almost mummified, as if she were a thousand years old.

•   •   •

They had to get out of St. Claire. That was all that mattered, the only thing Nicole dared think about. Getting out. Maybe in a day or a week or a month the impact of this night, the horror of it, would hit her and she would shatter, but she couldn't let that happen now.

Somehow she had gotten them back to the house, she and Duffy supporting Joanne between them. "Come on, Joanne, come on, Duffy, just a little farther. A hundred yards. Less. A hundred feet. Come on!" Joanne had calmed somewhat when Nicole found her abandoned clothes and put them on her, but oh, God, the relief when she had seen the light, still burning on the porch. Nicole had thought that Duffy was going to faint when he saw the blood on her face and body, but she had quickly reassured him. "It's all right, Duffy, I'm all right. A few scratches."

She hadn't told him it was Freya's blood.

Get clean, get freshly dressed, and get out. That was what they had to do now. While Duffy showered upstairs, his turn, Nicole was on her knees in the kitchen, repacking a couple of suitcases. Joanne, in a clean dry shirt and jeans, sat at the kitchen table, pale-faced, staring as if in a trance. As Nicole worked, she spoke soothingly and reassuringly to Joanne, touching her from time to time, but she got no response. The woman might have been catatonic. She had said only a few barely coherent words, something to the effect that Bruno Krull had raped her. She had been bleeding, and Duffy, though scarcely functioning himself, had done what he could for her.

Nicole rose to her feet as Duffy appeared at the foot of the back stairs. He still appeared to be in a daze. Nicole hurried to him and spoke in a low, urgent voice.

"Here's the story. We know nothing about what happened tonight. Nothing. Derek insisted on staying in St. Claire to work on his book, but Joanne decided to leave with us. She stayed with us last night so that we could get an early start."

"Nicole, we can't just go off—"

"The hell we can't! I don't want to be anywhere near here when they find those bodies. There are people around here who'll never believe that I'm not responsible—we'll be lucky if they don't try to burn this house down and us with it."

"We should go to the police—"

"Believe me, Duffy, the police will come to us soon enough. And what am I supposed to tell them? That I killed the woman I believe responsible for my father's death? But, no, please believe me, I didn't kill anyone else? Or that you and I and your little 'coven' of friends weren't part of some kind of crazy orgy that ended with everybody killing each other? Who's going to believe us, Duffy? Who?"

Duffy shook his head, and Nicole's heart went out to him, but she had to stay strong. If she didn't, they'd wind up trapped in St. Claire.

"You see, Duffy, we have no choice. We're going to leave here just as fast as we can, and when they come after us, we're going to hang together and hang tough. We can do it—"

"I'm not going with you," Joanne said.

When they looked at her, she hadn't moved, but tears were again rolling down her cheeks.

"Joanne—"

"I'm staying here. Bruno Krull raped me and killed my husband. And all the world is going to know it."

"But, Joanne . . ." Nicole hesitated. She knew she would have to handle this very, very carefully. She sat down at the table, facing Joanne.

"Joanne," she said gently, "Bruno is dead. You can't hurt him anymore."

"It isn't just to hurt Bruno. It's for Derek. He died for me. Okay, we had our problems, but he laid his life on the line for me, and for that, Bruno killed him. I want the whole goddamn world to know. He loved me and he died for me."

"I understand that, Joanne."

For a moment Joanne was overcome by tears again, but when she recovered she seemed calmer. "I think he wanted my respect. Not just my love but my respect. Well, he by God has got it!"

"He has the respect of all of us. And our love. Believe me."

"Then you do understand. I've got to tell about Bruno. And about Balthazar's part in it."

"Balthazar? Mr. Balthazar was there?" Nicole looked at

Duffy. He nodded, and her heart sank. This complicated matters.

Joanne saw, and smiled ruefully. "Oh, don't worry. You saved my life tonight, and I'm not going to involve you and Duffy. I'll simply say I passed out for a time and regained consciousness to find the others . . ." Joanne faltered, remembering the horror in the glen, but forced herself to go on. "For some reason I'd been spared, maybe left for dead. I found my way back to the cabin, and when I felt up to it, I went to a neighbor for help. That'll be close enough to the truth. And then I'll tell about Bruno and Balthazar."

All right, there would be no stopping Joanne from telling her story. Nicole had been afraid it might come to this. But there was still a way out. She considered her words carefully. If she didn't handle this just right, she couldn't blame Joanne for turning her down.

"Joanne, I'm going to ask you to do something for me."

"Anything. After tonight—"

"No, not because of tonight. I don't have that right. But I'm still asking. Go ahead and tell about Bruno. But not about Balthazar. Leave Timothy Balthazar to me."

Staring at Nicole, Joanne slowly shook her head. "I don't think I can do that."

"Listen to me. Timothy Balthazar is a very rich and powerful man. You may be able to hurt him, but if you try, he will destroy you. Even if Duffy backs up your story—"

"I told you, I won't involve Duffy or you."

"Knowing Duffy, I don't think you could keep him out, not if he thought you needed him, and then Balthazar would do everything he could to ruin Duffy. But if you will leave Balthazar to me . . ."

Dear God, she had never thought she would be saying anything like this. But the situation required it. And if it demanded that she be a braver and stronger person than she had ever been before, then she would have to be such a person. Her God and her grandmother asked no less.

She held up her right hand and leaned toward Joanne, looking intently into her eyes.

"Joanne, if you will leave Timothy Balthazar to me, I will promise you this. I promise, I vow, I swear to you that Timothy Balthazar will not go unpunished. I give you my solemn word as a St. Claire that, one way or another, I, Nicole St. Claire, will settle with Timothy Balthazar, and he will suffer everything he has coming. Before God and my grandmother, I do solemnly swear."

Some wordless communication passed between the two women. Duffy saw it, but he was still too foggy-minded to understand it.

"You really think you can do that?" Joanne asked after a moment.

"Yes," Nicole said, surprise in her voice, as if she were discovering some new and awesome power. "Yes, I really think I can."

"And you'd do it for me?"

"For you and Derek and all of us. For everyone who ever suffered that man's evil."

"Oh, God, if I could believe that . . ."

"Believe it." Nicole raised her right hand higher. "He will be punished."

A little smile began to play over Joanne's lips. Nicole smiled back, and Joanne's smile grew larger, became a kind of feral grin. For a moment Duffy had an impression of two fierce young wolves contemplating a kill.

"*Do it!*" Joanne said, and she slapped Nicole's right hand hard with her own.

The two women laughed softly and sat quietly for a moment, feeling that they had salvaged something from hell after all and that victory was waiting at the end of the night.

Then they stood up. They embraced briefly.

"I'd better get out of here," Joanne said, "and you'd better be on your way."

"I'll take you to your cabin," Duffy said.

"No. Best we don't take any chance on being seen together. I'll be all right." She kissed Duffy's cheek. "Take care of her, Duffy."

"You're a brave and wonderful woman, Joanne," Duffy said, hugging her.

"When will we see you again?" Nicole asked.

"I told you before," Joanne said, smiling. "At the wedding."

• • •

The dark nightmare images continued to haunt his mind . . . Derek . . . Lily . . . Bruno . . . Freya, Balthazar . . . the stranger with the bloody, gouged-out eyes . . .

. . . and then, suddenly, like a flash of lightning, that huge, beautiful wolflike creature, that fanged dire angel that had saved him . . .

Nicole . . .

No. A dream, an illusion. He, too, had been raised on tales of the St. Claires, their blood ran in his veins, but that those tales should be true—the enormity of such a thought was too much for him.

Yet somehow Nicole had saved him.

She was so strong. Even he, who loved her, would never have guessed her incredible strength. She was still his Nicole, but somehow the events of the night had changed her. It was as if where others might have been destroyed she had been made whole. He would ask her, sometime, what had happened to her, but not now. For now, it was enough to feel her strength flowing into him, a gift of grace.

Nicole drove. The rain came pounding down as they crawled through the deserted streets of St. Claire. When they reached the crest overlooking the town, it subsided, but lightning still flickered and thunder rumbled in the distance.

Nicole pulled over onto the shoulder and they got out. Duffy took a deep breath of fresh, storm-swept air, and his mind cleared as if a gentle breeze had blown away the fog.

Standing behind Nicole, he wrapped his arms around her, and they looked down into the dimly lit streets of St. Claire, perhaps for the last time. They were attuned, and he might have guessed her thoughts even if she hadn't spoken aloud.

"Good-bye, St. Claire," she said softly. "You were a good little town once, and I think mostly you still are. But the dark forces here have grown stronger over the years. So I've got to warn you. Leave the good people of St. Claire alone. If you don't, I may have to come back."

And then, Duffy found himself thinking, *and then, God help you.* Because this was no ordinary woman he was holding in his arms.

That reminded him . . .

"Nickie, what did you have in mind when you said Balthazar wouldn't go unpunished? Joanne seemed to understand, but I . . ."

Of course he knew the answer before he had even ceased speaking. Nicole went completely still in his arms, not even breathing, and neither did he. When she turned to look up at him, her eyes were troubled and he felt a profound sadness coming over her. He had an impulse to say, *Oh, Nickie, don't do it, you don't have to do it,* but he knew that wasn't true. She had made a decision and a promise, and now she felt a moral imperative.

When she shook her head and gently pushed his arms aside, he didn't try to stop her.

She walked a few yards away from him, almost disappearing in the darkness, and stopped, still facing the town but looking past and over it toward Balthazar's Mountain. She was silent for a time, and he knew that, however reluctantly, she was gathering up all her newly found strength of will and determination. He could feel it.

"Timothy Balthazar . . ."

She faltered and her head fell forward, but only for a moment. When she raised her head, Duffy could see her more clearly, as if a nimbus were forming around her, steadily growing brighter.

When Nicole spoke again, her voice had a note of sorrow. "Timothy Balthazar, hear me. You were my grandmother's friend. At one time, she, and my grandfather, loved and trusted you, and all of St. Claire looked up to you. But like your own grandfather long ago, you betrayed that love and trust, that honor and responsibility. Like your ancestor, you summoned up and welcomed the powers of darkness and destruction. Therefore . . ."

Her voice deepened and became firmer, not her usual speaking voice, yet strangely familiar to Duffy.

"Timothy Balthazar, for the pain and grief and suffering you have caused, for all the evil you have brought into the world, I, Nicole St. Claire, place this anathema on you."

Nicole paused, as if waiting to be told what she should say next, then straightened and slowly raised her hands above her head. When the words came, it was as if someone else, some dark avenging angel, were speaking.

"*Timothy Balthazar, for your sins, may this be your fate.*

"*May your dearest wish in all the world, your deepest longing of all longings, the one thing you most desire and cannot live without, never be granted—*

"*And may your worst nightmare, however terrible, come true!*"

As Nicole lowered her arms and pointed toward Balthazar's Mountain, the radiance surrounding her seemed to flair, and Duffy shut his eyes against it.

When he opened his eyes again, the light was gone and the night was silent. Yet Duffy could have sworn he heard in the distance, troubling the dark sky, a great cry of anguish and despair.

Head down, Nicole turned and walked slowly back to the car. She got in and closed the door. Shivering uncontrollably, she rested her head on the steering wheel. Duffy got in beside her and took her into his arms, and now his strength flowed into her, and he knew he still had something to give her. They had something, so very much, to give to each other.

"I never thought I'd do that," she said. "I never thought I could, and I never wanted to."

"But you promised Joanne."

"I promised. But if I've done the wrong thing . . ."

"You haven't. You only did what had to be done."

"What had to be done . . ." Nicole raised her head from his shoulder, and even in the dark he could see the pain in her eyes. "Duffy, what's happened . . . you do understand that it isn't over, don't you?"

"I know. The law will soon catch up with us—"

"No, not the law. We'll survive that. But afterward . . . I'm different, Duffy. I'm different, and I know now I'll always be different." She hesitated, closing her eyes. "Duffy, it's true. I'm . . . I'm a . . ."

"I know what you are, Nicole." As he said the words, Duffy found himself accepting the truth. The woman he loved was not a madwoman, not sick, not a case history. She was not to be explained by any of his textbooks. She was simply what she was: Nicole St. Claire, in some wonderful, mysterious manner known only to God, a daughter of wolves.

She nodded. "I've accepted it. But I'll understand if you ever decide you don't want to live with it."

Listening to her, Duffy realized that in the last hour Nicole had reminded him of someone, and now he knew who it was. It was her grandmother. Aunt Julia. Aunt Julia, who had done so much to make both of them what they were. Aunt Julia, who had tried so hard, he now realized, to make them worthy of each other.

"Nicole," he said with all his heart, "I know it's going to be tough, but I wouldn't miss one day, one hour, one minute of our life together."

Nicole looked at him for a long moment, reading his soul, and a smile came to her face.

"Then I'll promise you this," she said. "Whatever happens, for better or worse . . . we'll have a grand adventure!"

They kissed.

"I love you, Nicole."

"I love you, Duffy."

Nicole buckled up and put the car in gear. They moved forward.

The adventure began.

Epilogue

ITE MISSA EST

Even after that night, Timothy had not given up hope. Even after that terrible anguish that had overcome him before dawn, as if Julia St. Claire herself had pronounced an anathema on him. He had refused to give in to the sin of despair. Day after day and night after night, for weeks, he had sat at Alida's bedside, holding her hand, speaking softly to her, watching for any slightest sign of returning awareness, any stirring that might portend an awakening. But there had been none.

She was still beautiful, but all the wiles of medical science could not save that beauty forever, and Timothy could not bear to see it slipping away. Frank Stranger checked on her regularly, almost every evening after leaving his office, and Timothy knew that one of these evenings he, Timothy, was going to say, "All right, Frank. Enough."

"Minna," he said as he stood up at Alida's bedside, "tell Frank, when he gets here, that I would like to talk to him."

Tears glistened in Minna's eyes, and she merely nodded, as if she dared not speak.

"Rest well, my darling," Timothy whispered as he kissed Alida's forehead. It was the first time he hadn't promised her she would soon be back. Perhaps he would never make that promise again.

The police, the headlines, the hysteria . . . seven people slaughtered, five in a single night . . . one, Bruno Krull, known to have been his protégé . . . another, ultimately identified as the reclusive Freya Kellgren (strangely withered and shrunken), said to have been his former companion . . . and all of them acquaintances of this man who "jokingly" called himself a Luciferian. Had he really thought of himself as forever above suspicion? What hubris!

Not that they would ever prove anything. Joanne had identified Bruno as her rapist and Derek's killer, but she had been unconscious most of the time and apparently had never realized that Timothy was present. And Duffy, drugged, must not have recognized him. In any case, he and Nicole had wisely chosen to get on with their lives and say nothing.

The griffin tapestry was now just a gaudy piece of cloth hanging behind an altar. It communicated no mystery, no magic. It was dimly illuminated by the black candles on the ends of the altar, and Timothy, sitting cloakless in a pew, wondered why he had bothered to light them. The Prince of Power had, after all, turned his back on him.

Gone, he thought, with a bitter little smile; gone, all gone. . . .

Gone, his vaunted prescience. He hardly knew what was going to happen from one moment to the next.

Gone, his power over minds—to read them, to enter them, to influence them. Gone, his power to punish and reward.

Gone, his power to summon demons, even the god of this world himself.

All lost on the night of the Rapture, when he arrived back at his house to find himself an old and defeated man.

Gone, his political power. Questions and rumors about the killings abounded—they were said to have been satanic cult murders—and his influential friends now seemed to be distancing themselves from him. He might have driven the St.

Claires out of St. Claire, but there was no doubt that he had lost his hold on the community.

Ironically, his convocation was gone too. More than a few members suspected him of some involvement in the killings. They couldn't afford to be associated with him, and they no longer came running when he beckoned, no longer invited him to their meetings. They had, in effect, quietly excommunicated him.

He hardly cared.

No, that wasn't true. By rights, St. Claire was his, and the convocation was his, and he did care, he cared fiercely, profoundly, endlessly. The only thing in the world more dear to him was his daughter.

Then why had they all been taken from him? It was so unfair, all so unfair!

He couldn't help himself. He threw himself forward onto his knees and spoke aloud, desperately. "I did my best. I risked everything for you. You cannot say the Holland coven went unpunished, not even those who got away. As for Nicole St. Claire, the suspicion that she is a murderous madwoman will haunt her forever. So I ask you, why have you turned your back on me? Why? *Why?*"

The god didn't answer.

He didn't have to. Somewhere in Timothy's self-deceiving heart he already knew the answer. Had always known. And it had absolutely nothing to do with the coven or with Nicole St. Claire.

The real answer was quite different and quite simple. A biblical passage came to mind.

"And it came to pass after these things, that God did tempt Abraham . . . And he said, Take now thy son, thine only son Isaac, whom thou lovest, and get thee into the land of Moriah; and offer him there for a burnt offering . . ."

Abraham had not begged for his son's life. He had not attempted to bargain with his god or to read his secret intentions. He had not railed at him for being unjust. He had simply obeyed.

"And they came to the place which God had told him of; and Abraham built an altar there, and laid the wood in order, and bound Isaac his son, and laid him on the altar upon the

wood. And Abraham stretched forth his hand, and took the knife to slay his son."

Then and only then had the angel of the Lord stayed his hand. Then and only then had his god given him a ram caught in a thicket to offer up *"for a burnt offering in the stead of his son."*

Abraham had put his god before all else, even the life of his beloved son.

Timothy had not put his god or anything else before the life of his daughter. There had been times, while she lived, when he would have flung himself before oncoming trains or from high towers to save her. When her heart had faltered, his heart had cried out, *Take me instead!* He would have suffered all the tortures and torments of hell to save his daughter from them. No matter what promises he had made, in his heart his daughter had always come first.

That was his tragic flaw, that he had loved his daughter more than his god. It was the same flaw, he knew, that had caused his grandfather Isaac's downfall. Isaac Balthazar, for all his strength and dedication, had put his son Benjamin first—a mistake Benjamin had never made with Timothy—and as a punishment the Prince of Power had let the St. Claire anathema fall upon old Isaac like an avenging fury.

Now it was Timothy's turn. And there was absolutely nothing he could do about it.

With that realization, Timothy felt a great void opening up in himself. But it was not an emptiness that demanded to be filled, a hunger that asked to be fed. It was a sense of absolute loss, of complete futility, the knowledge that in loving his daughter too dearly he had thrown away any chance of saving her.

"Alida, forgive me . . .

"Lord Lucifer, forgive me . . .

"It is true. I have been arrogant. I loved my Alida too much, and I put my will before yours. But dear Lord, I have paid such a price. I have nothing left now, not even you. Even you have deserted me. Do with me as you will."

Timothy Balthazar was giving up, surrendering himself to his god utterly. He was a hollow shell, a man gutted and drained, and for the first time in many weeks a kind of peace came over him, the tranquility of defeat. After all, what more could fate or his god do to him? *"Ite missa est,"* he murmured. "It is finished. *Ite . . . missa . . . est."*

He never heard the doctor's car arrive.

Timothy wondered how he would get through the empty days ahead, days without Alida. Perhaps there would not be too many more of them.

The house was silent.

He felt a stirring within that silence, but he ignored it. He wanted only to be left in his dark solitude.

But the stirring became a rumble that could not be ignored. Somewhere overhead heavy footsteps reverberated, and Timothy seemed to hear someone calling his name.

More footsteps, closer.

Behind him the chapel door was flung open. Looking around, he saw Minna standing in the doorway, tears on her face. "Oh, Timothy," she wailed, "come quickly. A miracle has happened. A miracle!"

For a long moment Timothy felt totally paralyzed in both mind and body, as if the enormity of what Minna was trying to tell him was beyond his comprehension.

Then he was running from the chapel, following Minna, passing Minna, pounding up the stairs, calling out to Alida, calling her name aloud and shouting it in his heart. *Alida, Alida, Alida!*

Frank Stranger, his face pale, his large eyes almost out of their sockets, met him at the door of Alida's apartment. "Easy, Timothy, easy, it's too early to tell her condition, there were no advance indications—"

"I must see her!"

"Of course, of course. But gently, gently, quietly, she's so weak. Just for a minute or two—"

"Please, Frank, I must!"

"And you shall. You shall. But calmly, for Alida's sake."

For Alida's sake, yes. For Alida's sake, he could do anything. He breathed deeply, as if trying to inhale calm. Nearby, the nurse was trying to calm Minna. Heinrich had appeared in the doorway, his old lined face aglow with joy.

Finally Frank allowed Timothy to enter Alida's bedroom. He approached her bedside with all the awe and reverence and love that one's child, returned from the dead, deserved. Her eyes were barely open, but for the first time since she had been stricken he saw recognition in them. She was wasted and frail, yet to Timothy she had never been more beautiful.

He leaned over her. "Alida, darling."

Her mouth moved, silently at first, and when she spoke he could barely hear her: "Daddy . . ."

"It's all right, dear. You're going to be all right now."

"Daddy . . ." Her voice was rusty with disuse, as if even to whisper was painful. "Daddy . . . Daddy . . . I was in a dark place . . . so dark . . . and I couldn't get back." Tears came to her eyes. "Oh, Daddy, I couldn't get back!"

"It's all right. You're back now. And Daddy's never going to let you go away again."

"Oh, Daddy, I was so frightened!"

"There's no need to be frightened. Daddy is here."

Frank let him talk to her a little longer, then insisted that he leave. "She's very weak, Timothy. Even a little talk takes a lot out of her. I know it seems strange after all these weeks in bed, but she's got to get her rest."

Timothy understood, and having assured Alida that he would return soon, he allowed Frank to take him into the next room.

"Now, Timothy," Frank cautioned, "this is a wonderful thing, but I don't want you to get your hopes up too high. We don't yet know the effects of the coma, and there'll have to be tests and observation—"

"Oh, Frank, she's going to be fine! She's been given back to us, Frank. Have faith! As soon as you're done here, I want you to join Heinrich and Minna and me in the chapel. . . ."

Timothy didn't bother with the elevator. As he went down the stairs to his study, light on his feet as a schoolboy, he could feel his years falling away and his energy level rising. There was so much to be done!

In his study he made a number of quick telephone calls, spreading the good news and inviting—no, *summoning*—his lost followers to Balthazar's Mountain.

When he reached the chapel, Heinrich had already lit the candles, and they said a prayer together. Frank and Minna, in cloaks, soon joined them. As the four of them knelt at the communion rail, looking up at the magnificent fierce-eyed, bronze-winged beast-angel, Timothy foresaw the future. He would rebuild his convocation, making it more powerful than ever. He would draw to it other powerful convocations to form a great synod. And that synod would become the core of a great province, surely the greatest ever known.

And furthermore, if only as a matter of pride, he would reclaim the heart and soul of St. Claire for his own.

All of this he would give to his daughter Alida.

Timothy Balthazar's hopes, his ambitions, his elation, knew no bounds. Why should they? He had sworn he would have his daughter back, and he had her. Clearly, he was back in his master's favor and once again all things were possible for him.

His face hidden in the dark hood of his cloak, Timothy smiled. He felt almost as if he had tricked the devil.

And now, the girl thought, *and now* . . .

The doctor was right: she was terribly weak. But she was back, the memory of that dreadful darkness was already fading, and the dim light of the room struck her half-open eyes like a blessing.

With considerable effort, she managed to turn her head and call the nurse. Though the nurse was sitting in a chair only a few feet away, reading a magazine, she didn't hear that feeble whisper, and the girl tried again: ". . . nurse . . ."

The nurse looked surprised but pleased, and immediately hurried to the bedside.

The girl explained that she wanted "to . . . sit . . . up."

The nurse, a middle-aged woman with a pleasant vanilla-pudding face, looked dubious at first, but then smiled and said, "Well, why not?"

She raised the head of the bed a foot or so and then showed the girl the buttons with which, if she had the strength, she could raise or lower the head of the bed herself. She also showed her the button by which she could call for help should the nurse be out of the room.

"All right now?" she asked.

The girl smiled gratefully and managed to say "Yes."

The nurse left the room.

The girl lay still for a time, eyes closed, trying to gather up more strength. Then she opened her eyes and pressed the button to raise the head of the bed higher. The motor hummed softly, and slowly she came into view in the mirror of the dressing table on the other side of the room. Even in the dim light, she could see herself clearly.

She stared.

She had seen that face countless times, of course, but never before like this: so pale, so hollow-cheeked and sunken-eyed. And her body: so thin, so wasted. When she touched her ribs through her gown, she felt skeletal and she almost whimpered.

But then she smiled.

What did it matter what she looked like now? She was back. And she was only seventeen—she would soon recover. Her face would fill out and regain its color, her body would regain its strength and shapeliness, her raven-black hair would be long and silken. She would recover all her former beauty and more, much more. She would become a marvel of beauty, a wonder to behold, and then, and then . . .

Mirror, mirror, on the wall . . .

"Surprise, Timothy!" said Freya Kellgren.

ABOUT THE AUTHOR

JOHN R. HOLT has worked as an editor for a publishing house and for a literary agency, where he also directed foreign rights. He has published a number of books, some under the name "Raymond Giles." An often-transplanted midwesterner, he now lives with his family in Georgia.

REALMS OF FANTASY

The biggest, brightest stars from Bantam Spectra

Lynn Flewelling

The consummate thief, spy, noble, and rogue, Seregil of Rhíminee must save his world along with the aid of his loyal apprentice, Alec.

LUCK IN THE SHADOWS ___57542-2 $5.99/$7.99 Canada
STALKING DARKNESS ___57543-0 $5.99/$7.99 Canada

Maggie Furey

A fiery-haired Mage with an equally incendiary temper must save her world and her friends from a pernicious evil, with the aid of four forgotten magical Artefacts.

AURIAN ___56525-7 $6.50
HARP OF WINDS ___56526-5 $6.50
SWORD OF FLAME ___56527-3 $6.50

Katharine Kerr

The mistress of Celtic fantasy presents her ever-popular Deverry series. Most recent titles:

DAYS OF BLOOD AND FIRE ___29012-6 $5.99/$7.50
DAYS OF AIR AND DARKNESS ___57262-8 $5.99/$7.99

Ask for these books at your local bookstore or use this page to order.

Please send me the books I have checked above. I am enclosing $ ____(add $2.50 to cover postage and handling). Send check or money order, no cash or C.O.D.'s, please.

Name _____

Address _____

City/State/Zip _____

Send order to: Bantam Books, Dept. SF 29, 2451 S. Wolf Rd., Des Plaines, IL 60018
Allow four to six weeks for delivery.
Prices and availability subject to change without notice.   SF 29 7/97

REALMS OF FANTASY
The biggest, brightest stars from Bantam Spectra

Robin Hobb

One of our newest and most exciting talents presents a tale of honor and subterfuge, loyalty and betrayal.

ASSASSIN'S APPRENTICE: Book One of the Farseer
___57339-X $6.50/$8.99 Canada
ROYAL ASSASSIN: Book Two of the Farseer
___57341-1 $6.50/$8.99 Canada
ASSASSIN'S QUEST: Book Three of the Farseer
___10640-6 $22.95/$31.95 Canada

Michael A. Stackpole

An antique warrior, from 500 years in the past, is resurrected to save his kingdom from an evil he unwittingly propagated.

ONCE A HERO ___56112-X $5.99/$7.99
TALION: REVENANT ___57656-9 $5.99/$7.99

- -

Ask for these books at your local bookstore or use this page to order.

Please send me the books I have checked above. I am enclosing $____ (add $2.50 to cover postage and handling). Send check or money order, no cash or C.O.D.'s, please.

Name _____

Address _____

City/State/Zip _____

Send order to: Bantam Books, Dept. SF 29, 2451 S. Wolf Rd., Des Plaines, IL 60018
Allow four to six weeks for delivery.
Prices and availability subject to change without notice.   SF 29 7/97

REALMS OF FANTASY

The biggest, brightest stars from Bantam Spectra

Paula Volsky

Rich tapestries of magic and revolution, romance and forbidden desires.

ILLUSION ___56022-0 $5.99/$6.99
THE GATES OF TWILIGHT ___57269-5 $6.50/$8.99

Angus Wells

Epic fantasy in the grandest tradition of magic, dragons, and heroic quests. Most recent titles:

EXILE'S CHILDREN: Book One of the Exiles Saga
___29903-4 $5.99/$7.99
EXILE'S CHALLENGE: Book Two of the Exiles Saga
___37812-0 $12.95/$17.95

George R. R. Martin

The sweeping and exciting first volume, full of plots and counterplots, victory and betrayal:

A GAME OF THRONES: Book One of *A Song of Ice and Fire*
___10354-7 $21.95/$29.95

Ask for these books at your local bookstore or use this page to order.

Please send me the books I have checked above. I am enclosing $ ____(add $2.50 to cover postage and handling). Send check or money order, no cash or C.O.D.'s, please.

Name _____

Address _____

City/State/Zip _____

Send order to: Bantam Books, Dept. SF 29, 2451 S. Wolf Rd., Des Plaines, IL 60018
Allow four to six weeks for delivery.
Prices and availability subject to change without notice.   SF 29 7/97